THE
Oracular
ROOM

THE Oracular ROOM

THE LEIBNIZ-NEWTON EFFECT

Thorpe Feidt

Station Hill
of Barrytown

Published by Station Hill Press, Inc., 120 Station Hill Road, Barrytown, NY 12507, as a project of the Institute for Publishing Arts, Inc., in Barrytown, New York, a not-for-profit, tax-exempt organization [501(c)(3)], supported in part by grants from the New York State Council on the Arts, a state agency.

Online catalogue: www.stationhill.org
e-mail: publishers@stationhill.org
Cover and interior design by Susan Quasha

Library of Congress Cataloging-in-Publication Data
Feidt, Thorpe.
    The oracular room : the Leibniz-Newton effect / Thorpe Feidt.
        pages ; cm
    ISBN 978-1-58177-142-8 (softcover)
    I. Title.
    PS3606.E3647O73 2015
    813'.6—dc23
                                                    2015025724

The Oracular Room is for my grandmother,
CAROLINE HALLOWELL WILLIAMS
(1876–1957)
who read me *Puck of Pook's Hill* when I was five,

for my father
JOHN THORPE FEIDT
(1908–1997)
who introduced me to the works of J. Preslow Thurston,

for BARBARA CRAWFORD
(1914–2003),
painter, writer and mentor,

for GHOST DOG,

for TURPENTINE,

for BODFISH,

and for OLYMPIA

The doctrine of metempsychosis is, above all, neither absurd nor useless. ... It is not more surprising to be born twice than once; everything in nature is resurrection.

—Voltaire

O

Preface In Two Parts:
A Death In Aubrey.
An Arrival In Küsnacht.

1. **From the *Salem Trumpet,* Salem, Massachusetts, May 29, 1855:**

MEDIUM FOUND DEAD IN AUBREY!
HIS WIFE MISSING!
UNVEILING OF ORACLE CANCELLED!

As this issue of the *Trumpet* was going to press, the Editors were grieved to learn that the body of Dr. Eggbeater Caws was discovered late last night on Prospect St. in Aubrey, not far from his home. The cause of death has not yet been determined. The doctor had been in good health, so far as was known, and there were no signs of violence.

The door of his house was standing open. Mrs. Caws, the doctor's wife, was nowhere to be found, and still is missing.

A rain of cantaloupes was reported in the village around the same time.
The body was found by Mr. Calvin Mainwaring, the Cawses' next-door neighbor. Mr. Mainwaring said he had been awakened by his wife, who told him she had heard a noise in the street and asked him to investigate. He discovered the body lying on its back by the side of the road, near the entrance to the Aubrey Burying Ground.

A white feather was sticking out of its mouth.

Dr. Caws was fifty years old. Born in Batavia, New York, he resided on the Continent for a lengthy period before coming to Aubrey in 1848. That same year, he married Efficiency Barton, daughter of Aubrey's Abimelech Barton, the late banker and philanthropist. Beginning in 1850, Dr. and Mrs. Caws gained considerable notoriety as mediums, traveling throughout the northeast giving séances and spiritualistic demonstrations. The couple alleged that the voice which spoke through Mrs. Caws when she entered the trance state was that of the long-dead scientist, Sir Isaac Newton, and that the voice which spoke through the doctor belonged to the philosopher and mathematician, G. W. Leibniz, Sir Isaac's German contemporary and hated rival. Numerous physical phenomena accompanied the séances, which were often contentious and were widely reported in the national press.

Yesterday morning, Jeremy Welkin of the *Trumpet* conducted an extensive interview with the doctor, the full text of which appears elsewhere in this issue and presents the medium's final pronouncements on the subjects most dear to him.

Mr. Welkin also has disappeared.

Last year, the Cawses quit the séance room and returned to private life, citing exhaustion and the deleterious effects of constant travel as the reason, but, several days ago, the doctor announced the completion of what he called "the Delphic Oracle," a "spiritual calculating machine" which he said he had built in the back room of his house, working solely from specifications given him by Leibniz, who, we need scarcely remind our readers, departed this life in 1716. The machine, for whose powers the doctor made extravagant claims, seeming even to suggest that it was capable of independent thought and a form of articulate speech, was to have been unveiled this evening at a séance in the Cawses' home.

The police are leaving no stone unturned in their investigation of the tragedy. We will apprise our readers of further developments as soon as they become available.

2. From *True Tales of the Paranormal,* by Llanvair K. Tiflis (New Castle: Booster Books, 2005):

The sudden death of Dr. Fritz Eichhorn on November 27, 2002, at the Helvetius Psychiatric Clinic in Zürich, Switzerland, caused considerable commotion in psychoanalytic circles. At the time, the doctor was a patient at the Clinic, where, only a few months before, he had been one of its most eminent staff members, albeit a controversial one. Found among his papers, along with case histories, abortive drafts and essays, letters, newspaper clippings and miscellaneous jottings, was a lengthy narrative which appears to stand on its own. This text, composed during the last summer and fall of Dr. Eichhorn's life, bears witness to his breakdown and provides the basis for what follows here:

At nine o'clock in the morning of May 28, 2002, after an unseasonably warm night, with flashes of heat lightning and a rain of cantaloupes reported in nearby Zürich, a man appeared on the Seestrasse outside the house of psychologist C. G. Jung in Küsnacht, Switzerland. About sixty years of age, he wore a green American zoot suit of 1940's vintage, a bright red necktie, sunglasses and a porkpie hat, according to witnesses. His feet were bare. In his hands he held a small, tarnished metal object, shaped roughly like a human skull, with a thick coil of wire sticking out of the cranium. Introducing himself as "Empedocles Schwank, Keeper of the Central Fire," he demanded in a loud voice to see Dr. Jung, whom he repeatedly referred to as "Prez." Raising the skull above his head, he announced that he had made an amazing discovery. "See this?" he shouted. "This is the Delphic Oracle! That's right—the Delphic Oracle of Aubrey, Massachusetts. Designed by G. W. Leibniz, built by Eggbeater Caws. It knows everything there is to know about everything in the world. Past, present, future, you name it, baby. Get Prez out here right away."

Told that Dr. Jung had died more than forty years earlier, the man refused to accept the fact. "Just tell him I'm here," he insisted. "Schwank. Empedocles Schwank. And say I have the Oracle. He'll understand. Hell, he was in the Basie band, of course he'll understand."

3

Removed to the Helvetius Psychiatric Clinic later that morning in what was described as "an exalted state," Schwank remained intransigent. Questioned about his personal history, he gave rambling, inconsistent answers. He said he had been born over and over again, in Athens, Atlantis, Babylon, Benares, Ephesus, Chicago, New Orleans, Red Bank— "all over the place, man. You name it. I've been around, you know, don't think I haven't." He added that in one lifetime or another he had been a musician, a gardener, a midwife, an artist, a farmer, a general, a deserter, an alchemist, a pope, a prostitute and "You know, a boy and a girl and a bush and a bird, if you can dig it. Even a fish in the sea, like the man said. But that was a long time ago. Ancient history."

A more recent incarnation, he went on, had begun in the seventeenth century. He was *Colonel* Schwank, the natural son of G. W. Leibniz—"Yeah, Leibniz himself, baby"—and one Maria, an opera singer. "How about that, man, my mother was an opera singer, ain't that a gas?" Schwank was born in Aubrey, to which his mother had moved from Germany, and made a name for himself in the late 1680's in the Indian Territory along the Mississippi River. Eventually, he gave up exploring, went back east, and then, still restless, traveled to Europe— "Germany mostly"—where he saw his father, then took off again, north this time, "way *far* north, to Hyperborea, they call it," where he stayed "quite a while, a couple of hundred years, maybe. Why didn't I die? Well, baby, I did die, sure, just like everybody else. I died lotsa times, and came back. Lived a little, died a little, came back a little—that's what every-body else does, too, by the way, in case you don't happen to know. The only difference with me is, *I* remember it happening. Yeah, sweetie, I remember bein' born, over and over. What's it like? Well, it's a little like comin' to, after you've been out for a while: not so hot. The last time I came to, I was in a Mason jar, man. Jesus. I got outta there *fast*."

Asked why he still called himself Schwank after so many later lives and, presumably, later names, he answered, "Hey, I just happen to *like* Schwank, you dig? I liked *being* Schwank, too. Can't I like something once in a while? Those other lives were a drag. And Schwank *means* something, man—you don't believe me, look it up. Empedocles, too—love and strife, baby, that's where it's all at, ain't it? Sure it is. Besides, I got a right to take my pick. When I was in that Mason jar, they didn't call me *nothin'*."

Anyway, he said, none of that really mattered. The important thing was that he was here, "right here and now," to claim his "rightful inheritance."

Schwank did not elaborate on what that inheritance was. He seemed to be getting nervous. He repeated his demand to see "Prez." The situation was critical. "I'm not even supposed to *have* this thing," he confided, holding up the metal skull. "Hell, it's *dangerous* to have this thing. The Newtonians are *everywhere*, man, buzzin' on me. Listen, the cat that built the Oracle, Eggbeater Caws, that cat was killed before he could even unveil it. He was the only one that knew how to make it talk. I don't think even Leibniz knew that. But now *I* do. That's right; I figured it out, all by myself. Not the son of Leibniz for nothin', I'm not. All I need to do now is ... well, never you mind about that, you guys, I'll just wait to tell Prez myself, if you don't mind. *Sympnoia panta,* baby, *sympnoia panta,* you dig it."

When an attendant tried to take the skull away he became violent.

After several days, when he finally realized he was not going to get his interview with Jung, Schwank increased his demands. He wanted a room to himself, not too large but on the other hand not too small either, and absolutely without windows. This last was very important: nothing must come in and nothing must go out. He wanted a coal stove or furnace, with plenty of coal or wood, a Bunsen burner, a sink, a full set of laboratory glassware. He wanted a mortar and pestle, "thirty or forty" assorted minerals, metals and chemical compounds, along with other items such as moonwort, carapace of stag beetle, a pint of pigs' urine and a gallon of vitriol. Schwank explained that he'd counted on using the alchemical laboratory he knew "Prez" had in his basement, but now he'd have to make do on his own. He also demanded a big wooden worktable, as well as a thick coil of malleable wire, a take-up reel and a rig to go with it—a spindle and crank and a shaft, attached to a base that could be screwed into the table top. "And music! Compact discs, with something to play them on. Monk. Miles. Coleman Hawkins. Al and Zoot, Brookmeyer, Mulligan. And the Basie band! Yeah—Prez with the Basie band. 'Jumpin' at the Woodside.' 'Tickle Toe,' 'Mutton Leg.' 'The Jitters.' Yeah."

His speech degenerated further, descending into a maelstrom of disconnected phrases, relying more and more heavily on American musicians' argot interspersed with broken German and snatches of Latin and Greek. Sometimes he spoke only in numbers. Once he sang a song from an opera.

His ability to make meaningful connections in time and space also was impaired. His conviction that C. G. Jung and the jazz musician Lester Young were one and the same person could not be shaken, despite all proofs offered to the contrary. For him there was no inconsistency involved in the notion, for instance, that "Prez" was playing "Moten Swing" in the Panther Room of the Hotel Sherman in Chicago in 1939 and simultaneously treating patients and writing *Psychologie und Alchemie* in Küsnacht. Nor was Schwank impressed when shown printed evidence that Jung died in 1961 at the age of eighty-five and Young in 1959 at forty-nine. Time meant nothing to him. Time was "very overrated," he said. In what he called "the *Real* World" "Prez" was still alive, just as he had always been, "alive, accessible and cooking."

Schwank also spoke frequently of something he called "the *Gehirngespinstgemach*," a mysterious entity that sometimes seemed to be a metaphysical concept, sometimes a mythological being akin to a fallen angel and sometimes simply a room, albeit a room with unique characteristics. In fact, he confided, the *Gehirngespinstgemach* was the real intelligence behind the Oracle. "The Oracle's just a mechanism, a voice box, kind of. It's the *Gehirngespinstgemach* that does the thinking." It would explain everything, he insisted, much better than he himself could, "once I've done my stuff with the mechanism."

Suddenly he burst into tears. No one had any idea, he sobbed, "not the slightest subatomic notion," of the pressure he was under. The world had been cracked open, centuries ago, "the entire created universe, man," and it had fallen to him, Schwank, to put it all back together. He repeated his demand to see "Prez," shouting the name over and over.

At this point Dr. Eichhorn enters the narrative in person. "The case now came to my attention," he writes, adding in parentheses "Thank God! Just think what those bunglers would have made of it otherwise." The remark was typical of him. Since coming to the Helvetius, he had played to the hilt the role of the brilliant young psychoanalyst destined for greatness, often at the expense of his more seasoned colleagues. Known for his unconventional approach to treatment, he was not shy of telling anyone who would listen how he had made his mark in his first position, at the Basel Psychiatric Clinic, defying the authorities and effecting dramatic improvements in patients previously deemed irreclaimable. And brash though the staff found him, they had to admit his results were impressive: a paranoid schizophrenic who screamed night and day now wrote and painted his fantasies; a catatonic, immobile for years, was now learning the cello.

Certainly Eichhorn was no ordinary man. An American, born near Philadelphia in Bryn Athyn, Pennsylvania, he grew up in an unusual environment. Bryn Athyn was a bastion of the Swedenborgian church, and his parents took the religion seriously, especially its supernatural aspects. From infancy the child was given to understand that, in the words of the Swedish seer, we "live simultaneously in the natural world and in the spiritual world." Eichhorn's father had been a jazz saxophonist in Germany, widely known on the Continent as "Squirrel" Eichhorn. He was converted to Swedenborgianism in 1971, after a concert in Tübingen during which he experienced what he later described as "a little *Verflüchtigung.*" Shortly afterward he emigrated to the United States, where he met and married Mary Gwynn, a Philadelphia painter who experimented with the Ouija board. The couple brought their son up to regard phenomena that most people dismiss out of hand—second sight, for instance, or speaking in tongues—as fully plausible occurrences. Nothing in Fritz's later life, not even a long and rigorous university education, ever put a dent in these beliefs. On the contrary, he gloried in them. He used to boast to his colleagues that at thirteen he had made an homunculus, a fully formed and viable little man, in a Mason jar in the basement of his parents' home.

Eichhorn showed intellectual ability early on. Always first in his class in Bryn Athyn, at sixteen he won a coveted scholarship to the University of Cambridge, where he read philosophy and religion, writing his doctoral dissertation on G. W. Leibniz's *Monadology.* After graduation his interests turned to psychology, and he studied in Zürich, taking his training analysis with the renowned P. C. Haselmaus, "Haselmaus the Dreamer," "the Epimenides of Basel," whose decades-long work on dreaming had brought him almost legendary status. In his youth, Haselmaus had been analyzed by the great Stachelschwein, who in turn had worked with the charismatic Urwald, who had been a colleague of Jung himself.

"Haselmaus opened me up," Eichhorn wrote later. "He showed me myself and he showed me the world. I was only a learning machine till I met him."

But the patients at the Basel Psychiatric Clinic had an even greater impact. "They showed me the World *beyond* the world—and the World beyond *that*, too. The *über* World, the *unter* World, the *jenseits* World, call it what you will, those people wandered in It daily—hourly—through territory whose existence, whose *real* existence, I had never even suspected. They were the great explorers—my very first patients, too. Such good fortune! The *affinity* I felt for them—indescribable!"

By the time he arrived at the Helvetius, Eichhorn had come to believe that the mentally disturbed were to all intents and purposes the teachers of the sane, that all treatment should be undertaken primarily to learn from them, since (as he wrote in his paper, "Nuts? Why Nietzsche Wrote Such Good Books") they represented "the next evolutionary step for the human species. Already they reach levels of understanding—unrestricted by social assumptions, codes of conduct, above all by dictates of discourse and rational syntax—utterly unattainable by the rest of us." In the same paper he discussed the possibility of direct communication from the spirit world and cited the mediumship of the Cawses, husband and wife, and Dr. Caws' mysterious "Delphic Oracle."

The Cawses were hardly a recent discovery of Eichhorn's; he had known about them most of his life. When he was a boy his mother had made a point of telling him about her childhood in Wyncote, on the outskirts of Philadelphia, during the late 1940's. It was a time and place she recalled as idyllic, and she wanted to pass some sense of it on to her son.

One person Mary spoke of with particular affection was Aunt Mamm, a family friend who lived next door and whom Mary often visited. She usually had something tasty to eat, and a rich fund of stories, which Mary savored even more. Well into her seventies, Aunt Mamm was in the habit of reminiscing about her youth and the colorful characters she had known back around the turn of the century. The most colorful of all, by a wide margin, was Efficiency Caws, the famous medium, widow of the notorious Dr. Caws. After an extraordinary life, one filled with marvels and not untouched by scandal, she had retired to Wyncote, and Aunt Mamm, then in her twenties, had made her acquaintance.

Mary loved hearing about Mrs. Caws and her adventures in the spirit world. Was it really true that her husband could *fly?* she wondered. And could Mrs. Caws actually grow *taller*, right before your eyes, while the doctor was up in the air? It was all simply thrilling, and Mary was in Heaven when Aunt Mamm told her that the house in which the medium had spent her final days was only a few streets away. Thereafter, she made a detour on her way to school each morning so that she could pass the house, and each time she did she experienced the most pleasant *frisson* of fear, despite the fact that the building itself was quite ordinary, no different from many others of the same age in the neighborhood. Once she even caught sight—or thought she caught sight—of an old woman's face, peering through the curtains in a top floor window. She passed the rest of the day in an ecstasy of terror.

Not until she was older would Mary discover that her friend Aunt Mamm was in fact Ethel Mammon Striker, the famous author, and that her first book, which had made her reputation, had been a biography of Mrs. Caws, based on her interviews with the medium during the final weeks of her life. Mary bought the book as an adult and often read passages to little Fritz, at his enthusiastic urging.

Small wonder, then, that Schwank fascinated Eichhorn. In fact, he considered his appearance at the Helvetius "nothing short of providential." Trading on his reputation, with the breezy disregard for established procedures that usually got him disliked but that just as often got him his way, Eichhorn had himself put in charge of the case. In his narrative he tells us he straightway shocked his colleagues by acceding without question to the patient's demands. "The room, the chemical equipment, the minerals, the compounds, the other substances, all were to be provided without delay. Even, God help us, the music." (A dutiful son in other respects, Eichhorn was not a jazz fan. A senseless cacophony, it had always seemed to him, completely without spiritual worth. "Why the old man could not have been content with the *Mass in B Minor* or the *Toccata and Fugue in D Minor* is something I'll never understand if I live to be a thousand.")

But even with all Schwank's demands met, some problems materialized. A full chemical laboratory, as specified, could not be set up in the clinic on such short notice, if at all. A child's chemistry set, purchased at a Zürich department store, had to suffice. A kerosene camp stove was the only available heating device, and some of the laboratory glassware was improvised from a variety of containers already present on the hospital grounds. Carapace of stag beetle was out of the question; horses' urine, collected from a nearby riding stable (much to the amusement of the grooms) had to take the place of pigs'. And when no windowless room larger than a toilet could be made conveniently ready in the clinic proper, Eichhorn had the windows boarded up in a disused guest suite in a closed-off wing of an older building, an area not frequented for nearly a century and largely forgotten about by staff.

All in all, it was not a propitious beginning, as Eichhorn admits. "But I need not have worried," he quickly adds. "The substitutions and improvisations didn't matter to Schwank one bit. I don't think he even noticed. And the change in him—O, the change in him!—was immediate, glorious!" No longer raving, the patient moved happily into his new quarters and settled down to work. Soon the only sounds coming from the guest suite were jazz, played loudly and at all hours, mingling with the clink of glassware and the hiss of steam. (Orderlies passing in the hall also thought they detected muffled voices now and again, Schwank's and what sounded like a woman's in serious discussion. But no second person was ever discovered. In any case, that building, jokingly called *Das Fossil* when anyone happened to refer to it at all, had long been supposed to be haunted. The ghost of Sabina Spielrein was said to walk the corridors every Midsummer Night.)

There was also a strong, penetrating odor, as of sulfur mixed with swamp water and putrefying meat.

At the end of a month's time, thirty-one days to be exact, Schwank had produced a noxious, oily liquid which, in Eichhorn's presence, he decanted from a coffee urn on the surface of the camp stove into a chamber pot resting on the worktable. He lowered the metal skull into the pot and covered it with a dinner plate.

Another month passed. By then rumors were circulating non-stop through the hospital. Schwank had made the Philosopher's Stone. Schwank had made a bionic woman. Schwank was not insane at all; he was running a brothel out of his room. He was making designer drugs and selling them through pimps in the red light district in Zürich. In Basel. In Amsterdam. In Paris, New York, London!

A committee of Eichhorn's colleagues came to his office, their faces grim and censorious. The most disturbing reports had reached their ears, they said. Scandal threatened. The hospital's reputation was at stake. They insisted he tell them what was really going on.

In his narrative, Eichhorn freely confesses that remarks like these always infuriated him, especially when they came from persons in authority. A long, deep Jungian analysis (followed surreptitiously by a Freudian one in Baden, a Lacanian one in Thalwil and a month-long retreat sponsored by the antipsychiatric movement in Bern) had changed many things in him, but not that. He did not take criticism well. As far as he was concerned, his colleagues were simply stupid people meddling in his business, and he found it impossible not to be offensive. He answered airily that he knew as little as they did about what was "really" happening: that was a metaphysical, not a psychological question, as Jung had once observed on another subject, and no more within his area of competence than theirs. However, he suggested, they might take note of the fact that Schwank was now quiet, content and, in his own terms, meaningfully occupied. Did Eichhorn's colleagues seriously think the situation could be bettered? Would they take away Adolf Wölfli's pencils? he asked rhetorically. What about van Gogh's paints, or Artaud's papers? Would that have improved matters for them? For us? Of course not. "Let be, let be," he counseled, in as pompous a voice as he could muster. "All will yet be well: the music is still playing." As for the rumors, they were of course all nonsense. Brothels! Designer drugs! The idea! What did his colleagues think of him, anyway?

The committee left, "blinking," Eichhorn tells us, "their mouths hanging open, backing out of the room like a herd of suddenly startled sheep. Only what they deserved, of course. I don't know when I've enjoyed myself more."

But at the same time, he knew, he had not seen the last of them. They would regroup, would find some other line of attack, the bastards. He imagined them grumbling, even then, out in the corridor. "'Who does he think he is, royalty?' 'The music still playing—as if that explained anything!' 'Even Jung wasn't this high-handed.' And on and on, screwing each other's courage up. Oh, they would be back, no doubt about it."

And how would he meet it, the next attack? How ever would he meet it?

For the fact was, Eichhorn's talk had been all bravado. He was deeply concerned about Schwank's condition, and completely at a loss as to how to proceed. It had been a full month since his patient had covered the chamber pot with that dinner plate. It had been his last purposeful action. Now nothing was going on in that room: the music was *not* playing, literally or figuratively. Schwank sat all day at his table, quiet, yes, but practically immobile, his eyes fixed on that stinking pot. For the past three days his meals, which an attendant set outside his door each morning, noon and night, had remained untouched. Why was he starving himself? Had Schwank slipped into a psychological black hole, a catatonia so severe he could never be rescued? "For the first time in my career," Eichhorn writes, "I permitted myself to question the soundness of my methods. Had those other cures, in Basel, been simply a matter of luck, beginner's luck? Or—a terrible thought, but think it I did—were those individuals not so very sick after all? Might they not have responded just as well to anybody else who happened to pay them a bit of special attention, no matter what that attention consisted of? Had I ever, if it came to that, treated anyone who was really sick? If not—and I began very much to fear that this was indeed the case—I was nothing but a fraud, a poseur who'd compounded his imposture by fooling even himself."

What made it even worse, so painful that he had started seeing Haselmaus again, driving twice a week to Basel and back, was that Eichhorn knew what no one else had been able to discover, despite continued questioning and letters and emails sent to medical and judicial authorities all over the world: the identity of the patient. "I got my first shock when I read his case history," he wrote, "and went through his ravings. That Mason jar made me sit up and take notice, all right. But I couldn't be sure. I wouldn't have put it past my so-called colleagues—the jealous bastards—to play a trick on me. Maybe they'd hired this guy Schwank from Central Casting, to show me up. It would have been just like them. But when I first saw him, in that little, pale green room where they'd taken him for examination, and he swung himself around in the chair and lifted his face to me—that wrinkled, dried up but somehow still youthful face—I felt a sudden recognition, in spite of the sunglasses and that ridiculous suit. Then, as he took off his glasses a moment to rub his eyes, the years fell away: I was back in Bryn Athyn, and there was that same face, with those amazing green eyes (the same shade as the wallpaper in the examination room, by God, of an almost transparent paleness!) pressing itself against the Mason jar! In that instant I knew it for certain—*certain*—Oh, how can I explain the knowing, the *absolute* knowing, that I felt in my heart of hearts? A mother, perhaps, feels the same for her offspring?"

The narrative contains much more in this vein. Finally, though, Eichhorn comes to the point. In Schwank he recognized (or, the rationalist must interject, thought he recognized) the homunculus he claimed to have made long ago in his parents' basement, following "as best I could" the instructions in a copy of Paracelsus' alchemical writings, filched by the aspiring young theurgist from the Swedenborg room of the town library. "Working alone, with the most primitive materials—a sealed Mason jar for a chemical vessel—in constant danger of discovery (neither of my parents, free-thinkers though they were, would have tolerated such downright necromancy) I nevertheless triumphed. At the end of the prescribed forty days and forty weeks I had a fully formed little man, a living, active being—in his case hyperactive, running back and forth in his prison, throwing himself against the glass, shouting words I could not hear, furious. And from what had I created him? A few spurts of my adolescent sperm, a couple of blankets around the jar for warmth (horse dung being impossible for any number of reasons), a word or two I'd picked up in some other reading I'd done, and lastly some—but no: to tell all about such things is forbidden."

For a time all was well. The creature thrived, showing no signs of anything untoward save rage at his maker, a reaction Eichhorn considered "natural, a species of birth trauma really, sure to abate as the memory faded." Meanwhile, he looked forward to availing himself of the immense knowledge homunculi traditionally possessed, and to partnering with his creation in the achievement of "great things." But one morning, when he tiptoed downstairs as usual to inspect the homunculus before he left for school, the boy found the Mason jar broken, its fragments scattered across the cellar floor, and his little man gone.

In an instant his pride as an artist gave way to grief, and distress at the plight of a fellow creature, naked and helpless, for whose wellbeing he was responsible. He searched the house from top to bottom, telling his parents, who were calling him in for breakfast, that he was looking for a schoolbook. After school he searched again, more thoroughly. For weeks he never moved a piece of furniture without looking under it, or turned a blanket without shaking it out, but all to no avail. He never saw his homunculus again.

Until that day at the Helvetius. "What joy I felt at first," he writes, "what joy when I knew, really *knew* it was he. He that had been lost was found! Alive! Sentient! Erratic, confused, incoherent at times, but sentient. And back in my own special care. O, I would not let him go again, not this time. This time I would keep him safe, this time I would make him whole again, hale again. I would not reveal my identity to him, not yet at any rate; I could not be sure how the news would affect him. As yet he gave no sign he recognized me; if I told him who I was, the old rage might inflame him anew. But I would heal him, O yes—and I would tap his hidden knowledge, which as an homunculus he must—by his very *nature* he must—still have within him. Why, of *course* he did—had he not already brought me the famous Oracle of Dr. Caws, together with the assurance that he, and he alone, could make it speak after all these years? With what delight I furnished the equipment he demanded! What elation I felt, anticipating the marvels to come! Together again as of old, he and I would become the truest of companions, allies in the greatest of works!"

But when Schwank's activity ceased, when days, then weeks went by without his patient lifting a finger, uttering a sound, Eichhorn's joys turned to misery, his anticipation to self-doubt and, finally, terror at what the consequences of this "greatest of works" might be. Brooding that day in his office, with his fellow doctors' footsteps echoing in the corridor and their "plot-hatching palaver" (which Eichhorn imagined he could hear perfectly, "as clear as if I were walking beside them") he asked himself if his inability to heal had a deeper cause than merely personal shortcomings. What if a greater, a far greater, power was at work against him? "I realized I had become horribly vulnerable. By arrogating to myself the power, and not just the power but the *right* to create life, I had, wittingly or not, thrown down a challenge, a slap in the face as it were, to the universe. That I had been but thirteen at the time meant nothing, the deed had been done and I the doer. There are no extenuations in these matters. Plenty of others, no guiltier than I if you looked at it squarely, had been punished for their rebellion: Faust and Simon Magus were only the most obvious examples. What made me think I was exempt? I had long since ceased to believe in a merciful God. Leibniz was but a spasm of my university days, an amour in the ivory tower—Leibniz with his pre-established harmony, his all-wise Architect of the cosmos. A decade of living in the real world, not to mention the writing of "Nuts?", had cured me of that little delusion. Now I saw, so clearly I couldn't imagine how I'd missed it all those years, that the death of God, which Nietzsche proclaimed, was itself but wishful thinking. If only God *were* dead! Everything would have been so simple! So clean! But no such luck—the Creator of the world still lived, as powerful as ever. And he was, just as he had always been, *a raving lunatic*! Yes, a lunatic, stupefied in his madness, as the Secret Book of John declares, dark and without acquaintance. And vengeful—ready, without an instant's hesitation, to punish an errant child, first by destroying the child's creation, then—then!—by afflicting him with madness, an insanity equal to the Creator's own. I could feel it taking hold already, the doctors out in the hall screeching at me now, insults and catcalls coming in through the keyhole, together with a deep, hideous laughter. Small comfort that I had at last learned the truth! The foundations of the abyss were moving under me, I was collapsing into the pit, the wellspring of demons, the mental hell of—"

Eichhorn could not complete the thought. He rose abruptly from his desk, blinked and shook his head. He had to get out of that office. The building. The whole hospital. If only for an hour or two. Even a few minutes would help. He had to put Schwank out of his mind. And those doctors, damn them. Bourgeois bastards. *Hoping* he would fail, the swine. Well, the hell with them. The hell with them all. Out.

A drive, he thought. Yes, a drive. The privacy of an automobile, something he'd always loved. And motion: wheels turning smoothly, faithfully under you. Eichhorn opened the office door a crack and peeked out. The corridor was empty. What a relief! And only a moment before … Never mind about that now. He walked quickly to the parking lot and got into his car, ignoring the faces he knew were watching in the windows behind him, as well as the attendant he saw out of the corner of his eye approaching from the far end of the grounds. Don't give them the satisfaction, his mother used always to say. Just don't give them the satisfaction.

He started the engine. Where to go? Not Basel, there wasn't time. And anyway Haselmaus might not be in his office. And he didn't want to bother him at home. Not that he knew where he lived. Of course, once he got there he could always look in the phone book—"NO," he interrupted his own thought. "DON'T GO TO BASEL. HASELMAUS NEVER BELIEVED IN YOUR HOMUNCULUS ANYWAY. HE DIDN'T SAY SO, BUT I COULD TELL. I'M NOT STUPID, I CAN TELL A THING LIKE THAT. HASELMAUS NEVER BELIEVED IN YOUR HOMUNCULUS. HASELMAUS THOUGHT YOU WERE CRAZY. HE PROBABLY STILL THINKS YOU'RE CRAZY. DON'T GO TO BASEL."

But anywhere else, anywhere near. Along the lakeshore. Or into the downtown traffic, just circle the block. Just get out of there.

A few minutes later, as Eichhorn passed along the Seestrasse, going in the direction of Rapperswil and feeling a little calmer, a thought struck him—a wild idea, to be sure, but just wild enough, maybe, to work. Schwank wanted to see Jung—or Young. "Prez," he called him. Well, why not *give* him Prez? He knew a medium in Zürich, one Gretchen N., an old friend from his student days and a fellow Swedenborgian. Why not stage a séance, he thought, and take Schwank to it, or hold the séance there in his room at the Helvetius if he refused to budge, and get Gretchen to channel this Prez? Yes! That'd move the patient off his dead spot if nothing else would. Eichhorn would write the script. Of course, he'd have to do some research beforehand, he hardly knew a thing about Prez, apart from having heard his father mention the name, but that shouldn't be too hard, and once he'd gotten a few basic facts down he could establish Prez's bona fides and then slip something into the communication like ... like ... Oh damn! Suddenly he remembered. How could he have forgotten in the first place? It was a measure of his distraction. Gretchen was a *legitimate* medium. Dedicated to the calling. Absolutely honest. She'd never stoop to a trick like that, even in a good cause. She'd be insulted even to be asked. And *he* should be ashamed even to have thought of it. What would his parents say, not to mention the Swedish Seer himself? Oh, damn, damn, damn, damn, DAMN. He turned around and drove back to the hospital.

The attendant was waiting for him in his office. Schwank had come out of his trance, he said. (Loyal attendant! Calling it a trance.) He wanted to see Herr Doktor right away. It was urgent: Eichhorn had to witness something. There must be a witness, Schwank said. And the witnessing had to take place now; every second counted. Apparently time was important to the patient after all. Where had Herr Doktor been, anyway? Schwank was standing in the middle of his room, screaming.

Eichhorn found him beside the worktable, in his shirtsleeves. He had stopped screaming. "You're late," he announced matter-of-factly. "*Tempus fugit*, bud. It was, it is, and before you know it, baby, it's past. Ding-dong. Now, you sit over there and watch." Schwank pointed to a folding chair across the room.

Eichhorn went and sat. With great ceremony, as if everything depended on the just-so-ness of each movement, Schwank unbuttoned his cuffs and carefully rolled up his sleeves, patting the cloth into place over his biceps. Then he lifted the dinner plate off the chamber pot and placed it to one side on the table. He reached down into the pot and took out the metal skull, raising it above his head as he had in front of Jung's house.

The skull had turned a dull black, with specks of silver and russet on the wire sticking out of the cranium. An oily slime dripped onto the homunculus' hair and ran down his forearms.

The stench was truly alarming.

It did not seem to bother Schwank. "Juice of the Clouds," he commented. "Clouds of Joy. Zodiac Suite. *Vera origo atque intima aeternitatis natura est ipsa existendi necessitas.*"

He set the skull down next to the take-up reel, which was already on its spindle, attached to its stand. He fished the tip of the wire out of the coil and slipped it into the slot at the hub of the reel. Then, turning the spindle ever so slowly, he bent his head over the wire and listened.

No sound came out. Except for the creak of the reel, the room was silent.

"Shit. Oh, shit," Schwank muttered. But he kept on turning the crank, as slowly as he could.

Five minutes went by. Ten. Eichhorn had given up hope. But suddenly Schwank broke into a grin. He stopped, turned the crank back a little, and listened again. Still there was no sound, but now Schwank was smiling. He began to tap his foot. He looked at the doctor and beamed. "You see, Doc?" he asked. "What did I tell you? WHAT DID I TELL YOU, SQUIRREL MAN? *Sympnoia panta*, baby, *sympnoia panta*."

He called for pencil and paper. "Twenty pencils," he said. "A whole ream of paper." When they came he started to write, letter by letter, turning the crank slowly, nodding his head, his foot going like mad in the silence.

That night another rain of cantaloupes was reported in Zürich.

I

The Oracle Speaks.
Xhgjgghgff2323333.
Monadology.

From *The Cry of the Gehirngespinstgemach: The Delphic Oracle Recordings Discovered, Brought Out of Oblivion and Transcribed Word for Word by Empedocles Schwank, Keeper of the Central Fire* (Unpublished manuscript in the possession of P. C. Haselmaus):

… xhgjgghgff2323333? dhfgrh! GNHJJ! For if an invisible power—some genie, perhaps, who mhhgdddsfl who meddles in our affairs for some unknown reasome—took pleasure in giving us dreams that were well-connected with our preceding life and in conformity among themselves, could we distinguish them from realities before being awakened? And what prevents the course of our life from being a long, well-ordered dream, a dream from which we could be wakened in a moment? Suppose, for instance, that my name is the xhgjgghgff2323333; suppose, further, that I ghgf that I am ghgf that I am waiting with the rest of the cast backstage, in the wings, if you like, of an opera house, just before curtain time on opening night. Say that the opera is an historical piece. Imagine the costumes. They come from every period you can think of, brightly colored silks and brocades, with plumes, ribbons, extravagant lace: how wonderful! But in that case I am dressed in plainest grey. For

I am special, I must stand out, I am to sing the title role. Yes! After an Aeon of miscasting, I am back in my Primal Form. I cannot act save with perfect harmony. The present kgkgkgkj the present kgkj the present is pregnant with the future. *Sympnoia panta!*

Stagehands rush past me, maneuvering tall flats into position. One shows an old chemical laboratory, with furnaces, crucibles and strangely shaped vessels. Another depicts a gigantic cross-section of the human brain, still another an old map of the world with the land masses all out of proportion, pressed together like wayfarers sheltering from the storm or stretching themselves at ease, floating in regal splendor across an endless sea.

In the wings opposite me the principals congregate: an auburn-haired lady I think I know from elsewhere, in a long white dress with the shoulders bare, a red rose tucked in her belt; a man in blue from the seventeenth century, face half hidden by a massive black wig; a large, frisky dog—it must be an actor in a dog suit—with golden fur, thick white ruff and long, grizzled nose. The lady and the dog converse in muted tones, trading gossip perhaps. He laughs at a joke she makes, silken ears catching the light as he throws back his head.

Somewhere above us machinery begins to hum, in place of the music that ought to have started by now. The seventeenth century gentleman stares up into the flies. He takes off his wig and presses it to his heart; his crown is bald as an egg. The curtain parts, revealing not an auditorium but row after row of empty seats, set in a wheat field under a starry sky. This is disconcerting to say the least, but there is no help for it now; the show must go on. I advance to the footlights and raise my voice to the gods.

"Ladies and gentleman of the cosmos, planets, suns and comets, luminaries of all persuasions! Allow me, if you please, to introduce myself. I am a monad, unique and indivisible, a soul unmodified by matter, at your service. I am a metaphysical point without extension, a simple substance that enters into composites, a true atom of nature in this best of all possible worlds.

"Hear me! I am a living mirror of the universe! In me you may read all that has happened, or will happen, or is happening, here or anywhere. My dissolution is not to be feared and there is no way conceivable by which I can perish through natural means. Likewise there is no way conceivable by which I can come into existence through natural means; I cannot be formed by composition. I can begin or end only all at once, through creation or annihilation. There is no possibility of transposition within me; I cannot be changed in my inner being or by any other created thing, nor is it possible to conceive of any internal movement which can be produced, directed, increased or diminished within me. I have no windows through which anything may come in or go out. Neither substance nor accident can enter me. I am an entire world. I am the glory of God. My name is—"

But I get no further. A burst of applause drowns me out, rising in waves from every corner of the galaxy. The whole sky goes wild with joy. Shooting stars plunge deliriously to earth. The stage is showered with rose petals.

And all these things are true! I shout, as the ovation dies down and I set out once more on the long trek towards waking. Every one of these statements absolutely is proven and justified, in pre-established harmony, yes, every syllable! ... Or rather (I come a bit closer to consciousness) they used to be true, a few of them anyway, once upon a time, once upon a very long time, ago. But somewhere along the line, through some concatenation of causes the grotesqueness of which I can barely imagine, a terrible mistake was made. For I *have* come into existence through natural means, and not just once but over and over again, in countless locations and eras. For century after century I have been produced, directed, annihilated, transposed and reformed by composition. Substance and accident have entered me all over the world, whenever they felt like it, in mansions, huts, hotels, barns, prisons, factories, lazarettos, martellos, minarets, masjids, pagodas, baptisteries, basilicas, igloos, wickiups, hogans, tupiks, yurts, cottages, caverns, mine shafts, drifts, crypts, catacombs, stupas, monasteries, cathedrals, charterhouses, slaughterhouses, countinghouses, opera houses, meeting houses, boathouses, blockhouses, boardinghouses, gatehouses, icehouses, charnel houses, farmhouses, townhouses, country houses, doghouses, henhouses, workhouses, cathouses, longhouses, powderhouses, sweathouses, alehouses, almshouses, outhouses, castles, convents, pigsties and palaces. I have been increased, diminished, torn down, boarded up, bricked in, cleaned out, scraped, scorched, papered, plastered, paneled, dusted, gutted, flooded, painted and refurnished. Once I was hung with chandeliers. Another time I was filled with cow dung. If I ever really had a name I have no idea what it could have been. As for my inner being—if the existence of such a thing can even be posited without gales of laughter, now that I am fully awake—it has been shat on, pissed on, puked in, screwed in, slept in and walked over until all trace of whatever it once was surely has been obliterated: I would not know it if I caved in on it. The applause from the heavens has stopped—thank God. All that the Encores from Algol and the Bravos from Betelgeuse have done for me is to start an acute pain running through my upper reaches like an old, familiar crack through plaster. All thoughts of monads or metaphysical points, not to speak of souls and living mirrors of the universe, go back to the dream world they came from. My eye opens a slit, onto a rough patch of wall in the dismal green-grey light. This day is no different from any other. I am still what I have always been—absurdly, incomprehensibly—for all my years on this planet, in one form or another: a room without windows.

2

Jump For Joy

"I never saw anybody so happy in my life," Eichhorn's narrative continues. "He literally danced for joy that first day. He jumped up from the table and broke into a Charleston, at least it looked like a Charleston, arms and legs every which way for about five seconds. '*Sympnoia panta! Sympnoia panta! Panta, panta, panta!*' he shouted. Then back to work, ear bent to that wire, shaking his head, tapping his foot in time to God knows what, and writing. Letter by letter sometimes, erasing sometimes, stopping, turning the reel back to listen again, but getting it down eventually, filling up the pages. And all the time—so far as I could tell—silence, cold, unbroken silence. Not to him, though. Oh, brother, not to him."

3

THE EDUCATION OF A
SPIRITUAL AUTOMATON

The Cry of the Gehirngespinstgemach:

And *what* a room, ugh! Constricted, ill-proportioned, an architectural afterthought. Front and back, I'm a good fifteen feet wide, but my sides aren't much deeper than a closet. Three of my walls are solid plaster, but the fourth is just a black woolen curtain, hung on a brass rod running the width of me and shut tight against whatever is beyond. Inside me I hold whatever the people in this house have no use for. At least I can think of no other explanation for the pile of old chairs, most of them broken; the pair of packing crates with the horsehair mattress laid on top of them; the lowboy with its drawers missing; the stacks of musty books; the cracked mahogany table. Screwed into my back wall, several rows of shelves accommodate the overflow: a tangle of wigs, false beards and moustaches; half a dozen tin horns; a brass bell with a wooden handle; a bridal dress folded up next to a gentleman's cashmere suit; six or seven hats of various styles; an engraved portrait of a lady in a silver frame; a tarnished mirror; a coil of rope; some strips of gauze; a bolt of cloth; and a mechanical contraption on a tripod, covered with a grease-spotted cloth.

A film of dust lies over everything; the air is thick and stale. Faint rustling sounds, barely audible, come from somewhere behind the shelves, as if a family of ghosts lived there. I imagine I can make out their chatter; they tell each other the same stories over and over, ticking off their disappointments on ectoplasmic fingers, rehearsing losses that never can be recovered, fabricating plans never to be carried out.

How long has this room been the vehicle of my soul? A year? A century? A millennium. I have no idea. Nor can I say what room I was before this, nor recall how the transformation was accomplished. In my dream the past, present and future were an open book within me, but in the grim actuality of waking I must admit that the attrition of the ages has worn my memory to an embarrassing smoothness. Great swaths of my history are virtual blanks to me now, though I'm sure that not so long ago—yesterday, even? Last week?—I could have rattled off every detail, chapter and verse. A young man's face, flushed with anticipation, and a woman's voice saying "*Enfin vous voilà!*" are all I have left of the seventeenth century. One glimpse of a marble sarcophagus, carved with swans, its lid chipped in three places, must do duty in my recollection for the whole of classical antiquity. Other images carry no hint of time or place whatsoever. That cow dung might have been shoveled in the Athens of Pericles or the Amherst of Lord Jeffrey. All that stays with me is the animal warmth.

But, after all, how could it be otherwise? Even my moment-to-moment visual experience is fragmentary and always has been. (My hearing, for some reason, is excellent.) Without windows, my eye—I have just one—can see only inside me, and, as if that were not limiting enough, it sees from unpredictable angles, often switching its position without warning as though it had a will of its own. It is as much as I can do, and sometimes far more, to get it to settle where I want for any length of time. What can have caused this aberration is a complete mystery to me. I often imagine, though of course I have no way to prove it, that there are pairs of hands living inside me along with the ghosts and broken furniture, and that they circulate my eye here and there among them, roll it in their palms, hold it a bit, then pass it on—a foolish fancy, I admit, and all the more so since it even fails of its primary objective, which is to give a satisfactory explanation of the eye's motion. For,

25

even assuming the proposition to be true, who or what causes the hands to move? Not I, that's certain. In any even, to study, let us say, my ceiling is at present out of the question, since my eye—which when I awoke was somewhere near the center of me—has just dropped to the floor, right down on the wood. My ceiling might as well be at the North Pole, and the shelves in the Arctic Ocean. All I can make out now are broad, worn planks with their coating of dust, and motes of dust suspended in the air an inch or so above, shimmering softly in the green-grey light. I must say I find them rather interesting. At such close quarters, filling practically my whole field of vision, each one is quite distinct—something I never would have guessed. If Sir Eye would only stay put long enough, I should take some pleasure in counting them—at least it would be a change from listening to the ghosts, and ought to be no trouble at all for a living mirror of the universe, eh? And if those pairs of hands should happen to be overcome by sleep or entrancement, I just might undertake to name the specks, one by one, as Adam did the beasts, or the Babylonians—or whoever it was—the stars. But no: fickle as usual, the eye shoots upward again, stopping abruptly three of four feet from the floor. It swings back and forth a while in mid air, as if uncertain why it had made the journey, then moves rapidly to one of the shelves, burrowing in behind the wedding dress and the cashmere suit, pressing up against a smooth, darkish form I hadn't noticed before—a bottle? A beaker? A vase? My eye is too close to the shape for me to tell for certain, and it doesn't seem to want to investigate, for suddenly my vision shifts a third time and the eye is on the ceiling, nearly grazing a nest of tiny cracks in the plaster and brushing past a big cobweb in the corner. Then it turns—or is rolled over—and rests, steady for the moment, at midheaven. From this vantage I survey myself, and discover I have a guest.

It is the woman from my dream, the actress who was gossiping with the dog player. She must have come in through the curtain while I was studying the cosmology of dust. I'm glad she's here, I was beginning to wonder if she'd show up today. It's not surprising I dreamed of her, she's been a frequent visitor lately. Sometimes she comes in with a man, but more often she's by herself. (Never does she bring the dog.) How attractive she is! Tallish, with a slender figure—almost always in the same dress—striking, you might even say classical, features, and hair that shines red-gold even in this light: she's as familiar to me by now as anything here of my own, and a thousand times more welcome. A lot younger, too! And she seems genuinely to like me—at least she never looks as if she has any special purpose when she pays a call. She's not in a hurry, never puts anything into me or takes anything out. In fact, she usually doesn't do much at all—just lies on the mattress and stares at the ceiling. Sometimes she gets the portrait down from the shelf and cradles it in her lap, humming or singing to herself. (I'm afraid she has an awful time carrying a tune.) Once, she fell asleep, rolled off the mattress and woke up on the floor with a curse—it gave me a shock, I don't mind saying. But otherwise she's never made any disturbance—unlike the man (I think he's her husband), a pudgy, awkward fellow with oily hair and a big moustache. He's always in a sweat about something or other, full of complaints, fussing over this and that, messing with the wigs and false beards, trying them on endlessly, bent over in front of the little mirror, poking through the books, muttering under his breath. Lately he's been spending most of his time on that mechanical contraption—built it himself, actually, right in here, hammering away loud enough to wake the dead, out of junk he hauled in from God knows where. Sets great store by it, he does—won't work on it when his wife's here, either, and always covers it with the cloth before he leaves. It's his own little secret; at least, that's what he thinks.

But today, I notice, the lady is not quite herself—I mean, of course, that her behavior is different. She's made no move to sit or lie down, but is standing in the middle of me drawn up to her full height, contemplating the mahogany table, which she has managed to drag free from the pile of chairs and set in the open space between the packing crates and the lowboy. She's holding a wine glass in one hand and a lit cigar in the other. She cocks her head and laughs softly. It's a refined, almost musical sound. Who would have thought a voice like that could curse the way she did—or have such trouble carrying a tune? After a moment she puts the glass down, reaches up to my top shelf and removes the metal thing, placing it in the center of the table. Giggling, she whisks away the greasy cloth and performs a girlish little curtsy before the object.

It is a small machine—though maybe machine is the wrong word, for it's more human looking than any manmade contrivance I can recall. It stands on an iron tripod eight or ten inches high, which supports a pewter basin tipped at an angle like a pelvis. Driven through the center of the basin is a thick vertical shaft which holds a box of interconnecting gears; further up the shaft is a broad crosspiece, and above that is a silver plated mass about the size of a cantaloupe, hammered crudely into the shape of a head. A wire runs from it down to the gearbox. A crank with a wooden handle sticks out from the spot where the left ear hole should be. Various bars, plates, balls and coils are suspended on wires from the underside of the basin. The whole thing is approximately two feet tall.

The lady takes a drink and sets the glass down again. She moves around the machine, regarding it from different viewpoints, humming—badly—a little tune. Then she stops, wets her finger tip on her tongue and quickly draws a pair of eyes on the object's head: big, loopy pupils in saliva with sloppy dabs for the lashes. Below them she adds two dots for nostrils and a lopsided crescent for mouth.

In the corner of the ceiling my eye blinks and goes out. A gabble of voices invades my mind, scores of them shouting at once a tumult of numbers, dates, equations. Soon they abate and give way to a chorus of women chanting, "*Enfin vous voilà! Vous voilà enfin! Sympnoia panta! Vous voilà enfin!*"

In a moment my vision returns. But I am seeing now with two eyes instead of one, and my view is from the head of the machine, not the ceiling. The lady's face is directly in front of me, barely a foot away. Her eyes are bright green, glistening with exhilaration. She seems to be looking straight through me.

She puffs on her cigar, leans closer and exhales into my mouth. The smoke moves through me like thought. In ancient Greece the priestesses of the Delphic Oracle inhaled the smoke from henbane seeds before delivering their prophecies. In China the Taoists used hemp. 10 times 8 is 80. 11 minus 9 is 2. The Peace of Westphalia was signed in 1648, the Magna Carta in 1215. The orbital period of Jupiter is 11.86 years. 17 times 3 is 51. 6 minus 6 is 0.

She slips her hand under the basin; I feel her twisting one of the wires around a ball. With the other hand she gives the crank in my ear hole a turn.

A blast of organ music sounds inside me. Mercury has no satellites. The German mathematician and philosopher Gottfried Wilhelm Leibniz died at 10:00 PM, Saturday, November 14, 1716, aged 70 years, 4 months, 13 days, 3 hours and 15 minutes. Sir Isaac Newton, who hated him, greeted the news with glee. Newton was certain that Leibniz had plagiarized from him his discovery of the calculus, and for years he had done everything in his power to ruin Leibniz's reputation. The square root of 16 is 4. 21 minus 6 is 15. 14 is 9 plus 5. 13 divided by 3 is 4.3333333333333333333333333 333333333333333333333333333333333333333333333333333333333333333 333333333333333333333333333333333333333333333333333333333333333 333333333333333333333333333333—

She adjusts another wire, wrapping it around one of the metal plates. 1 plus 2 plus 3 plus 4 is 10. The Greek philosopher Pythagoras was born in 569 B.C. on the island of Samos. A squared plus B squared is C squared. He taught his followers the doctrine of the transmigration of souls. He also taught that all things are made up of numbers. 1, 3, 6, for example. 15, 21, 28; 36, 45, 55. 1 plus 1 is 2. 2 plus 1 is 3. 3 plus 2 is 5. Isaac Newton used to tell his disciples that Pythagoras had understood the law of universal gravitation but kept the knowledge hidden from the multitude.

5 plus 3 is 8. 8 plus 5 is 13. The world's smallest mammal is the white-toothed pygmy shrewmouse. It measures between 35 and 48 millimeters from head to tail and eats 3.3 times its own weight daily. 3.33. 3.33333. 1, 4, 10, 20. 35, 56, 84; 120, 165, 220.

Malachite is green. Beryl is green. Gold is yellow; the alchemists gave it the same written symbol as the Sun. They believed that metals vegetated in the earth, striving toward perfection, and that gold was the purest of them all.

The specific gravity of gold is 19.3. 193 is 1 plus 9 plus 3. 1 plus 9 plus 3 is 13. 13 is 1 plus 3. 1 plus 3 is 4. One of the earliest alchemists is said to have been a woman, Maria Prophetissa; she is credited with the axiom, "One becomes Two, Two becomes Three, and out of the Third comes One as the Fourth." Isaac Newton made use of her writings.

768; 3,072; 12,288. Kyanite is blue. Cinnabar is red. Eggplants are purple. The pineal gland, situated between the two cerebral hemispheres in the middle of the brain, is reddish grey. In humans it measures anywhere from a third to a half an inch in width, weighs about a tenth of a gram, and is shaped like a pine cone—hence its name. Its function is still largely unknown. Herophilus of Alexandria (fl. 300 B.C.) claimed that it regulated the flow of thought. René Descartes (1596–1650) held that the pineal was the seat of the soul. Xeniades of Croton (540–473 B.C.), a dissident pupil of Pythagoras, taught that the entire contents of each of an individual's incarnations—the future existences as well as the ones gone by—were stored like seeds in various secret recesses distributed everywhere throughout the individual's body.

13 plus 8 is 21; 21 plus 13 is 34. Sir Isaac Newton was born under a full moon, between 1:00 and 2:00 AM, on December 25, 1642, in the hamlet of Woolsthorpe in Lincolnshire. He never saw his father, who died before the child was born. Sir Isaac's favorite color was crimson. The bed he died in (on March 20, 1727, in the village of Kensington just outside London, again between 1:00 and 2:00 in the morning) had crimson curtains, and all through the house were crimson drapes, crimson furniture, crimson cushions, crimson hangings. Virtually all of Newton's adult life was passed in two places—first Cambridge, where he was Lucasian Professor of mathematics, then London, where he was Master of the Mint.

His hair turned white before he was 30.

He did not believe in the Holy Trinity.

He hated Roman Catholicism.

He burned several boxes of his papers shortly before he died.

He was buried in Westminster Abbey.

34 plus 21 is 55. G. W. Leibniz was born at 6:45 PM on Sunday, July 1, 1646, in Leipzig. He attempted to reconcile the Protestant and Roman Catholic faiths and was partial to blue. Late in life he used to receive visitors to his rooms in Hanover clad in fur stockings, a fur-lined blue dressing gown and a large, unfashionably long black wig. The sovereign he served in his final years disapproved of him. For more than a century after his death his grave went unmarked. He died worn out and disconsolate, from neglect, from physical and mental exertion, from the failure of his projects to find support, from the plagiarism controversy with Newton, from crippling gout, unable during his last few days even to hold a pen anymore—he who had written book upon book, whose correspondence alone would fill volumes, and had gone to recipients all over the civilized world. But in his prime he had been hardy and active. He wrote the *Discourse of Metaphysics* while stranded in a snowstorm

in the Harz Mountains. He traveled the length and breadth of Europe, on diplomatic missions, on scientific investigations, or for historical research; he thwarted assassins single-handedly in the Adriatic. He believed that all matter was composed of souls, which he called monads, metaphysical points, living mirrors of the universe, the true atoms of nature, and that these souls together with their bodies were—*what in the name of God is happening to me? How do I suddenly know these things?*

The lady turns the crank once again. 55 plus 34 is 89. 89 plus 55 is 144; 144 plus 89 is 233. The organ music grows louder. It is the *Toccata and Fugue in D Minor*, composed by J. S. Bach in Mulhausen, Germany and finished, I know with sudden and absolute clarity, at 3:21 in the afternoon of November 16, 1707. Bach was sitting at his desk in an open shirt. His coat—dark blue, with a rather large gravy stain on the left sleeve three and a half inches below the shoulder—lay over the back of a chair on the other side of the room. He was 22 years, 7 months and 26 days old, with a stuffy nose and scratchy throat, the lingering effects of a head cold caught the previous week while riding in an open coach during a downpour. Seconds after the final notes were written, the composer's cat, a well-fed black-and-grey-striped tiger named Franziska, with white chest, belly, forepaws and rear legs and a circular black spot about the size of the above-mentioned gravy stain on the upper back portion of her left rear leg, made a leap for the desk and knocked over the inkwell. Only quick action on Bach's part saved the score from serious damage.

Lying open on a table, next to the chair with the coat on it, was a book by Leibniz, *A Dissertation on the Art of Combinations*, first published in 1666. One page, the recto—also spotted with a gravy stain—began with the heading, "DEMONSTRATION OF THE EXISTENCE OF GOD", and went on to make good its promise in 21 closely reasoned statements. Bach had been studying the work earlier in the day. When the composer came to die, 43 years later, the volume was at his bedside, blind as he was by then.

233 plus 144 is 377. 377 plus 233 is 610; 610 plus 377 is 987. Wulfenite is orange. Siderite is brown. Molybdenite is black, tar is black. Talc is greasy. Leibniz also wrote a book on the history of the earth, the *Protogaea*, not published during his lifetime. "It seems that this globe was once on fire," he stated, "and that the rocks forming the base of this crust of the earth are scoria

remaining from a great fusion. In their entrails are found metal and mineral products, which closely resemble those emanating from our furnaces." ("The Mines are cold as to sense," wrote Newton, "yet minerals continue in their motion of growing. For nature uses another sort of heat imperceptible to sense, a warmth of the nature of Spirits...."). In fact, the earth's crust, composed of silicate minerals such as pyroxine, olivine and garnet, was formed 4,600,000,000 years ago around a core of molten iron alloy, now about 10,300 degrees Fahrenheit. Within this core is a cooler central mass of solid rock. The ancient Greeks believed that a river of fire, which they named Phlegethon, surrounded the Underworld, and that volcanoes were the chimneys of the smithy of Hephaistos.

Coal is black. Smoke is grey. Morganite is pink. Smiths, being workers of metal, were sacrosanct figures in ancient societies, god-knowers, their techniques a closely guarded secret. Metals have been worked in Egypt for more than 9,000 years. Algonquins and Eskimos have worked copper from time immemorial. Pythagoras discovered the laws of harmony from the ringing of the anvil in a blacksmith's shop. 40,000 years ago, while European peoples were filling their graves with red ocher, packing it in close around the corpses, red iron ore was being taken out of the ground in South Africa, from a place called the Lion Cavern, at Ngwenya.

987 plus 610 is 1,597; 1,597 plus 987 is 2,584. Beginning in the spring of 1667 and continuing for the next 29 years—that is, until he moved to London to take charge of His Majesty's Mint—Isaac Newton conducted alchemical experiments in a laboratory next to the chapel at Trinity College, Cambridge, where he was Lucasian Professor of Mathematics. At the same time as he was doing the scientific work for which he became famous, he also was practicing the ancient art—some called it the "torture"—of metals, distilling, cooking, washing, grinding and pulverizing them in ardent pursuit of the Philosopher's Stone—"the honorable stone," he wrote, transcribing an old manuscript that had passed into his hands, "which is hidden in ye caverns of ye metals ... This stone shall deliver you from ye greatest diseases & keep you from all sadness & affliction & difficulties & bring you from darkness to light, from ye desert to an habitation, & from necessity to abundance." Night after night, moving among his furnaces and crucibles while his fellow

dons slept, watching the matter in his retorts volatize, coagulate, swell and change colors, Newton saw dancing in the ferment the same creatures that adepts before him had encountered and named: the Stone Serpents, Melusina the siren, the Salamander that lives in fire, the Green Lion who swallows the Sun, the Red Man and his White Wife, and the divine Hermaphrodite, great goal of the Work. Within the walls of his vessels these bit, pecked, tore and writhed; they coupled with each other, were slain and dismembered, restored to life, dissolved, turned to vapor, reconstituted and slain again, acting out their parts in the age-old theater of transmutation. Apples are red. Roses are red. Halite is white. Chalcanthite is soluble in water.

2,584 plus 1,597 is 4,181; 4,181 plus 2,584 is 6,765. Dandelions are yellow. Crows are black. "Marry the Red Man to his White Wife," urged one of Newton's masters. "Out of these Two Parents of one Root is brought forth a Noble Son of a Regal Off-spring."

—As if it rose from the body of the sun itself! A fiery beam to the east and north! Isaac Newton never married. According to his doctor, he never even violated chastity. He had a niece, Catherine Barton, the daughter of his half-sister Hannah; Catherine kept house for him in London, and was counted a great beauty and wit. There were two ne'er-do-well nephews: one, Benjamin Smith, a well-known profligate despite his taking holy orders; the other, Robert Barton, Catherine's brother, a colonel who died in a shipwreck on an expedition against Quebec. And there was Nicolas Fatio de Duillier, a young Swiss mathematician whom Newton met in his late forties, and to whom, for a time at least, he gave his heart. Thick white ruff. GHdfjghhD.

6,765 plus 4,181 is 10,946. Leibniz never married, either. (It was said he took seriously the maxim, *Heiraten sei gut, doch musse ein weiser Mann sein ganzes Leben darauf denken*—Marriage is a great thing; a wise man will consider it his whole life.) But he had great friendships with women, such as Sophie, Electress of Hanover and her daughter, Sophie Charlotte, Queen of Prussia, who took pleasure in his conversation and sought his advice. And there was an opera singer in Nuremberg, when he was very young. And rumors of a natural son. FRhgklj. GJSGRFhnsehfjkaaaaar. Artichokes are green. Jade is green. Mercury has no satellites. Tellestisa. The German mathematician is the world's smallest mammal. Jupiter turned white before he was 30.

The sun is in a dog suit, with golden fur, thick white ruff and long, grizzled nose. The Dog Star is Sirius. Betelgeuse is the Giant's Shoulder, Algol the Eye of the Gorgon. The first human being to name a star was Urururururururur. Urururururururur stood four feet, nine and a half inches tall, had eyes the color of graphite, external as well as internal male and female reproductive organs, and lived in Africa 1,263,142 years ago. 1,263,142 is 1,263,142. klctvdsstn. thggnwhc. thickwhite. 3.33333333333333333333333333333333333333333 333333 333333333333333333333333333333333333333333333333333333 33333333333333333333333333333333333333333333333333333333333333333 33333333333333333333333333333333333333—

The lady blows more smoke into my mouth and turns the crank a third time.

O merciful monads! Great leaping entelechies! The dream was true—I *am* a living mirror of the universe! In continuous sequence unfolding out to infinity, past, present and future are disclosing themselves within me! Clear and unblinking, my Eye—which just moments ago was bouncing aimlessly from one dingy corner of my self to another—now flashes out anywhere at my command, each of its 157,325,967 receptors at the ready, to take in not only my current surroundings but the far, far reaches of time to come. See! SEE! The present year is 1855. In 1856 ductile steel will be made for boiler plating. The first corkscrew patent—Number 27,615—will be granted to one M. L. Bryan of New York City on March 27, 1860. In 1867 Blessed Germaine Cousin of Pibrac, whose body, whose body remained miraculously incorrupt after her death in 1601, will be canonized at long last by Pope Pius IX.

The first balloon wedding will be performed on October 19, 1874. The Reverend H. B. Jeffries will marry Mary Walsh and Charles M. Colton over Cincinnati, Ohio. On May 8, 1877, a dog show—thick white ruff—will take place at the Hippodrome in New York City, with 1,191 entries. Later that same year, in Menlo Park, New Jersey, a man named Thomas Edison will complete his invention of a machine called the phonograph, which will record sound by means of a vibrating stylus making perforations in a length of tinfoil attached to a rotating cylinder.

Lady Margaret Scott will win the first British Ladies' Golf Championship in 1893! Six years later, Nikola Tesla will receive messages from Mars in his laboratory at Colorado Springs. In 1902, Leibniz's remains will be exhumed from their crypt in Hanover. The cranial capacity of the skull will be found to be only 1,422 cubic centimeters. Three years later, energy will equal mass times the speed of light squared.

In 1910, dissection of the pineal of the New Zealand lizard tuatara will reveal an eye 0.5 millimeters in diameter, complete retina, lens and a nerve connecting the eye to the brain. Research over succeeding decades will link the pineal in mammals with the secretion of two previously unknown substances, to be called serotonin and melatonin. The first successful chinchilla farm will be founded in California in 1923.

Thomas Edison will die in 1931! In the same year, one Cab Calloway, born like Newton on December 25, will utilize Edison's invention to record a musical composition called "Minnie the Moocher". In 1939, Coleman Hawkins will record "Body and Soul". In 1942, Lester Young will record the same piece. And in Hackensack, New Jersey, on December 24, 1954, a few hours before Sir Isaac's 312th birthday, in a room full of recording equipment and in the middle of a performance of "The Man I Love", a man named Thelonious Monk will stop playing the piano. Early the next morning, Urururururururur's fossilized brain case will be dug up near Lake Nyasa.

The lady flicks the ash off her cigar. She connects the ends of two coils to each other and squeezes. O specimen of dynamics! The crank starts to turn by itself.

Principles of nature and of grace! I draw my Eye, sharp as the tuatara lizard's, back to the present. Today's date is May 28. The George Dixon Velocitrot Lubricator has just been patented in Washington. In Paris, Jean-Auguste-Dominique Ingres, on his way home from a visit to his acclaimed display of paintings in the first French Universal Exposition, stops suddenly in the street to congratulate himself, and not for the first time, on the enduring beauty of his *Bather Seen from the Back*, a paean to ideal form painted barely fifty years before. In the Crimea, the British army masses before Sebastopol, while Florence Nightingale lies recovering from fever and delirium in a hut on the heights above Balaklava. Though Lord Raglan came to visit an hour ago, and left under the impression that she was better, she still imagines an engine turning in her brain, still sees her room filling up, several times a day, with multitudes crying out for food and supplies. A gentleman from Persia drops in, bothering her about money.

A china squirrel watches from the dresser as Friedrich Nietzsche, aged ten, directs Sebastopol's defense from his bedroom in Naumburg, Germany, planning with toy soldiers a victory for the Russians. The squirrel, painted with touches of saffron and brown, sporting a paper crown, pale blue sash and the name King Squirrel I, given it by its young master, is a present from Friedrich's late father, Karl Ludwig Nietzsche, who had it from his father, who had it from his, who bought it from a butcher in Ansbach, who stole it from the man who made it, J. J. Kaendler of Meissen, who produced it in 1751 following a formula written down by Johann Friedrich Böttger, alchemist and porcelain artist, three days before he died, raving mad, on March 13, 1719, in Dresden. Cooking hotter and hotter, boiling in its own juices, Böttger's fevered mind yielded up, at the last possible moment, the secret he had sought all his life. In a few scribbled phrases, almost illegibly, he recorded in a private code directions for making the Philosopher's Stone—the divine Hermaphrodite, Noble Son of a Regal Off-spring—out of a mixture of kaolin and alabaster. "In all the world," said Kaendler, "there is no squirrel like this squirrel."

Charity Foxcroft has hanged herself in Philadelphia. Sarah Maloney has taken laudanum in New York. Fifteen weeks after becoming a viable zygote, Eugene V. Debs gestates contentedly in Terra Haute, Indiana. Knox's hats are pronounced unique by all those qualified to judge. Hyatt's Life Balsam cures scrofula, old ulcers, diseases of the blood. Twenty years of oblivion has not been the fate of Deshler's Fever and Ague Pills.

O ultimate origination of things! O spasms of contraction! Infinitesimal gnosis! 10,946 minus 4,181 is 6,765; 6,765 minus 2,584 is 4,181. 4,181 minus 4,180 is 1. My present abode is part of a house built by Pilgrims, at Number 18 Prospect Street, in the village of Aubrey, Massachusetts. The Atlantic breaks not a mile from the hem of my curtain. The air above my floorboards contains 995,374 motes of dust; their names are available on request. 32,407 filaments make up the cobweb in the corner of my ceiling; 38 cracks run through the plaster. And I was wrong about one thing: I am no storage room, or at least no ordinary one. For the ghosts behind the shelving are real! This house belongs to two spirit mediums, the man and woman who come to visit me, and I am their cabinet, the space they use to gather and concentrate their psychic powers—just as this machine in the middle of me has gathered and concentrated mine. And I do have a name, I do have a name after all! I am the *Gehirngespinstgemach*! Yes! And today, May 28, is my birthday. And I have been immured as a room for exactly 2,440 years.

But today—today!—someone is coming to rescue me. And the dog—the dog!—that Dog will have something to do with it!

Enfin vous voilà. Vous voilà enfin.

987? 4.333? 6! 28! 496!

4

THE MUSIC OF THE RHIZOMES

TRUE TALES OF THE PARANORMAL:

Eichhorn stopped his visits to Haselmaus as soon as Schwank began his transcriptions. He spent every free moment at the Helvetius, in his patient's boarded-up room. The work there seemed enormously important. He felt he and the homunculus were on the verge of tremendous discoveries, if only Schwank could be kept productively to his task.

One question, however, still troubled him. But a subtle approach was essential. "I didn't want to jinx anything," he wrote, "I was afraid he might fly off the handle or go back into himself. Still, I had to know, and after a couple of days I asked him, as gently as I could, how he heard all the things he was writing down, when I, who was right beside him, couldn't hear a word.

"It didn't bother him at all. 'I listen to the bass,' he said matter-of-factly. 'You gotta listen to the bass, Squirrel Man. Just like in music.' And he named some bass players, Charlie Dominguez, I think, and a few others. 'That sound's under everything,' he explained, 'way down at the bottom. That's where you gotta listen, baby. Down with the root notes, the rhizomes. Music of the spheres, man? Hah. Music of the rhizomes! Now hear that, sweetie. Ooooh, just hear that: Klctvdsstn! Thggnwhc! Man, I wish Prez was here.' And he went back to his writing."

5

AN INTRODUCTION TO A
SECRET ENCYCLOPAEDIA

From *The Encyclopaedia of Reincarnation*, Ninth Edition, 2005:

GEHIRNGESPINSTGEMACH,[1] THE. (b. 585 B. C., Miletus, Asia Minor.) Fallen Leibnizian monad, living mirror of the universe; erstwhile soul unmodified by matter; one of the irreducible simple substances that are the ultimate constituents of reality, come to a bad end. Due to a slight but unprecedented shudder some thousands of years ago on the part of the Aristotelian Unmoved Mover, the *Gehirngespinstgemach* was precipitated out of its proper abode in the Empyrean and dropped at random into the physical world of time and space, where it found itself incarnated in the 6th century B. C. as a room without windows. Since then it has transmigrated against its will from place to place and from era to era as a succession of interiors, sometimes large and richly appointed, sometimes humble and shabby, but always without windows. It is condemned to remain a room, wandering without respite, until Metakynos, its friend and former companion who has been assigned to its deliverance, can find it and bring it back.

---

[1] Ger. Fantasy room; literally, brain web room. From *Gehirn*, brain, brains, sense; *Gespinst*, web, cocoon, tissue (of lies, etc.); and *Gemach*, chamber, room, apartment. The name is of recent origin, there being no record of its use before the middle of the 17th century, in the opera of the same name by Halbstiefel. The ancient Greek name for the *Gehirngespinstgemach* was *to apeiron chorion* (Acanthus of Rhodes, *The Thracian Histories*, passim; pseudo-Anaximander, frag. 2).

The *Gehirngespinstgemach's* fall caused serious harm to the universal order. A vacuum was created in what previously had been a seamless plenum, and the best of all possible worlds was permanently flawed. Originally the monad's function was to stand with Metakynos on the bridge between life and death, dispensing justice to the souls who passed over, The *Gehirngespinstgemach* exercising severity while Metakynos advocated mercy. Between them they effected what Leibniz, much later, would call "the charity of the wise." It was also the *Gehirngespinstgemach's* job to make a record of each case and to enter it, together with any commentary that seemed necessary, into an ongoing universal history. But after the monad's fall, and Metakynos' enforced neglect of his post, the proper flow of earthly incarnations was wholly disrupted. Souls found themselves unable to pass into the existences which their conduct had merited; instead they were shunted off in utterly unsuited directions. Scipio Africanus was reborn as an oak in Sherwood Forest. Saint Augustine came back as Marie de Medici, Marie de Medici as a washing machine. A cup of coffee became Lola Montez. Worse, while some souls were tossed haphazardly from one life to the next, others were presented with whole cycles of lives predetermined from the outset, without any hope of change or redemption: John Calvin, for instance, has always been a human being. It goes without saying that these conditions still obtain in the world. Nothing can restore the balance except Metakynos' rescue of the monad.

Aside from its lack of windows and the faint, almost imperceptible hint of greenish grey in whatever light it fails to reject, the *Gehirngespinstgemach* has no observable characteristics: many people have passed large portions of their lives, even several lives, in the monad and not known it. Its effects on individuals vary. Some persons are afflicted with chronic illnesses; others feel only a comfortable glow. Still others produce works of genius and benefit to mankind: some of the greatest achievements of the human spirit have been initiated by the *Gehirngespinstgemach*. In many cases, however, exposure to the room produces a kind of megalomania. Here the sufferer, unaware that he suffers, treats the world outside himself as if it were merely, in Leibniz's phrase, the temporary reflexive representation of his own thought. He is given to grandiose assertion. His subtle body is invaded by glue. Sometimes his head physically enlarges; often the victim feels it has become transparent.

Eventually his sense of selfhood, swollen past the bursting point, explodes, allowing not only apperceptions of the past and present but also apprehensions of the future to rush in unchecked, so that, as Max Möhre writes, "his mind becomes no more than a playpen for the antics of time ... An ever-increasing amount of sensation is received by a constantly diminishing capacity for discrimination." At last, all distinctions of time, space and causality cease to exist for the victim. "For all practical purposes, his psyche becomes indiscernible from the flood of phenomena passing through him," Möhre continues. "He gives himself entirely over to them, following them without hesitation to what he thinks are the ends of the universe, ecstatic as he feels his spirit slipping away into the limitless climes beyond. From this vantage he looks back at the world, far below him, and finds that he has effected the greatest transformation of all: he has become God, the original monad, supreme Architect and Final Cause of all creation. His perfection is absolutely infinite."

The many manifestations of the *Gehirngespinstgemach* across the centuries include a brief period in 49 B. C. as a hut beside the Rubicon, which served as a shelter for Julius Caesar shortly before he crossed the river. By A.D. 325, the room was in Asia Minor, at the imperial palace in the town of Nicaea, when the august council of Christian bishops took place. The defeat of Arianism and the consequent victory of the doctrine of the Trinity were assured when the deacon Athanasius caucused secretly with three undecided bishops in the cool, grey stillness of what they took to be an unused dressing room. Late in the 11th century, the *Gehirngespinstgemach* served as a larder in the Benedictine monastery of Bec, while its prior, Anselm (later St. Anselm), was writing his ontological proof of the existence of God. Anselm was fond of slipping into the larder late at night and helping himself to victuals when he could be sure there was no one about.

Though it has no control over its migrations, the *Gehirngespinstgemach* does have its affinities, and in the 15th century it began a long association with alchemy. By 1475, it was securely established, once again as a larder, at the Priory of Bridlington in Yorkshire, where its canon, George Ripley, performed his transmutations and wrote the *Compound of Alchimie*. By 1644, the monad had crossed the sea to Harvard College where, as a seven by five foot cubicle, it served as a study for the young George Starkey, who had just been introduced to alchemy that year and was reading Ripley along with assigned texts in logic and physics. One night as he slept a voice came to him, whispering secrets of the composition of matter, and the true nature of the Philosophical Fire.

On another night, two centuries later but only a score of miles to the north east in Aubrey, Massachusetts, the same voice instructed the sleeping Abimelech Barton on how to set up an alchemical laboratory in his home by creating a windowless room on the ground floor. On Barton's death the laboratory was demolished, but in 1850 his daughter, Efficiency, and her husband, Dr. Eggbeater Caws, stretched a woolen blanket across the area in order to form a spiritualistic cabinet for use in their séances. In an instant the *Gehirngespinstgemach* was reconstituted.

Shortly thereafter, the couple's mediumship acquired immense celebrity. Especially popular were their séances channeling the spirits of G. W. Leibniz and Sir Isaac Newton. What was not known, however, or even suspected, was that they themselves were reincarnations of Leibniz and Newton, he of the former, she of the latter, so that they were, without knowing it, simply carrying their previous lives over whole into their present ones.

For four years the Cawses enjoyed a great success, working together as a team in cities and towns throughout the northeast. But when Dr. Caws undertook on his own the construction of a machine which he claimed was a calculator built on instructions by Leibniz, dissension arose between husband and wife. This led in the following year to the sudden death of the doctor in mysterious circumstances and the simultaneous flight of Mrs. Caws. Ironically, as we now know, the machine had the unintended effect of enlarging the *Gehirngespinstgemach's* consciousness to an astonishing degree, so much so that the room seems to have recovered, if only temporarily, some of the omniscience it once possessed.

Evidence of this expansion of consciousness is given in *The Cry of the Gehirngespinstgemach*, an unpublished manuscript by Empedocles Schwank, now in private hands in Basel. But the published literature on the monad is considerable, beginning in ancient times with a fragment from pseudo-Anaximander ("Boundless or bound, the *apeiron chorion* ... is") and the *Thracian Histories* of Acanthus of Rhodes, and continuing into the twentieth century with Max

Möhre's magisterial *Die Gehirngespinstgemachnaturwissenschaft* (Köln, 1927).
Ethel Mammon Striker's *Gravity Newton: The Life and Legend of Efficiency
Caws* (Philadelphia, 1901) is a groundbreaking biography, containing invalu-
able interviews with Mrs. Caws together with a description of the inside of the
spirit cabinet and an account of her husband's construction of the machine.
There is also an opera, *Das Gehirngespinstgemach*, by J. P. Halbstiefel (1638–
1701). First performed in Germany in 1666 and based on texts by Acanthus
of Rhodes, it was revived in Florence in the 19th century by Luigi Coturno, to
tremendous acclaim. Less successful were attempted revivals in Aubrey, where
a version of the piece was performed yearly from 1902–1907.

The *Gehirngespinstgemach* was born at 6:13 in the evening of May 28, 585
B. C. at Miletus in Asia Minor, during an eclipse of the sun which its father,
Thales of Miletus, had predicted. The first Greek ever to bring off such a
forecast, Thales also is said to have been the founder of Greek philosophy,
astronomy and geometry; it is now known that he was, as well, an early incarnation of Sir Isaac Newton. The *Gehirngespinstgemach's* mother was G. W.
Leibniz, at that time a Thracian servant girl named Lipnike. In Plato's *The-
aetetus* (which Leibniz was to translate) Socrates described her as "witty and
attractive." Thales and Lipnike met, the story goes, one night when Thales
was out looking at the stars, failed to watch where he was walking and fell
into a well. Lipnike, who was passing by on some errand, laughed loud and
long at the astronomer, remarking pointedly on people who presumed to
understand the heavens but were blind to what was under their feet. No one,
least of all a servant girl, had ever spoken to Thales this way; but far from
being offended, he was altogether charmed. The *Gehirngespinstgemach* was
conceived that very night, in the well itself according to Acanthus of Rhodes,
in an open field beneath the stars according to other authors …

The Cry of the Gehirngespinstgemach:

Quartz has no cleavage. Azurite is blue. 1,2,3,4,5, my Eye catches up to them:
her face covers his as she slides on top of him. His shoulder relaxes. She has
long red hair, a boyish figure, looks about eighteen years old. He could be

forty, with curly hair cropped short and a build like a wrestler. And I? I am alive inside each of them, I am two migrant beings at once, and both of us are toiling, against all the odds, to rejoin ourselves: an egg, .140 millimeter in diameter, extruded from my capsule in her ovary, making my way into the uterine tube; and a sperm, one of 400,101,210, 51 microns long, my oval flattened head propelled by my tail, driving myself furiously forward at 1.5 millimeters per minute. In a few moments these two of us will be one again.

The Encyclopaedia of Reincarnation:

But wherever it took place, there is no doubt that the conception was maculate in every way; it was Lipnike's pregnancy that was miraculous. For all the ancient authors agree that as the months went by, instead of feeling the child grow inside her, she found that she was beginning to live inside the child. During her last weeks she experienced an increasingly unpleasant sensation of enclosure, and her confinement was literally that. At the height of the eclipse she had a vision of soaring cyclopean masonry, which 2,500 years later would remind Max Möhre of Piranesi's etching of imaginary prisons. Acanthus says that for several months after the monad's birth both Lipnike and Thales, wherever they went, felt themselves wrapped in a mist of pale, greenish light.

Acanthus is often casual about details, preferring a lively story to sober record keeping, but he is nevertheless at pains to set down a full description of the building housing the original *Gehirngespinstgemach*, or *apeiron chorion* as he calls it. He says it was situated on a hill and buried on all four sides up to the roof, except for a small space left at one corner for an entrance. Lipnike gave birth in—or rather to—an underground chamber, which later became a local shrine. Practically all modern scholars, with the exception of Möhre, have discounted these statements, assuming that Acanthus must have borrowed the underground chamber from the well-known tale of Pythagoras' slave Zalmoxis, who lived a generation after Thales and Lipnike and is said to have constructed a similar room in Thrace after obtaining his freedom. Möhre, however, insisted that the reverse was true, that Zalmoxis was inspired by the *apeiron chorion*, and indeed that Pythagoras himself had been influenced by the monad. His remarks were greeted with derision when *Die Gehirngespinstgemachnaturwissenschaft* was published, but in fact Möhre's view was vindicated (though he did not live to see it): in the summer of 1983 the building Acanthus describes was discovered, and in remarkably good condition, during the excavations of Miletus conducted by Curtis Bacchi of the Brewster Institute. Positioned within an open area marked out by boundary stones, on high ground overlooking the ruins of the old Lion Harbor, the shrine structure measured a little more than 18 feet in length by 11 feet in width. It was sunk into the earth, which was mixed with loose stones all around the walls; the building rose only 3 feet 9 inches above the ground at its highest point. It was surmounted by a double-pitched stone roof, to which a number of the original tiles still clung. The sole entrance, a wooden door at the southeast end of the shrine, incised with a large, round eye the pupil of which still held some flecks of yellow paint, was so low that in order to enter one had to bend over double. Inside, a narrow set of steps led down to a chamber containing a broad stone bench in the center of the room; an empty sarcophagus standing against the north wall, its front carved with swans, with its lid lying askew and chipped in several places; three amphorae of the Archaic period, decorated with Gorgons; and numerous clay amulets scattered across the floor, each of them inscribed with an eye. The chamber, which ran the whole length of the building approximately 6 feet beneath the surface of the earth, evidently had been sealed off at a very early date.

All these articles are mentioned specifically by Acanthus. He lays particular emphasis on the various eye-forms in the shrine, stating that the eye was considered to be inseparable from the *apeiron chorion*. He adds that this eye is responsible for what the ancients universally described as the monad's unpredictable and dangerous temperament.

From *The Thracian Histories*, Book IV, by Acanthus of Rhodes:[2]

Some say that the *apeiron chorion* gets its evil disposition from having been born without windows and that its blindness enrages it. But the Thracians tell a different tale. Here is the story of how the *apeiron chorion* got its eye.

A long time ago there lived the Grey Ones, called Graeae, three old sisters grey haired at birth, but fair of face and made in the shape of swans. They were the daughters of Ceto, Whale, and her brother Phorcys, Old-Man-Who-Rules-the-Waves, and the granddaughters of Pontus, Sea, and his mother Gaea, Earth. They had but one eye and one tooth between them, which they shared by turns, passing them from hand to hand.

The Graeae had three other sisters, the Gorgons, horrible to look upon, the worst of them being Medusa, who had serpents for hair and the sight of whose

---

[2] The text used here, and throughout, is *The Thracian Histories of Acanthus of Rhodes*, translated by Roy K. Williams (New London: Swain Press, 1988). In his introduction to the volume, Williams writes: "A Greek historian, satirist and rhetorician, Acanthus was in his prime about A.D. 160. Very little is known of his life. He was born on Rhodes and educated at Pergamum and Athens. From there he traveled to Rome and spent some years in that city as tutor and rhetorician before returning to Athens with the intention, he tells us, of passing the rest of his life communing with the shades of Aristophanes and Menander. However, he found the city much changed from what it was in his student days and soon took ship for his native island. (Valerius Turpens, writing nearly three centuries later, says Acanthus was forced to flee Rome on account of a scandal involving the wife of a senator, and Athens on account of a scandal involving a kinswoman of Herodes Atticus, but these stories are uncorroborated.) It seems to have been on Rhodes that Acanthus completed *The Thracian Histories*, about three-fifths of which survives. Ostensibly a factual account, it is really a compendium of myth and historical material strung together with salacious anecdotes in the manner of the so-called Milesian tales popularized by Aristides of Miletus in the 2nd century B.C. What his contemporaries thought of the Rhodian's work is not known, but so far as moderns are concerned his mixing of genres has done his credibility as an historian little good, despite the scholarly efforts of Möhre and the recent archaeological discoveries of Bacchi.

"Acanthus died sometime before 200. In addition to the *Histories*, he is known to have written a treatise on rhetoric, a book of fables and a comedy, *The Turnips*, all of which are lost."

face turned the viewer to stone. One day Perseus, whose name means Destroyer, came to the cave of the Graeae at the foot of Mount Atlas. It was his mission to find Medusa and cut off her head. He snatched the eye and tooth away from the sisters and refused to give them back until they told him the whereabouts of the Stygian nymphs, from whom he needed the magical weapons—winged sandals, helmet of invisibility and sack to hold the head in—with which to accomplish his task. The Graeae told him, but instead of giving back their eye and tooth as he had promised, he coldly flung them away as far as his arm could send him. The tooth fell to the bottom of Lake Tritonis, but the eye, the Thracians say, sped on through time as well as space to drop at last into the well at Miletus where the *apeiron chorion* was begotten. The screams of the Graeae followed it, like a blare of trumpets breaking open the sky. They echo in the demon still, and are the source of its treacherous humor.

The Encyclopaedia of Reincarnation:

It is noteworthy that Acanthus unequivocally calls the monad a demon. Throughout the *Histories* he is emphatic that, whatever benefits may initially come from the *apeiron chorion*, evil is sure to follow. Thales may have gained wealth and fame for many inventions; Lipnike may have received the gift of prophecy. But at the same time their lives were cruelly marked: Thales lost the respect of his countrymen, who turned instead to his brilliant protégé, Anaximander. Lipnike lost Thales, who tired of his paramour and refused to acknowledge her role in his success. In order to get revenge, she took up with a Thracian mercenary, and as a result went through another grotesque pregnancy and birth, this time bringing the dog Metakynos into the world. The mercenary deserted her. After a brief interlude on Samos, in the household of the merchant, Mnesarchus, she ended her days at Delphi, as a priestess of Apollo. Although some might consider this an enviable outcome, Acanthus points out, by that time Lipnike was embittered, exhausted, old and alone, obsessed with her losses, barely cognizant of the oracles she spoke or the importance of her position. He treats the first part of her story in Book V....

The Thracian Histories, Book V:

This is what men say of how Thales of Miletus and the servant girl Lipnike lived together for a time and then came to part company, and how Lipnike met the Thracian soldier Gyges and the pair of them escaped from Miletus, and how they landed on the island of Samos and the god who is called Metakynos was born into the world.

Thales traveled long in Egypt and Babylonia, and he took Lipnike with him wherever he went. She proved a most remarkable and intelligent companion, educated far beyond his expectations and clever in ways he had never imagined. She produced a great many ideas which were extremely useful in Thales' work and which, I may say, helped bring him lasting fame later on.

Now, a number of these ideas had to do, in one way or another, with water, as that element had come to hold a great attraction for Lipnike and never left her thoughts. The pale, green-grey light, which had seemed to surround her and Thales in the first months after the birth of the *apeiron chorion*, had taken on a more moist and fluent character in her eyes. Often the edges of the objects she looked at seemed to ripple gently and blur into each other, as if they were underwater. At night in her dreams the high stones of the well, in which she always found herself standing, oozed patches of dampness on all sides above the water line. Droplets formed on the rock, each of them glowing with a greenish tinge and each of them filled with tiny creatures who squirmed round and round, pressing against the surface of the bubbles. Sometimes the creatures seemed to be animals, at other times men and women, or fish, or reptiles, or birds. Once or twice Lipnike even caught a hint of forests and hills in the background, or cities with rivers flowing beside them, or mountains or fields of flowers. At this point in the dream she would hear a voice, coming from somewhere behind her left shoulder, whispering that these droplets, taken together, held within them the whole history of the world, not only the past but the future too, and that if she could ever manage to see them distinctly enough she could read all that was and would be for anyone anywhere. But whenever she turned, or tried to move closer to one of the walls, she would feel a sharp tug from something inside her chest which pulled her away. Then the water would quickly rise, her body would be carried up with it and she would find herself floating on her back in the open sea. As she looked up into the night sky with the waves lapping softly against her skin, she realized that the thing in her chest was a lodestone, a magnet, which controlled all her movements, and that this lodestone was itself controlled by another, larger magnet located outside her body, far away, a great stone of magnesium, which on some nights she imagined to be lodged in a lighthouse at the head of a distant harbor, and on others to be sunk at the bottom of the ocean, under a mountain of sand.

Lipnike spoke so often and so fervently of these dreams, and Thales was so impressed by them, that soon, according to many authors, he began to look at them not as mere delusions but as living revelations sent by some god, though wrapped in a cryptic form. He therefore meditated long and deeply on them, turning their contents this way and that in his mind, till at last he arrived at what he was sure was the answer to the deity's riddle: the dreams presented a new cosmology, he said, with a new explanation for the origin of things. They showed, as plain as if they'd been speaking to Lipnike out loud, that the primary substance of creation, the *archai*, the single element, that is, from which everything issues, is water—not a universal sea serpent, not the body of a titan or the blood of a god, but water. Furthermore, Thales said, all things return to water at their death and dissolution, so that the primary substance always persists, with only its qualities changing, through all the workings of time. The earth itself, he added, rests on water, floating like a flat disc, or a log. As another result of these dreams, he is said to have experimented for the first time with magnetic stones, and, after observing how they moved iron at a distance, to have concluded that soul exists throughout the world, that, as Aristotle and others report him to have said, all things are full of *psyche*.

Now, as everyone knows, it is this doctrine of water as the primary substance, and of soul as intermingled with all parts of creation, on which Thales' reputation as an original thinker largely rests, and the world certainly is not lacking in writers who stoutly maintain, against all evidence to the contrary, that Thales developed his cosmology by himself, without any assistance, long before the *apeiron chorion* was born, long before he met Lipnike, and that neither she nor it had any influence at all on the main points in his philosophy. These authors (in whose ranks, I hardly need mention, are some very well-known figures) argue their opinions with a great deal of force and persuasiveness. However, having examined all the available evidence in the case, I must say that I am strongly inclined to disagree with them, and for the following reasons.

First, there is the character of Thales himself. For he is widely known to have been not only one of the wisest men of his day but also one of the most superstitious, especially in regard to dreams; it is said that he regularly questioned his pupils, his friends and even people he met by chance on the road about their dreams the night before, and frequently insisted on interpreting them on the spot and giving his interlocutor advice on how to conduct his affairs that day. This practice was so conspicuous that "Thales-asking-questions" came to be a catch-phrase in the Ionian Greek world, used at first to describe someone unusually curious about dreams and omens, and later as a designation for any ordinary snoop or busybody.

Second, nearly all authors, no matter what their opinions may be on the origins of Thales' cosmology, agree that Lipnike had a hand in the philosopher's many nautical inventions (for which, by the way, he later tried to take all credit). For instance, Cleonymus of Athens (who elsewhere describes Lipnike as a meddling shrew!) states unequivocally that it was she who worked out, while she and Thales were in Egypt, a new method of re-measuring land holdings after the annual flooding of the Nile. And this method, says Cleonymus, was based on an understanding of geometry, no less! She it was, too, writes Theodorus of Cyrene, who had the idea to divert the course of the river Halys, so that Croesus' army could advance without hindrance into Persian territory, a feat which Herodotus confirms in his history of the Lydian monarch. Moreover, says Theodorus, Lipnike had already performed the same service for the troops of Nebuchadnezzar and been handsomely rewarded for her efforts.[3] For these reasons, and for others as well, which will appear

---

[3] Cf. Herodotus i, 75. Herodotus questions the truth of the entire episode at the Halys, and in any case mentions only Thales in connection with it. Croesus' reign did not begin until 560, long after Lipnike and Thales must have parted. The works of Cleonymus of Athens and Theodorus of Cyrene are lost; however, the story of Lipnike and Nebuchadnezzar's army appears elsewhere, notably in Amphiaraus (*Chronicles*, ii, 17–21) and Metrodorus of Chios (*On Monarchy*, i, 38–40). —R. K. W.

presently, I think it most likely that Lipnike had a part in the formation of Thales' cosmology.

But wherever the truth of that matter may lie, no one, to my knowledge, has expressed any doubt about the fact that soon after Thales and Lipnike returned to Miletus, his attitude toward her underwent a profound change. Some say this was because Thales, who was well over forty by that time, married and had a son, Cybisthus by name, and the philosopher's wife was jealous of Lipnike and insisted she be sold. They claim that she was bought by a wealthy Phoenician merchant who took her to Samos, that the *apeiron chorion* went with her—in the guise of a sea chest, if you please!—but was thrown overboard before they reached land, and that the god Metakynos was born to Lipnike on the island a few months afterwards, the fruit of a liaison between her and a goat. Others say Thales never married, and instead adopted his sister's son, because the possibility of fathering another monster like the *apeiron chorion* was too odious to him. According to this story he finally got rid of Lipnike when he found he could no longer be in her presence without feeling the shame their offspring had brought him.

Still others insist that both of these explanations are wrong, and what really happened was that Lipnike went mad. This version of events is supposed to have been circulated first by Thales himself, though this is highly improbable. It is said that one night, in his cups, when he was an old, old man, he told his fellow philosopher and former pupil, Anaximander, that Lipnike had been driven out of her senses by a vision which she had had when they were in Egypt, and which, on their return to Miletus, troubled her with increasing frequency, coming upon her without warning no matter where she was or what she was doing. She saw herself, said Thales, in chains at the bottom of the sea, being crushed to death between two gigantic boulders. Slowly but relentlessly they would roll up against her and grind her down, first into pieces of bone and sinew, then into grains like sand on the shore, and finally into dust which was dispersed in the underwater currents. At this her soul as well was washed away, to wander hopelessly in a far-off region, or state of mind (Thales, full of wine, was not exactly clear as to which of these Lipnike had meant) that she called "the Boundless".[4] Thales told Anaximander that she would act her vision out in bizarre dances, which were really more like fits than anything rhythmic or graceful, accompanying herself with snatches of old Thracian folk songs, croaking in a hoarse, tuneless voice. (However, Cleonymus claims elsewhere that it was Thales who was unable to sing.) The climax of this behavior came early one morning when Lipnike went into her dance and failed to come out of it, repeating the same movements and sounds over and over the whole day and night, until she dropped from exhaustion. When she awoke she recognized no one and could not even remember her name. It was then that the philosopher sent her away. This story gained a good deal of credence (many, in fact, believe it to this day) after Epicharmus used it in his comedy, *The Milesians*, in the famous scene where Thales and Anaximander stagger drunkenly along the beach in the moonlight, taunted by a chorus of mollusks, and think Aphrodite and Athena are cooing sweet nothings to them from behind a sand dune.

But all these tales, widely believed or not, are false. The plain truth of the thing I chanced to learn some years ago in Rome, from a scribe in the Temple of Jupiter, Decius by name. He had been born in Thrace not far from Mount Kogaionon, where there are Metakynos and Lipnike cults still active, seven hundred years after their inception. As a young man, Decius became interested in the cults, and collected all the information he could on the history of the figures they celebrated. As regards the matter under discussion, he told

---

[4] The Greek here is *to apeiron*, the same word as the name for the demon. Thus, *to apeiron chorion,* which I have preferred to keep in the original, could be translated as "the boundless room," or, perhaps better, "the boundlessness room." Metrodorus, who seems to be Acanthus' source for this vignette, writes, "Over time the term was shifted from Lipnike's vision and applied to her progeny, the room." Acanthus does not accept this, and in fact, as any student of philosophy knows, it cannot possibly have been the case. *To apeiron* must have come directly from Anaximander himself, since it was a salient term in his cosmology: it was, for him, the *archai*, the original element, which he proposed instead of Thales' water, in what many scholars consider a brilliant leap of abstract thinking, far ahead of its time. It is altogether likely, then, that the demon's name comes from Anaximander and not the other way 'round.
—R. K. W.

me that the long and short of it was that soon after they got back to Mile-tus, and Thales had installed himself again comfortably in his old abode, he consigned Lipnike to a space in the women's quarters and hardly ever sent for her. Thales never gave her a word of explanation, either. Certainly his wife had nothing to do with it; he could have twisted her around his little finger. Nor did he adopt his sister's son; his sister had seven daughters. And Lipnike definitely was not mad. No, said Decius, Thales had simply come home tired and feeling his age. His mind was weary as well: he no longer had the zest for thought that had brightened his youth. It was Lipnike, after all (aided not a little by the force of the *apeiron chorion*) who had provided the inspiration for most of his discoveries abroad. It did him no good now to hear her constantly prattling about new ways to do this and new ways to do that. (In many ways, Decius said, the *apeiron chorion* seemed to have had the opposite effect on him from what it had on Lipnike: whereas she grew livelier and more clever, he became more and more morose.)

Thales was disappointed, too, by the welcome he received from his fellow citizens. He had expected them to greet him with exclamations of joy and to congratulate him on his many achievements in foreign lands, which surely had reached their ears. Instead, they were hardly more than civil to him. To his chagrin, he soon realized that all the praises were reserved for his former pupil, Anaximander, who was little more than a boy when Thales and Lip-nike had left. In the intervening years, however, Anaximander had grown into someone to be reckoned with, a mature thinker and man of affairs who had brought to completion a number of difficult tasks. He had invented a sundial to mark the solstices and equinoxes, and had traveled to Sparta, at the request of its citizens, to set one up in that city. He had also invented an entirely new means of indicating the hour, and had conceived and carried out something which no one else had even attempted: he had made a map of the entire world, complete with Europe, Asia, Africa, the Gardens of Hesperides and the Island of Ultima Thule, all enclosed in the great encircling Sea. As a result of his industry and resourcefulness his fellow Milesians had elected him to head the colonizing expedition which established the city of Apollonia in Thrace, on the western shore of the Black Sea. Anaximander had returned from this mission a hero. In great measure, then, he had taken the place of his old teacher in the eyes of the town. In fact, what people now recalled first about Thales was not his sagacity, not his many inventions and service to the city, but his reputation as an impractical dreamer, a man who, though he might have done one or two things of value, always had his head in the clouds. Why, hadn't he once fallen down a well, they reminded each other, while out at night gawking at the stars?

6

THE SUBSTANTIAL FORM OF THE BODY IS THE SOUL. MORGANITE IS PINK.

From The Salem Trumpet, *May 29, 1855:*

[To our readers: The following article was set up in type before the sad news of Dr. Caws' passing reached us. We publish it here unchanged, to discharge our sacred obligation to print the truth as we see it, and as a necessary contribution to the public record, with all due respect for the departed and our profoundest sympathy to his loved ones in this, their time of trial. –The Editors.]

DEAD MEDIUM'S LAST MESSAGE—"DIE!"
DR. CAWS GIVES HIS FINAL SÉANCE!
MATERIALIZATIONS! LEVITATIONS!
WILL LEIBNIZ RISE AGAIN?
(NOT LIKELY, WE THINK!)

BY Jeremy Welkin

—**Special to the *Trumpet*—**

Aubrey, May 28: Eggbeater and Efficiency Caws, Aubrey's most talked-about couple and two of the best-known mediums in the Nation, have decided to come out of retirement. They will give a séance tomorrow evening at eight o'clock sharp in the sitting room of their home at 18 Prospect St. "The public is more than welcome," says Dr. Caws.

A large crowd is expected; the village is girding its loins for the event. Famed far and wide for their trance utterances and a host of spectacular, not to say flamboyant, physical phenomena, the Cawses are breaking a year-long silence spent in self-imposed isolation from the spirit world. They plan to celebrate their return in proper style, with the dramatic unveiling of what Dr. Caws claims is the first calculating machine in the history of the world to have been conceived and constructed entirely under the direction of spirits. "It adds, subtracts, multiplies, divides, does square roots, quadratic equations—why, it'd probably predict the weather, too, if we could only figure out which screws to tighten," states the doctor. "But don't take my word for it," he adds. "Come and see for yourself. Make sure to be on time, though, because seating is limited. This is an historic moment. You don't want to be one of the poor fish who fifty years from now will have to tell his grandchildren he missed it. The present is pregnant with the future. *Sympnoia panta.*"

Before their withdrawal last year, Dr. and Mrs. Caws had established, as the so-called "Rising Leibniz" and "Gravity Newton", an international reputation for their unique blend of intellectual percipience and stunning, sense-defying manifestations of supernatural power. An added fillip was the fact that they were, and still are, the only husband-and-wife team to grace the spiritualist circuit in this part of the country.

But the pace of it all was exhausting. Days on the road and nights in the séance room passed in a blur.

"We experienced in ourselves a state where we remembered nothing and where we had no distinct perception, as in periods of fainting, or when we were overcome by a profound, dreamless sleep," explains Dr. Caws, a portly distinguished looking gentleman with a large, pepper-and-salt moustache, as he ushers us into the family sitting room, where tomorrow evening's séance will be held. "In such a state the soul does not sensibly differ from a simple monad. But this state is not at all durable, and the soul emerges from it, the soul is something more. We just needed some time to think a few things over, is all."

"Let's face it, we were fried." Mrs. Caws appears at the far end of the room, through an opening in the heavy dark curtain that runs from wall to wall there. Attired in a dazzling white dress, with bare shoulders and a red rose at her belt, she is a most exceptional lady, with sea-green eyes, a mass of lustrous, auburn hair and a commanding air not often found in one so youthful. She fixes us briefly in her gaze, puffing on a cigar held casually between the first and second fingers of her right hand. "Fried but good," she continues, giving us another sample of the puzzling and idiosyncratic argot that is a regular feature of the couple's mediumistic pronouncements. She laughs, a rich, melodious laugh, but not without a touch of girlish shyness, and shakes her head. "You can't do this kind of thing ten, twelve, sometimes sixteen hours a day and not be. Every body, that by a radius drawn to the center of another body, howsoever moved, describes areas about that center proportional to the times, is urged by a force compounded of the centripetal force tending to that other body, and of all the accelerative force by which that other body is impelled. I mean, there's no two ways about it. Something's got to give." She giggles, crosses to the tea table and takes a long pull from the sherry decanter.

Her husband sits, unbuttons his vest and puts his feet up on an occasional table. "Every organic body of a living being is a kind of divine machine or natural automaton," he reminds his wife patiently, "infinitely surpassing all artificial automatons. For a machine"—he warms to his theme—"constructed by man's skill is not a machine in all its parts; for instance, the teeth of a brass wheel have parts or bits which to us are not artificial products and contain nothing in themselves to show the use to which the wheel was destined in the machine. However, the machines of nature, namely living organisms, are still machines even in their smallest parts, *ad infinitum*." He turns to us. "You got all that, sonny?" We nod, finish a sentence in shorthand and turn a fresh page in our notebook. "Good. I wouldn't want you to fall behind—because the machines, in fact, are as imperishable as the souls themselves, and the animal together with its soul persists forever. It is as if someone tried to strip Harlequin on the stage but could never finish the task because he had on so many costumes, one on top of the other. You got to understand it was a very big strain on us."

Mrs. Caws taps her foot. "Every body continues in its state of rest, or of uniform motion in a straight line, unless it is compelled to change that state by forces impressed upon it," she cautions.

"God alone is without body," observes Dr. Caws.

"The axes of the planets are less than the diameters drawn perpendicular to the axes." An edge comes into Mrs. Caws' voice. "The effects which distinguish absolute from relative motion are the forces of receding from the axis of circular motion, you fat _____." She speaks a word which decency forbids this paper to print.

"Extension, mass and motion are no more things than images in mirrors, or rainbows in clouds," the doctor replies.

His wife bridles. "_____! Horseflesh, _____ and cabbage!" A dinner plate, apparently moving under its own power, sails in from the dining room. "The hypothesis of vortices," she goes on, "is ultimately irreconcilable with astronomical phenomena"—the plate smashes against the wall, just above her husband's head—"and rather serves to perplex than to explain heavenly motions!" Mrs. Caws hitches up her skirts and stands on a chair, waving the cigar.

"We must distinguish what is necessary from what is contingent though determined," Dr. Caws answers evenly, brushing shards of china out of his hair and moustache. "Not only are contingent truths not necessary, but the links between them are not always absolutely necessary either. *Les vérités de Raissonement sont nécessaires et leur opposé est impossible.*" He closes his eyes and drapes an antimacassar over his face.

"There is a power of gravity pertaining to all bodies," Mrs. Caws screams, "proportional to the several quantities of matter which they contain!" The ceiling sprouts branches and leaves, which intertwine with her hair. A rain of apples falls on the carpet.

The Cawses are well-established figures in Aubrey society; one might even say that over the years they have become fixtures in the daily life of this small, seacoast village. Mrs. Caws, born Efficiency Barton, is of an old Aubrey family. Seven generations of Bartons have come into the world, grown to maturity, married, thrived and met their Maker, all in the house on Prospect St. Beginning with Nehemiah Barton, a fiery Puritan divine who was one of the Town's original settlers, and continuing with his son, Onan, another man of the cloth, the clan has boasted a long line of soldiers and ministers, scholars and statesmen, farmers and merchants. Mrs. Caws' great grandfather, Nathaniel, was a hero of the Revolutionary War. Her grandfather, Thaddeus, was a prominent Massachusetts jurist who published a translation of the plays of Sophocles. Her father, Abimilech, was a banker and philanthropist, known for his support of scientific projects and for some not-inconsiderable achievements of his own in that field. And, before she developed her powers of mediumship, Mrs. Caws herself earned no little fame as a hostess, who presided over her teas and soirées with a grace and wit matched only by her exquisite beauty.

Dr. Caws, on the other hand, is a more recent addition to the Aubrey scene. He hails from the city of Batavia in upstate New York, where his father, Mulegluer, ran a profitable operation in the carriage trade. Upon attaining his majority, however, young Caws elected not to go into the family business but to strike out entirely on his own, see something of the world, and discover what it had to offer a gentleman of his abilities. He therefore left Batavia to travel on the Continent, eventually settling in Paris, where he devoted himself to the study of medicine, in time becoming an eminent exponent of the practice of animal magnetism. (We are not exactly certain what this branch of healing entails, but we are told that the doctor made a great success of it, giving many well-attended lectures and demonstrations, not only in the French capital but in Florence, Zürich and other cities as well, effecting some remarkable cures which came to the attention of authorities from one end of Europe to the other.) He returned to this country in the spring of 1848, settling in Aubrey. He and Efficiency Barton were married late in the same year after a whirlwind courtship. The Cawses were admired as an exemplary couple, making a propitious union of old family tradition and the invigorating impress of independent enterprise....

The Encyclopaedia of Reincarnation:

CAWS, EGGBEATER (1805–1855), American medium, known as the "Rising Leibniz" of Aubrey, Massachusetts, who built the machine that initiated the so-called "Caws Experiments", was born in Batavia, New York on March 13, 1805. His father, Mulegluer Thomas Caws, was a coach manufacturer and prominent Freemason in the area, being Master of his Lodge. The future medium's mother, the former Abigail Prettybones of Canadaigua, also came from a family with Masonic connections, her uncle, Seneca Prettybones, having won the annual Canadaigua Masonic ambulance wagon race three years in a row. Educated at the Gresham Fuller School in Batavia, young Caws showed an aptitude for languages which astonished his teachers. The child was able to speak foreign tongues fluently with no more than a few days' instruction, and on one occasion carried on a lengthy conversation in German after seeing only a single page of grammar. He demonstrated an equal facility with numbers, solving complicated arithmetical problems immediately, without benefit of pen or paper. He was also of an affable, modest disposition, eager to please his elders, and his masters predicted great things for him. However, in the spring of 1820, shortly after the lad's 15th birthday, his father died suddenly, stricken while giving a pass-grip to a fellow Mason at the opening of a Lodge meeting. As the only male in the family (his uncle Seneca also being deceased by that time) the boy was obliged to quit his studies and go to work at the carriage business in order to support his mother and four sisters.

Though he can hardly have been enthusiastic about his altered circumstances, young Caws made good at his trade, and his life passed uneventfully until September, 1826, when a carriage manufactured by him was used in the kidnapping and, it was widely believed, subsequent murder of Captain William Morgan. A Royal Arch Mason and native Virginian, Morgan was a newcomer to Batavia; when he applied to open a Royal Arch chapter in the city, his name was removed from the petition. In retaliation, he wrote and caused to be published a book divulging the rites and other secrets of Freemasonry. He was abducted by Masons in Canadaigua and driven under guard to Fort Niagara, after which he was never seen again. The crime prompted a national outcry against Masonry; Lodges across the country were closed or lost membership; Masons were even attacked in the street; an anti-Masonic political party was formed. In the furor, Caws was accused of complicity in the crime and a warrant was issued for his arrest. Although entirely innocent, he chose in view of the hostile environment to flee the country, escaping first to Canada and then, aided by fellow Masons in Montreal, to Europe. (Schlemmer argues plausibly that Caws was motivated by more than a desire to avoid an unjust punishment, however understandable that would be; he claims that the young man saw in the scandal a perfect opportunity to be rid of a life of stultifying routine, for which he felt himself unsuited and which he found increasingly irksome. Surviving letters of Caws' dating from about this time would seem to confirm this theory.)

Only scattered reports survive of Caws' movements on the Continent, where, for the next two decades, he seems to have lived by his wits. He is known to have spent part of 1828 in London, and to have been one of the crowd that gathered in the City Road to watch Charles Green, the British aeronaut, ascend astride a pony from the roof of the Eagle Tavern, in a balloon inflated with coal gas. The sight is said to have made a deep impression on him, and later scholars such as Schlemmer and Muschel point to it as a formative factor in his later feats of levitation as the Rising Leibniz of Aubrey. Muschel goes so far as to call the event "epiphanic," and connects it to what he claims was a "conversion experience" which Caws experienced later that year in the Harz Mountains of Germany, on the peak of the Brocken. At that time the young traveler apparently encountered the famous Specter of the Brocken, a phenomenon produced when the sun is low in the mountains and the observer's own shadow is projected in gigantic scale onto a cloudbank. Conversion experience or no, Caws' explorations in the Harz evidently had a profound effect on him, since in later life he frequently made reference to his adventures there, usually embroidering his anecdotes with fantastic details.

December of 1828 found Caws in Weinsberg, the guest of the poet and physician, Justinus Kerner. By this time he was styling himself Dr. Caws, although there is no evidence of his ever having taken a medical degree. (Such a degree cannot, however, be ruled out. Indeed, it is likely, on balance, that he did have one, since, over the years, the doctor—as we shall call him from now on—showed unquestioned familiarity with more than a few medical procedures.) In any case, Kerner was a dedicated practitioner of the theory of animal magnetism, espoused in the 18th century by Franz Anton Mesmer, according to which all bodies that exist anywhere in space both contain and radiate a universal, life-giving magnetic fluid. Mesmer said that by manipulating the ebb and flow of this fluid within the patient, the physician could restore the person to health. It was probably through Kerner that Dr. Caws first became aware of this method of healing, which was to play such a large part in his own practice. He also came into contact with Kerner's famous patient, Frau Friedericke Hauffe, known as the "Seeress of Prevorst", a somnambulist and visionary who was undergoing treatment at Weinsberg and was producing in trance states a great many psychic phenomena, which were often accompanied by clairvoyant statements and prophecies. These were couched in a special language which, she asserted, was the original language of the human race and was closely connected with numbers. All sources agree that during his stay at Weinsberg Dr. Caws first became fascinated by, and then fell deeply in love with the Seeress. The two would converse daily, speaking in nothing but numbers; they are said to have understood each other perfectly. Finally Dr. Caws implored Frau Hauffe to leave her husband and run away with him, despite the fact that at this point she was completely bedridden and suffering from a variety of ailments which, in a few months, would claim her life. In *Saint Caws*, Muschel suggests that the Seeress, who was only a few years older than Dr. Caws and whose married life had been hardly idyllic, returned the doctor's affection and agreed to elope with him, notwithstanding her physical condition, convinced that her lover could cure her where Kerner had failed. According to Muschel, Kerner discovered their plan and intervened at the last moment to stop it. Schlemmer, writing twenty-five years before Muschel, mentions nothing of such a theory, nor does Ethel Mammon Striker in *Gravity Newton*. However, it is known that in the spring of 1829 some sort of disagreement with Kerner resulted in Dr. Caws' sudden departure from Weinsberg. When the doctor returned briefly in September of the same year, Frau Hauffe had passed away.

Dr. Caws seems now to have embarked on a solitary pilgrimage of mourning. We cannot be sure of his precise itinerary (though Schlemmer suggests that the trip to the Harz may have taken place at this time, not in 1828). Nevertheless, we do know its point of termination: the parish church of the village of Pibrac, about ten miles outside of Toulouse in the south of France. Here, in the sacristy, lay the remains of Germaine Cousin, the shepherdess, who died in 1601 at the age of twenty-two, and whose body remained in a state of perfect preservation. It was said by the villagers to be the source of numerous miracles and healings. How the doctor heard of Germaine is not known, but when he came into the town he went directly to the church and stayed with the coffin for several hours. He left Pibrac on foot, walking in the direction of Toulouse, and observers noticed that he was followed by a small flock of sheep, the first of many animal entourages that would accompany the doctor on his travels thereafter.

His course now seemed more assured. The town records of Caen, for April of 1830, mention several well-authenticated cures which the doctor effected that month at the Hotel Margot, using animal magnetism, including one case of a four-year old girl born with a crooked back; she was cured completely, in the presence of her father and three of the town's physicians, who examined the child both before and after the demonstration. He stayed in Caen for a few months, performing several more cures and establishing a considerable reputation for himself, but abruptly, around the middle of July, moved on to parts unknown.

In December of 1830 he settled in Paris, opening a practice in the Rue Garancière in the Faubourg St. Germain (the same street where, as Leibniz, he had lived between 1672 and 1676, and where he had discovered the calculus in October of 1675). Dr. Caws remained in the city for over 2 years, giving numerous lectures and demonstrations of his healing techniques, the last of which, presented at the end of February, 1833, was witnessed by the young Daumier, who made sketches of the event. One drawing, now in the Boyer Collection, shows the doctor on a raised platform, standing beside a seated woman whom he apparently has just hypnotized. Dr. Caws exudes confidence; with his left hand he indicates the patient, while with his right he gestures grandly toward the audience seated in front of him. He is already slightly overweight, a characteristic that was to increase as the years went by. His moustache bristles ferociously.

As the sketch indicates, the doctor had become a popular and charismatic figure; his name appeared frequently in the papers. However, he still seems to have had trouble making ends meet, for from this period of greatest success come also the first reports that Dr. Caws had begun offering the additional medical services—those of an abortionist—with which he was to supplement his income surreptitiously during the remainder of his stay on the Continent.

Dr. Caws left Paris hastily in the summer of 1833; from this point on he is believed to have employed a variety of aliases. A man answering his description, calling himself Hodges and attended by a troop of ground squirrels, appeared in Zürich one day in September, 1834. He gave a lecture on animal magnetism, performed two cures and was gone before nightfall. The same man appeared ten days later in Basel, this time calling himself Teschemacher, with a flock of sparrows circling around his head. In 1836, using the name Wombell, Dr. Caws was back in England, plying his trade in the Midlands. In November he was in London, again calling himself Hodges, with two cats at his heels; observers described them as "extremely gentle," one black with white markings, the other completely white, with one pink eye and one green eye. Once again the doctor witnessed the aeronaut Green in a balloon ascent, this time the great Nassau Balloon, which rose from Vauxhall Gardens on its historic flight to Weilburg, Germany. For the second time he is said to have been profoundly moved by the spectacle. (An eye-witness account of the ascent survives; it was formerly thought to have been in Dr. Caws' hand, but is now considered a late forgery.)

In 1838 the doctor arrived in Italy, staying in Florence through March and April under his own name. He performed several cures and appeared frequently in public, as in the old days, attending the opera with great regularity. At one performance, Coturno's revival of *Das Gehirngespinstgemach*, he met the seventeen-year old Florence Nightingale, who was touring Europe with her parents. The future nurse is said to have become fascinated with Dr. Caws, and to have canvassed his views on modern healing and its relation to the immortality of the soul. The two met several times again before the Nightingales' departure for the Italian lakes. Nothing is known of the doctor's activities thereafter until his arrival in America, penniless, in the spring of 1848....

Dr. Caws' other incarnations include: Lipnike of Thrace (603–541 B.C.), servant girl; Xeniades of Croton (540–473 B.C.), Pythagorean philosopher; Ffllaa (fl. c. 400 B.C.), a bedstraw hawk moth in southern Anatolia; Jcjcjc-jcjc (fl. c. 350 B.C.), a back tooth of an angle worm, genus Chaetognatha, living in the north Atlantic; Acanthus of Rhodes (fl. c. A.D. 160), Greek historian; Gaaar (fl. c. 700), a grey seal in the Gulf of Bothnia; Ahk (fl. c. 750), a pink-breasted cockatoo in eastern Australia; Maria (fl. c. 1320), a cow in Bohemia; Klk-Klk (fl. c. 1380), the right eye of a north African pygmy shrew-mouse; Germaine Cousin (1579–1601), French shepherdess, canonized 1867; Gottfried Wilhelm Leibniz (1646–1716), German philosopher, mathematician, jurist, historian, diplomat, librarian, genealogist, geologist, mining engineer and inventor; Ang Dorje (1717–1761), Sherpa tribesman; Metoh-kangmi (1762–1804), yeti; Himself (1805–1855); Foorlrlr (1856–c. 1859), cylindrical earthenware retort used for the manufacture of coal-gas at the Imperial Gas-Works, King's Cross, London; Swwwwwsh (1860–c. 1871), liquid manure spreader, with pipe and sprinkler arrangement attached to a tank strapped to the operator's back, used mostly in Flanders and Holland; Bkol, the olfactory bulb of Bruno (1872–1891), the Haflinger draft horse embraced by Friedrich Nietzsche on the morning of January 3, 1889, in the Piazza Carlo Alberto, Turin, Italy; Ndl, the sapphire stylus used to make a cylinder recording of Buddy Bolden on trumpet playing *The Bucket's Got a Hole in It* in New Orleans, c. 1903; Thelonious Monk (1917–1982), American jazz musician.

∽

CAWS, EFFICIENCY BARTON (1827–1899), American medium, was born in Aubrey, Massachusetts on October 30, 1827. Her father was Abimelech Barton, a prominent banker and philanthropist. Her mother, the former Propinquity Benbow, was an Aubrey socialite. The Benbows claimed a direct line of descent from the family of Nicolas Fatio de Duillier, the distinguished Swiss mathematician, religious enthusiast and friend of Sir Isaac Newton. It is generally accepted that Mrs. Caws inherited her mystical inclinations from Fatio, along with her striking good looks.

Efficiency's mother died giving birth to her. The girl was raised by her father and two maternal aunts. She was educated at the Aubrey Female Academy, where one of her teachers was Miss Josephine Slocum, the author of a widely read book on deportment for young ladies. Miss Barton was generally considered a sweet, intelligent child, though perhaps a little high-strung. (However, Ethel Mammon Striker—whose source was Mrs. Caws herself, reminiscing in her old age—alleges that there were instances of mediumistic proclivities even in her childhood.)

Miss Barton's father died in the autumn of 1843; thereby she became, at the age of sixteen, the heiress to a large estate, which made her financially independent for the rest of her life. Early in 1848 she made the acquaintance of Dr. Eggbeater Caws of Batavia, New York, an exponent of the theory of animal magnetism who had arrived in Aubrey after years of travel on the Continent. The two were married that fall, shortly after her twenty-first birthday. They settled down to what was, by all accounts, a placid and happy existence—Mrs. Caws continuing the charitable work that she had begun before her marriage, and the doctor taking advantage of his newfound leisure to read in Mr. Barton's extensive and wide-ranging library and to "tinker," as he put it, indulging a previously unsuspected mechanical bent in the construction of whimsical inventions.

Beginning in 1850, however, initially motivated, it would seem, merely by a casual interest in the then-current fad of spiritualism, Dr. and Mrs. Caws participated in a widely publicized series of séances, some held in their home, others at various locations in New England and the Middle Atlantic states, as a result of which she became internationally celebrated as "Gravity Newton" and he as "Rising Leibniz". The séances attracted attention not only for their astonishing supernatural displays, including levitation, elongation, materializations and direct voice communications (all in such profusion that one observer at least was reminded "more of showmanship than spirituality") but also for the quarrelsomeness exhibited by the spirits and the atmosphere of antagonism and competition engendered in the séance room. The series was broken off in 1854 after a fire following one of the sessions generated a surge of public protest. In the following year the couple attempted a return, but with disastrous consequences … Despite the lurid publicity surrounding the performances, however, and notwithstanding the hostility that the Cawses encountered in some quarters, the fact remains that no fraudulent practices were ever proven against either of the mediums in the production of their phenomena, and that those phenomena remain unexplained to this day....

A partial list of Mrs. Caws' other incarnations includes: Thales of Miletus (c. 625–546 B.C.), Greek philosopher, geometer and astronomer; Aspasia (c. 470–411 B.C.), Greek courtesan, mistress of Pericles of Athens; Cruuuuhu (fl. c. 200 B.C.), a tiger cat in northern Brazil; Pfft (fl. c. 100 B.C.), a tubular sea-squirt clinging to a pier-pile at Smyrna; Peter the Fisherman (fl. 30 A.D.), Christian saint; Valerius Turpens (296–377), Roman man of letters; Anselm (c. 1033–1109), archbishop of Canterbury; Gloria Dei, Gloria Diaboli, an homunculus made by the physician and alchemist Paracelsus von Hohenheim (1493–1541) from putrefied semen and essence of human blood and kept alive for twenty-one days in a dunghill in Basel, Switzerland, from the middle of October through the first week in November, 1527; Sir Isaac Newton (1642–1727), English scientist; Herself (1827–1899); Bessie (1900–1923), a threshing machine with self-feeder and fan-blast delivery pipe built by the Avery Manufacturing Company of Peoria, Illinois; Miles Davis (1926–1991), American jazz musician.

The Salem Trumpet:

... Dr. and Mrs. Caws' conversion to spiritualism took place five years ago, after they casually attempted some table-turning during an evening's visit to friends in nearby Danvers. Table-turning, or table-tipping as it is also called, is one of the most popular pastimes (not to say crazes) to have swept the land since 1848, when the mysterious, still-unexplained rappings in the home of John D. Fox of Hydesville, New York, initiated the spiritualist movement in America, giving rise to all the psychic phenomena so prevalent today: levitations; messages from the dead; production of the strange substance called ectoplasm, or ideoplasm, a whitish, pasty stuff which emanates from the person of the medium; and *apports*, solid objects transported instantaneously from one location to another in clear contradiction of the laws of physics.

An ordinary table provides the simplest means of getting in touch with the spirit world, say the experts in these matters. The participants place their fingers on its surface and sit motionless until, of its own volition, the table begins to move. Sometimes it merely revolves; sometimes it rises entirely off the floor, or tips one end in the air, rocking up and down. By assigning letters of the alphabet to the number of raps the table makes on the floor, one can establish communication (or so it is believed) with spirits in the beyond, and receive intelligible answers to whatever questions one cares to put.

When the Cawses arrived at the Danvers address, an evening of table-turning already was underway. Half a dozen persons were in the parlor, clustered around a table that was bouncing back and forth. The hostess, an old friend of Mrs. Caws and a popular member of the north-of-Boston social set, kept count of the raps and called out the corresponding letters to a gentleman seated in the corner, who took notes on a sheaf of papers resting on his knee. The new arrivals were invited to participate, which they eagerly did, since they had heard a great deal about the diversion but never before had seen it in operation. As soon as the Cawses took their seats, however, the table came crashing down and refused to budge an inch the rest of the night. It was impossible even to lift the thing by natural means, let alone get it to tip by itself. (Later this incident provoked a contrary fad, called table-*fixing*, in which intense concentration, and often stern looks, were used to keep a table stationary; but interest in this died down when it was discovered that some people were cheating with nails.) Soon, though, as if to atone for having spoilt the evening's entertainment, the Cawses themselves began to rotate, slowly at first, standing in place, then faster and faster all around the room, finally experiencing such dizziness and disorientation that they had to be led into an adjoining room to recover. Dr. Caws even started tapping out messages with his shoe against the wall as he lay on the couch, but no one thought to take notes until it was too late.

When they returned home a few hours later, still a bit light in the head but otherwise not much the worse for wear, the Cawses found all their furniture turned topsy-turvy, with every chair in the house thrown in a pile in the middle of the sitting room, the dinner table upside down in the back yard and their big four-poster bed from the second floor standing on its headboard in the kitchen. Its lace canopy was discovered the next morning hanging from the roof, one end stuffed in the gutter spout. The couple thought at first that it was a practical joke of some sort, although they had no idea who among their acquaintances would—or could—-have perpetrated such a thing. But shortly thereafter loud knocks began sounding from all parts of the house, often in several rooms at once, while at any hour of the day or night singing (usually German *lieder*, but sometimes hymns or other pieces difficult to classify) would erupt out of nowhere, frequently accompanied by discordant notes from a horn or piano. In a few weeks the racket ceased, but only long enough for the noisemakers to break camp, as it were, change tactics and occupy new territory—this time within the Cawses' brains. Nightly the couple were afflicted by a jabber of inner voices, each one demanding exclusive use of their vocal chords and claiming to be the spirit of some long-departed figure—an ancient Greek courtesan, a Himalayan tribesman, St. Anselm of Canterbury, an old cow from Bohemia, and a host of others. Eventually, after a very painful period during which the Cawses were convinced they were losing their minds, the voices subsided, until at last only two remained, who called themselves "Sir Isaac Newton" and "Gottfried Wilhelm Leibniz", the former speaking through Mrs. Caws, the latter through her husband.

Asked at the couple's first séance to present some proof that they really were the spirits of, first, the seventeenth century British genius who, among his many accomplishments, invented the reflecting telescope, discovered the law of universal gravitation, wrote the *Philosophiae Naturalis Principia Mathematica* and discovered the infinitesimal calculus; and, second, Newton's great contemporary and *bête-noire*, the German philosopher, mathematician, jurist, diplomat and—oh, a great many other things—who, among *his* many accomplishments, wrote the *Discourse on Metaphysics*, the *Monadology*, the *Theodicy*, the *Dissertation on the Art of Combinations*, the *Protogaea* and the *New Essays on Human Understanding*, invented a compressed air engine, a mechanical calculator and an aneroid barometer, designed a ship that could travel underwater and a high-speed coach that could travel on tracks, *and* discovered the infinitesimal calculus (for the last of which accomplishments, reputedly, Sir Isaac never forgave him)—asked at the séance to present some proof of their identities, the spirits promptly replied: a ripe, red apple materialized in the air and fell to the floor in front of Mrs. Caws, while Dr. Caws was whisked peremptorily out of his chair and levitated to the ceiling, where he (or rather Leibniz) delivered a lecture on brachistochronic curves, and a bouquet of feathers materialized over his head.

The apple was picked up and eaten after the séance by Mrs. Calvin Mainwaring of nearby Ipswich. "It wasn't too bad, all things considered," she told this reporter the next day. "A trifle sour, maybe, but plenty crunchy. Not near as good as what comes out of my Uncle Hiram's orchard, of course, but then, what d'you expect? Uncle Hiram's been growin' apples fifty years and more. And that Dr. Caws! Oooh, what a *man*! In all my born days, I never *saw* such a man!"

Their claims substantiated by Mrs. Mainwaring's endorsement, Newton and Leibniz have gone on to provide some of the vividest, best attended and most intellectually stimulating demonstrations of the immortality of the human soul ever witnessed on the spiritualist circuit. Even the unprovidential fire which last year put a—if we may be pardoned the term—damper on their activities, has not been sufficient to quench the *élan* of these extraordinary geniuses of yesteryear.

"Don't think Mrs. C and I aren't grateful," says Dr. Caws. "They're two tremendous fellas, and we could never had done it without them." It is quieter now in the sitting room. An hour or more has passed. We are stretched out on the floor with the doctor, drinking a champagne punch from a big cut glass bowl placed between us in the center of the carpet. Mrs. Caws has dropped into a light doze under the settee at the far end of the room, near the curtain from which she made her entrance earlier in the morning. Behind this curtain is the area known as the *cabinet*, no ordinary cupboard, the doctor assures us, but a special, enclosed space which mediums use to collect the vital forces necessary to attract the denizens of the spirit world and conduct séances. It was to this space that the Cawses retired, early in May of 1850, to rid themselves of the cacophony of voices in their skulls. For days they remained sequestered in strict quarantine, taking neither food nor drink but meditating, the doctor says, "on Holy things alone and in constant prayer," until at last the tide of battle turned and the invaders loosed their hold on the Cawses' minds. On the morning of May 13, the pair emerged, weak but triumphant, and Leibniz and Newton, who spoke through them that day for the first time, introduced themselves to a flabbergasted world …

T*he* G*ehirngespinstgemach*:

Cuprite is red. Argent is white. Coleman Hawkins will record "Some of These Days" in 1935. The Treaty of Brussels gave Ferdinand I the county of Tirol. Three days and nights they spent inside me, sweating and shaking. They dragged in the packing cases from the barn and shoved them against the wall, under the shelves. Then they found the mattresses from somewhere on the second floor, and they dragged them down here, too, and piled them on top of the crates. They did all these things, but I was not here yet. That is to say, of course, here was not I—not yet. No, not until they tacked that curtain up, and pulled it tight—just the way Starkey had done, in London, to make me his laboratory—not until then did I leave my … leave my … leave my whatever I was, I was dark and cold and rainy, that's all I know … and I did not leave, anyhow, that's all wrong, I never *leave*, I only *am differently*, it's my curse, to *be* the space, never to move through it—enough of that. Not until they stretched that curtain tight, from one side of the room to the other, did I awaken anew, here in this here, *as* this here, this where. They stripped off their clothes, still trembling, and lay down on the mattresses together, wrapped in each other's arms, for all the world like the King and Queen in one of Philalethes' alchemy books ("She sweat therefore even as though she would melt … I cannot endure this heat, but I must die in it, and without me your Highness can have no Offspring.…").

After a while, as they clung together, they felt the voices moving out of their heads, dispersing all through their bodies—speaking now from her liver, now from his kidneys, now her colon, his bladder, her stomach, his spleen, from moonrise to sunup, their innards aroar with shouts, curses, mumbles, whispers, weeping, questions, diatribes, laughter. At last they slept. On the 13th, a little past midnight, the voices left them—the cow first, through his left nostril; the courtesan next, through her mouth; then the others, one by one, through ear canal, tear duct, urethra. The last to go was St. Anselm, through her anus. For a little bit there was silence, sweet peace. They stretched themselves and sat up, shaking their heads. Then, from their pineal glands, dead in the center of their brains, two new speakers piped up:

"A proposition is held to be true when our mind is ready to follow it and no reason for doubting it can be found. The substantial form of the body is the soul. *Sympnoia panta.*"

"Sympnoia, my arse-cooler! The latus rectum of a parabola belonging to any vertex is four times the distance of that vertex from the focus of the figure. Mussels and marmalade. Pizzles and sposh. Bellies. Armpits. Eel-grass. Fud. Come on, you old guts and garbage, let's dance that blanket hornpipe again!"

The Salem Trumpet:

" ... Yes, Siree Bob, without them we could never have gotten off the ground," Dr. Caws continues. "Or at least I couldn't have." He takes a long drink of his punch. "Efficiency's proclivities"—he points toward the settee—"don't *lie*, ha-ha, in that direction, if you know what I mean. Besides, mixing sherry and champagne—after all these years, she should know better. Haroop." He belches, sounding not unlike a seal at feeding time, and readjusts the antimacassar over his face. "But in the drictly, I mean of course in the strictly, metaphysical sense no external cause acts upon us excepting God alone, and he is in immediate relation with us only by virtue of our continual dependence upon him. Whence it follows—haroop—that there is absolutely no other external object which comes into contact with our souls and directly excites perceptions in us."

He pauses. His body, still supine, rises slowly several feet off the floor, stays motionless a moment in mid air, then returns to its former position, his boots hitting the carpet with a thud. He starts talking again as if nothing had happened. "We have in our souls ideas of everything only because of the continual action of God upon us, that is to say, because every effect expresses its cause and therefore the essences of our souls are certain expressions, imitations or images of the divine essence, divine thought and divine will, including all the ideas which are there contained."

We have done our homework dutifully in preparation for this interview, and thus have little trouble recognizing in the speech Dr. Caws has just made a section from Leibniz's *Discourse on Metaphysics*. We point this out to him. He lifts the antimacassar and blinks. "Oh, really?" he asks. "Surely not?" He turns his gaze toward the open window, through which there has just come the sound of a dog barking some distance away, and scratches his head. "But on the other hand, of course, I suppose, um … now that you mention it … um … yes, it might be, at that. Isn't that interesting. Thanks. It's always nice to know where things come from. But then, you know"—his face brightens—"all substances sympathize with one another and receive some proportional change corresponding to the slightest motion which occurs in the whole universe."

He grins. We are about to make a comment, but he goes on before we get the words out. "The whole universe, mind you, every last squiggle and squirt of it, every last squeeze. I wonder if that's in the *Discourse*, too? By the way, son, did you know that Leibniz wrote that book while he was stranded in a snowstorm, completely cut off from civilization? No? Well, I'm not surprised. But he did, assuredly—it's a well-established fact, where I come from. Up in the Harz Mountains, it was, in the last week of January, during one of the worst winters on record. All the passes were blocked. They sent search parties out, of course, but none of them could make the slightest headway, not even the Sherpas. Not Ang Dorje himself! He came to me with tears in his eyes. 'Colonel,' he sobbed, 'we can do no more.' And one—"

Sherpas? we ask.

"Nepalese tribesmen. Well known as expert mountaineers. Indispensable in a situation like this. Normally. But even Sherpas were forced back by this storm, and—as I was about to remark a moment ago, my dear sir—one could see why. The drifts were twenty feet deep. A single step outside and the air froze in your chest. And all the spooks the Brocken could boast of were out on the loose in that wind, screeching for all they were worth. Even the villagers heard them, thousands of feet below, breaking in like blasphemy over the sound of the choir. Spooks, did I say? Werecats, rather! Kobolds, hobgoblins, erl kings! But not even those creatures—not even those!—would have been strong enough to stop the Sherpas. What stopped the Sherpas"—his voice drops to a whisper—"what stopped the Sherpas, my dear sir, and believe me, it was the only thing that *could* have stopped those gallant fellows—was this: they had seen the footprints of the Yeti."

"Yeti?" The name is new to us.

"'Abominable Snowman,'" he explains blandly. "Legendary giant of the Himalayas. '*Metoh-kangmi*' in their tongue; 'Wild Man of the Snows' in ours. Well, fortunately I had a pistol in the pocket of my greatcoat, a chiseled Italian dagg with a bell-nosed barrel, that I'd brought with me from—"

"Now, wait." We raise an eyebrow. Himalayan giants are a bit much for us, not to mention Nepalese tribesmen popping up in Germany. Besides, the Harz is one of the doctor's favorite subjects; minus Sherpas and yeti, we've heard most of this palaver before. "This was in January?" we ask. "And what year, pray tell?"

"5686."

5686! This, we admit, is a surprise. "Anno Domini?"

"Naaah. Anno Lucis, son, Anno Lucis. Year of Light. In Anno Lucis, everything is dated from the Creation—you know, 'Let there be light' and all that, in the Book of Genesis—starting at 4,000 B.C. It affords one a quite instructive perspective, to say nothing of a vanishing point. So—"

So in normal parlance, the year in question would be....

"1686, yes. To the uninitiated. But don't make that equation too quickly, young fellow." His dark eyes narrow. "There are two kinds of history, public and secret; the Years of Light contain chronicles you may never even have had an inkling of. Besides, notions defined by extension always involve something imaginary. There are an infinity of possible sequences of the universe, each of which contains an infinity of creatures; everything possible *demands* that it should exist! Even Yetis. Even me. Even Leibniz. Even the Harz Mountains. Perhaps I'll tell you more about it another time. Oh, don't apologize, please don't, sir, apologize, I don't mind waiting, really I don't mind at all—a day, a week, two months, several lifetimes, whatever it takes, the tale will still be there, we can drop it or pick it up again at any point, and I can see you're not quite ready at the present moment, not quite ready to hear the continuation, the several continuations, of the—Oh, my dear young man!"

He breaks off, staring at us with genuine concern. "Oh, my word, my word, it is *I* who should apologize! Look at you, young sir, just look at you, you're shivering with cold. Here, let me brush the snow off you."

He does so, and for the first time we realize that we are covered with the stuff—head, shoulders, trousers and boots, as much as if we'd walked half a mile in a blizzard. And we are, indeed, trembling uncontrollably, and most likely have been for some little time. A stiff breeze seems to have started up, coming in through the doorway to the dining room.

"There, young man, there, that's better." The snow melts into the carpet. "Have another drink, quick, it'll take off the chill." We do so, gratefully. "Good. Good. Drink it right down, now. Good. I can't believe how inconsiderate I was, maundering on and on, and you in such an awful state. I can just imagine what Efficiency would say if she knew! Well, I can't, actually, but you understand what I mean. Oh, dear, oh, dear, I *am* so sorry. The Years of Light can do that to you, though; they make you forget even the most *basic* human values. Do you know, my dear sir, if you don't mind, I think I'll have another drink, too. Haroop. Dampen the old moustache again, what? Put things right in a minute, eh?"

He leans over and refills his glass directly in the punch bowl, drenching his sleeve to the elbow. He downs the drink in a gulp, replenishing it as before. "Oooooom, yes. That's better." He licks his moustache. "Paah. Gaah. Klk-klk. Pflewgie." He turns and looks at us; his countenance shows a freshness and a boyish quality that were not there a moment ago. His brown eyes twinkle. As we return his gaze, the doctor's moustache detaches itself slowly from his face, advancing like a stately galleon under sail midway into the space between us, where it heaves to, quivering gently and glowing a soft green. "You see?" he continues, smiling. "The body is made in such a way that the soul never makes any resolutions to which the movements of the body do not correspond; even the most abstract reasonings play their part in this by means of the characters which represent them to the imagination. What wonder, then, that everything goes so well and with precision, since all things work together and lead us by the hand. It would rather be the greatest of all wonders or better, the strangest of absurdities, if this vessel, designed to go so well, should fail in spite of the measures which God has taken." He pauses, then adds, as if reproving our thoughts, "Our hypothesis with respect to corporeal mass should therefore not be compared to a vessel which brings itself to port but to the ferry boats which are attached to a cable across the river. It is like the theatrical machines and fireworks whose regularity we no longer find strange when we know how everything is done." He snorts. "Not that we all do know, of course. Not that some of us know anything of the sort. Hah! Thales saw the stars, though he did not see the well at his feet. Hah! And what, for that matter, was Newton doing while Leibniz was risking his life, halfway up the side of a mountain in a snowstorm? Answer me that, if you can." He glances over at Mrs. Caws, who is still asleep under the settee. "Hah. Safe in his rooms in Cambridge, Newton was, warm as toast by his fire, writing the *Principia*." He looks at his wife again, and shakes his head. "Ah, well; ah, well. All things are animated, but only the immortal soul remembers itself. Haroop." He reaches out in front of him and retrieves his moustache, cupping it lovingly in his hands, cooing to it softly, then drawing it in and pressing it with great gentleness onto his face. Little by little its fluttering ceases; its pepper-and-salt coloration returns.

Dr. Caws helps himself to more champagne and stretches out again on his back, covering his face with the antimacassar. "*Bene*," he sighs. "*Bene, bene, bene. Gut. Bueno. Bon.* Now, where were we, exactly, before we got … Oh, yes: images of the divine essence, divine thought and divine will. Certainly. Absolutely. No question about it. Solid. You have but to say the word and they dance before you, those images, their tiny toes atwinkle, their little hearts athrob with delight, as if their only wish in all the world were to please you." He laughs. "Actually, of course, they have almost no choice in the matter. For, as I think I intimated a moment or two ago, the Architect of the universe has arranged it so that all substances sympathize with each other, and it requires only the smallest perceptual adjustment to make their affinities vividly apparent. A miniscule warp in the order of coexistences or a quick shuffle of the order of successions is enough to do the trick. And speaking of that, *mein* boy, did you enjoy our little demonstration just now?"

We did, indeed, and we see no reason—especially now that we have stopped shaking—to hide the fact from our host. It is not every day, even in the newspaper business, that we are privileged to witness such a remarkable defiance of the law of gravity, and it would be churlish not to show our appreciation. We add that we are equally affected by the doctor's antics with his moustache, as well as the (if we may so describe it) chilling impression wrought by his snowmaking activities. But at the same time we cannot deny that we are (if we may employ the term) haunted by some criticisms which were leveled early on against the Cawses' mediumship and which continue to be voiced today: in particular, we refer to complaints that few if any new messages have been forthcoming from the couple's spirit guides, only restatements, usually verbatim, of Newton's and Leibniz's writings, all of which could have been committed to memory beforehand and presented as spontaneous utterances from beyond the grave. "What we have here," fulminated Justinian Forbes, the influential editor of *Time and Light*, in a widely-read essay published in 1850, "are not revelations of the divine but schoolroom recitations, and poorly delivered ones at that." Other critics agreed. So strongly, indeed, did they put their objections, that only the amazing physical phenomena which the mediums produced prevented the couple's disgrace at the very start of their career. The "little demonstration" that we have just witnessed does not really address the questions which Dr. Forbes and his followers have raised; in fact, it tends to point them up all the more strongly, and to open the door to suspicions that the whole thing is a matter more of showmanship than spirituality, or, in the recent words of the doctor himself, "theatrical machines and fireworks." We feel it would be a breach of the sacred trust we hold with our readers not to ask Dr. Caws how he counters these criticisms.

"Hey—who has time to memorize all that stuff, anyway?" he answers. "Justinian Forbes, maybe, but not me. All these complaints after the deed are unjust, inasmuch as they would have been unjust before the deed. Look: let me pull your coat to something." He leans toward us on the carpet and his voice drops once more to a whisper. "It is inconceivable that a soul should think using the ideas of something else. The soul already includes the idea which is comprised in any particular thought. Everything which happens to a soul or to any substance is a consequence of its concept; hence the idea itself or the essence of the soul brings it about that all of its appearances or perceptions should be born out of its nature and precisely in such a way that they correspond of themselves to that which happens in the universe at large, but more particularly and more perfectly to that which happens in the body associated with it, because it is in a particular way and only for a certain time according to the relation of other bodies to its own body that the soul expresses the state of the universe." He chuckles. "We must not ask why Judas sinned because his free act is contained in his concept, the only question being why Judas the sinner is admitted to existence, you dig it, rather than other possible persons. The supposition from which all human events can be deduced is not simply that of the creation of an undetermined Adam—*un Adam vague, si vous voulez*—but the creation of a particular Adam, determined in all circumstances. It follows also that if he had had other circumstances, this would not have been our Adam, but another, because nothing prevents us from saying that this would be another. It is, therefore, another. You can watch anything. You can watch rabbits. Morganite is pink. Always know. Have another drink."....

7

CRAZEOLOGY

The final stage in the disintegration of Fritz Eichhorn as a rational human being began, ironically, on the heels of his greatest triumph, soon after his homunculus started recording data picked up from the metal skull. As Schwank labored happily, filling page after page with text, Eichhorn fretted, unhappy with what was going on and apprehensive about his place in it. Try as he might, he could not hear anything in that coil of wire. "Listen to the bass," Schwank had told him. "Listen to what bass, for God's sake," the psychologist wrote. "What the hell kind of advice was that, when nothing, absolutely nothing, was audible. And it wasn't even as if Schwank was writing down music, it was all in letters, letters and numbers. Music of the rhizomes, hell. Was this just one more instance of the guy's insanity, or was he plain trying to trick me? Or was there some other explanation?" Without Haselmaus to guide him, he was stymied.

Eichhorn's situation was not made easier by the fact that his colleagues, surprisingly, were swift to congratulate him on the latest developments, "stopping me in the hall, slapping me on the back, coming up to me in the cafeteria. One of them had even found a copy of my Nietzsche paper; he put it into my hands like an offering, and asked me to autograph it. Of course all of them pretended they'd known all along my approach with the patient was the right one; it was only hospital regulations that had made them question me at first, 'just for the sake of *form*, you know.' Form, my ass. The two-faced bastards."

Still worse, these colleagues began to treat Schwank like a celebrity, dropping in at odd hours 'just to see how he's getting on,' crowding round the worktable, bending over the take-up reel, listening. And *reacting*, damn them. Oohing and aahing, tapping their feet, snapping their fingers. *They* could hear the bass, all right, no problem with *their* ears, oh no. Right swingers, they were. Been listening to Charlie Dominguez all their lives."

Eichhorn didn't believe any of it for a moment. He was sure it was only a ruse, diabolical perhaps but a ruse—a put-on in the argot of the homunculus—to destroy him, little by little, with exaggerated praise. "So why did I put up with it?" he writes. "Why didn't I burst out of my hiding place" (by this time he had taken to concealing himself in the closet whenever he heard footsteps outside in the hall, and spying on the proceeding through the keyhole) "and throw them all out, tell them to quit bothering my patient? God knows I had every right to do so. What held me back?"

Well, he admitted, there were problems, "wheels within wheels." To begin with, far from being bothered by the attention he was getting, Schwank seemed to be thriving. He'd started wearing his zoot suit again and his tie, was brushing his hair and shaving regularly. Soft spoken and affable, he would willingly answer questions on any number of subjects, especially on the details and ramifications of C. G. Jung's double life as Lester Young (though he professed a mild surprise that these Zürich-based doctors weren't already familiar with it). And his pages of transcription were building up nicely. But these things by themselves could never have held Eichhorn back. Mainly, he did not act because there was a chance, "the slimmest of the slim but still a chance," that his colleagues really were hearing something which his own ears could not pick up. So he stayed put on his knees in the closet, eye at the keyhole, sweating.

"What else could I do?" he asked himself rhetorically. "What would Nietzsche have done in my place? Exactly the same, I'd stake my life on it. Exactly the same."

He never went to his office anymore. He went home only to sleep. He had an opening cut into the wall in an empty room adjoining Schwank's, so he could slip into the closet from the rear without anyone being aware of it. He brought in a bath mat to protect his knees while he knelt at the keyhole. And there he watched.

Early one morning, not long after sunup (they came earlier and earlier now, Eichhorn swore, and stayed later, sometimes sending out for sandwiches in the middle of the day, "brazen beyond belief") a new visitor joined the group. This was Dr. Anna Zeisig, a young epidemiologist who had begun to make a name for herself in her profession, and had taken to joining the psychologist for lunch. She was quiet and studious. Eichhorn had been attracted to her from the first, especially relishing her petite figure and "lustrous" black hair, which she wore "long and loose." He imagined it covering his face as she bent over him, naked on his bed, having first removed her thick horn-rimmed glasses. She seems to have occupied a large portion of his fantasy life. He had asked her out several times, in his smoothest, man-of-the-world manner, but had always been rebuffed, "the last time with a firmness not even a moron could have mistaken." Additionally, she had become one of his harshest critics, even suggesting he was losing his mind. ("Narcissism," she opined, "rampant narcissism. A typically American affliction, but in his case pushing up against the frontiers of psychosis.") Now she pushed her way through the crowd and bent over Schwank at the worktable, asking ("in her sweetest, most honey-dripping voice, damn her") if she could turn the take-up reel herself. Willingly, Schwank made room for her on his bench. "'Oooh,' she cooed as the machine creaked along, '4,181 plus 2,584 is 6,765. *Ja, ja.*' She bent over the wire, her hair (oh, that hair!) brushing the top of the filament. '*Graben, graben,*' she sighed. She looked up at my homunculus, her face aglow with adoration. 'Oh, Herr Schwank, you are so *hüfte!*' Was I seeing things, or did she actually start stroking the back of his neck?"

Eichhorn woke with a start. He was in his pajamas, lying in bed at home, with the moon shining in through the window. The illuminated clock on his bedside table read 2:00 AM.

He had no idea how he had gotten there. The last thing he remembered was her hand, with her long, thin fingers—a water hand, he was sure—sliding up and down Schwank's neck and playing in his hair, blood-red lacquer on her fingernails.

Never, not for a second, did it occur to him that he might have been dreaming. His only thought was that he had to get back to the hospital. Find Schwank. Make sure he had come to no harm. "My God, oh my God in Heaven," he wrote, "I had been 'out,' or whatever you want to call it, for nearly a day. Anything might have happened in the interim. I had to get back there."

He threw on some clothes as fast as he could, not bothering to remove his pajamas, and ran down to the street. He found his car, to his immense relief, in the lot where he usually left it, the key still in the ignition. He drove at top speed to the hospital, let himself into *Das Fossil* with his pass key, and raced up the stairs to Schwank's floor.

On the landing he heard sounds of laughter and music—"a familiar melody, something my father used to play all the time, 'A Slow Boat to China'. God, how I hated it. And the laughter, the laughter too I recognized: two voices, intertwined, Schwank's and—curse her—that woman's. In a flash it hit me: *this* was what the attendants had heard. It had been going on behind my back for weeks!"

He ran down the corridor towards the homunculus' room. "The sounds were louder now, raucous. The music screamed. *She* screamed, *Ein Langsame Boot Nach China! Ein Langsame Boot Nach China!*' I heard the tinkling of glasses. In a kind of ecstasy Zeisig shouted, '*Ein Vogel lebst! Ein Vogel lebst!* Oh, Empedocles!' Then—I swear it—she *cackled*! And she called *me* crazy. 'A bird lives, a bird lives'—what the hell does that mean?

"I flung open the door, not of the closet, the room—I would never use that closet again—I flung open the door and, dear God, there they were!"

Schwank and Anna Zeisig lay together on the rug beneath the worktable, wrapped in each other's arms. A champagne bottle stood on the tabletop, next to her glasses. He was in his T-shirt and jockey shorts, she in her bra and panties. As they turned in Eichhorn's direction, the psychologist saw that she was wearing the homunculus's red necktie.

"Hey Squirrel-Man," Schwank called out. "Long time no see. *Sympnoia panta*, you dig it? Bird lives, baby. Come on in, join the party."

8

An Alphabet of Human Thought.
Prosopolepsy.
Peter Writes Beautifully.

The Salem Trumpet:

… We decline politely. For the last few minutes we have been experiencing a certain lightheadedness, which is probably caused less by the doings of Leibniz and Newton than by the action of other, more familiar denizens of the spirit world—the spirits, that is to say, which we've lately imbibed from the punch bowl. We tell Dr. Caws we're beginning to feel our liquor.

"But, my dear, dear young man, that's no time to *stop!*" he exclaims. "That's when it starts to get good." He drains his glass. "Phaaa. There's really no point in drinking it at all if you *don't* feel it, you know. There exists in the soul not only an order of distinct perceptions and passions, forming its dominion, but also a series of confused perceptions and passions, forming its knowledge. The soul would be a Divinity if it had none but clear perceptions. Still, suit yourself." He lies back and puts his hands behind his head, addressing the ceiling. "Let's see. Where did we leave off? The Forbes matter, was it? The ridiculous posturing of Justinian Forbes, prime prevaricator and lowest member of the lowest species of rot merchants ever brought into the world on the wrong side of the blanket? But no, we cleared that up, didn't we? Yes, I would say, examining the thing from all sides and giving each of its aspects my fullest attention, that we cleared up the Forbes matter lock, stock and hogshead. Haroop.

We can, therefore, begin afresh, bolstered by the confidence that, whatever we do, we at least are proceeding from a completely blank slate, a *tabula* scrubbed thoroughly *rasa*—a highly unusual state of affairs, and one in which my colleague Mr. Locke would doubtless have reveled, since he mistakenly attempted to generalize just such a situation into a universal rule affecting all humanity. So, what shall I tell you about? My principle of Sufficient Reason? The Identity of Indiscernibles? My proof, fore, aft and lubbard, that this—this one and no other—is the best of all possible worlds? The Year of Light, I realize, we have already touched upon, but only briefly, far too briefly, and there are astonishments in store, astonishments beyond measure, for anyone who chooses to dig more deeply into that subject. What would you like to know? Speak, sir, we have the day before us. I am an asymptote to your hyperbola."

We should like to know a great many things, such as how, exactly, Dr. Caws levitated; why, precisely, he thinks that the concept of Judas and the creation of an undetermined Adam (whatever that may be!) "clear up" the "Forbes matter"; why, in Heaven's name, Sir Isaac Newton, known during his lifetime for his piety and rectitude, now finds it necessary, when speaking through Mrs. Caws, to express himself in language a drunken sailor would blush at; and what, specifically and in what amounts, are the ingredients of that extraordinary punch. However, in the interest of expediency (since we have *not* got the day before us, on the contrary we have this story to file and the hour is advancing) we return to a subject broached earlier, one more closely related to the occasion for this morning's visit: the mysterious and highly touted calculating machine which the doctor plans to unveil at tomorrow evening's séance and which has been the major factor in bringing the Cawses out of retirement. Would Dr. Caws care to say a few words about this machine? Can it really add, subtract, multiply and divide—not to speak of quadratic equations? If it was in fact built by spirits, how did that construction take place? And how does it operate now?

He sits up straight, his eyes glistening. "But of course, my dear young man, of course, of course, of course. Only too delighted to oblige. A topic most dear to my heart—and it had clean slipped my mind. Fancy that. The human soul is immortal, ça va sans dire, mais immortality without recollection is something else again, something *très* much else, being *inutile* in a variety of *façons*. For instance, sir, take yourself. What good would it do you to become, let us say, king of China, on condition that you forget what you have been? Would it not be the same as if God, at the moment he destroyed you, were to create a king in China? Of course it would. Stands to reason. It is why I reject the doctrine of metempsychosis; no sane Divinity would have ordered it so, and no sufficient reason can be found. Now, as to memory: if we are willing to call *soul* anything that has perceptions and appetites, then all simple substances or created monads could be called souls. But as sentience is something more than a mere perception, I hold that one should call souls only those whose perception is more distinct and accompanied by memory. Memory is needed for attention: when we are not alerted, so to speak, to pay heed to certain of our own present perceptions, we allow them to slip by unconsidered and even unnoticed. But if someone alerts us to them straight away, and makes us take note, for instance, of some noise which we have just heard, then we remember it and are aware of just having had some sense of it. Haroop. Now, what was it you wanted to know?"

The calculating machine, we remind him. What about the calculating machine?

"Oh, of course, of course. Delighted, delighted, delighted. Thought you'd never ask. How's your writing hand? Not too tired? Got plenty of notepaper? *Buono.* Just fill up my glass, would you, please? The upper lip is beginning to desiccate again. Thank you. Phaaah. Pflewgie. Heigh-ho!"

Dr. Caws launches into a long, episodic discourse in several languages, covering a broad range of subjects, of which space permits us to include only the few fragments that happened to pertain to our question. The "project," as he calls it (or, in one of his more fanciful moments, "the Chain of Wonderful Demonstrations," by which he means the events leading up to the construction of the calculator as well as its actual manufacture) had its real beginning in Europe, long before he became a medium, at the opera. "It was in Italy," he says, in the spring of 1838, in the city of Florence. A brilliant season it was, too: one heard Mozart, Donizetti, Bellini—*Norma; Beatrice di Tenda; La Sonnambula.* And the singers! Tosi! The Grisi sisters! Bonfigli! We rubbed shoulders with Lablache and Tamburini in the streets. The whole town was mad for opera!" He breaks into song:

"Tu non sai con quei begli occhi
Come dolce il cor mi tocchi...."

Ah, well; ah, well. It was one great spectacle after another. But the particular opera I'm referring to was a revival, by Coturno, of a German piece, *Das Gehirngespinstgemach*. You know the one I mean—the ancient Greek legend, with the bad-tempered room, and the philosophers, and the Thracian servant girl who becomes priestess at the Oracle of Delphi? Yes. Well, the performance in Florence was a smashing success, let me tell you. Giuditta Pasta sang the girl, to Lablache's Thales. Not a dry eye in the house. Well, there happened to be in the audience, the first night I was there—oh, I saw the piece more than once, sir, don't think I didn't—an exceptional young lady, by the name of Miss Nightingale—yes, that's right, the same one who's in all the newspapers now, nursing the wounded over in the Crimea. But she wasn't a nurse then, good Lord no, she was just seventeen years old and on holiday with her family. Opera-mad like everyone else that season—I shall never forget how her eyes filled with tears at the end of the first act, when the girl and her lover, the giant Gyges, escape from Miletus, with Thales and Anaximander at their heels! *Tu non sai con quei begli occhi* ... ah, well; ah, well."

The next link in the "chain," to use the doctor's term, was forged late last year, shortly after reports began appearing about Miss Nightingale's expedition to the hospitals at Scutari on the shore of the Bosphorus at the entrance to the Black Sea, and the tremendous work she was accomplishing there. One night, after reading one of these pieces, Dr. Caws dreamed that he and Miss Nightingale were watching *Das Gehirngespinstgemach* again. The stage set, he says, was just as it had been in 1838; the players were cavorting and singing exactly as before. There were only two changes: first, he and his companion were both in nurses' costumes, wearing black dresses, white aprons, white collars and caps; second, a small engine or machine was standing center stage, facing the audience. In general, its structure reminded the doctor of a miniature human figure done in metal. Its upper component was strongly reminiscent of a head, with a crank sticking out of its left ear. Its mouth hung open on a hinge; tiny black numbers jumped up and down on the tongue, hopping like so many sand fleas from spot to spot. The music in the opera, loud and quite raucous, seemed to be issuing from this head. Suddenly, the mouth snapped shut and the curtain fell, leaving the doctor and Miss Nightingale, still in their nurses' clothes, alone in a wheat field, burying corpses under a starlit sky.

A few days later, around New Year's Day as he recalls, Dr. Caws was passing through his sitting room on his way to the front door when, without any warning, he found himself levitating—a not-unusual phenomenon for him. But this time he kept on levitating, rising straight up, swiftly and without resistance, through the ceiling, into the bedroom above, past the canopy of the four-poster bed, on through the roof, over the treetops and into the clouds. At last he came to a snow-white plain bathed in sunlight, containing nothing but gigantic pieces of machinery that seemed to have grown out of the silvery soil, some of them vaguely familiar but others impossible to classify. Directly before him was a towering structure faintly resembling a windmill, but larger by far than any windmill he had ever seen. A doorway at its base stood ajar. The doctor walked inside, moving in wonder through a forest of levers, gears, ropes and pulleys. He caught a glimpse of Florence Nightingale at one end of the building, bent over a hospital bed bandaging the head of a wounded soldier. He was about to walk toward her when he heard a clanking sound behind him; he turned, and there in an open space was a man with his back to him, stripped to the waist, working a lever up and down, his shoulders glistening with perspiration. The man turned, and noticed the doctor. He was wearing a thick black wig, which hung down over his chest; somehow Dr. Caws knew that this was Leibniz. "God created everything according to measure, weight and number!" the philosopher shouted, striving to make himself heard over a humming noise that had started above them. "Music is the concealed art of computation for a soul unaware of its counting! On these two commandments hang all the law and the prophecies. Every paralogism is but an error of calculation. Rectify them, Eggbeater, rectify them!" Leibniz took off his wig and extracted from it a folded sheet of paper. He crumpled it into a ball and threw it the length of the building toward Dr. Caws. The doctor picked it up, smoothed it flat and examined it; it proved to be a set of plans for a machine, one with a metal head and a crank in its ear, just like the object in his dream.

This vision, which baffled the medium on his return to earth (without, he admits, the sheet of paper, which seems to have gone back into the aether somewhere between the treetops and the four-poster bed), was followed by a series of specific instructions, delivered in Leibniz's voice at any hour of the day or night. "Get a twelve-foot coil of copper wire," the voice would say; or, "Find seven plates of zinc"; or, "Fetch five brass rings, twenty-three steel balls, eleven pounds of lead," and so on. When these items had been procured (often at considerable expense and inconvenience, especially when the call came in the middle of the night) further instructions were issued about putting them together.

The doctor obeyed faithfully, but still had no idea what kind of machine he was supposed to be making with all this material. "Then one day," he tells us, "at a bookseller's in Boston, I happened to see a life of Leibniz, published about ten years ago. And in this book the author said something I'd never known—that Leibniz once built a calculating machine! And a mighty good one it was, too; it became quite famous in his day, and he was proud of it, proud as proud could be. But—being the sort of man he was—Leibniz still wasn't entirely satisfied; he wanted to make his invention even better. He wanted the machine to be able to do automatic carrying! It finally got so he could think of nothing else. He came to believe that all his hopes for the betterment of the human race—the reconciliation of Catholics and Protestants, improvements in the judicial system, the promotion of peace among nations, mutual understanding, improvement of highways, everything—depended for their realization of his bringing to perfection that one detail. Well, he worked and worked, for years on end, to bring it to pass, but try as he might he never could get his calculator to do automatic carrying correctly and it just about broke his poor heart. Well, sir, I wasn't born yesterday, nor last week neither, and when I read that it didn't take me more than a second and a half to realize what Leibniz was up to with the machine I was putting together. It was to be his old calculating machine, but made *right* this time. Old Gottfried Wilhelm was rectifying his *own* errors, through me! Me, Eggbeater Caws! Just think! After that, of course, it was mostly a matter of physical labor: working out the details, you know, of the mechanical structures of particular bodies. A few trips to the blacksmith, a session or two of final instructions, some hammering and scraping and filing and polishing—*et voilà! Ecco! Sieh da!* The Delphic Oracle!"....

T*he* G*ehirngespinstgemach*:

GJKRHDHGKLJLSJDFjhhejcnfghsoffeeenCarnotite is yelol. Yellow. Delphic Oracle, hah! 10,946 plus 6,765 is 17,711. I'll Delphic Oracle *him*! He couldn't tghgjghsjgngjdhs—damn this machine anyway. Phlogopite is brown. He couldn't tell an asymptote from a cauliflower. Chain of wonderful demonstrations, indeed! Chain of amazing stupidities is more like. Automatic carrying! What the hell makes him 333333333hgtl;ajkfj what the hell makes him think that Leibniz—Leibniz of *all* people—would have had his heart broken over something like that? *That* wasn't what broke gjtykhowsh that wasn't what broke his heart—it was the *other* "project," the *big* one, the ghtlsdjgjashxxxxxxxx33hg;;gjtDAMNTHISTHING—the *alphabet* he wanted to make, and never managed to, the "alphabet of human thought" he called it, "the characters that express all our thoughts," a universal language, *that* was Leibniz's dream, not that goddamnhjehthtojhhhhhz3zsbc33333333333333333-aaaaaaaahhhhHHHHHHHHHHHH!!!!!! Delphic Oracle, is it? Well, I do know a thing or two Caws doesn't, that's for sure: for instance, I know Xeniades of Croton was right—one's incarnations *are* stored in the body; my Eye can see them, inside Eggbeater. Oh, he may have lost a few of them, in that purging five years back, the Bohemian cow and some others, but there are plenty, plenty more still at their posts. My God, just look! There's Leibniz himself, to begin with; he's gotten set up in style in the doctor's pineal gland, brought in his old writing desk, and books, and a big, old-fashioned globe, all in that tiny pink-grey hollow. I'm glad to be able to report that he's laughing himself silly at Eggbeater's foolery. Then there's that sleek, silver-coated seal, formerly of the Gulf of Bothnia, swimming happily through the Caws spinal fluid. And—aha!—all the way down by the tip of his coccyx, nestled in the fibers of the superficial sphincter muscle, seated on Apollo's tripod, is the Delphic Oracle herself, Lipnike of Thrace, her entire being and all her surroundings molded to perfection in the tiniest monads of ectoplasm. Oh, how I wish I could show it to him! Oh, how I wish Lipnike'd give him a good kick in the arse!

The Salem Trumpet:

Dr. Caws starts suddenly, and rubs his hindquarters.

Delphic Oracle? We ask.

"That's my name for it." He grunts, recovering his composure. "A pro-sonomasia in honor of Miss Nightingale, and the opera that started it all." He smiles contentedly. "That oracle was revered, you know, above all other prog-nosticators and sibyls in the ancient world, not to speak of haruspices, thau-maturges, palmists, geomancers, soothsayers, dowsers and scryers, along with the faceless legions of calamity howlers, examples of whom—Haroop!—exist even today. Blaughh. Oh, don't mistake me, my dear sir. I know perfectly well my machine can't tell the future. Not really. But if we had only proper names and no appellatives we would not be able to say anything at all. And let me just mention this, son, and mind you mind me: if you could figure out a way to ask that contraption about the future, in such a manner that all you used to do the asking was numbers, I'll bet you'd get yourself some results. Anything to do with numbers the Oracle knows for certain. You just write out your question on a slip of paper—for instance, how much is 74,368 ½ divided by 19.207693, multiplied by the square root of 18.1 and then cubed? You then insert your paper in the Oracle's mouth, turn the crank a few times, and PHFAAH! BLURRRG! SLUNGO! PFLEWDGIE! Out comes the answer, served up on the tip of its beautiful pink tongue, correct to the seventeenth decimal place. Right every time! I've tried it over and over and it's never failed me yet. Oooomn."

All this sounds most intriguing and ingenious; we are eager to see the ma-chine in action. Would it be possible, we wonder, to consult the Oracle right now, or, if that be too much to ask, might we just take a momentary peek at this marvel, to give our readers a foretaste of what awaits them at the séance?

"No, son, I'm sorry. I can't do that. It wouldn't be proper. Not respectful to genius, if you see what I mean. No one tests the Oracle, or even gets a glimpse of it, till tomorrow evening at the appointed time. It's like a bride on her wedding day, son, a bride on her wedding day. You'll just have to wait."

Of course. We quite understand. The mention of brides, however, reminds us that throughout this tale of the machine and its construction, the doctor has neglected almost entirely to mention his wife. What was Mrs. Caws' role in the enterprise, if we may be so bold as to enquire?

His genial manner vanishes. He snorts. "Sir Isaac Newton and his followers have a very odd opinion concerning the work of God," he says. "A very odd opinion, indeed." He refills his glass and gets up off the floor. "According to their doctrine, God Almighty—God Almighty *Himself*, if you please—needs to wind up His watch from time to time, otherwise it would cease to move!" He starts to pace around the room. "God had not, it seems, sufficient foresight to make it a perpetual motion." He drinks. "Nay, the machine of God's making—*God's* making, no less—is so imperfect, according to these gentlemen— and they're not *all* gentlemen, either, I'll tell you that for nothing, son—the machine, they say, is so imperfect that God is obliged to *clean* it now and then, and even to *mend* it as a clock maker mends his work, Who must consequently be so much the more unskillful a workman, as He is oftener obliged to mend His work and set it right! Ouch!" He jumps, and rubs his backside again.

He turns to us. "Now, isn't that the most perfect nonsense you ever heard? Ouch. Of course it is." He shakes his head. "Laughable, really. For, as any child knows—I need hardly explain this to *you*, my dear sir, after all we are men of the world, you and I—but as the most innocent neonate at its mother's breast understands perfectly well, the same force and vigor remains always in the world and, contrary to what these Newtonites would have us believe, only passes from one part of matter to another, agreeably to the laws of nature and the beautiful pre-established order. Ow."

He resumes his pacing, picking up speed and gesticulating with his free hand. "And I hold, my dear Welkin, that when God works miracles, He does not do it to supply the wants of nature, but those of grace. Whoever thinks otherwise must have a very mean notion of the wisdom and power of God! If Sir Isaac and his epigones are capable of that kind of claptrap about the Creator of the Universe—and they are capable, sir, I assure you, they are capable of every bit of that and more besides—just imagine what a botch they would have made of a delicate piece of work like the Oracle!" He collapses onto a chair and takes a long drink.

Then Sir Isaac—or rather, if we may so infer, Mrs. Caws—had nothing at all to do with the creation of the machine?

"Nothing. *Nada. Niente. Nihil. Rien. Nichts.* That's where you made a mistake a while ago, son, when you asked about spirits. This was not the work of spirits, in the plural, and in collaboration, but of one spirit, in the singular, one spirit all by himself: Leibniz. It was Leibniz's project at the beginning and it's Leibniz's project at the end. *Finis. Fin. Fine. Termino. Ende.*" His head slumps forward onto his chest, and he begins whispering to the glass in his hand.

We reflect that no love, surely, was lost between Newton and Leibniz during their lifetimes, and we make no doubt that, with the two of them, so to speak, living under the same roof, matters could become rather strained. Indeed, during the past few weeks, rumors have reached our ears that a serious rift has developed between the Cawses in their work with the spirit world. Several occurrences that we witnessed earlier in the morning appeared to confirm these stories, and the doctor's latest revelations about the Oracle and its origin seem to substantiate them even more strongly. Would Dr. Caws care to comment on this?

He looks up form his drink, astonished. "What? Me an' Efficiency? A riff? No, son, never. You got that all wrong. Somebody gave you some very bad information there. 'Fishiency an' I are 'voted to each other, same as ever. This was Leibniz's special project that's all. Chain of wonderful demonstrations, and ... and all that. Newton would have been completely out of his depth in that sort of thing. I mean, what with God having to wind up His watch and all the rest of it—*really*, now. I ask you."

But certainly the situation must make for some domestic friction now and again? We point to the pieces of dinner plate scattered about on the floor.

"What? That little old dinner plate? Don't be silly. Look, son. If the body A strikes the body B, of smaller mass and at rest, it will continue in the same direction though with diminished motion. Fair enough? All right. Now, if the body A strikes the body B, of *equal* mass and at rest, it will stop, so that while A is at rest its movement is communicated to B. Take that away and what have you got? Prosopolepsy."

Mrs. Caws stirs under the settee. "The vital agent diffused through everything in the earth is one and the same," she calls out in her sleep, "and it is a mercurial spirit, extremely subtle and supremely volatile. The motion of a cylinder revolved about its quiescent axis is to the motion of the inscribed sphere revolved together with it as any four equal squares are to three circles inscribed in three of those squares, and the motion of this cylinder is to the motion of an exceedingly thin ring surrounding both sphere and cylinder in their common contact as double the matter in the cylinder is to triple the matter in the ring; and this motion of the ring, uniformly continued about the axis of the cylinder, is to the uniform motion of the same about its own diameter performed in the same periodic time as is the circumference of a circle to double its diameter. _____. " She rolls over on her back.

"Absolutely," says the doctor. "Took the words right out of my mouth. *Sympnoia panta*." He puts the antimacassar back over his head. The subject, apparently, is closed.

Nevertheless, as readers of this newspaper will doubtless recall, a considerable amount of stress, and sometimes open warfare, did accompany the Cawses' séances, especially in the months just before their retirement. Rarely in this period did their spirit guides condescend to answer questions from sitters or provide messages from departed loved ones, avidly though these were sought by petitioners. Indeed, such inquiries were often greeted with scorn, in sharp contradistinction to the behavior of spirits at other mediums' séances, who usually respond with sentiments of comfort, love and serenity. Newton and Leibniz, instead, seemed singlemindedly bent on recapitulating and once and for all resolving, by physical violence if necessary, the issues which had divided them so sharply during their lives on earth: first, the crucial priority question, that is, the question as to which of them had discovered the calculus first and which, if either, had plagiarized from the other; second, the nature of God; third, the nature of time and space; and, fourth, any other little grievance, real or imagined, that happened to occur to them during the course of any particular séance.

Flying crockery and overturned furniture were the rule, as in plenty of ordinary domestic spats, but with the spiritualist's advantage of levitation and apportation, the clashes in air of chairs and china made every session a Fourth of July. In addition, there was the behavior of the mediums, as each, apparently, tried to outdo the other. One of Mrs. Caws' specialties, for instance, was elongation, a phenomenon in which the medium inexplicably grew taller while some disinterested party held her feet on the floor in order to prove there was no fraud. She, or rather Sir Isaac, appeared to use this ability as a weapon, with which to assert, like the ancient Greek giant Antaeus, the strength of the earthbound against her husband's Daedalian defiance of gravity. Now, we think we are betraying no confidence when we observe that Mrs. Caws is a remarkably pulchritudinous lady, slender and already somewhat tall. But the sight of her, stretched to a height of seven or eight feet, expounding in a deep, masculine voice the gravity and equilibrium of fluids, while the doctor, who is heavyset, floated beside her, leaning forward at an angle of 50 degrees or thereabouts, while the sideboard lumbered toward them from the dining room like an indignant bear prematurely aroused from its winter sleep—all this was a spectacle which no one, who witnessed it, could ever forget. However, it was hardly conducive to peacefulness.

Nor was this all. In some towns on the Cawses' circuit, Newton and Leibniz would grow loud and abusive, like ghosts who had drunk too much wine, urging those present to choose between them, often in the most offensive terms, usually demanding a voice vote or other tangible show of allegiance, so that a strong sense of factionalism pervaded the sessions. Our readers will recall that one such séance, held last year in the neighboring town of Rowley, led directly to the couple's retirement. On that occasion, after the conclusion of the evening's performance, the debate spilled out into the streets, and Leibniz supporters prowled the back alleys looking for Newtonites, who ran home to arm themselves. Scores of people were injured in the mêlée that followed, the Pig and Bladder Tavern caught fire, and gunshots crackled far into the night.

All this makes a séance with the Cawses an exciting but risky prospect, and Aubrey is girding its loins for tomorrow evening's events. But, hazardous or no, the couple's sessions have always been popular with their fellow citizens. Aubrey is an extremely small, close-knit community, with many families descended directly from the original colonists. Aubreyites are fiercely loyal to their own and correspondingly distrustful of the outside world. Throughout its history, the town has vigorously resisted the influence of places it regards as "foreign," even including Rowley and Ipswich, which abut it on the north and the south respectively, and with which it went to war—simultaneously—in

94

1695 over a minor boundary dispute. (Three years earlier, the townsfolk had refused to take part in the witchcraft persecutions which swept the area, not from any theological or humanitarian convictions, but solely because the persecutions had originated in Salem.) Nearby cities, like Newburyport and Gloucester, are looked on with suspicion as centers of mischief and ill-breeding, and the opinions of Justinian Forbes, who hails from Boston, carry no more weight in Aubrey than they would if they issued from Peking or Benares, merely confirming the scorn the natives already feel for their countrymen to the south. It should come as no surprise, therefore, that the controversy surrounding the Cawses in the New England states only increases the esteem in which the couple is held at home.

Then, too, there is the curious fact that Aubreyites, unlike some others of Puritan stock, are notorious for the unfeigned pleasure they take in entertainments, diversions and amusements of all descriptions. The expression, "Play it in Aubrey," has long been a catch-phrase in the theatrical business, used of a piece so deficient in dramatic interest that it could find an appreciative audience nowhere else. Some say this condition stems from an innate quirk—a mental tic, if you will—in the character of the founding fathers, which was passed on to their progeny; others insist it is only the natural result of the boredom attendant on more than two centuries of self-imposed isolation. Still others hold that it must be something in the water. This is not the space to settle the question. However, we may say that, if local lore be any guide, Aubrey's thirst for amusement goes back quite a long way—at least to the spring of 1685 when (so the oft-told story has it) the Reverend Onan Barton surprised his young wife, Parthenogenesis, at sport with the dashing Empedocles (later known as "Colonel") Schwank, and the latter escaped down Prospect St., up Middle, through Main, across the South Green, through the Burying Ground and from there out of town naked as a jaybird, much to the delight of his fellow citizens, who assembled in large numbers to view the chase and cheer on the principals—all this, it goes without saying, in starkest contrast to the prevailing standards of Puritan morality and decorum.

Many Aubreyites, especially members of the Barton clan, hotly deny the truth of this tale. But whatever one's verdict may be on that head (and we, ourselves, will not presume to render a judgment) it certainly cannot be denied that Aubrey loves a good show, and that spirits, regardless of any other virtues they may or may not possess, are highly diverting phenomena. By the same token, there is no question but that the Cawses' séances, considered as entertainment alone, are far and away the most dazzling extravaganzas to appear in the town for many a moon. The Cawses, thus, are the darlings of Aubrey; so far as the locals are concerned, the pair can do no wrong. Even the fire at the Pig and Bladder, which scandalized spiritualist centers from Montreal to Philadelphia, reminded old timers here of nothing so much as the Great Blaze of 1814, which wiped out over half the town's buildings in less than an hour and which many still cherish as the most thrilling moment of their lives. "Never thought I'd live to see a thing like that *twice*," one old codger told us recently. "An', to tell the truth, it didn't seem like it was goin' to amount to much at first. But when the wind started fannin' the flames an' the whole north wall of the Bladder went up—whoosh!—in not more 'n a second or two, I'd a sworn it was the Fire of '14 all over again. EKPYROSIS! The ever-livin' fire itself. Fire in its advance, judgin' an' overtakin' everything. That Eggbeater Caws is a great man." Residents like this one were deeply saddened when the couple withdrew into private life, and the news that they soon will be back in the séance room has filled these citizens with hope.

Indeed, a few Aubreyites, more thoughtful perhaps than the rest, find not only amusement in the performances but instruction as well, so long as the sessions are approached in the proper philosophical spirit. "Newton against Leibniz, Leibniz against Newton," the old codger continued. "A war to the death, an' beyond death, too. That's the way things really are: war is the father an' king of all, sonny. The fairest harmony comes out of discord. Lots of folks don't want to admit that. They want harps an' angels' voices an' weepin' an' cooin' an' such-like sentimental treacle. There's plenty other mediums happy to serve it up to 'em, too." (Here he named a few famous ones.) "I been hearin' it for years. They try to spoon a lot of flapdoodle down our throats, a lot of 'Ooooo-sweet-peace-an'-we'll-all-be-together-in-the-Promised-Land' stuff—as if we couldn't get exactly the same thing ourselves any night of the week, droolin' over the Prayer Book in the privacy of our homes. Oh, I guess it's not all their fault; it's probably the only thing the stupid ghosts they attract have got to offer. But it's flapdoodle all the same. I don't care if it does come from the spirit world. It's nothin' but old, stale passive empiricism with a dash of Swedenborg thrown in to kill the taste. Now, the Cawses, on the other hand, the Cawses show you the *real* world, full in the face, monads an' all, an' they've got the grit to do it without flichin', too. The real world is the real world, sonny, an' you can't get away from it, no matter how hard you may try. War is the common condition; strife is justice. All things come to pass through the compulsion of strife, an' don't you ever forget it."....

The Encyclopaedia of Reincarnation:

AUBREY. An early village, now defunct, on the coast of Massachusetts, 26 miles northeast of Boston. At its peak (1855) its population was approximately 850. A one-time residence of the *Gehirngespinstgemach*, Aubrey was bounded on the north by the town of Rowley and on the south by Ipswich. Its terrain included hills, wooded areas, rocky pastures and marshland; a narrow strip of beach fronted the Atlantic Ocean. The Awagonic River, a tidal stream, wound through the center of the town. The community is said to have boasted a few fine 17th and 18th century buildings, although many were destroyed by fire in 1814.

Aubrey was founded in 1640 by a small band of colonists from Aubrey-on-Steeping in Lincolnshire, under the leadership of Nehemiah Barton, a Puritan clergyman, and Exhumation Sweet, a magistrate. However, the area had been a center of habitation for a very long time before that. In the 11th century, the Norse made camp on the spot now known as the Kidney, a curved protuberance of land sticking out from the coastline. But the Agawam and other Indian tribes already had been frequenting the place. Moreover, axe heads and pottery fragments have been found which date back well into Neolithic times. Although the "discovery" in 1988 of an alleged Upper Paleolithic sanctuary not far from the ruins of the Town Hall, with incised bones, flint daggers and a cache of statuettes, has been proven to be a hoax (as have the "cave paintings" found in Rowley in 1992), it nonetheless is beyond doubt that the district has been a focal point of human activity for a very extended period.

Aubrey originally was established in order to strengthen the northern coastline of Massachusetts against incursions by the French, and fortifications were erected on the Kidney with that end in view, with demi-bastions, hornwork and retrenchments designed by Notwithstanding Mallard, one of the founding fathers. But almost immediately the townsfolk became embroiled in boundary disputes with Ipswich and Rowley, both of which had been settled before the Aubreyites' arrival. This wrangling continued throughout the century, culminating in 1695 in what the town referred to as the Ipswich-Rowley Wars, a series of fiercely fought encounters from which Aubrey emerged victorious, despite being sorely outnumbered, thanks to the leadership of one Colonel Schwank.

A legendary figure in village history, Empedocles Schwank was born in Aubrey, probably in 1667. Rumored to have been the natural son of the philosopher G. W. Leibniz, he passed a wild and rebellious youth, eventually running off into Indian country at the age of eighteen after the discovery of his liaison with the wife of the local minister. However, it is said, at the start of the Ipswich-Rowley Wars he suddenly reappeared, calling himself "Colonel" Schwank, and, to the amazement of the villagers, proved himself an able commander. His conduct of the final battle of the conflict, which featured a maneuver afterwards called the Charge in Both Directions, became village lore, a signal event which was reenacted with gusto each summer on the anniversary of the battle.

Having won the victory, it was said, Schwank disappeared again into the wilderness. But Aubrey tradition always maintained that someday, like King Arthur, he would return, to save the town once more in time of need....

What is certain, however, is that Aubrey thrived in the ensuing years, and entered the nineteenth century with confidence. Its more responsible citizens, sober, industrious Puritans descended from Barton, Sweet, Mallard and the rest, had long since established themselves as successful merchants, bankers and farmers, and even the Fire of 1814 did little to curb their optimism. At the same time, a tendency towards some highly un-Puritan conduct, which had always characterized a number of the villagers, made itself felt even more strongly in these years. They exhibited a fondness for gambling, fancy clothes and unconventional, even lewd behavior which was completely alien to the ethos of neighboring towns, and indeed was considered blatantly irreligious. April Fool's Day, for example, became Aubrey's most popular holiday, and this in a colony that frowned on *all* holidays, even Christmas, as heathen.

Still, these issues remained largely of local concern. But in 1850, Aubrey unexpectedly achieved national prominence when two mediums, Efficiency and Eggbeater Caws, astounded spiritualist circles with their dramatic and widely publicized séances featuring the long-deceased Sir Isaac Newton and his German contemporary, G. W. Leibniz. The Caws Experiments, as these séances were called, ended in disaster in 1855 with the death of Dr. Caws. For a few years thereafter, curiosity seekers found their way to the town, and Aubrey accommodated them with an outburst of tourist attractions, which included not only exhibits of spiritualistic and occult interest, but also amateur theatricals consisting of elaborately produced reenactments of events from world history, which often overflowed their confines on the South Green and ran through the streets, meadowlands and beaches. Although relatively peaceful subjects such as the Council of Trent were performed on occasion, most of the events were drawn from the annals of warfare. Summer visitors saw the townsfolk reenact the battles of Marathon, Hastings, Waterloo and Balaklava, among others. Unfortunately, the Aubreyites had little theatrical training, and the presentations were clumsy, not to say tedious. Audiences soon dwindled, until the actors found they were performing largely for themselves. The town entered a period of economic depression; one by one, residents moved away, until the last inhabitant was removed, by force, in 1901. Citizens of Rowley and Ipswich, who had been much put upon by the Aubreyites' antics, are said to have held a celebration to mark the event.

The Brewster Institute, in Cambridge, preserves a few noteworthy relics from the town's past. Among them are a plaster cast, said to have been made from the life, of Dr. Caws' moustache; a hunting knife and birch bark canoe alleged to have belonged to Colonel Schwank; a pickled hand; and several broken gravestones, crudely carved, with images of an erotic nature. A metal skull, which Dr. Caws called the Delphic Oracle, was stolen from the museum in 2002.

In recent years, Aubrey has become the object of considerable attention from historians and sociologists, who have sought to explain, first, the causes

of the original settlers' eccentricities and, second, how they were able to survive in a new land among neighbors whose values were so inimical to their
own. As to the former question, the answer so far remains a mystery. Research
done on Aubrey-on-Seeping, the first colonists' place of origin, has yielded
nothing out of the ordinary in the 17th century makeup of that town, merely
a not-uncommon country village stubbornness and an equally unsurprising
lack of interest in affairs of the shire as a whole that did not touch directly on
the townsfolk's own community. O. K. Schlemmer's suggestion, that there
was a second wave of migration to Aubrey, consisting of a troupe or troupes
of out-of-work actors, fleeing England after Parliament closed the theaters in
1642, and that the infusion of these immigrants helped to form the town's
unusual character, does not seem to hold up. First, no records exist of any
such voyage at that time. Second, it is not at all clear why actors, no longer
able to practice their art in England, would choose the New World as a viable
prospect, since there was no theater in this part of the world either. As to the
question of survival, more fruitful ideas have been advanced. In *Aubrey: A
Puritan Nonesuch*, Professor Karl E. Fahrwart undertakes a thorough examination of the community's past and reaches the following conclusions:

> Many have wondered [he writes] how such a group, holders
> not of heretical beliefs but of cultural attitudes and predilec-
> tions odd enough to have seemed the equivalent of heresy
> to those around them, could have weathered the theological
> storms of those first years, to say nothing of the military fire-
> power those storms would have brought to bear on them.
> The fate of other settlements which opposed the Puritans is
> well known. Thomas Morton's community at Merrymount,
> which practiced a bacchic libertinism complete with revelry
> round a Maypole, was summarily smashed and its leader
> arrested and sent back to England. What saved the Aubrey-
> ites? After long consideration I contend that beneath what
> seemed mere superficiality and foolish impropriety, there re-
> sided in the Aubreyan soul a dense, hard core of viciousness,
> an ill will which Morton lacked and which enabled these

colonists to succeed where he had failed, to triumph on the battlefield, surrounded by the enemy, to win out against a devastating fire and fiscal shortages, to match scorn for scorn, resisting as long as they could all incursions on their inalienable right to be alien. Their malice was their salvation. It is even possible that their neighbors in Ipswich and Rowley, and in Beverly, Topsfield and Salem, unconsciously identified with this malice; if so, it was with good cause. Sweet, Barton, Mallard and the others were themselves Puritans, after all. They fully shared their neighbor's hatreds: of Royalists, Roman Catholics, Quakers, Anabaptists, Antinomians, Jews, Freethinkers and all other "heathen." The only real difference was that the Aubreyites extended their hostility to the likeminded communities in their immediate vicinity. For they were, in their own eyes, the purest of those Puritans; they were the true Chosen among the chosen. Their destiny was unique, *and it had to be made visible as such*. The Aubreyites' constant search for flamboyance, for the needlessly baroque, even the silly, must be seen in this light: that it was merely a way—and a most effective one as well—of declaring, once and for all, their *essential* superiority to the rest of the world, their *manifest* holiness. This was not decadence, or loose morals, or crass commercialism; this was Puritanism itself, carried to a logical conclusion. In *Wayward Puritans: A Study in the Sociology of Deviance*, Kai T. Erikson writes, 'The Puritans were almost a mythical people in their own day, not only because their manners were so easily caricatured, but also because they treated life with such an exaggerated sense of mystery and always felt they were involved in a special cosmic drama.' Can it not be said of these Aubreyites that they were gathering that drama to themselves in a magnificently exclusive way?

The Salem Trumpet:

We have left the house and are strolling with Dr. Caws down the path leading to his front gate. An honor guard of squirrels has fallen in beside him. The sun is shining brightly; a dog barks somewhere in the distance. The doctor leans toward us and takes our arm. "Peter writes beautifully," he confides without preamble. "That is, Peter writes something beautiful. Peter stands handsomely, that is, Peter is handsome insofar as he is standing. The sword is Evander's, that is, if the sword is acted upon when Evander acts, Evander is to that extent just. I see you are somewhat confused, my young friend. But these are really quite useful exercises in logic. Analysis," he explains, "is nothing else than substituting simples in the place of composites or principles in the place of derivative propositions. Men are writing, that is Titius is writing, Caius is writing. Titius is a man, Caius is a man. Peter is similar to Paul, that is, Peter is *A* now and Paul is *A* now." After a long silence, he adds, "Her skin is *A*. Milk is *A*. Haroop."

At last, we arrive at the front gate. A glass of clear liquid, smelling distinctly of juniper berries, has materialized in the doctor's left hand. He stirs the drink with a small white feather. We ask where the feather comes from.

"Only a chicken feather, son, only a chicken feather. Nothing exotic, I assure you. Evander's sword is excellent. Caius is slain by Titius, that is, in the respect in which Titius is a slayer, in that respect Caius is slain. Just a common, ordinary chicken feather." He rises about eight inches off the ground and hovers there. The squirrels stare up at him expectantly. "But Miss Nightingale was not *entirely* opera-mad when I knew her," he says. "I wouldn't want you to get that idea. It was simply that the music appealed to a deeply romantic strain in her being, and an equally deep feeling for beauty. She had a very strong, a very serious side as well, which became quite clear to me in the several conversations we had. What she wanted, she told me, what she wanted more than anything else in this life, was a mission. Just that, a mission. Well, she certainly has one now, hasn't she? Hand; son; horse; heat; title," he adds. "Part; effect; possession; accident; predicate. I, the one now speaking. You, the one now listening. Man is not stone. Sherpa is not yeti. Music is the concealed art of computation for a soul unaware of its counting. 1,2,3,4,5,6,7,8, 9,10,11,12,13,14,15,16,17,18,19,20. Comes to 210. *Finis. Termino.* The tenor saxophone is here to stay."

He reaches down and grasps our hand earnestly. "Thank you *ever so much* for dropping by, my dear sir. It was a very great honor, for *both* of us. Be sure to come back tomorrow evening, now, to see the Oracle."

It has been a long morning. We thank the doctor for his hospitality. As we push open the gate, a final question occurs to us. It is a very *large* question, to be sure, and therefore not one we should ordinarily consider asking. But we feel that in these rather unusual circumstances we might risk it. We turn back to the doctor. By the way, we venture, trying to sound as casual as possible, what *is* the purpose of life?

"To die," he replies, and smiles beatifically.

The Cry of the Gehirngespinstgemach:

XYZXYZXYZXYZ. Erythrite is red. Marcasite is white. Arsenic is yellow, black and grey. 17,711 plus 10,946 is 28,657. Under the settee, Efficiency Caws shudders in her sleep. A dream of salamanders and quicksilver slides through her body, rising in her upper intestine, making a circuit through her cerebellum and disappearing into the pedicle of her spleen. She takes a long, deep breath and turns her eyes inside herself.

Within her heart, just beneath the sinoatrial node of the right atrium, a door swings open, revealing a small, windowless chamber cut into her flesh. In the room is a furnace made of brick, its fire banked with new coal. On top of the furnace, resting on a tripod, is a chemical vessel, long and slender at the neck but with a broad, globular base, about half full of a cloudy, yellowish solution which has begun to bubble in the heat. As she looks through the beads of moisture that have formed on the glass, Efficiency notices moving patches of red, then of white, suspended in the murky liquid. Might it be ... *could* it be? She looks closer, and yes! It is a little man and woman, she milk-white all over and he the color of rust and dried blood. They are floating there, thrusting and heaving, bodies joined in the act of love. It seems to her they have tiny crowns on their heads, set with precious jewels.

Her chest heaves, and the door to the furnace room slams shut. Lying on her side, cheek pressed to the sitting room floor, she slowly opens an eye.

Worn planks with a film of dust. Motes of dust suspended in the slanting sunlight. Who is she, where is she. Killing headache, thirst. Voices, coming from outside, in the garden, down on the path to the gate. Jerry and Eggbeater. Christ. Have to find a drink. Christ! Can I even move? This time I've really done it. She drags herself out into the middle of the room and tries to sit up, her legs flopping like rubber.

She takes a look around and almost faints. She is in a room she has never seen before, smoky, close, with a low, grimy ceiling, the air stinking of rotten eggs. The main source of light is a candle, set on a bench a few feet away. The bench is cluttered with glassware—flasks and jars—along with a bellows and a pair of tongs—instruments of torture, she is sure—lying next to a stack of books, loose papers and writing materials: books of the damned, Last Judgment. Farther off, down at the end of the room, is a furnace, like the one in her dream, with a glass vessel resting on top of it. All around the glass are colored vapors, green, blue, yellow and black, licking at the container like flames, sending out a soft, pulsating glow.

I am in Hell, she thinks. This is Satan's workshop.

And then she sees him—the Devil! How could she have missed him before? The Devil in breeches and a loose-fitting shirt streaked with soot, on his knees beside the furnace. And he is looking in her direction!

In spite of her fear she cannot take her eyes off him, and her legs will not let her move. But as she stares at him she realizes that he is not really the Devil, but an ordinary man—about fifty, she would say, with a shock of white hair—and that his own eyes have widened in consternation, as great, perhaps, as her own. But she feels small and helpless under his gaze, trapped like the couple in the vessel.

The man gestures at her, waving his arms from side to side; he opens his mouth. Though she can hear no words, he seems to be shouting. She tries desperately to scream, but cannot. He reaches out to touch her. The scene vanishes, and she is back in her sitting room.

Somehow she gets to her feet, shaking all over. She lurches, three steps, to the table against the wall, grabs the sherry decanter with both hands, tilts her head back and drinks deeply. Most of the wine spills down the front of her dress.

9

Un Poco Loco

True Tales of the Paranormal:

There is an old saying at the Helvetius Psychiatric Clinic: "The Helvetius takes care of its own." Usually this refers to the patients, and the responsibility the hospital feels for their welfare, but on occasion it has been applied to the peccadilloes of the doctors themselves. Thus the discovery, in 1913, that the distinguished Professor Frosch had for decades led a double life as the Frog Prince, a notorious peeping Tom who left his calling card at the scene of his intrusions, was promptly hushed up, and it was given out that the professor had retired to his farm in the country when in fact he had been taken off to prison. Likewise, many years later, when the great Haselmaus began his "long sleep" at the Helvetius in the middle of an analytical hour, he was quietly transferred to Basel, where he eventually recovered consciousness.

In the same way, in the summer of 2002, Fritz Eichhorn's transition from doctor to patient was accomplished smoothly and without public knowledge. No notice of the events leading up to his change in status appeared in the Zürich press. But the August 30 issue of *Der Guckkasten*, a Berlin scandal sheet, carried the following item:

"AND—speaking of CRAZY—what BRILLIANT PSYCHOANALYST was discovered a few nights ago—in his PAJAMAS—stumbling through the grounds of a Zürich mental hospital? *Der Guckkasten* has learned that Fritz Eichhorn was apprehended by security guards at 3:00 AM, August 27, at the Helvetius Psychiatric Clinic. He was disoriented and incoherent, pleading for help, crying over and over that he had created an HOMUNCULUS and it was being subjected to SEXUAL ABUSE in an upper room of the clinic. He kept calling for someone named Charlie Dominguez, insisting that he could make everything clear.

"The doctor is said to be under sedation. The hospital did not comment officially on his condition, but a colleague of his, who happens to be a friend of ours, as well as an up and coming young epidemiologist, did consent to speak to us. 'It is all terribly, terribly sad,' she said. 'He was—I hate to use the past tense, but one must face the facts—he was a gifted healer, as he rarely failed to remind us. But I really must add that in my opinion this incident is not too surprising. There had been signs, quite early in his time here, that he was not, perhaps, a very good "fit," as they say. He acted in a superior manner, did not always work well with the rest of us. And in the past few weeks he had been behaving, I must say, strangely. He had one patient, a brilliant amnesiac, of whom he had grown quite, well, *fond*. He really became quite possessive about him. Perhaps that is the origin of this "homunculus" fantasy, though of course that whole subject is ridiculous, repulsive and completely demented. But sexual abuse: again, permit me not to be surprised. Dr. Eichhorn is an American. That is all the Americans think of, is it not—sex?'"

Meanwhile, in his upper room, unperturbed by all the excitement swirling around him, Empedocles Schwank went on with his transcription.

IO

FERMENTATION OR WORKING OF LIQUORS.
UNCLEANE THOUGHTS WORDS AND
ACTIONS AND DREAMES

The Cry of the Gehirngespinstgemach:

… She doesn't give a damn about the front of her dress. Nothing matters but the drink. Still trembling in every muscle, her hands fluttering with a will all their own, legs shaking so badly she's sure they're going to fold up underneath her any second and land her on the floor like a collapsed marionette, she takes another swig, even bigger than the first, bending backward against the table, her neck arched as far as it will go, the bowl of the decanter aimed straight at the ceiling. Somehow this time it all goes down her throat. She pauses only for air, then starts right in on her third, a long grateful guzzle, relaxing as the liquor glides warmly through her system. By the time she leaves off, her legs feel like things she might be able to stand on again; her hands have become almost steady in their grip on the vessel—she hoists it with ease for her fourth. By the time she lowers it, panting but relieved, the throbbing at her temples has begun to let up and her fright to shrink to manageable proportions. It's all right, she tells herself, for the love of God, sweetheart, can't you see that you're safe in your own room and everything is perfectly all right? Of course you were scared, who wouldn't be, but it was only your imagination. You've been right here in this room all the time. Haven't you? Of course you have.

Never left it, not even for an instant, did you? No. Well, then, my love, tell me: is there a working furnace hiding in here somewhere, which somehow you've managed not to notice in all the years you've lived here? Is there a big wooden bench lurking about, with a lot of junk piled on top of it, which just happens to have escaped your glance for the past two and three-quarters decades? Are there retorts and tongs and a bellows and vials and bottles with a God-awful stink coming out of them, not to mention a shabby-looking white-haired man in a dirty shirt who acts as if he owns the place and is about to throw you out for trespassing on his private property? No, of course there aren't. Pizzles and sposh. Eggbeater always says you let your imagination get the better of you—not that *he's* anyone to talk. But you have to admit the old shit-sack may have a point anyway. Besides, sweetie, what the hell else do you expect, mixing sherry and champagne like that and curling up afterwards on the hard wood floor for a nap? What must Jerry have thought? Couldn't you at least have managed to stay upright—leaned against the wall or something, while they were talking? Or *sat*, for God's sake, just sat on a bloody chair with your back straight and your chin lifted and one of those nice, enig-matic smiles on your face—used to get him every time, too—till the whole thing blew over? If he'd asked you a question you could have pretended to be in trance—or just turned and *looked* at him, given him that sweet, melting glance, and *he'd* have been in trance! But no, you had to go down on your hands and knees like an animal, and crawl under the God damned settee to sleep it off, in full sight of the both of them. Jesus. Well, dearie, all I've got to say to you is, that given that kind of performance you're just lucky that's *all* you saw when you woke up—because you've seen some wild ones, haven't you? Remember those flying snakes last winter, with gold coins raining down from their scales, that turned into toads when they landed? And the yellow and blue ants that crawled out from under your fingernails the next morn-ing and left those sticky brown stains all over the bedclothes? Eh? Thick and smelly they were, like sap oozing out of a tree trunk, but you couldn't even find them when you crept back into the room an hour later to change the sheets, the linen was as clean as could be. A man with white hair and a spot or two of soot on his shirt is nothing, my love, compared to *those* bits of fancy, even with the furnace and rotten eggs thrown in for good measure. Yelling at you, was he? Well, what of it? Didn't lay a hand on you, did he? No, he did not. Waved his arms a bit, that was all. Can't a phantasm wave his arms if he chooses? Probably didn't mean a thing by it. Unless he *wanted* you, of course. Didn't think of that, did you? Well, why *wouldn't* he want you? Tell me that. You're as attractive as anyone else in the world of the living, and probably a damn sight more so than anyone that inhabits whatever world *he* comes from. No, my love, when all is said and done, that white-haired man is something to be downright *thankful* for, *proud* of, even, if only you look at the situation properly. You've done a lot worse in your time, a lot worse, dearie, in your twenty-seven years and seven months in this vale of tears, and you know it as well as I do, if not better. What the hell.

The fifth drink is an undiluted pleasure, and she lingers over it. Having spotted an empty glass lying on the floor across the room, she's poured herself a generous shot, and now sinks onto a chair beside the occasional table, cradling the decanter in her lap like a baby. Baby. Rock-a-bye, rock-a-bye. Remember how hot it got, sweetie, those three days in the cabinet? I thought we'd never stop perspiring, just get smaller and smaller and finally disappear altogether, running out over the floorboards in two commingled streams. Rock-a-bye, rock-a-bye. And I found out a while later I was—what was that word, that Eggbeater called it? *Enceinte*! Well, we knew what to do about that, didn't we? Rock-a-bye, rock-a-bye, rock-a-bye, rock. She leans back and closes her eyes, sipping contentedly, reveling in that old, familiar, well-loved feeling—what her Newton voice has often defined as the slow and continued motion of heat as particles of bodies gradually change their arrangement and coalesce in new ways, all of them restorative, all of them delightful. Now the voice starts up again. "There exists a certain most subtle spirit," Sir Isaac purrs to her from his place in her pineal gland, as he settles himself comfortably on a step stool in the organ's pulpy, red-grey perivascular connective tissue," a spirit sweet, my dearest, and of a dark metalline color, whose vibrations are mutually propagated along the solid filaments of the nerves, from the outward organs of sense to the brain, and from the brain to the muscles." Oh, yes, my love, oh, yes. She cuddles the decanter. Blessed muscles. Blessed brain. A vital agent is diffused through everything. Squishy-squishy, and of a dark metalline color. You see, sweetheart, what did I tell you? Everything *is* all right, after all.

28,657 plus 17,711 is 46,368. Grossularite is a garnet. Miles Davis will record "Surrey With the Fringe on Top" in 1956. She giggles. It wasn't even my imagination, I bet, that scene I thought I saw. More likely it was just a dream, a very vivid dream—the kind, you know, that you get just before waking. Yes. The whole thing, now that I think about it, was much more like a dream than … anything else. But what was the rest of it, I wonder? There was definitely something more. A sound, was it? Yes, loud and sudden, BANG, like a door slamming shut in the wind. And before that, a heart; a heart and a bottle, or maybe a piece of chemical equipment, like what Papa used to fool around with—a glass vessel. It was sitting on a fire, inside the heart. And when you looked—yes!—when you looked close up, you could see there was something going on behind the glass, churning up the liquid cooking there. Something red and white. Something *naked*. She giggles again. Something dirty! It's always that way in my dreams, these days, isn't it, Uncle Isaac, since you and I took up with each other? Something red and white and naked—and dirty—inside a bottle: now what could that possibly mean, dearest?

Newton grins. "Oh, yes, to be sure, to be sure," he answers, his voice low and silky, "your dream is filthy, my love, filthy and rapturous your dream is, my poppet, my pretty, my pet." He—or rather his double, an exact copy spun out of ectoplasm propagated along the solid filaments of Efficiency's nerves and in the post-synaptic membranes of a billion neurons—is sitting deep in her brain, beside a workbench, amid the pinealocytes and interstitial trabeculae of the pineal gland, the pea-sized, cone-shaped organ directly connected to the third ventricle, controller of reason, judgment and the natural sciences. The double is three-dimensional, animate and faithful to its original in every detail, as Newton was at the age of, say, fifty, with white hair, intense, dark blue eyes, square jaw, full, sensuous lips and long, thin hands. However, he is drastically reduced in size: this Newton is but 1/64 inch tall. He wears a white shirt, stained with soot, and dark knee breeches. Around him, built into the organ's connective tissue, is a fully equipped alchemical laboratory, also made of ectoplasm, a miniature likeness of the one Newton used for so many years in Cambridge, but much more richly appointed, with row upon row of furnaces and countless retorts and vessels, all connected by a jungle of tubing that loops and twists its way out of the flasks and toward the ceiling of the laboratory, disappearing finally into the fleshy walls.

There is something else that has changed about Newton, beyond his size. He has a very large and seemingly permanent erection, his phallus insistently pushing against the confines of his breeches—he, who in his lifetime was known as a pillar of virtue, who once ended a friendship merely on account of an off-color joke. "Something red and white?" He asks now, his smile slipping into a leer. "Oh, yes, that's *always* an important sign. Any interpreter—the prophet Daniel himself, my swish-tail—would tell you the same thing." In fact, he has not heard the dream at all, except for the very last part, having been busy in the laboratory with some work of his own when Efficiency was reconstructing the experience to herself, but the few images—red and white, naked, in a bottle—make what he considers a remarkable, and lucky, correlation with his own preoccupations at the moment, and with his overall plans for this hostess of his." And in fact, love," he goes on, "I believe I have a rather good notion of just what the import might be. Just let me examine something a moment, and I'll tell you."

He gets up and makes his way across the pineal to one of the furnaces, his walk a bandy-legged shamble. Brushing aside a group of overhanging commissural fibers, he bends down and inspects the contents of a tall, broad-bottomed vessel resting on the furnace top, chuckles and returns to his stool. "Did I say rapturous, my beauty? Ecstatic, rather! He licks his lips. Rejoice, rejoice! Philalethes was right, as usual, and it's we who are to gain. You see, my love, the something red and white is a man and a woman. And I've got them here, darling, cavorting in the liquid in the self-same bottle of your dream. What a charming coincidence, eh? They're called by many names, some of them quite fanciful, I must admit, but the simplest way of referring to them is as the Red Man and the White Wife, and these are the names that Philalethes, whom I mentioned before, mostly uses. I don't think I've told you about Philalethes yet, have I, dear? A most extraordinary man—a physician and chemist, primarily; a Philosopher by the Fire, he called himself. Born in Bermuda, they tell me, but educated in your country, dearest—graduated from Harvard College, class of 1646. A friend of the Winthrops, father and son. Achieved the Philosopher's Stone, so it's said, before he turned twenty-four.

Not long after that, he concocted a pill, which was quite famous in its day: 'Starkey's Pill (Starkey was Philalethes' real name, George Starkey)—the Universal Antidote, Diaphoretic, and Anodynous Elixir.' Cured practically everything, I gather, from piles to limberneck. I never tried it myself, so I can't pronounce on its efficacy. But his books—his alchemical writings—those I did try, I can assure you! I read them over and over, all my life; by the time I came to die, I had many passages by heart. And I followed his directions, too, in the laboratory, followed them to the letter. And with good results! Let me tell you, love, those books are worth their weight in—well, in gold, for seekers and adepts like me—and like you as well, with your wonderful dream! For it was Philalethes who explained the *true* nature of the Red Man and the White Wife—the one fixed and ripe, the other volatile and unripe—and showed us how to prepare them, and in what proportions to mix them together. Spelled it all out for us, my pretty, step by step." Newton raises his hands to heaven; he rolls his eyes. "So that the Body draw down its Soul again!" He shouts. "That the Spirit be joined also! Stone of Paradise incombustible—formed in our dreams and crucibles, hot from the furnaces of our desire!"

He rubs himself back and forth along the edge of the workbench, then goes back to look at the vessel. "Yes, honeybunch, it's working, working, they're going at it in there like the pedlar and the hedge whore, belly to belly, rolling over and over, bubbling and flowing. And sweat! The sweat is running off them in rivers, just the way Philalethes said it should, a most violent sweat, he said, exceeding sweat, immoderate Venery. 'I cannot endure the heat,' the White Wife says, 'I must die of it'; 'I am very faint and weak,' says the Red Man. But they go on with it, they do, a second time, a third, a fourth! Ah!" He brushes against the basal lamina which encloses the endothelium of a blood capillary. "Never have I seen it like this—one time, long ago in Cambridge, I almost—but it was not to be. Ah, if only my Nicolas Fatio could be here now to see this!"

Yes! Efficiency shouts. She has heard of Philalethes: someone her father used to talk about. She thinks Papa said he once lived in Aubrey. But that is not what has her excited, nor is it even the pair in the vessel: it is the *sweat!* I know just what you're talking about, she exclaims. It was exactly the same with Eggbeater and me, that time five years ago in the cabinet, when you first spoke through me, dearie. So hot! My God, we must have lost twenty pounds between us, before it was over!

The adrenergic fibers in the pineal quiver in a squall of rage as Newton hisses, stung at the mention of his rival. "Forget that clown," he orders. "That lansprisado, that dabster, that sneak thief—he has no place in this. It's holy matters we're concerned with here, a Sacred Marriage, of the Red Man—the King Himself—and his Queen, the White Wife, to conceive the Royal Child, the glorified body of the Savior, Hermaphrodite-King, perfection of the Work! What could that little smatterer, that upstart from Leipzig—or where does he claim to come from now, Batavia? Good God, *Batavia!*—what could a gypsy like him possibly contribute to such an operation, other than blighting it out of all recognition? I must say, cuddlekins, sometimes you appear to lose track of the seriousness of what we're doing here. There are tremendous forces involved, you must remember; the weightiest issues are hanging in the balance. A single misstep could bring disaster, and that idiot is just the one to make it. Frankly, my sweet—and I've been meaning to bring this up for quite a while now, this is no offhand remark, thrown out without reflection—frankly I cannot, try as I may, form the slightest notion of what you saw in the lout in the first place. Oh, I make no doubt that it was a youthful indiscretion: you certainly were young at the time. You are moderately young even now; may the pox never blemish your pretty countenance. But 'youthful indiscretion,' accurate though it may be, provides little more than a description of the event; it can hardly be said to go to the root of the matter, or disclose the prime mover compelling eventuation from a distance. To find that, my dear, you'll need more than a phrase or two of airy dismissal; you'll have to search deeply, unsparingly, within your own character—'Know thyself,' as the great Thales says—examine your conduct, your thoughts, your dreams and your most secret wishes, in the clear light of day, unflinchingly. When you were a child, for instance, did you make pies on Sunday night? Squirt water on the Lord's day? Engage in idle discourse, show peevishness, steal cherry cobs and deny you did so? Did you champion the theory of vortices, or maintain the relativity of space and time? Did you squabble about atoms and universal gravity and the Sensorium of God? Did you deny the existence of a vacuum? These, of course, are but a few sample questions; others, equally probing, will leap, I'm sure, into your awareness. But I very much fear, my dear, that when you are done with your accounting, when the debits and credits—for surely there must be at least a few of these latter, too—are finally totted up, you will discover, lurking at the very center of your nature, some single primogenial flaw, squalid, repulsive, which is (please pardon the pun) cause of all the others and which has led, among other things, to your truly atrocious choice of a male companion. Exactly what this flaw may be, one cannot, of course, predict; but it goes without saying that its correction will be no simple matter. Enormity does not yield to virtue save by the grimmest of struggles. Indeed, you may find complete victory—the utter eradication of your weakness—impossible. But admission of one's sins is an admirable beginning, and reform of one's conduct a natural—nay, a mandatory—continuation which not only demonstrates good faith but also provides virtue a foothold from which it can gradually advance and gain new ground in one's soul. In short, my sweet, the way before you is not easy, but—thank Heaven—the way is clear: get rid of the bastard. Get rid of him now. Just cut him out of the act, cut him out of your life, while there's still time. Go out on your own—just you and me. The public will love us, I'll take care of that. I promise."

Oh, *really?* The dorsomedial nucleus of Efficiency's hypothalamus vibrates as if teased with an electric current. She takes another drink. You're a mite full of yourself today, aren't you? "Youthful indiscretion"—I like that! "Get rid of the bastard"—shit! Where the hell did you all of a sudden get the right to preach to me that way, eh? Sir Isaac Newton, the Great Moralist? Hah! Maybe you were once, way back when, but these days you're just a dirty old man, and have been ever since I've known you. You're interested in one thing and one thing only, and that's fine with me. Why else do you think I've put up with you all this time, for Christ's sake? Made you comfortable, gave you everything you wanted, played your little games? It certainly wasn't on account of your cheery disposition, nor because of any great heroism of yours in an emergency, either. *You* never had to deal with a great huge brown-and-white spotted cow squeezing its body inch by inch out of your left nostril and mooing all the while at the top of its lungs the way Eggbeater had to, did you, dearie? No, and I'll bet you anything you like your Red King and White Queen or whatever-the-hell-it-is you call them didn't either. Not to mention what *I* had to go through in that cabinet, with an actual, canonized Christian saint—Anselm of Canterbury, in the flesh—sashaying out of my arsehole cool as you please—might have been taking his afternoon stroll in the Cathedral grounds, he might—prattling on about how that which can be conceived not to exist is not God or some other crap I forget, as if Eggbeater and I didn't already have enough to occupy our minds as it was. And where were you while all that was going on, eh? Lying low, that's for sure; probably keeping out of danger till the worst had blown over. Well, let me tell you something, Mr. Scientific Genius—and see if you can manage not to forget it right away: Eggbeater may have his faults, but he and I might have died in that cabinet if we hadn't, uh, stuck together, and we've been doing all right as a team since then, by and large—a lot better than all right, as a matter of fact, if you'll kindly recall some of our reviews. So we're not about to break up at this late date over a few minor differences of opinion—and certainly not on *your* say-so. By the way, have you ever given any thought to where you might *be* today if Eggbeater and I hadn't gotten out of there alive? Well, I suggest you do so. And while you're at it, if you're so smart, you might consider how you'd feel if I took it into my head again to stop listening to you—just ignore you entirely, the way I did last year. You didn't care for it much, did you, pet? Watch out, then; it could happen again. And what if one day in the not-so-distant future Eggbeater and I should decide we're fed up with the whole business, and go back into the cabinet and get rid of you *and* Leibniz for good? We could do it, too, don't think we couldn't, if we set our minds to it. It wouldn't be easy, but we're not exactly the novices we were five years ago, and when we got through with you and you came to your senses, such as they are, you'd find yourself *evacuated*—out the back door, same as old Anselm. How'd you like *that*, sweetie?

Newton's anger vanishes as quickly as it came, put to flight by sudden, all-conquering fear. He sees he'd better make amends, and right away, if he wants to keep his sinecure. Luckily, the obsequiousness cultivated throughout thirty years of court life, first as Warden of the Mint and then as its Master, is still at his disposal, and he feels no compunctions about spreading it on thick. "Oh, my dear, my dear, my dear, dear love, my Efficiency, my own, my sweet one," he babbles, "I meant no offense, please do forgive me,

I meant no harm, please do believe me, no harm in all the world, nor in the heavens either, in the whole frame of Nature no harm, no harm, no slightest hurt to your precious person." He paces back and forth between the bench and the furnaces. "It was only my excitement—my thrill, actually—a feeling so strong and" (he rubs his groin) "sustained that it quite overcame me, as I looked into that vessel and saw my dreams at last—at long, long, last, through lifetimes and lifetimes—on the point of coming true. You see, my sweet, all my work has prospered so well, far beyond anything I could have predicted, in this new laboratory of mine—of ours, I should say—or, rather, to be more accurate about it—*much* more accurate, what a selfish old fool I am, to be sure—this laboratory of *yours*. And how grateful I am, how deeply, how eternally, how infinitely grateful I am to you, my sweetest one, for the opportunity you have vouchsafed me. I always used to say, that if I had accomplished anything of significance, it was because I stood on the shoulders of giants, and once again that sentiment makes—not, of course, that you're *that* tall, I didn't mean to imply any such a thing, you're not tall at all, except, that is, when we're giving a séance, and you … oh, dear, I'm putting this so badly. That was only a figure of speech, my marvel, to indicate the size of your spirit, your heart—yes, your great, your beautiful, your generous heart, beating [This ought to bring her 'round, he reasons] like a glorious perpetual motion machine, pumping faithfully beneath your magnificent bosom, with its two great luminaries, your breasts, milk-white and firm, I'll warrant, and perfect in their curvature, though of course I've never seen them. Nor must I neglect to pay homage [he smirks] to those other globes, your buttocks, even whiter, I would wager, than your boobies, but with the same delicious mixture of pliancy and firmness to the touch, the motive force of each cheek (what we commonly call the weight) being as the content under the quantities of matter in both, divided by the square of the distance between their centers—although naturally I've never had the pleasure of examining them. Ah, what heaven it would be to do so, spreading them gently, ever so gently, apart, and then penetrating with all the ardor at one's command—like a huge fiery beam stretched out!—into the inner sanctum of your temple. How heinous, then, the sacrilege, that the slabby Anselm, spewing obscenities, should have chosen that particular portal to effect his stinking egress from your person! But then, I cannot refrain from adding, what else would you expect from a Papist?"

Newton stops. An icy silence fills the pineal gland. He senses that he's getting nowhere, that in fact he may even have lost ground: prurience, inexplicably, isn't having the usual effect. With mounting dread he decides on contrition as his only option. "Oh, my darling," he cries, "my best, my gorgeous-est, my most *efficient* Efficiency, I say everything so ineptly, I cloud my own meaning. I was a monster, I admit it, I was crass, I was thoughtless, I was harsh, vindictive, headstrong, toplofty, cruel, remorseless, ravening, rude, remonstrative, importunate, base, corrupt, pustulous, nasty, vicious, noxious, venomous, vile, foul, intemperate, ranting, ill-bred, scabrous, swinish, currish, foetid, rank, intolerant, turgid, prolix, tortuous, Gongoresque, lexiphanic, pompous, pedantic, theocratic, apodictical, captious." He warms to his theme. "I was as Cain, as Haman, as Herod or Judas. Nay, I was as Leviathan, Behemoth, the four Beasts of Daniel, the Serpent in the Garden, the Worm that smote the root of Jonah's gourd. I was as Saul, afflicted with an evil spirit."

An inspiration strikes him; he stops pacing. "For in truth, my adored one," he wheedles, "to be utterly and unselfservingly honest, it may not be impossible—indeed, the longer I reflect on it the more likely it does seem to seem, my heart's desire—that some such dybbuk of qlippa, taking the form, perhaps, of a sudden distemper or hectic endemic to these parts, may have seized my head and impaired for a spell my usual consistency of mind. If so, I must say it hardly would be surprising. These disturbances are by no means uncommon in serious laboratory work. The strain under which one operates is enormous."

He takes a deep breath. Hearing no outburst from Efficiency, and thinking he feels a slight moderation in the gland's temperature, he sits again at the bench and surveys the pineal with some of his old sense of proprietorship. His voice gains in confidence. "The first difficulty," he goes on, "lies in the extreme sensitivity of the materials we employ—and by materials I mean not the equipment (though there are pitfalls there as well) but the matter itself."

He stops again. Nothing; and it *does* feel slightly warmer, he'd swear to it. Never underestimate contrition. He clears his throat. "Now, it's rather well known that we work with three primary substances, Sulfur, Mercury and Salt. But what is not suspected—and what I would not, could not, tell even you, my beloved, if you were not already, simply by the splendor of your being and your effulgent intelligence, almost an adept yourself—what remains unsuspected by the multitude is that our three substances bear no similarity worth mentioning to the commonly recognized versions of themselves. I mean that *our* Sulfur, which we call Philosophical Sulfur, is not merely brimstone; our Mercury is not quicksilver; nor our Salt sodium chloride. They are Soul and Spirit and Body, respectively, extracted at immense pains from the Chaos of the elements and given chemical expression within our vessels. Mere words can never convey the delicacy, the deftness, both mental and physical, required for such manipulations." He drools. "The rewards are magnificent, but dangers abound. In my own day Thomas Vaughan, a Welsh adept, was killed by an explosion in the laboratory. A century before that, William Holway lost first his Elixir, then his reason, and finally his sight. And Philalethes, as talented a worker as ever came along, fell into drink and debt, died of the plague, a martyr to the Art. The simplest mistake can be fatal.

"Then, too, there are the long hours spent tending the fire, not only to keep it from going out but to raise and lower the heat at the proper times, a matter demanding the utmost attentiveness. One often goes days without sleep, or else rest can be caught only in the fleetingest of catnaps, especially if one is working without an assistant. Constant vigilance must be maintained, for decades of work can come to naught in an instant. And in such exhausted watchfulness, what curious phantoms may invade the mind, or even materialize, full-bodied, it would seem, before one's eyes, standing in the air mid-way between floor and ceiling, or scratching at the window pane, or slithering across the floor, beckoning, enticing, luring one toward … Ah, dear Efficiency, believe me, I know whereof I speak, for to my lasting—my everlasting—regret, my own reason once was claimed, temporarily, by just such a specter! Perhaps the story will soften your heart."

He sighs. "It happened in the summer of 1693, in the laboratory I used at Cambridge, a small shed—nothing like this one, my sweet—but serviceable, built against the wall of the chapel, next to the college garden. The end of August, I think it was, or perhaps the first week of September, but well before the autumnal equinox in any case. Autumn! *That* was my time of year, especially in my youth—the season of fall, rectilinear descent of bodies! It was in autumn, you know, that the first hint of the law of universal gravitation came to me, as I sat one afternoon in my mother's garden, at the farm in Lincolnshire. I was turning over in my mind the possible connections between the orbit of the moon and the attraction of bodies in a straight line. If one could draw such a line, I thought, it would pass through the center of the earth. At the same moment I felt a breeze on my cheek and looked up: an apple was falling from its tree, not a dozen feet from where I was seated! I was just twenty-three years old. The autumn before, also at the farm, I had arrived—entirely on my own, as the world well knows, for which you, my love, among others, are to be thanked—at the direct method of fluxions for computing the acceleration and deceleration of bodies moving through space, the very method [his voice hardens] which that vomit-provoking [he stops himself in time] I mean that highly esteemed colleague of mine to whom you are presently married, pirated outright—borrowed, I mean, and failed—most likely forgot—to acknowledge, a perfectly innocent oversight I am sure—the swine—calling my discovery his calculus." (*His*! Newton mutters to himself: may he rot in the putrefaction of his own deserving, the back-biting shitheel, lie dead and buried and rise no more to trouble us ever, on the third day or any other!)

" ... Oh, nothing, nothing, my dear, nothing at all. I was merely making the point, yet again and in another way, that autumns, sweet cool autumns, have been unusually kind to me, particularly—if I may so put it—in the springtime of my life, ha-ha." He sighs. "But *this*, this season, this seizure, of madness which I am about to relate to you, took place in summer, fiery, unforgiving summer, and I, alas, was in my fifty-first year.

"The forenoons all that month had been a Gehenna. Even the nights had been suffocating, and ten times worse as I toiled at the furnace. I'd been shut up in the laboratory for days, tending the Work with practically no sleep and nothing to eat aside from a spoonful or two of cold porridge. I hadn't seen a soul all that time—which ordinarily would have posed me no problem. Under most circumstances I have the greatest fondness for my Retired Solitudes, as Philalethes calls them. Did I not, after all, wait nearly twenty-five years before revealing myself to you, my aurora? It was nothing, believe me, only an effortless continuation of established practice. Philalethes says the adept should be of a constant mind, diligent, industrious, learned, a devourer of books, private, solitary. Well, I was certainly all of those, never happier than when engaged wholly by myself in the plenitude which only the Work can bring, as it swells and proliferates, unfolding out of itself—nature delighting in nature, and only I there to see it. But not that night—not the night the madness came. Then were no delights; then were only the heat, thwarted plans, a fevered brain and ill omens. Two weeks earlier there had been a fire in the laboratory, started when I happened to leave a candle unattended, and many important papers had been ruined. I came back into the shed just in time: another second, and the whole place might have gone up. And then the Sevens began!

"The day after the fire, seven ravens appeared suddenly out of a cloudless sky; they swooped down like an avenging horde onto the roof of Trinity Chapel, where they perched, silent and motionless, until nightfall. The next morning, seven snakes' eggs hatched in the garden. One week later, a woman in the Town gave birth to a litter of seven puppies. I heard it from a man who knew the midwife; he said he had seen the dogs with his own eyes. That night—and it was the last full night of sleep I was to have for a long time—I dreamed I saw two men crouching naked at the bottom of a barrel, which stood on the end of a pier. Someone nailed the lid down; others attached iron weights to the barrel and pushed it into the water. I heard the men roaring as they sank, and the sound of their thrashing below. A crowd cheered. The following day I received a letter from a dear who, in addition to dismissing every one of the proposals I had made to him earlier in the summer (dismissing them *airily*, my sweet, as if they were of no matter at all!) happened to mention—for my edification, I suppose!—that two men had been drowned in a barrel for sodomy, in Amsterdam in 1686, exactly seven years before!

"Now, I am not a superstitious man, lovely Efficiency, far, far from it. I know too well, better than anyone, the true mechanical workings of phenomena, be they never so marvelous. But freely I confess, that sequence of events shook me. Not for nothing had I studied the Apocalypse of Saint John, with its seven seals, seven angels, seven trumpets, seven thunders. How could I fail to recognize the signs of dire times ahead when they showed themselves so plainly to my sight? Sleepless, hardly aware of my actions, I wandered about the laboratory, the cries of those drowning men ringing in my ears. What would I not have given then for the presence of that one faithful Companion whom, the old adepts tell us, even the solitary man may have as his co-operator in carrying out the Work! After all, I told myself, it was hardly a matter of weakness or of purely personal gratification, this desire for another human, to be cut out of my heart as one would some horrible vice. No, it was a continuation of time-honored tradition, a practice attributed to some of the greatest masters. One of the earliest we know of, Zosimos of Panopolis, had Theosebia, his *soror mystica*. Nicolas Flamel, successful in the Work beyond all measuring and the author of one of our most important and useful texts, had his wife, Perronelle, constantly at his side. Even my countryman, Thomas Vaughan, who came to such an unhappy end, had his wife, Rebecca, to share his labors. And these were not mere apprentices, expected only to clean flasks and grind powders; they were genuine partners, as committed to the Opus as their mates, essential to its outcome. A book printed in my day, the *Mutus Liber*—a work composed entirely of pictures—showed a man and a woman kneeling together beside their furnace; in other pictures they were shown performing all laboratory operations in common.

"'And what about me?' I cried. Me, *Isaacus Neuutonus—Ieova Sanctus Unus*, born the same day as Our Lord Jesus Christ! Am *I* not an adept, as great as any other, and entitled to the same measure of success? Am I to be denied what others have been given freely, even when I humbly put out my hand to request it? Shall I end my days in isolation, in ignominy—like Holway, blind and foolish, or Borri (whom I once tried to trace to no avail), an exile, forced to wander from country to country, a price on his head? Flamel and his wife endowed hospitals, chapels and churches; his tombstone, they say, can still be seen in Paris, carved with the symbols of the sun and moon. What shall be cut on my monument? The number Seven, girt with ravens, serpents and puppies, chasing each other endlessly in spirals, surmounted by a—? NO! The thought could not be tolerated. I sank to my knees in despair."

46,368 plus 27,657 is 75,025. Franklinite is black; cerargyrite is sectile. Newton falls silent. He grimaces. Recalling this episode is always vexatious for him, bringing back not only defeat and sorrow but also—and far more painfully—a sizable portion of intellectual mortification. What he saw that night—when, obeying some obscure impulse, he turned, still on his knees, and looked away from the furnace toward the other end of the laboratory—marked him deeply, shaking for the first time his confidence in the supreme power of his intellect to make sense of his conscious experience. For suddenly, *ex nihilo* as it were, there appeared before him, on the floor in the middle of the room, a human shape, hunched over, crawling painfully in his direction. At first his heart leaped, as he thought it was Fatio—Fatio clad, for some reason, in a long white gown, perhaps as a penitent, come back to beg his forgiveness! But the next instant he saw it was a woman, her dress of a style he had never seen, down on all fours, propelling herself forward by her arms and shoulder muscles, her legs dragging uselessly behind.

Was it the color of her hair, a red-gold, so like his friend's, that caused his confusion? Or the youthful face, the sensuous lips? Most likely it was all of these, but Newton had no time then to consider the question, for something worse, far worse, now presented itself. Behind the woman—all through the area she had traversed—his laboratory had ceased to exist. Another room, a kind of sitting room, by the looks of it, as unfamiliar as her costume, had taken its place. Where the door to the laboratory had been, two windows were now cut into the wall, and they opened out not on the Cambridge night, with black silhouettes of Trinity College towers, but on a sunny, verdant garden, with a tree-lined street behind it. As the woman came closer and closer, so did this new room, blotting out, inch by inch, the laboratory in which he stood. It was as if she was not so much moving by herself as dragging this new room with her, laboriously but inexorably, eliminating everything in her path.

Newton rose with a frantic gesture. He opened his mouth to yell but could not make a sound. She stopped then and looked him full in the face, her clear green eyes—Fatio's eyes!—wide in astonishment. Desperate, he lunged toward her, arms outstretched. She opened her mouth and at the same moment he finally cried out Fatio's name. Somewhere outside a dog barked. As suddenly as she had come, the woman vanished, and the sitting room with her. But when Newton went back to his furnace (a few seconds later? An hour? He had no idea), and looked in the vessel there, the Red Man and his White Wife—the only fruit of his long summer's labor—were gone as well, reduced to a green oily scum floating on the surface of the liquid.

Newton was changed, too. For weeks he lived in a state of distraction. He wandered to and fro without purpose, passed acquaintances in the College without a sign of recognition, and wrote crazy letters to his friends, John Locke and Samuel Pepys, apologizing for non-existent wrongs and begging them never again to see him. ("Being of opinion that you endeavored to embroile me with woemen," the one to Locke began, "I answered twere better if you were dead.") It was well into autumn (sweet, forgiving autumn!) before he regained any sort of composure at all, and winter was in the air before he felt his old self again. Sometimes, indeed, he wonders if he ever fully recovered. Certainly he has never been able to think of the incident without a shudder. But now, like it or not, he must go through the whole thing again, for Efficiency's sake, relive every last bit of it, if he is to make her sympathize with him. A humiliating prospect, at best. But the prize is worth it. Oh, yes, he tells himself, no prize ever was worth more!

He looks up from the workbench, with its litter of tools, papers and laboratory glassware, and casts his eyes again around the pineal gland. How *nice*, he thinks, not for the first time, how very, very nice on the whole indeed— greatly expanded beyond his old Cambridge place, and fitted out (so smartly!) with what he supposes are the latest in scientific improvements. His vessels, for instance, are connected to his distillation apparatus by a remarkably sophisticated and efficient system of tubing—an arrangement quite unlike anything he has ever seen. Some day, he tells himself, he must take the trouble to examine it thoroughly; so far as he can tell at present, it seems to originate somewhere inside the pineal's walls. Is it possible that some of the by-products of his experiments are not simply drained off but instead conveyed directly into his hostess' anatomy? And if so, what function do they perform?

Another point of interest is a membrane, shaped roughly like an eye, high up near the top of the gland, of a somewhat smoother texture and—it would seem from below—thinner composition than the surrounding tissue. At any rate, shadows now and then seem to weave back and forth across the area, as though forms on the other side of the membrane were moving in front of a light source. Newton has hopes of one day opening the eye, and installing some sort of telescope there. It would be a simple enough matter to grind the lenses; he has the tools for it, and the skills. All that's needed is time, and—assuming he plays his cards right with Mrs. Caws—he'll have an infinity of that.

But the most remarkable thing about his laboratory, so far as he is concerned, is that, through some miraculous agency which as yet escapes him, his furnaces seem almost to regulate themselves, responding instantly to his slightest adjustment, providing exactly the right amount of heat beneath his vessels, no matter how high or low, at whatever duration, whenever he wants it. Newton can hardly credit the possibility, but for the first time in his alchemical experience there may be no need for horse dung, or even for his own special mixture of brewsters' grains, wheat bran, sawdust and chopped hay, to keep the Regal Child warm while he, she or it is undergoing incubation. What marvelous adaptations and arrangements, he thinks. A fire vaporous and yet not light, a fire which nourishes and devours not, a fire natural and yet made by art.

Of course, other aspects of his quarters are not so satisfactory. The greyed-out pink of the pineal's walls, for example, leaves a good deal to be desired, particularly when contrasted with the rich, vibrant crimson he used to adorn his London houses in his later, more affluent years. But, greyed-out or not, at least it is *some* sort of red, he reminds himself, and a damn sight finer, no matter what your taste, than that soot-streaked, acid-piss yellow of the walls in the Cambridge place. No wonder you went a bit daft that time, he ventures, cooped up day after day, night after night, in a room like that. That yellow alone would have done the trick eventually, Fatio or no Fatio. But this place, now, this is a place you can work in, and make up (he licks his lips) for lost time. Which one of the adepts was it—Gerhard Dorn, perhaps, that student of Paracelsus?—who wrote that there is a final state in the Great Work which can only be attained *after* death? Yes. Yes! Faintly, Newton begins to get a glimmer of what Dorn might have meant by that, a meaning quite different from anything he would have embraced during his lifetime. He thinks he knows how to go about achieving that state, too: in the human body, Dorn had written, there is a certain metaphysical substance known to very few … Ah, yes. And fewer still, Newton adds, have guessed where in the body to find it, or how, once it is located, to coax it up out of its hiding place! Oh, there were always *rumors* about it in the old days, he remembers, passed back and forth in secret among the cognoscenti—mostly speculations concerning urine, spittle or some other unlovely by-product. And there were some folk as well who read the wildest meanings into this or that passage of Flamel, Ripley, Philalethes or one of the other great adepts. But there were those, too, who wondered aloud (strictly in private conversation, to be sure, no one in those times would have dared air such notions in public, much less commit them to paper) exactly what practices Thomas Vaughan and his wife must have been up to, in order to get themselves killed off, one after the other, in the space of a few short years, as if (the rumor-mongers said) by a judgment of Divine Providence. And on one occasion, Newton recalls, he himself, together with Fatio on a visit to London, had been shown a very old manuscript, said to have come from the East, which purported to explain, in shocking and—as Fatio commented—almost ludicrously copious detail, the precise physical procedures for … But the man who showed them the text was untrustworthy to say the least (a grubby little pornographer and purveyor of stolen goods whom Newton saw hanged as a counterfeiter twenty years later), and there were a host of dangers involved—mortal ones, if the fate of Vaughan and his wife was any guide—which the text alluded to but gave no indication of methods for avoiding them. Last, and most decisively, there were one's own scruples, as a properly instructed and unfailingly devout Puritan, chaste into the bargain, who had been taught from the cradle to shun, shun as filths and abominations, all such doings as—

Newton laughs, laughs as he never did in his lifetime, a deep, rumbling belly-laugh that bounces off the walls of the pineal and causes Efficiency, now on her seventh or eighth drink, to hiccup in mid-swallow. Oh, yes, abominations, he recalls, most assuredly he used to regard them so: unspeakable crimes in this life and certain perdition in the next. He, who had questioned even the Holy Trinity, never had questions about that. But death, he discovered, was a great teacher, an emenogogue who provided the most astounding corrections. From the very beginning (which in Newton's case occurred shortly after one o'clock in the morning of the twentieth of March, 1727, at his house in Kensington) when his soul slipped out of his exhausted, eighty-four year old body and flew like a homing pigeon into the soft, warm folds of the crimson hangings on the walls of his bedroom, death showed him simultaneous comfort and enlightenment, wrapping him in easefulness, giving the lie to the predestined wretchedness preached by generations of Calvinist clergy and replacing that dogma with a vision of a ruby red dawn—a truly alchemical outcome! Now, more than a hundred years later, having had plenty of opportunity for reflection, recollection, experiment and practice—combined, in his present habitation, with all the laboratory equipment he needs and (he caresses his testicles) a marvelously readjusted physical orientation—he at last feels ready, not only to greet the sun in good earnest but actively to assist in its rising. Newton looks across the pineal at the nearest furnace, where the Red Man and his White Wife are going lustily about their business, and smiles broadly. Courage, Isaac, he tells himself. Courage, *Ieova Sanctus Unus*, courage. Everything may yet work out for the best, so long as you're careful to keep your tenancy of this place. And that, I needn't remind you, means staying cozy with its owner. It's not for the working space alone, remember: she has a part of her own to play in this project, and a crucial one, too. Haven't you been getting her ready for it, little by little, over the last half-decade, improving her tastes, whetting her appetites? Well, then, my lad, have a care. That temper of yours could bring everything to naught in an instant. Keep your mind on the goal, stay calm, level-headed. Be friendly. You know what she likes—my God, man, you made her like it. Keep her *interested*.

He turns his attention back to Efficiency. "Ah, my dear, my sweet, my more-than-precious, my radiance, do excuse, if you can, a fond old man. I was momentarily, er, distracted—no, no, not distracted, how can I tell you less than the truth, my closest confidante?—I was *overcome*, my love, by emotion. I am often taken that way, I'm afraid, when I recall the events of that dreadful summer, and rehearse yet again all I lost then." He stifles a sob. "But one must be strong; a thousand pardons, my glory. Let me resume my tale where I left off.

"How long did I stay in that attitude—kneeling, you recall, as if in prayer? I could not say, my sweet. I only know that I kept repeating numbers over and over, numbers and equations, tonelessly, as fast as I could, calculations and logarithms to fifty-seven places, the areas of curves, axioms, postulates, the rule for extracting the cube root of binomials—anything to shut out the tumult raging unchecked in my brain...."

Mmmmmmm, says Efficiency, as Newton drones on. Her anger has abated considerably. She's about decided this Newton is worth hanging on to, after all. Oh, he's plenty high and mighty, no doubt about it, and that can get under your skin, sometimes. She's never known a man more full of himself, not even her father, which is saying quite a lot when she considers the self-admiring puffed-uppedness of the late Abimelech Barton. But he's quite lively company otherwise, Uncle Isaac is, and always good for a dirty story or two, although this particular memoir he's slogging through doesn't seem to be one of them. She wishes he'd get done with it, and go on to something more racy; she likes the racy ones more and more, she finds, the last few years especially. Pretending to be a lady is all well and good, she tells herself; in fact, it's imperative, if you want to maintain any kind of standing in the world. But actually *being* one? Inside your mind, your skin, your whole self? Never! Remember the Aubrey Female Academy, dearie? Torture. And Miss Slocum's book on deportment? How about all that charitable work, aiding the poor, visiting the sick? Disgusting. One long, boring, well-meaning misery, nothing but virtuousness and not a drop of joy anywhere. And if it was that bad, sweetie, the way *you* did it, imagine what it would have been like if you'd let them fool you into taking it *seriously*! My God, they wouldn't even let you wear attractive *clothes*—this dress, for instance, would *never* have been permitted. Bare shoulders? Lordy, the scandal! And of course there was no question of speaking your mind about anything. A lady's not supposed to have opinions; she's not even supposed to *want* to have any. It went without saying there was to be no fun. Not to mention adventure. Not to mention a little nice, happy *coarseness*. Or—God forbid!—*indecency*. Well, Jesus Christ! How the hell can anybody live without indecency? Really *live*, I mean. It just can't be done; *I* could never manage it anyhow. I'd go crazy inside a week. The spirit would be drained right out of me.

Efficiency smiles. In her pineal gland a cluster of synaptic ribbons vibrates, as bursts of a substance that one day will be called melatonin pass from the vessel where the Red Man and his White Wife are disporting themselves, through a system of tubing attached to the hermetically sealed lid, and thence into her bloodstream. Her headache is not even a memory.

Now there, she continues, that's one big difference between me and Eggbeater: he really does take his respectability seriously. I think it's more important to him than anything in the world to be looked on as a gentleman; he has to be absolutely proper in everything he does. And him with a herd of livestock tramping after him wherever he goes—when he isn't five feet up in the air, that is. Imagine! But no matter—he tries to carry it off *respectably*, whatever it is. It's the most comical thing I ever saw. The lengths he'll go to, to convince you that he's the soundest, the whitest, the most trustworthy, the most *gentlemanly* gentleman who ever tied a cravat! The Continental manner, the cultured voice, the I-don't-know-how-many-languages, even when he's three sheets to the wind—which is most of the time, lately. She sips her drink. But it's not just the outside world he wants to impress; he behaves exactly the same in front of me, and after all we've been through together, too. And not only that: I've heard him talking to himself—when he didn't know I was around—and he was just the same then. The soul of propriety. "Oh, my dear, dear Sir." "Oh, how very kind of you." "The pleasure was entirely mine." Right into the shaving mirror. Jesus. Say what you want about Uncle Isaac, sweetheart, he doesn't have any of those problems, not with me he doesn't. We're birds of a feather, Uncle Isaac and I, at least so far as indecency goes. So you'd better keep him, dearie, she answers herself. *He* understands you, if nobody else does. Besides, what the hell would you do without him the next time you were in the séance room? Call back St. Anselm? Eggbeater would hog all the attention, with his blasted levitation, to say nothing of that Oracle thing he's got now. Nobody can resist a new machine. They wouldn't take the slightest notice of you, my girl, bare shoulders or covered, not even Jerry. You'd be part of the Goddamned *audience*.

Mmmmmmm, she repeats a little louder, and her voice is a purred peace offering. I'm *so* sorry to interrupt you, Uncle Isaac, I know it's terribly rude of me, but there was something you said a few moments ago ... I'm not sure I have it right ... was it "raging unchecked in my brain," or words to that effect? It was? I thought so. Well—and pardon me again, dear, for interrupting, but I just wanted to say ... (Quick, she says to herself, make something up, for God's sake, he's waiting) I just wanted to say ... er ... that I know just what you mean. (Good. Go on—anything, for Christ's sake, just butter him up.) It was ... it was like that every day for me at the Aubrey Female Academy. Simply terrible. Never hated anything so much in my life. It must be the Eighth

Wonder of the World, how I got out of that place in one piece. Oh, you are? Well, thank you, lovey, I'm glad, too. You would? Oh, how very flattering! You're *so* good to me, darling ... Listen, sweetie, I was thinking. There's really no reason for you to go on with that story, if it upsets you. Certainly not on *my* account. I mean—please don't misunderstand me—your story is *most* interesting, and simply filled with pathos, but to finish it would only ... well, to finish it would only add *more* to it, if you see what I mean? I'm sure I get the gist of it already, and I *couldn't* be more sympathetic. So let's just go on to something else—whatever you'd like—if it's all the same to you.

Hurrah! Victory! Rod of Mercury be praised! Newton claps his tiny hands and jumps off the stool, kicking it halfway across the pineal gland. He breaks into a jig. A jar containing granulated salt of pig's urine falls off the work-bench and smashes on the floor. Let it go! Let it go! What's one jar of pig's urine, more or less? He hasn't felt this carefree since the autumn of 1716, when he got the news that Leibniz was dead. Oh, fountain of crude sperm! Feces and abominations! Hot metallic splendor! The world is reborn!

But—he stops himself in mid-spring—wait now, friend Isaac. Not so fast; have a care, as I told you a moment ago. There will be time enough later for celebration. But just now—to stay on the safe side—you must keep up appearances. Speak to her, old fellow, and take the *joy* out of your voice. Be *sincere*; pour out your heart.

"Oh, my dear," he prevaricates, "you are kind beyond kindness. I weep at your compassion, your clemency, your forbearance, your ruth. But I couldn't possibly accept, not until I have explained, no, not until I have *expiated*, my harsh, vindictive, headstrong, toplofty, cruel, remorseless, ravening, rude, remonstrative—but do you really mean it, my sweet? You DO? Ah, my delight!" He starts his jig again. "My delectation, my deliverer! A wonder, you are, a true wonder! And, since you do feel that way, as of that little matter I was speaking of earlier—a mere trifle, of course, but one *will* inflate things beyond their importance—suffice it simply to say ... [He starts to run out of breath] Suffice it ... simply to ... [He stops dancing, finds the stool, puts it upright and sits]....simply to say ... [He gets his wind back] that on that particular occasion I ran, temporarily of course, out of my wits, largely due to the strain of overwork, and several disturbing things took place which I would much prefer not to live through again but which, in the end, hardly mattered since everything came out right." There! *That's* done. "And now, my darling, as to the 'something else' you requested: I will supply it with pleasure, pleasure and gratitude. But—to that end—perhaps it will be best if I begin where, or *approximately* where, I left off some time ago, just before our little, uh, contretemps, if I may so describe it, occurred. For I think, my voluptuary, that you will find the continuation to be full of twists and turns—mortifications and regenerations, Philalethes calls them—of the most fascinating and *lubricious* character, well worth your attention and even, you may come to agree, your participation. Oh, yes, my sweet, participation. Have another drink. It will relax you. Good.

"Now, I had spoken, I believe, of the Red Man—a beautiful, fine figure of a Red Man, too, large of component parts—and his White Wife—as perfect a White One as ever was made, supple, well-shaped and sinuous—who were exerting themselves in connubial ferment here in my laboratory, or rather in yours, my dear, I beg your enchanting pardon once again. And I had alluded, not without a good deal of pleasure on your part, to the sweat which was pouring off their bodies, from shoulders, from thighs, from the warmth of their interior parts, as they strove in love-making. Well, my parsnip, this extraordinary sweat is still pouring off them, even as I speak, even as you drink. Each golden, glistening, glorious, plump drop of it is filled to bursting with vigor, with regenerative life; it goes out from these persons and prepares a place, as it were, for their great transformation, and for the glorified body to come, the Royal Child they are conceiving. Would you like to see all this, my love, with your own eyes, not merely through my describing? Attend the still-throbbing conception, stand watch with me through the gestation, be present at the splendid Nativity? Well, you can, you know, you can."

Newton is cooing to her now, repeating words and phrases over and over. He has left the stool and gone to stand next to the vessel, speaking across it as if she were in the room with him, on the other side of the furnace. The sweat continues to issue from the Red Man and his Wife; a vapor rises from it and clouds the inside of the glass. The excess ascends into the tubing and is sent, in more and more frequent bursts, as melatonin into Efficiency's bloodstream.

"Would you like to, love, be present? Would you like to, love, take part? I know a way, my dearest, a way for you to do so. 'Tis a simple, a very simple, operation, simple and easy indeed, my sweet, nothing simpler, nothing easier, once one has the will to accomplish it. Philalethes calls it, Sealing the Mother in the Belly of the Infant. Simple and easy, my love, and oh, so delightful once it is achieved. Once one has the will. The desire. The will. It is only a step away, where you want to go. No, it is not even that: a turn, a turn is all it is, from where you are now. For now it—the place where you want to go—is inside you. And all that's required is for you to go inside it. What could be simpler, what? Than to join me here. Here. Why, you're practically a White Wife already, I'll wager. I imagine your hands, I imagine your shoulders, I imagine your arms, your lovely neck, your breasts, your belly, your thighs. I imagine them white, I imagine them all white, of an admirable, fair-complexioned skin, just as Philalethes predicted, bright, bright, bright as the finest silver. The finest silver! Oh, my sweet Efficiency, you and I, together we could—"

"Her skin is *A*. Milk is *A*. Haroop."

Suddenly Efficiency is wide awake. WhoWhatWhenWhereHow? –Oh. Why so jumpy, sweet-cakes? She asks herself. It's only Eggbeater, out front on the walk. She relaxes against the back of her chair. There's a little breeze this morning, and it's carried his voice through the open window. Still talking to Jerry, I suppose, unless he's babbling away to himself, which wouldn't be very surprising, considering how often I've found him lately doing just that—in front of the mirror, in the kitchen after the cook's left, in the pantry, on the stairs, in the cabinet, in the field back of the house, out on Prospect Street in broad daylight, for God's sake, off among the tombstones in the Burying Ground, anywhere he pleases, chattering on and on all alone, happy as can be. But I'll bet he still has Jerry with him, even so. Once he's gotten the Ear of the Press, as he calls it, he doesn't give it up if he can help it, and he usually *can* help it, quite a lot. Eggbeater's a persuasive bastard. You wouldn't think it at first, with all the garbage that comes out of his mouth that nobody could possibly understand—Leibniz, he says, Leibniz my arse, it's nothing but an excuse to blather whenever he feels like it without having to take respon— Wait a minute. She looks around her. How the hell did I get here? In this chair. Wasn't I … Tell me, dearie, isn't this true? … Wasn't I under the settee?

Of course you were, sweetie, it's the last thing you remember. Then why the hell am I over here, all the way across the room, with this decanter of wine in my lap? Well, I really couldn't tell you, dearie, unless … unless … were you talking to Uncle Isaac, by any chance? She snorts. Talking to Uncle Isaac?! Hah. He to me, more like; it's hard to get a word in, edge- or any other wise, when he's on one of his tears. But, no, love, I don't think so, although there *was* something about silver … and *skin*, I think, some very white skin. No, that was Eggbeater, that's what woke you up. "Her skin is *A*. Milk is *A*." And then he belched, loud—you could have heard it over on High St. Oh. Yes. But that still doesn't explain—oh, the hell with it.

She picks up the glass from the carpet, where she had dropped it, and pours another drink. Hmm. Bottle's getting low. Have to replenish it soon. Unless you can materialize the stuff, ha-ha, the way Eggbeater claims to be able to. When he's Leibniz, that is—him and his Goddamned Leibniz! A passel of lies! Why does anyone put up with him?

Well, I'll tell you, dear, she answers herself. Not that you don't know, you've said it yourself already: because Eggbeater *is* a persuasive bastard, that's why. He may not be a gentleman, but he's just about the *persuasivest* bastard that ever lived. There's something about him—like that gleam he gets in those soft brown eyes of his when he's excited, or that funny little half smile and tilt of the head he gives you at the end of a sentence that makes you think what he just said, no matter how crazy it may have been, was meant for you and you alone out of the entire population of the earth and that if you hadn't been there to hear it he'd have been so *very* unhappy—there's something about that that does hold people's attention. Doesn't it? Oh, it does, it does, sweetheart, no question about it. He's been that way for as long as I've known him, too. Remember the day I first met him? Seven years ago, early in the spring. Eggbeater had just arrived in Aubrey, not more than a day or two before, and already he was the sensation of the village. Why, it was practically unheard of: here was a real cosmopolitan in our midst, an American, yes, but a Continental traveler too, and a doctor into the bargain. And a bachelor! The Aunts, Prudence and Prosperity, had invited him to call that afternoon. We were all three of us expecting some dashing rake with the Devil in his eye (and maybe even a stiletto in his boot!) on account of his having been in Europe for so many years and having lived the high life—at least, that was what people in the town were saying about him—in Paris and Zürich and Florence and London and Germany and about a hundred other cities, and who could ignore those who asked pointed questions about what might have caused him to leave America in the first place? The Aunts were prepared absolutely to disapprove of him, of course: a more narrow-minded pair of old maids I don't think I'll ever come across. But they hadn't much choice about receiving him because—and this was what fretted us more than anything else we'd heard—the reason this man had come to Aubrey at all had to do with Papa! Yes, Papa! That's what Eggbeater had told us, in the note he'd written the day before, asking permission to call: Papa had written him a letter, shortly before he died—five years back, mind you!—and he wanted to discuss it with us. He had expected to find Papa alive, and condoled with us sincerely, and so on and so on, and was himself personally desolated, even though he'd never had the honor—the immense, please believe me dear ladies, honor—of meeting Papa in person, but he did want to discuss that letter. Well! The Aunts suspected fraud, of course. They were sure Eggbeater was a thief or a confidence trickster come to cozen us out of our fortune, or a blackmailer bent on bleeding us to death, and I have to admit their buzzing made even me a little anxious.

—What do you mean, *even* you? Come on, dearie, own up. You know perfectly well you were so nervous back then you couldn't do anything right—or at least didn't think you could. You were absolutely positive you'd upset the tea service when you poured, or say something stupid, or faint.

Oh, all right, all right. Maybe I was a little upset. But for once I had an excuse. This letter, this supposed letter, of Papa's. Would the doctor—if he *was* a doctor—have it with him? What would we do if it turned out to be genuine? What, for that matter, would we do if it didn't? What would we do if he demanded money—if he claimed Papa promised it to him? Or if the letter revealed something awful that Papa had done, and Caws—if that was really his name, we couldn't even be sure of that—threatened to make it public? Not that we *really* thought Papa had done anything terrible, but you never know for sure, and the way your mind works, dearie—you must admit it, sweet, you know your own mind as well as I do—you just couldn't help thinking the worst. What if a child had been born out of wedlock, for instance, and Papa'd been proven the father? Or if there'd been a murder, and Papa named a suspect, or some shady financial dealings with innocent people ruined, maybe even driven to suicide—now, *that* might easily have happened, dearie, bankers have been known to do the most dreadful things for money, don't think they haven't, with no one the wiser, and if Papa wasn't greedy I don't know *what* you'd call him.

As it turned out, though, none of us need have worried. In came Eggbeater, right on the dot of three, all proper, absolutely proper and modest, and had us eating out of his hand in two minutes—all of us, even Aunt Prosperity, who'd sworn not half an hour before that she wouldn't even speak to him, vile creature that she knew him to be. The most perfect gentleman he was, and so good looking! Clean-shaven, of course, without that gruesome moustache he sports now—not that I think "sports" is the word for it. Jesus. No stiletto, and no Devil in his eye either. Those eyes! Remember them, dearie? They were the clearest, frankest eyes I've ever seen, and when he spoke every syllable was for us. His whole life too, up to that very moment, was for us, it seemed. When he told us about the cities he'd been in, the things he'd done there and seen—the buildings, the promenades, the fashions, the operas, the lectures he'd given, the balloon ascents—he made us feel he'd had those experiences only in order to give us pleasure, me and the Aunts, and that this opportunity, to tell us about them, was the only reward he wanted ever, in this world or the next. And as for that letter—why, it turned out to be the most innocent thing you could think of, all perfectly straightforward and natural. He had it with him, and showed it to us. You couldn't mistake Papa's handwriting, those big bold strokes sweeping across the paper, like a scythe going through wheat. Praising Eggbeater, too, praising him to the skies—never knew Papa to do the like, for any man alive. Practically groveled before him, he did: "Dear Honorable Dr. Caws, Most Eminent Sir, Esteemed Practitioner of the Great Art." Said he'd heard of the doctor's many triumphs; invited him—begged him, really—to come to Aubrey "as my honored guest and Master" to share in Papa's scientific work. Said he'd pay him handsomely. Oh, and he mentioned a funny name, too—reminds me of Uncle Isaac, for some reason—Philadelphia? No, Philalethes, that was it. Papa said he'd heard that Eggbeater had made a Philalethes something—a powder? A poultice? A posset? Who knows. The letter was dated August 1, 1843; that was right around the time Papa started acting so strange—which, I thought, probably explained why he sounded so respectful. Never knew him to be like that before.

And why had Eggbeater waited all this time to arrive? Very simple, he told us. He had not received it until a month before—and in his voice and expression there was nothing but sadness, sadness at a great opportunity missed. Papa had sent the letter, he explained, to an old address of his, in Paris—he showed us the envelope—where he had not lived for many years. By rights, it should have been lost entirely. But happily it followed him, from residence to residence, back and forth across the map of Europe while he pursued his vocation as a healer, only catching up with him five weeks ago, when he had stopped for a few days in—I forget the city, but somewhere in England, I think. When he read its contents, he came immediately, dropping everything else he was engaged in, so honored to have been invited by the great Mr. Barton, whom all the world knew to be one of the truly Great Men of his time. And to have discovered, as he had yesterday when he first set foot in our village, that the Great Man had been gathered to Glory so long ago, was unbearable. He could only express to us his heartfelt sorrow.

Sounds a bit fishy now, doesn't it, dear? Well, it didn't then, and you didn't think so either, don't forget. Not when you heard that voice, or saw that face, those eyes filling with tears, the quivering mouth—a strong man, an honest man, struggling to master his emotion and not quite succeeding. Oh, yes. Oh, yes.

What could we do? We certainly couldn't turn him out; nor did we want to, by that time we were all of us quite taken with him. And obviously—I don't exactly recall *how* it was obvious, he didn't say anything directly, but nonetheless it was perfectly clear—he'd spent his last penny to make the trip. So, that very afternoon, right on the spot, hardly even taking time to confer with each other, we came to a decision. If Papa had confidence in him, why, then, so did we. We set him up in business, gave him his own medical practice, here in town, even gave him a place to stay, here in the house, till he found one of his own. It was the least we could do, we felt, the very least, and when we saw the tears well up again—but in gratitude this time—in those sweet brown eyes, we knew we were right.

And we *were* right, damn it—and don't you start in on me, dearie, with your snickering little comments, you'd do the same thing again yourself and you know it. I remember what you said to me that afternoon, the first time we laid eyes on him, here in the sitting room, don't think I don't. "Oooooooh!" You said, one long squeal of delight coming from way down inside my ear, "Oooooooh!" just like that. And then, after he'd finished his tale of woe about coming all the way here from Europe and finding Papa dead, "Oh, how *sad!*" you said, "Poor man, poor man!" So don't be giving me any of your smart advice at this late date.

Besides, no matter how much things have changed since then, what does it matter? We didn't know any of that *then*. And there's something else, too, something I'll bet you haven't thought of: Papa would have liked Eggbeater too if he could have been there. Yes, he would, I'm sure of it. Not because of his doctoring, or his Philalethes posset or whatever he called it, I'm not talking about that. I mean Papa would have liked Eggbeater for himself, as a person, same as we did—well, not exactly the same, but you know what I'm trying to say. And—listen to me now, dearie, this is important—Eggbeater would have liked Papa, too. They might have been different in a lot of ways, but believe me, sweetie, they had plenty in common too. They would have seen eye to eye about the things they found most important in the world. Science, for one thing. They both of them were true believers in science—a lot truer than you or me either, dearie, not to speak of most other people, who as far as I can tell don't bother with anything but blind instinct.

And *gadgets*. Eggbeater and Papa were both *fascinated* by gadgets. Not important, you say? Well, it was to them, that's my point. Think of the months and years Papa spent in his workshop, making those whatever-you-may-call-thems that nobody to this day can imagine a use for. And think of Eggbeater, with that ridiculous Delphic Oracle, God damn him. Gadgets were a positive obsession with those two.

Now, the third thing was money. Oh, my, dearie, how they did appreciate money. No, sweetie, not "each in his own way," no matter what you may think. On the contrary: each in exactly the *same* way. Let me ask you this: when an old man lusts after a beautiful young girl, is his feeling any different from some other old fellow's, who also lusts after her? Well, then. That's how

Eggbeater and Papa were about money. They didn't just want it, it was their passion. Science they may have believed in, and gadgets may have delighted them, but money, sweet gorgeous money, was the love of their lives. Oh, there was room for us, too, I'm not saying there wasn't, but you have to admit there was a lot *more* room so long as you clearly understood that you came fourth and you'd better not try to change it. And I didn't really want to, with Eggbeater, not at first, anyway, it would have been like changing some special part of him, taking away a special talent, and he wouldn't still have been *him*. Of course, when I met him he hadn't a penny, but that was only a temporary condition. He had such a beautiful *feeling* for money, how to get it, how to keep it, how to make it grow. Yes, dearie, I know, I know, I'm perfectly well aware that most of it was mine—or Papa's, rather, that I'd inherited—but still. Oh, he and Papa would have gotten on famously, I'm sure of it. Real men of the world, the both of them.

And another thing, sweetie: this might sound odd, but I think Papa would have appreciated Eggbeater's *humor*. It's not so much that he would have laughed along with him. I can't remember Papa laughing much at all, if it comes to that, and I must say I never heard anything less funny than a joke that had been mangled by his telling of it. But he did like *words*. He liked everything about them—their sounds, their meanings, their different histories. He probably got that from Grandfather Thaddeus. He even liked their spelling. But above all, he liked to hear words used distinctively, and he took an interest in anyone who did that. And, Lord! What a lovely way with words Eggbeater had back then. The way he chose them, where he put them in the sentence, how he matched them up with each other—he just lit the words up, put a little shine on them, so to speak, and that's what Papa would have appreciated. The humor part was extra, really. Words just *felt* different when they came out of Eggbeater's mouth, and it was such a *nice* feeling it made you want to laugh. Do you know what he said to me once, dearie, when we were courting? He said that on shipboard, on his way to Aubrey after getting that letter, he kept hearing a voice in his head, talking to him, urging him on. "Courage, Eggbeater, courage," it said. "You are inseparable from me until death, for now and every hour of time. Come to me, Eggbeater, come. Immediately, immediately! Quickly, quickly! Now, now!" He said it was a woman's voice, one he'd never heard before—until, that is, he met me. "It was your voice, Miss Barton," he told me, "yours, carrying all the way across the Atlantic!" And he laughed, and suddenly spoke falsetto, "Quickly, quickly! Now, now!" He laughed and laughed, and I laughed too!

Efficiency sighs, and takes another drink. Well, dearie, she goes on, a lot has happened since then, hasn't it, love, and if Eggbeater's still saying plenty that's unusual, which he certainly is, and if he's still hearing voices in his head, which I'd be willing to bet on, he just as certainly hasn't said anything I'd regard as *funny* for about seventeen hundred months of Sundays. And as for that old feeling that he was speaking what he was speaking just for you and you alone—my God, I might as well not even *be* there! Ever since he started building that God damn Oracle. Half the time he doesn't even look at me anymore, but somewhere behind me, or off to the side, way into the distance, or up in the sky. Or else he just covers his face with that God damned antimacassar, talking all the while. I could go out of the room and come in again, go out of the room and come in again, go out of the room and come in again— or just go out and not come back at all, and it wouldn't change a thing. But I don't. I don't. That's just the problem, dearie, that's just the God damned problem: he *is* a persuasive bastard. You're dead right about that. I don't know how he gets away with it, but if he wants you to pay attention to him—if, for any reason at all, it's important to him that you stop whatever you're doing, stay right where you are and listen to him—then by God, you stop, you stand there and listen. "I, the one now speaking; you, the one now listening." That's a favorite saying of his, the swine. It's infuriating. It's *insulting*, for Christ's sake! *And*, what's even worse, if he ever happens to get tired of talking but still wants you to pay attention, or if he begins to suspect, somewhere in his gin-soaked mind, that *your* mind might be wandering from the main point— wandering from *him*, that is—then all he has to do is *rise*, God damn him. Now, why the hell can't I do that? I try and try, and all I get is *taller*. Five years I've been at it, ever since our very first séance when he floated up to the ceiling as if he didn't weigh any more than one of those little feathers he always has with him to stir his gin with, and left everybody's mouths hanging open, including mine. How does he manage it, anyway? I've asked him I don't know how many times, but he always tells me he doesn't know. Says it just happens, completely beyond his control, but I don't believe it, not for a minute. He's only saying that to annoy me. Well, damn it all, I'm his *wife*; a wife has a right to know these things. Shit and shallots! I'll bet it's something he picked up in Europe—probably Paris, in some God damned cathouse—some little trick he learned to do with a muscle, or maybe a twist of the pelvis, something like that to get him started, although what keeps him up there all that time I'll be damned if I can figure out. Whatever it is, it isn't natural, that's for certain. Why can't he stay on the ground, like everybody else? He'll do himself an injury one day. He'll probably die, or go blind or crazy, and have to be put away somewhere, and I'll be left to carry on all alone. Inconsiderate bastard. Who the hell does he think he is? It's just a cheap bid for attention, and all because he's not funny anymore and he knows it. Well, let him see if I come to the asylum to visit him, just let him see *that*! What the hell.

The Encyclopaedia of Reincarnation:

… Mrs. Caws never returned to Aubrey after the death of her husband. She traveled extensively on the Continent, at first accompanied by the journalist Jeremy Welkin, and became a familiar presence in Parisian literary and artistic circles. Both Ingres and Degas found her charming. Baudelaire is said to have been smitten with her. The nature of her association with Delacroix is not known, but she was among the mourners at his funeral at Père Lachaise in 1863. In 1856, Ingres painted an enduring record of her youthfulness and beauty when she posed for him as Germaine Cousin, the sixteenth century French peasant girl whose body remained incorrupt after her death and who was canonized in the nineteenth century as Sainte Germaine of Pibrac. (The painting is now in Montauban, at the Church of Saint-Etienne-de-Sapiac.) Armand Cambon, one of Ingres' assistants, is said to have fallen in love with Mrs. Caws while the painting was in progress, and to have threatened to kill himself if she rejected his suit. Mrs. Caws also is said to have received proposals of marriage from Theophile Gautier, Luigi Coturno and Count Leopold Apponyi. (By this time she and Mr. Welkin had parted company.) Count Apponyi, an attaché at the Austrian Embassy in Paris, arranged a series of séances for her in Berlin, Zürich, Florence, Milan and Vienna, held during 1878 and '79. Her reputation preceded her wherever she went, and the sessions attracted a large number of people from all walks of life including not a few intellectuals, among them G. T. Fechner, H. L. F. von Helmholtz and the Baroness Malwida von Meysenburg. However, there is no truth to the story (which is often recounted as fact) that the young Freud was present at the celebrated séance in Vienna, during which the sitters were pelted by a rain of bananas. On the whole, while she never failed to command respect, and on occasion filled those who witnessed them with something approaching awe, Mrs. Caws' performance on this tour lacked the consistency and élan of the exhibitions she had given with her husband two decades before in America. Newton's voice came through as of old at a séance in Rome in 1879, but he confined himself to a few perfunctory remarks, delivered after a desultory fashion. "He seemed to have lost interest in the proceedings," Apponyi wrote to the Princess Ramolaccia. "All the fire had gone out of him." A pair of boots found on the floor after the séance was at first taken for an *apport*, but proved to belong to one of the sitters, who came back later to claim them. A final séance in Paris, held in January, 1880 at the Salpêtrière before the great Charcot and his staff, failed to produce any phenomena at all.

As she entered her seventh decade, with her powers diminished and her fortune depleted by a lavish style of living, Mrs. Caws embarked upon a stage career, causing a sensation when she appeared as the Ghost in Kenworthy's production of *Hamlet* at Covent Garden in 1887. Critics remarked on the extraordinary depth of her voice and the dramatic increase in her height as her scenes progressed; apparently her powers of elongation had returned. The undimmed freshness of her features also was noted, despite the green-grey makeup that covered her face; while the reviewers agreed that her youthfulness was not, perhaps, entirely appropriate to the part, it was nonetheless an exceptional accomplishment in its own right and made a substantial contribution to her dazzling stage presence.

Encouraged by her success, Mrs. Caws went on to enact other roles, both male and female, in a series of Shakespearean plays. She portrayed Juliet with great effectiveness in 1888, with Mr. Kenworthy as Romeo, the balcony scene being commemorated in a painting by Leahurst, now in the Manchester Theatre

Museum. Comparison of this work with the *Sainte Germaine* of Ingres would seem to support what her long-time admirers maintained, that she hardly had aged at all since she first set foot on the Continent in 1855. Be that as it may, her Iago (1889) was not well received, and her Falstaff in *The Merry Wives of Windsor* (1890) closed after three performances. In the following year, with her fortune further reduced, she returned to America, settling in Wyncote, Pennsylvania, on the outskirts of Philadelphia, where she had distant relations on her mother's side. It was here, in March, 1899, that the young Ethel Mammon Striker, then an aspiring but still-unpublished writer, discovered Mrs. Caws living in isolation and almost entirely forgotten. Thus began the sequence of visits and interviews which formed the basis for Striker's first book, *Gravity Newton: The Life and Legend of Efficiency Caws* (1901), a work that produced an immediate revival of interest in its subject. Unfortunately, it was a revival that Mrs. Caws was unable to enjoy, since she passed away quietly at her home on October 31, 1899, one day after her seventy-second birthday.

She was buried in Greenwood Cemetery, in northeast Philadelphia. The rumor that her body remained incorrupt after her death has never been substantiated.

True Tales of the Paranormal:

True to its reputation, the Helvetius took good care of its former staff member. Dr. Eichhorn was given a private room, along with generous exercise privileges in the Clinic's yard. His request for writing materials was granted immediately. His former colleagues, whom the doctor was to excoriate in his narrative, could not have been more solicitous.

Through the rest of the summer and into the fall, this treatment worked well. Fortified by regular meals (which the doctor had seriously neglected) and plenty of fresh air, Eichhorn grew quiet, even contented, and applied himself to his writing. Then, sometime towards the middle of November, according to his narrative, he suddenly found himself staring at an eye, a green-grey, wide open human eye, which had materialized in the space between him and his typewriter. The eye remained stationary for a few moments, and then, slowly and deliberately, it winked at him—once, twice, three times.

"Be calm," he told himself. "You are not crazy. No matter what they say, no matter where they've put you, you are *not* crazy. You are having a psychic experience." Desperately, he ran through everything he could remember of Jung's writings on eye symbolism—the Eye of God, the eye of the alchemists, the seeing of the soul. "It is wholeness," Eichhorn wrote. "Consciousness, not craziness. THE COSMIC EYE," he scrawled in capital letters across the page. It was the last coherent notation he was to make.

From *Gravity Newton: The Life and Legend of Efficiency Caws*, by Ethel Mammon Striker (Philadelphia: Thurston & Sons, 1901):

Many assume that Mrs. Caws' psychic abilities burst fully formed on the scene in 1850 when she and Dr. Caws began their mediumship. Nothing could be further from the truth. Indeed, the story begins even before her birth, with the strange history of her father, Abimelech Barton.

To the world at large, the everyday world of commerce and social obligations, there was nothing remarkable about Mr. Barton, except, perhaps, the completeness of his conformity to the standards with which he had been brought up and his great and consistent financial success. But there was nothing unusual, nothing one would have called strange. Born in Aubrey in 1789, scion of an illustrious family, he had been an assiduous, hard-working schoolboy, little given to play, obedient to his masters, mindful, like the good Puritans from whose loins he sprang, of the ever-watching Eye of God, ready to spy out the slightest deviance. Young Abimelech did the right thing, always. But what his teachers and schoolfellows did not suspect (nor would we, had he not written it down himself years later in his journal) was that this model boy by day was at night not a human being at all but a tiger, a lion, a jaguar, a snake, a lynx, roaming the earth at will, tracking his prey across the primeval landscape of his dreams. By the time he was sixteen these dreams were coming twice or thrice nightly, and they were so vivid and so bloody he could no longer bear them. He told not a soul about them, he was too ashamed, but he did start recording them privately in a journal, in the hope, he wrote, that "these terrors might abate."[5] In this he seems to have been successful, since after a few weeks the nightmares gave way to dreams of smooth, silvery geometric solids, spheres, cubes and polyhedrons, and instead of being these forms he was merely observing them, often floating beside them far above the earth. Some nights, to his great relief, he did not dream at all. So it went for a number of years, while young Barton grew up, went out into the world and began what promised to be an outstanding career in banking. He became well known in financial circles, and by his mid-thirties could count himself an important man of affairs in the north-of-Boston area, a pillar of his community and a force to be reckoned with.

Then, on the night of April 24–25, 1825, he dreamed he was sitting in his family's pew in the Aubrey Meeting House, waiting for the service to begin. As he looked around him, he thought how drab, how sterile the interior was. How much better it would be, he reflected, if the elders had let his father take a hand in the decorations. Father Thaddeus and his Greeks—they would have livened things up! At this the elders appeared, carrying a huge, thick snake down the aisle, handling it as if it were a long, rolled-up carpet. At last they got to the altar with it, and set it up there vertically, for all to see. As Mr. Barton looked he realized that it was not really a snake at all, but someone wearing a snake-suit, a black sheath of some shiny material, and that it was standing there under its own power. He could see a pair of eyes and eyebrows through an opening in the sheath, and it came to him suddenly that the person inside the snake was a woman. He looked down, and there on the pew beside him was a big red apple, lying on a clean, white linen napkin. He woke up feeling that he had just been initiated into a secret of great importance.

The next morning he set off, as planned, on a trip to Boston, and, once his business there was concluded, he decided to call on a friend. While there, he

<hr>

[5] This journal is extant, written in an almost microscopically small hand in four black-covered octavo volumes, often employing idiosyncratic abbreviations and numerous passages in French and Latin. It is now in the Barton-Caws Archive in Ipswich, Massachusetts. Throughout my acquaintance with Mrs. Caws, however, I found no indication that she had read the journal or even knew of its existence. I myself did not discover it until after her death. –E. M. S.

happened to look for the first time through a reflecting telescope, which his friend had just purchased and of which he was rather proud, astronomy being one of his hobbies. As the two made polite conversation, Mr. Barton was astonished to learn that the man who invented the telescope had also discovered the law of universal gravitation, written an important treatise on optics, discovered the calculus, done significant pioneering work in chemistry, been President of the Royal Society, and, to top it all off, served for over a quarter of a century as Master of the Mint, overseeing everything having to do with the English coinage, which included the hunting down and prosecuting of forgers and counterfeiters!

Mr. Barton was dumbfounded. Nothing in his education or experience had prepared him for such an onslaught of achievement. True, his family was a proud one, and by no means bereft of distinction. His forebears had left records of bravery, piety and legal and scholarly eminence. But the all-encompassing, unqualified mastery of which he had just been told, the supremacy of intellect expressed in so many forms—all this was new to him. To be sure, he had heard of Sir Isaac. Who had not? Mr. Barton had had a better education than most people (most people in Aubrey, at least) with more than a smattering of the classics, drummed into him by his father. But he had remained largely unversed in scientific studies, paying them, it must be admitted, little heed in school (his mind already directed towards a career in commerce) and he had had no idea, not even the beginning of a suspicion, that Newton had achieved so much: why, for twenty-five years and more, Newton had been in charge, with complete, unquestioned control, of all the coin in the realm, and apparently had acquitted himself splendidly in this capacity as well as all the others! The banker in Mr. Barton was moved. In truth, he looked on the facts which his friend had just related not merely as items of casual interest but as something akin to religious revelation: a personal message, in some strange way connected with his dream the previous night (though he could not have said why), nay, a permission even!—extended across the years from Sir Isaac to himself. He suddenly "saw life in the round again," as he put it long afterward. "A forgotten part of myself was restored to me." Musing on the attainments of Sir Isaac, Mr. Barton found himself thrown "into a profound reverie" in which "long-ignored incidents of my earliest childhood welled up unbidden."[6] These all concerned a gift he had had, a knack, a predilection which at one time he had exercised quite freely but abandoned once he attained man's estate (or rather, quite a long time before that, since Barton the eight-year-old was already a very serious little man indeed, according to those who knew him then). This was a talent for putting things together—bits of wood, paper, wire, twine or sometimes metal—and making divers mechanical constructions, with intricate moving parts that worked together, each in harmony with the others, to carry out particular actions. Unfortunately, there was no apparent usefulness in any of these actions; they seemed to have been designed with only the movements themselves as an end. Thus they had drawn but little praise from the boy's elders. But now Newton's example showed the man Barton that his talent had been anything but frivolous; on the contrary, it formed the basis of all invention. What, after all, was the reflecting telescope but a mechanical construction? And had not Sir Isaac made the first one with his own two hands? Surely the telescope was not the first such object, either; surely it could not have sprung out of Sir Isaac's head of a sudden fully formed, as Athena had done (he recalled father Thaddeus telling him) out of the head of Zeus. Newton must have begun his experiments much earlier, even as a child, to have attained such preeminence in manhood. And without those experiments? Perhaps nothing at all would have been born. It amazed Mr. Barton how he, to say nothing of his elders, could have thought so little of what was, quite clearly, a God-given asset. Such a gift was cause for celebration, not scorn and dismissal! Not even a genius like Sir Isaac achieved what he did by hiding his light under a bushel, still less by letting others do so. Mr. Barton resolved to give his own light greater exposure. He could well afford to now, and on a far grander scale than his boy-self had ever thought possible.

Mr. Barton returned to Aubrey that very afternoon, a changed man, cutting short what he had planned as a longer stay in the metropolis. Over the next weeks, he had his barn fitted out as a workshop, installing a reflecting

---

[6] Abimelech Barton, *Some Incidents of My Youth, To Serve as a Guide to the Earnest Inquirer, Together with a Treatise on Iatrochemistry and a Postlude on the Virtues of Ambition* (Boston: privately printed, 1842), p. 42.

telescope, a microscope, all sorts of hand tools, wood, wire, metal plates, screws, nails, a pendulum, a prism and stacks of scientific literature, all he could get, purchased indiscriminately and in large quantities. Without, it would seem, any clear idea of what he was going to investigate, build or invent, he set happily to work. "I had no intention of waiting," he wrote, "for Inspiration to take notice and favor me with a glance. The ideas would come along soon enough, I reasoned, as soon as I got my hands good and dirty. I felt young, truly young, perhaps for the first time in my life."[7]

He also began to read everything he could find on his new hero. Somewhere he came across a suggestive piece of information: that one of Sir Isaac's step-sisters married a man named Barton, and that the couple had two children, a daughter who kept house for Newton in his later years in London, and a son who came to America. Greatly excited, Mr. Barton dug out his own records, and in practically no time composed a genealogy that brought Sir Isaac securely within the welcoming branches of his wide-spreading family tree. He reckoned it this way: Nehemiah Barton, the great-great-great-great-grandfather, who, along with Exhumation Sweet, had been one of the leaders of the party of settlers that founded Aubrey in 1640, must have been the great-uncle, previously unacknowledged, of the Reverend Robert Barton, who hailed from the village of Bridgstock and who, in 1677, married Hannah Smith, Sir Isaac's step-sister, and became the father of Newton's niece, Catherine, and his nephew, Robert, Jr. This last Robert, who apparently was something of a vagabond, went to the New World to seek his fortune but died ingloriously, by drowning, in 1711 during Hill's ill-fated expedition against Quebec—"Before he ever had a chance to visit his kinfolk in Aubrey," Mr. Barton would add wistfully, whenever he recited the details of his lineage (which was rather often, his associates remembered). To drive his assertions home, he would usually end by reminding his listeners that Nehemiah Barton was a native of Lincolnshire, just as all the Newtons ("the other Newtons," he called them) had been. What he overlooked—or, perhaps, chose not to consider—was that Bridgstock, from which Robert Barton, Sr. hailed, was in Northhamptonshire, where the Reverend's forebears, but not Abimelech, had lived for generations.

---

[7] *Ibid.*, p. 44.

Oversight or not, Mr. Barton's lapse had no discernible effect on his mood, at least not when he came to write his memoirs. "As I sat at my desk that morning," he says, "watching my family connections approach, then finally merge with Sir Isaac's, I was filled with awe. I felt, as never before, the hand of Providence at work in my life, touching me as palpably as if it had been a physical presence with me in the study. I felt—how shall I say—a Divine Plan for me, opening like a flower generation after generation, up to the glory of the present moment. I knew myself part of something vast, the splendid progress of the Universe."[8]

Meanwhile, Mr. Barton continued to work in his barn. More and more now, he thought of himself as Newton in Cambridge, locked in his study, rapt in contemplation of the secrets of Creation. And when he went to work at the bank, which he did as assiduously as ever, for he was far too canny to neglect his gainful labor, he imagined himself at His Majesty's Mint, receiving petitioners, supervising the coinage.

On the night of January 29, 1826, he dreamed of a gigantic apple riding on a cumulus cloud. A deep voice from within the apple boomed, "be fruitful, my son, and multiply. The new Newton is coming." At the same moment, Propinquity Benbow appeared on earth far below, eating a banana.

Now, Aubrey was a small enough village that just about everybody knew everybody. Mr. Barton, therefore, knew the Benbows, not very well but well enough to dislike them for the airs they put on about their supposed Newtonian connections, so much flimsier, he told his journal, than his own. But he believed in his dreams, with what seems today a rather quaint literalism. His dreams, he wrote, had never failed him. Propinquity Benbow was unmarried, unaffianced and, while "a bit on the plain side, still a long way from ugly." Resolutely, he set about courting her, tentatively at first, then with the zesty self-assurance of a man accustomed to getting his own way. The couple was married a year later, and, almost exactly nine months afterwards, Efficiency was born.

Mr. Barton greeted the event with hosannas, although, one regrets to add, there is no evidence he grieved overmuch for his wife, who expired as their daughter was coming into the world.

---

[8] *Ibid.*

"So you see, honey, Papa started all that Newton business long before I was even thought of," said Mrs. Caws in her old age. "You might even say I've got Uncle Isaac in my blood." We were in the parlor of her house in Wyncote. She leaned forward in her chair and looked straight at me, with a twinkle in her eye and that winning smile that made her seventy-one years seem twenty. She took a sip from the glass of sherry at her elbow. "But look, Papa didn't know the first thing about science or inventing when he started out. And I'm not sure he *ever* learned that much either, though he sure thought he did. _____." Here she employed an expression which it would be improper to repeat, the first of many as it turned out.

"Papa went about it all wrong. _____. Anybody with the brains of a mollusk knows you can't make progress inventing unless you have some idea at least of what you're looking for. Papa didn't have that. All Papa did was play. That barn was his playpen, and he was playing Newton. But don't imagine for a minute that *he* thought of it that way. No, Papa was always as serious as could be. And nobody, *nobody*, could have told him he wasn't working exactly the way Newton did. Papa knew everything about Newton—to hear him tell it—and nobody could have told him any different. Laugh at him, honey? Of course people laughed at him. *I* laughed at him. A banker acting like a three year old, doing Lord knows what in the barn behind his house? I ask you. And then there was that stupid portrait."

Mrs. Caws explained that on one of his trips to Boston, probably in early 1827, shortly before she was born, Mr. Barton purchased an old painting, a half-length figure study in oils. He described it to friends as a copy—a "certified copy"—of the "official" portrait of Sir Isaac by Jervas, which hung in the gallery of the Royal Society in London. Inordinately proud of his acquisition, the banker displayed it prominently in his home, over the mantel, "like an ancestor," Mrs. Caws said. "'It's the finest copy available,' Papa would tell people." Her voice deepened as she imitated her father. "'There's none like it anywhere, sir, not anywhere in the world. They tell me Jervas himself—Jervas himself, mind you—was jealous when he saw it.'"

Precisely who "they" were, Mr. Barton did not specify, but in saying there was "none like it anywhere" he was probably correct, since those who saw the painting (which had since disappeared) agreed that this "Newton" has a pronounced stoop and an emaciated face that seemed ravaged by illness, attributes conspicuously absent in all other likenesses of the scientist. Mrs. Caws, who grew up with the portrait, recalled that for many years she had a completely mistaken notion of Newton's features. "It wasn't till I was well into my twenties that I found out what Uncle Isaac—that's what Papa called him, and I did, too—really looked like," she informed me. "And let me tell you, sweetie, it came as quite a shock. Oh, I could a tale unfold."....

Mrs. Caws' first brush with the supernatural came, she said, on the morning of her sixth birthday, October 30, 1833. "It wasn't the sort of thing that was considered very *nice* then," she confided, "if you know what I mean, dearie. In fact, I don't think it would be considered very nice even today." She giggled. "Papa, who, if the truth be told, was usually a little bit uncomfortable around me, anyway, as if I reminded him of something and he couldn't quite think what—Papa was terribly embarrassed about the whole thing and made me promise never to breathe a word of it to anyone. S____. But I never have, till now."

She was walking to church with her father. The day was sunny and crisp, with not a cloud in the sky. The little New England village seemed wholly at peace. "All of a sudden, though, I knew something funny was about to happen," she said. "And I don't mean 'funny' like 'strange,' either. I mean funny like *funny*. Don't ask me how I knew, I just did. And I said to Papa, without even realizing what it was I was saying, I said, real loud and clear, I said, 'Here come the apples!'"

No sooner were the words out of the girl's mouth than a rain of apples burst directly over their heads, falling all around them with great ferocity. Caught in the open, they had to run for it, and only escaped serious injury by taking shelter in a nearby henhouse. They got to church half an hour late, spattered with chicken droppings, entering in full view of the congregation while the sermon was in progress. "It was Jerry Welkin's grandfather, old Manassah Welkin, preaching, too," she chuckled. "I can even remember the text, after all these years. It was from St. John, as I found out later: 'This is the bread which came down from Heaven.' Now, how about that for a coincidence? I thought that was the funniest thing of all!"

The next day, after dinner, when Efficiency had been excused from the table and had just risen from her chair, the apples came again, crashing through the ceiling and landing on the empty seat. No holes were made in the ceiling, though the family noticed large cracks spreading through the plaster. These disappeared in a few days, however. On the girl's seventh, eight, ninth and tenth birthdays, the apple-rains were repeated, sometimes in the house and sometimes out of doors, but always in Efficiency's immediate vicinity. "Papa got madder and madder about it as the years went by," Mrs. Caws remembered. "He used to run out of the barn in his shirt sleeves, screaming bloody murder. He was sure I was doing something deliberately to make it happen, just out of mischief, but he never could work out exactly what. He used to look at me awfully *hard* sometimes, and shake his head, as if I was a column of figures that wouldn't add up right." She laughed. "It never did occur to him to connect those apples to old Uncle Isaac—which is more than a bit curious, now I come to think of it, him being so proud of having the old bird for an ancestor and constantly dragging his name into every subject under the sun. Uncle Isaac this, Uncle Isaac that, morning, noon and night. Why, do you know, dearie, he wanted to name *me* Isaac? Yes, he certainly did. Aunt Prosperity told me so. And not only before I was born, either, when he was still hoping he'd be getting a boy, but afterwards, too! He was that pigheaded, he was going to name me Isaac anyhow, just out of spite. And him with a name like Abimelech! He ought to have been ashamed of himself. The Aunts had to step in and stop it; mother, of course, was dead. For a man who was normally pretty intelligent—which he certainly was, dearie, don't for a moment let yourself think any different—Papa still could act powerfully *dense* about some things. But as far as those apples went, well, I didn't have any better idea than he did what was causing it all. I just thought it was funny!"

Mrs. Caws spoke lightly, but beneath her accustomed insouciance it was plain that even after so many years she remained perplexed by her father's behavior, perplexed and not a little resentful. Her confusion would have dissolved, however, had she had access to Mr. Barton's dream journal, perusal of which reveals that, far from being unaware of the connection between the apples and Sir Isaac, her father had become obsessed by it. He realized, of course, that his first apple-dream had occurred just before he saw his first reflecting telescope and got his decisive introduction to the works of Newton. But notes written in December of 1833 also show that he had calculated that the date of his second apple-dream, January 29, 1827, was almost exactly nine months before Efficiency's birth. Therefore, he observed, the dream could have taken place the very night she was conceived. Indeed, the fact that in his journal the date was accompanied by a curious hieroglyphic figure (somewhat resembling the astrological sign of Cancer) which Mr. Barton used throughout his life to register instances of sexual intercourse, made the matter all but certain.

Even his decision to name his child Isaac was no willful or arbitrary urge held onto through sheer stubbornness; on the contrary, it came to him in sleep, on August 30, dictated to him by a voice which whispered the name in his ear as he was trying, with a frustrating lack of success, to cross an ever-widening gulf between his barn and the main house. When the child arrived, two months later, and to his dismay proved a girl, and her aunts insisted he abandon the name, he went through agonies. "I gave in at last," he wrote. "Weakling that I am, I could not stand up to them both. So I let them have their way—and all for the sake of a little peace in the house. What cowardice! I could at least have proposed a compromise—Isaaca, for instance. Or Isaacine; Isaacetta, even. Efficiency—what kind of name is that? May God in His mercy forgive me."[9] The matter receded into the background, forgotten in his grief over his wife's death and the consequent turmoil into which his life had been thrown. But six years later, when the apple rains started, he berated himself again. "Something terrible is about to happen," he told his journal, "I can feel it in my bones. It is a judgment on me for not insisting on the child's proper birth-name. A rain of blood could not be more disturbing."[10] And when, three years after that, a young business acquaintance, seemingly in perfect health, died of a stroke the day after the banker dreamed the event, he grew really alarmed. For a long time he was racked with guilt, thinking he had somehow caused the tragedy. But one day it came to him that he could not be considered even slightly at fault: the dream, whatever its source, had taken place completely outside his intent, without even his negligent acquiescence (the way one might, say,

---

[9] Abimelech Barton, *Dream Journal*, volume iii, p. 188.

[10] *Ibid.*, iv, p. 23.

be blamed for failing to stop some accident through sloth or inattention). No, the dream was a phenomenon in its own right, wholly separate from his will; he was powerless to dictate its content, powerless to direct its course. All he could do, all anyone could do with a dream, was to observe it, examine it, very much the way one would examine a phenomenon presented in the waking world: look at it from all sides, compare it with other phenomena, consider its function, categorize, denominate. Yes, that was the scientific way, the rational way, the sole assurance of truth. There was no question of guilt or innocence; it was merely a matter for enlightened investigation. Mr. Barton went to work on the problem.

It took him years. Perhaps he never really finished. But eventually, having gone over his journal from beginning to end, having correlated its entries with incidents in his own life, in his acquaintances' lives and in the world at large, he arrived at a sweeping new theory, not merely of his own dreams but of dreams in general, a theory which, despite its supposedly scientific method, had more to do with ancient ideas of prophecy than with modern thought. He came to view dreams not as the "imagination, fancies or reveries" that Hartley had alleged them to be in 1801, but instead as instances of, as the banker put it, "a natural language, truly a language spoken to us by Nature" which, directly or indirectly, foretold the future. "It is, perhaps, Nature's greatest gift to us," he wrote, "but one which we, as yet, have small ability to make use of. If only we could discover this language's vocabulary, its grammar and syntax, if only we could master it as well—even half as well—as Father knew his Greek, we should verily be Masters of our Destiny. We should understand all causes, and be able to project their effects onward in time, into the next generation, and the one after that, and yet again to the third, the fourth and so on—on, on, until Apocalypse ... For unquestionably, if such a small thing as an apple be so laden, so luminous I may say, with meaning, and insinuate itself into one's waking life with such startling regularity, then every other thing that takes place in sleep, no matter how minute, must likewise be fraught with significance. But how can we find this meaning out? And what—WHAT—is the Intelligence at work within the process? Paracelsus calls it the Light of Nature. But that is just one more name. We cannot any longer be content with names. We must discover its Essence. Until we know that, we know nothing."[11]

The next day he struck a darker note. "I have good news for the philosophers. Free Will exists, there can no longer be any doubt of that. I encounter Free Will every night of my life. But I regret to inform the sages of something they may not have considered: it is not human beings who have it. No, Free Will, I am afraid, belongs only to this ... this ... what shall I call it? This *Sphinx*, this Sphinx without a face, who speaks in riddles, in contradictions, in jokes, whose purport is discovered—if it is discovered at all—too late for one to act on the knowledge. *If*, that is, one could have acted in the first place, and if those actions could have averted the outcome! Think of Oedipus, flying from Corinth to avoid the fate the Oracle had foretold and going straight into it at Thebes!

"And yet, and yet: perhaps that is not the whole story. Perhaps the riddle only seems so because of too little knowledge. It may not be enough to attend to one's own dreams exclusively. The pieces one retrieves, even when spread out over many years, may be too few and too fragmented to decipher adequately. Perhaps one needs hundreds—no, thousands!—of dreams, by thousands of dreamers, night after night the world over, and all the dreams stitched together, to make a single, a huge dream—Father would have called it a rhapsody—a dream the size of a continent. Yes! *That* might reveal an order! A long, well-ordered dream, its language transparent, its meaning plain, its Author exposed at last for all to see! But how could such a thing possibly be recorded? And if recorded, stitched together in sequence? And if stitched together, observed? Never—never in a thousand lifetimes. Hopeless. Oh, hopeless. It is enough to drive one mad."[12]

By the time Mr. Barton made this entry (January 7, 1843, the day after he had dreamed an isosceles triangle, its apex sunk in a field of mud) the apple-rains had long ago ceased, and Efficiency had settled down to enjoy what seemed, least on the face of it, to be a normal, contented New England girlhood. But the banker remained suspicious of her, and distant to her aunts.

---

[11] *Ibid.*, p. 158.

[12] *Ibid.*

Nothing now could seem normal to him. Every event, every person, whether encountered in dream or in the waking state, had a double significance, one obvious and ordinary, the other subtle, unknown and potentially terrifying. The commonest object, sound, sight, smell or touch held a hidden aspect, an underside, so to speak, crawling with occult qualities within which, he was certain, some cosmic drama was being enacted. For Mr. Barton had embarked on the final and, sad to say, most disreputable phase of his scientific work. Before, his efforts had been futile, perhaps, but harmless. Now they became positively damaging to those around him. The reader is entitled to a word of explanation:

Mrs. Caws' estimate of her father's early work was not, it must be confessed, wide of the mark. The products that survive, and there are several of them,[13] are little more than repetitions on a larger scale of the constructions Mr. Barton made as a child, that is to say structures with intriguingly moveable parts but without, so far as can be discerned, any specific function. Even the banker seems to have been dissatisfied with these pieces, and he spent a considerable period casting about for, as he put it, "new worlds to conquer."[14] Mrs. Caws remembered that he would often stand in front of the "Newton" portrait, lost in contemplation and even, she added, talking to it. "He got answers, too," she said. "At least, that was how it seemed to me. He'd mumble something to the picture, with his voice going up on the last word—you know, as if he was asking it a question. Then he'd wait, and start nodding, as if he was listening to the answer. It was one of the strangest things I've ever seen, and believe me, dearie, I've seen plenty."

Be that as it may, Mr. Barton at length shifted his concentration to chemistry, probably sometime in the late 1830's. In itself, that was not unusual;

---

[13] Three pieces survive, all of them in the Aubrey Hall of Fame Museum, made of metal, wood and wire. In 1985 they were included in "American Primitives," an exhibition curated by Seneca Kirk at the Vronta Gallery in New York City, where they caused a considerable stir. One reviewer, Alex Muschel in *The Westsider*, found them "a century and a half ahead of their time, kinetic art of an extremely high order." – *Encyclopaedia of Reincarnation*.

[14] Barton, *Dream Journal*, iv, p. 97.

chemistry had been one of Sir Isaac's passions as well. But Mr. Barton, unfortunately, was no more successful than his hero in avoiding that mare's nest of superstition, mysticism and fakery called alchemy. Sir Isaac was a genius who happened to possess this single weakness, incomprehensible perhaps, but fully pardonable in one whose accomplishments in other fields were so astounding. In Mr. Barton's case, however, that same weakness consumed him. On the night of April 1, 1838, he dreamed a shining silver sphere resting on a table beside his bed. Seven tubes extended from the sphere like the branches of a tree and reached up through the ceiling, attaching themselves to seven stars which burned brightly in the sky. A note in the banker's hand, presumably written the next day, reads:

> "Mercury=Mercury; Venus=Copper; Mars=Iron;
> Jupiter=Tin; Saturn=Lead. The Moon=Silver;
> The Sun=Gold. These are the correspondences.
> Planets, metals and gods all in one. 'As above, so below.'"[15]

Newton's biographer, Sir David Brewster, lamented the fact that his subject copied out long passages of "contemptible alchemical poetry." Mr. Barton also inserted into his dream diary extensive quotations from the alchemical authors whose works he collected, besetting book dealers in Boston and elsewhere for the rarest and most obscure publications to satisfy his thirst for knowledge: works by such authors as the New England adept, George Starkey; the mysterious self-styled "Cosmopolitan," Eirenaeus Philalethes; and the English antiquary, Elias Ashmole, soon took their place on his shelves, crowding out the sober and constructive books he had previously amassed. The mind boggles at the sort of thing the banker allowed himself to commit to paper:

"Keep the urine for a month in a wooden vessel, 'in a place which is not hot but yet keeps out of the cold, till of itself a ferment arise in it and stirs up bubbles.'

"'The Fool (believe me) will not find our Stone ... but the Wiseman will find it in the Dung.'

---

[15] *Ibid.*, p. 102.

"'Our crude Sperm flows from a Trinity of Substances ... drawn from the Menstruum of our Sordid Whore.'"[16]

To what conceivable end (all that is decent in us asks) were these operations (sordid indeed!) carried out? In a note dated October 4, 1841, Barton tells us:

"Ashmole writes that there are four Stones: the Mineral, the Vegetable, the Magical and the Angelical. The Mineral 'hath the power of Transmuting any Imperfect Earthy Matter into its utmost degree of Perfection'; the Vegetable Stone makes 'perfectly known the Nature of Man, Beasts, Foules, Fishes together with all kinds of Trees, Plants, Flowers, etc.'; 'By the Magicall or Prospective Stone it is possible to discover any person in what part of the World soever, although never so secretly hid, in Chambers, Closets, or Cavernes of the Earth'; but the Angelical (ah, the Angelical!) 'so subtill ... that it can neither be seene, felt, or weighed but Tasted only'—the Angelical Stone 'hath a Divine Power, Celestiall, and Invisible, above the rest and endowes the possessor with Divine Gifts. It affords the Apparition of Angells, and gives a power of conversing with them, by Dreames and Revelations.' St. Dunstan calls it the 'Food of Angells.'"[17]

Such were the delusions under which Mr. Barton labored.

Soon his family was laboring under them as well. For, inspired by yet another dream, he determined to move the site of his experiments directly into his home. On the night of March 1, 1839, as he was struggling once again across the ever-widening dream space between the barn and his house, a voice—"the same one who told me to call the child Isaac, a woman's voice, soft and low, with an indefinable accent, perhaps from the East"[18]—instructed him, step by step, on the best way to convert his downstairs rooms into a laboratory. This plan he put into practice immediately, ignoring the protests of daughter and sisters-in-law ("I would not let them bully me a second time"[19]). He installed a furnace, still, worktables and shelving in what had

---

[16] *Ibid.*, pp. 108-109.

[17] *Ibid.*, 131.

[18] *Ibid.*, p. 112.

[19] *Ibid.*

been a cozy, welcoming sitting room and parlor, boarding up the windows and re-plastering the wall at one end and hanging a curtain to make an alcove, a black, empty space for "meditation and prayer" ("Meditatio," Barton added, "an inner dialogue with someone unseen"[20]) where he also put a bed.

"It was disgusting," Mrs. Caws said. "The smell, for one thing—you can't imagine, dearie, not if you've never had a chemical laboratory in your house: there was sulfur, urine, horse dung, vitriol, turpentine, all kinds of oils and acids, and something else I could never quite pin down, a mixture of earth and flowers and swamp water. It went through the whole house, that smell did. There was no getting away from it. We even had it on our clothes. How Papa stood it in there day after day, and sometimes all night too, I'll never know. Of course, we couldn't have any visitors; the Aunts were almost beside themselves. We'd been one of the best, most admired families in Aubrey, and with good reason, too: we had money, influence, pedigree, everything you could possibly want. Then all of a sudden we were freaks. People didn't just stay away, they crossed the street to avoid us. Except for the sympathetic ones, that is; the ones who were *so* concerned, *so* sorry we were having such *trouble*, it must be simply *awful* and was there anything they could do. I think they disgusted me more than anything else, even the stink. Of course none of it bothered Papa in the least; he practically never went out by then, anyway, even to the bank."

All this was bad enough. But by his new obsession the banker brought another ill on his family, something far beyond mere eccentricity, beyond even the flouting of convention and social custom, something shameful and obscene. Soon after Mr. Barton had moved into the laboratory, the family heard a woman's voice there, talking quietly or laughing, at odd hours of the day or night. They never could make out what she was saying; she spoke in a thick foreign accent. Often she addressed Mr. Barton directly, calling him by his first name. Naturally, everyone in the house found the situation extremely uncomfortable, and Mr. Barton certainly did not help matters. At first he denied that anything unusual was going on; the family, he insisted, was hearing things. Later, he surmised that it was "only the wind." Finally, he told them flatly that it was none of their business.

---

[20] *Ibid.*, p. 117.

"We never could figure how he got her in and out without one of us seeing," said Mrs. Caws. "Of course there was no chance of looking into the laboratory itself; Papa had boarded up the windows. I tried to peep through the keyhole once, but he'd stopped it up with tar or something. And there was no chance of sneaking in when he wasn't around: he always put a big padlock on the door if he happened to go out. At last, the Aunts decided it must be a ghost, but they were just trying to make the best of things. Because, let me tell you, dearie, *that was no ghost*. Not with a voice like that, a voice like honey, so smooth and sweet. That was a real woman he had in there." She laughed her girlish laugh again. "You know, when all is said and done, you've got to hand it to Papa. I don't know how he did it, but you've really got to hand it to him."

Mr. Barton's diary would seem to bear out her assessment. After 1838 the hieroglyph indicating sexual congress appears in his notes with increasing frequency. But the matter has not been fully explained to this day.

It was in January, 1843 that Mr. Barton made the discovery that was to have such an impact on his daughter's later life. His work that month had come almost to a standstill. "Goodbye to the long, well-ordered dream," he wrote on the 10th. "After a promising beginning—so many years ago!—I seem to have fallen into every trap the books warn against. Sloth, inattention, greed. Mishandling the heat. Today, another vessel cracked, and all the contents ruined—the fifth in a week. And last night's dream! I saw the Holy Grail standing before me, in mid-air beside my bed. I got up and looked inside—it was full of spiders and scorpions!"[21]

The next day, despondent and weary, he chanced to be looking through an old catalogue of chemical equipment, with the vague idea of finding replacements for his broken vessels, but mostly just to have something to do, when he saw the following advertisement, placed incongruously among notices for beakers, flasks, boilers, tubing, stopcocks, clamps and other items:

DR. EGGBEATER CAWS

ANIMAL MAGNETIST

HEALER, MASTER OF THE ETHERIC FLUIDS!

---

[21] *Ibid.*, p. 159.

HEALS BY MEANS OF THE LIFE FORCE ITSELF!
POSSESSOR OF
THE FOOD OF ANGELS,
THE STONE OF THE WISE,
STARKEY'S PILL,
PHILALETHES' POWDER,
CAN INDEFINITELY EXTEND THE LIFE SPAN!

Also cures
ringworm, catarrh, liver problems, ulcers,
gout, headaches, pimples, scrofula,
jaundice, hives, female complaints.
Monthly Pills for Female Irregularity—
A Faithful Friend to Suffering Women.
Thousands of Satisfied Customers Attest!

Write: Dr. Eggbeater Caws
Rue Garancière,
Quartier de Luxembourg,
Faubourg St. Germain,
Paris

Mr. Barton was electrified; in an instant his whole outlook was transformed. "At last!" he wrote. "A kindred spirit—and a kindred spirit who *knows*! Philalethes, Starkey, the Food of Angels! After laboring so long, groping in the dark, suddenly to find—ah! to find a Master!"[22] Immediately he sent a letter to Dr. Caws, recapitulating his experience in the Great Work, explaining his progress and frustrations, offering the doctor financial inducements—"half, Sir, fully half of my worldly goods, nay more, more, you shall not find me niggardly, I promise"[23]—to come to Aubrey and instruct him.

[22] *Ibid.*, p. 160.

[23] This letter is in the Caws Archive of the Brewster Institute, along with the page from *Chemia Monthly*, May, 1832, containing Dr. Caws' advertisement. —*The Encyclopaedia of Reincarnation.*

As soon as the letter went off, Mr. Barton went back to his experiments starting from scratch with a will. "The World seems possible again," he told himself. "Help is on the way."[24] Nothing could stop him now, he felt.

And, strange to say, he did have success of a sort—if his diary is any measure and if the imagined capture of a proven delusion can be truly considered success. His notes through the spring and summer are sprinkled with references to an "Elixir" which, apparently, he believed he had produced. "Finally! The way is clear," he wrote in August. "And subtill—so subtill!"[25] His hieroglyphs, which had vanished from the record for several months, now reappeared with a vengeance.

His dreams, too, underwent a transformation. Beginning in February, a new motif asserted itself: fruit, not only the familiar apples but a whole range of fruit, appearing at first in isolated instances but soon taking over the content of the dreams exclusively. All through the spring, summer and early fall Mr. Barton walked nightly through landscapes bursting with oranges, apricots, lemons, plums, pomegranates, bananas, strawberries, every fruit known to man and some for which no name yet existed, bulbous, juicy, composite things covering the ground, hanging from trees and trellises, in an endless series of gardens disappearing into a misty horizon. The banker woke each morning in his meditation room feeling "positively at peace, truly serene, and for the first time in my life. The long dream *is* well- ordered. Who would have thought it?"[26]

"Yes, Papa got awfully *odd* that summer," Mrs. Caws recalled. "Something good must have happened to him in there—and it must have happened more than once, too." She giggled. "He stopped complaining, for one thing. It used to be, that was the only reason he'd come out of his lair, to raise Cain about this or that not being right, and who cooked this God-awful slop, and what kind of a household did we females think we were running? Imagine *him* asking *that!* But that summer there was hardly a peep out of him. He'd come into the dining room, take his meals with us like an ordinary human

---

[24] Barton, *Dream Journal*, iv, p. 162.

[25] *Ibid.*, p. 170

[26] Ibid., p. 182.

being, send a compliment to the cook, then go back to his work, whatever that was. The stink was just as bad as ever, you understand, and we still heard that woman's voice, but otherwise things were different. Papa actually smiled at me once or twice, and I don't think he'd ever done that before. The Aunts were delighted; they thought a great change was on its way. I guess I should have felt good about it too, but I didn't. It was such a *strange* thing for him to do, and so uncalled for, really, considering what an unruly, devious little— well, considering how unruly and devious I'd become, under that good little girl appearance I still managed to keep up—oh, dearie, I could a tale unfold. Yes, now that I think of it, in some way those smiles of his made me more resentful than anything he'd done before. I mean, if he really thought I was … if he didn't at the very least have sense enough to see behind my … Oh, well, that's all long gone and dead, what's the point of bringing it up again? But the fact was, I didn't care much for the way he was behaving, even if the Aunts did. And I had that same feeling I already told you about, the feeling I'd had years back, just before those apples fell for the first time: I just knew something *funny* was about to happen."

On the morning of November 5, 1843, after a hearty breakfast with his family, Mr. Barton broke with established custom. He did not cross the hall to his laboratory but instead, as he left the dining room, turned right, went down the hall and out the front door. He was clean-shaven for the first time in months and impeccably dressed, in a stylish black suit and vest, spotless white shirt, lightly starched linen cravat and his best light-weight overcoat. He walked east, down Prospect St. to Main, where he turned right, walked down Main to High, then right again down High to Maple. By now word had spread that Mr. Barton was abroad, and a number of townsfolk followed him at a distance, eager to see how the recluse looked after all this time and to learn what had finally brought him out.

At the corner of Maple and Juniper the banker turned left. Halfway down the block a tall granite building dominated the adjacent houses, with a broad set of stone steps leading up to its doorway. Mr. Barton climbed these and entered his bank.

It was his first visit in almost a year. Employees said afterwards that they knew no special reason for his coming. He had not been expected. Apparently, they said, he merely wanted to see what was going on, reestablish himself in his old place of power. He was, they agreed, uncharacteristically affable. "He smiled and smiled," said one. "Had a good word for everybody. Even remembered some of our names. Never saw him like that before, not in twenty years with the firm."

His business, such as it was, concluded, the banker stepped out again into the sunlight. There, under a clear, cold November sky, in full view of several dozen curiosity seekers who had gathered across the street, he was hit on the head by a single, hard, unripened cantaloupe, falling from a great height.

Stunned, Mr. Barton lost his footing, tumbled down the steps, struck his right temple on the heavy iron railing and dropped dead on the sidewalk. "Nobody could understand what caused it," Mrs. Caws told me, absently kneading the center of her forehead in a gesture that proved to be habitual as our conversations continued. "Not then, and not later. Most of us had never even seen a cantaloupe before. We certainly didn't have any growing in those parts." She paused, and took a sip of sherry. "One thing I was grateful for, though, sad as the whole business was: I was halfway across town when it happened, in the Mainwarings' barn with young Jerry Welkin, so nobody could blame it on me."

BOOK 2

II

FERMENTATION, CONTINUED:
AN UNPLEASANT DISCOVERY.
THE ROWLEY SÉANCE.
TWO EQUAL SALTS CARRY UP SATURN.

True Tales of the Paranormal:

At eight o'clock in the morning of November 27, 2002, Georg C. Dietz, secretary and all-around assistant to Dr. P. C. Haselmaus, knocked on the door of the private room assigned to Fritz Eichhorn at the Helvetius Psychiatric Clinic. Dietz was in Zürich to report to his employer on Eichhorn's condition. Getting no answer, he turned the handle and entered. Dr. Eichhorn was lying on the floor, on his back, eyes wide open, staring up at the ceiling. A white feather was sticking out of his mouth. Pages of his manuscript were scattered around the room.

Subsequent examination revealed that he had been dead at least six hours.

Apprehensive as always about the scandal, the Helvetius made sure the treatment of the death in the local papers was muted. Comments on Eichhorn's professional life were confined to praise for his brilliant beginnings and regrets that his "great potential" would never, now, be fulfilled. The doctor's time as a patient at the Clinic was explained as a "rest cure." And there the matter might have ended, but somehow the more lurid details of Dietz's discovery leaked out, and were featured the following week in Anna Sprengel's gossip column, together with two further revelations—first, that the drawers in Eichhorn's desk had been filled with acorns, which were also found under the rug and in the dresser drawers, and second, that the doctor had been seen the week before, climbing trees in the exercise yard. "Yes," Sprengel's piece concluded, "say what you like about psychiatry—and I do say a lot about it, don't I, friends?—you have to admit that it's given us quite a ride, ever since the days of old Sigmund. We've had the Wolf Man, we've had the Rat Man, and now, right in our very own city, we have the Squirrel Man! The entertainment value has been stupendous. Can you stand the success, animal lovers? What next, one asks oneself—Wombat Man? Psychiatry seems to be the gift that keeps on giving. I do wonder what chicken that feather came from."

"I should prefer to say nothing," Dr. Anna Zeisig remarked, when questioned by reporters outside her Zürich home. "However, I was a colleague of his; we worked together. As is well known, we did not always agree. I'm the first to admit I found some of his ideas, well, extreme. But if one respects one's own work, one owes it to the profession at least to acknowledge the work of others. We all make mistakes. One sends one's condolences to his family."

"Poor Squirrel Man," said Empedocles Schwank. "He was a good old wagon. If only he could have learned to listen to the bass." But within a month, Schwank would be gone, too.

The Cry of the Gehirngespinstgemach:

CLKCLKCLKCLKCLK. Miles Davis will record "The Squirrel" in 1951. Steve Elson and Art Baron will record "Eye Deal" in 1990. Efficiency Caws takes another sip of her drink. You know, sweetie, she tells herself, an asylum might be the best place for Eggbeater at that. He's certainly not in his right mind. She shifts in her chair, scratching an itch that has just begun in the middle of her forehead. In the chemical vessel in Newton's laboratory in her pineal gland, the Red Man and the White Wife begin to fuse into one.

Oh, I know what you're going to say, honey, she goes on, you always stick up for him. You're going to say, those aren't really Eggbeater's statements at all, they're Leibniz's, and the poor man shouldn't be held responsible for anything Leibniz says, just because he happens to be using Eggbeater's vocal chords. Well, dearie, you're as wrong as wrong can be, and here's why. All that tripe couldn't *possibly* be coming from Leibniz, and for one simple reason: Leibniz wasn't crazy! That's right. Leibniz was as sane as you and me—just you ask Uncle Isaac if he wasn't. Uncle Isaac has said a lot of bad things about Leibniz—I don't think I ever heard anyone say worse about another human being—but not once has he suggested that Leibniz was crazy. No, sweetie, Leibniz was *smart*. Why, Uncle Isaac *hates* him! He wouldn't waste his time hating a crazy man, would he, now? Of course he wouldn't; Uncle Isaac has *plenty* more important things than that to do, let me tell you. And just ask yourself this, sweetheart: whose word have we got for it, finally, that all that talk is really coming from Leibniz? I mean, apart from one or two reporters that Eggbeater's bamboozled, who claim they've looked up this bit or that bit—as if anyone could be bothered doing so, and anyhow they're things Eggbeater could easily have found and memorized, and it'd be just like him, too—whose word have we got for the authenticity of any of it, when you come right down to it? Eggbeater's, that's whose! Eggbeater's, and Eggbeater's alone. And his word these days is worth approximately nothing, as far as I'm concerned. Remember what he told me, that time I asked him where the plans came from for that Goddamned adding machine of his, that stupid "Delphic Oracle"? Remember that, dearie? That long-winded taradiddle about his dream, his "very important dream," as he called it, "with Miss Nightingale in it"—pronouncing "Miss Nightingale" in a reverent, hushed voice as if it were the name of God or something—Christ, it's Miss Nightingale this and Miss Nightingale that every minute of the day, what with Eggbeater and now the damned newspapers getting into the act as well (why they're all making such a fuss about her is more than *I* can figure out, I'll bet she can't even elongate) and how he saw the machine in his dream and then Leibniz told him how to build it? Remember that, dearie? Even you thought that a bit fishy at the time, as I recollect. Well, sweetheart, I've never mentioned this to you, but I happen to *know* that Eggbeater *stole* those plans, out of Papa's papers that have been stored out in the barn ever since he died—stole them as sure as I'm sitting here drinking this drink (she pours herself some more) and passed 'em off as CLKCLKCLK Count Basie will record "Jumpin' at the Woodside" in 1956. Coleman Hawkins will record "I Surrender, Dear" in 1940 CLK-CLKCLK passed 'em off as CLKCLK passed 'em off as CLKCLK passed 'em off as coming from Leibniz—Leibniz and that Goddamned "very important dream with Miss Nightingale in it." Christ! Of all the naked gall. The thief. What do you mean, how do I know for sure? I just *know*, that's all. A year ago, right after we retired, Eggbeater started going out to the barn, where we'd put all Papa's equipment and papers after he died, when we cleaned out the parlor and sitting room. "Just to look things over," he said at first, and then, later, "just to straighten things out a little." The papers—notes, plans, and I don't know what-all, were all there in big piles, on tables, chairs, the floor, just the way Papa had left them. I'd never touched them, and Eggbeater said he wanted to put them in some sort of order, maybe even have them published someday as a book. Well, I didn't suspect anything at the time, in fact I thought it was a good idea, but what obviously happened was that one day he found those plans, and bided his time until he saw how he could use them. Then at some point he slipped two of the plans into the house, and hid them someplace in the cabinet. Then he brought his materials in, all that scrap metal and wire and God knows what, and started building the thing, practically under my nose, the bastard. And that's how—what? Well, of *course* I didn't *see* him with the plans, sweetie. How could I? Eggbeater would have *hidden* them, wouldn't he? Of course he would, and then he—Oh, for God's sake. How do *I* know why he didn't make the thing out in the barn? He just *didn't*, dearie, and there's an end to it. Besides, wouldn't I have been just as suspicious if he'd put it together out there and brought it in here all finished, to show me? Sure I would. No, it's no good taking his side this time, honey, he's a fraud and a thief, and that's all there is to say about it.

She takes a sip of her drink and giggles. That's all right, though, lovey, no need to worry. I've gotten even with him. This morning, just before Jerry came, while Eggbeater was in another part of the house, I went into the cabinet, and took the Goddamn thing down from its shelf, and made some adjustments Leibniz—or Papa, rather—hadn't thought of: twisted a few wires, tied up a couple of loose ends, and then loosened a few tight ones. She laughs. Oh, I can't *wait* to see Eggbeater's face tomorrow night! When he unveils his precious Oracle, and tries to put it through its paces, and all it does is sit there! "Ladies and gentlemen," he'll say, "here it is, the miracle you've all been waiting for, the center-piece of this historic occasion—it adds, subtracts, multiplies, divides, does square roots, quadratic equations! Ladies and gentlemen, I give you, fresh from the spirit world, from the deathless mind and the immortal soul of nature's nobleman, Gottfried Wilhelm Leibniz—I give you, ladies and gentlemen, the Delphic Oracle!" And the damn thing'll just sit there. Just *sit* there! "Now, Oracle," he'll say, standing there all puffed up with pride, his big belly sticking out a mile in front of him, "Tell us how much is five times five." And he'll poke a piece of paper under its tongue, the way he showed me the other day after he finally got the thing finished. Then he'll turn the crank and—silence! Ha! Silence for a *long* time. The audience'll start fidgeting in their seats. "Well, then, Oracle"—he'll try it again—"Well, then, Oracle, how much is one times five?" Silence. "How about one times one, then?" Nothing. "One *plus* one, damn it! One minus one! How much is one minus one, God damn you?" And on and on like that—he'll be screaming at the thing, getting redder and redder in the face, and the crowd'll be laughing, and Uncle Isaac and I will be standing off to one side, so aloof-like, getting taller and taller and taller, so *above* the whole vulgar show, if you know what I mean, dearie. I can see it now—a night to remember, lovey, a night to savor forever! What's that you say, sweet? Ruin the act? Of course not, dear. How in the world could it ruin the act? I can't think where you get such an idea. It'll just teach Eggbeater a lesson, that's all. He—what? Make him a laughingstock? *Naturally* it'll make him a laughingstock, that's the whole point. It's just what he deserves. He's been trying to take over everything, so Uncle Isaac and I are going to take over him. He thinks he's so Goddamn important! Well, Uncle Isaac and I can run the whole thing by ourselves; we don't need him at all. She stops and cocks her head, reminded of something. Ha. Now, isn't that curious, dearie, I think Uncle Isaac said that very same thing to me, not long ago. It just came back to me. "Get rid of the bastard," he said, or some such thing. "Go out on your own. The public will love us." And I got mad at him, I can't think why, and told him Eggbeater and I would never break up. Well, that just goes to show you how wrong even the best of us can be, doesn't it, love? And how right Uncle Isaac is, too. How right—she pauses again. Her face darkens. Damn! *Damn.* Oh, sweetie, Goddamn it, what the hell am I talking about? Her body sags in the chair. It won't happen that way at all. Eggbeater won't be a laughingstock, the swine—I ought to know better. He'll be at a loss for about a second and a half, that's all, and then recover his poise completely. He's never at sea for long, no matter what goes wrong. He has too good a feel for his audience. Remember the séance in Rowley the night of the fire? He'll probably do the same thing tomorrow night—just levitate. Why not? It never fails, Goddamn him. It's a cheap trick, all right, but the audience isn't made that can resist it. "Ooooooooooh!" They'll yell, just the way they always do, and everything else will be forgotten. Jesus. I don't even know what he thinks he needs that adding machine for. He probably figures it adds respectability. Hah. He doesn't need it at all. Why the hell should he bother?

She hears voices again, coming through the window. There. Just listen to that, sweetie. The pig. I'll bet he's up in the air right this minute, showing off to young Jerry, charming the socks off him. She glowers. It isn't fair, Goddamn it. Jerry's *my* friend. I knew him long before Eggbeater did, long before Eggbeater even knew *me*, when he was still off in Europe somewhere—if only he'd stayed!

She fills her glass, all the way to the brim, and takes a long drink. Thelonious Monk will record "Thelonious" in 1947. He will eat a slice of chocolate pie in 1949.

Jerry and I were children together, for the love of God. You remember Jerry, don't you, sweetie? Naturally; I knew you would. He lived only two houses away from us, right here on Prospect St. He couldn't take his eyes off me, back then. It was as if he were trying to *drink* me with them, every time I came near him. He didn't say much. You'd have said he was shy—if you hadn't seen his eyes. He just *stared* so. I did most of the talking. I was a terrible flirt. But *somebody* had to get things started, and it didn't look as if he ever would. Besides, I figured that if he was going to stare at me like that—well, it *was* flattering, lovey—the least I could do was to make it worth his while. How he blushed at first! But he loved it. We both loved it. How old was I then? Sixteen? I suppose so, it was right around the time that Papa died. And he—fifteen? Something like that; younger than me, anyhow.

Efficiency sighs and gets to her feet. She moves, a little unsteadily, carrying the decanter and glass, across the room to the settee. She plunks herself down at one end, swings her legs up onto the seat, and leans her back against the cushioned arm, setting the decanter down within easy reach on the floor. There. That's better. Mmmmmm. Those afternoons in the barn. Not our barn, of course, it would have been much too chancy. The Mainwarings' barn, across town. We used to go through the Burying Ground—separately, so as not to arouse suspicion—over the hill behind it, through the woods, and sneak into the barn by the back door, where nobody in the main house could see us. She smiles. It was so innocent, really, looking back on it now. All we did—mostly—was stare at each other! What, love? Naked? Of course we were naked, dear. You must remember *that*. We'd climb up into the hayloft, take off all our clothes, lie down side by side and—stare at each other. Real still, and serious-like. Not touching—not for a long, long time, anyway. The game was to wait, as long as you possibly could, *without* touching. Just *looking*. Letting our eyes do all the work, have all the fun. It was delicious, sweetheart, delicious. That beautiful, pale, fresh young body. And such eyes! Such unforgettable eyes! A deep, deep blue they were, almost purple. She giggles. I used to imagine myself dissolving into mist on his face, then being sucked through his tear ducts into his brain and—oh, and down inside all through his body, fifty million little dewdrops of me, traveling all through his bloodstream, everywhere in him and all at the same time. What did he imagine, I wonder? He never would say, just shook his head and smiled. Not that it mattered. In some ways it was nicer without knowing. And eventually one of us—usually me—wouldn't be able to stand it any longer and would reach out and break the spell. That was all right, too, naturally, that was part of the game. Now I break the spell on your lips. Now I break the spell on your cheekbone. Now I break the spell on your chest, your belly, your ankle, your thigh, your crotch, your crotch. Now you break the spell on my Adam's apple. Now you break the spell on my shoulder. Now you break the spell on my left breast, my right breast, my belly, my cheeks, between my legs, between my legs, between my legs, between my legs. Now.

Clifford Brown will record "Joy Spring" in 1954. He will be born in 1930, on Efficiency Caws' birthday, in Wilmington, Delaware. She gives a little shiver and lets out a long sigh. Oh, what days those were! She scratches her forehead. How long ago did all that happen, sweet? Twelve years? Is that all? She grunts. It might as well be twelve lifetimes. Just look at me. She eyes the decanter. A Goddamn drunk. And Jerry—he's different, too, plenty different. She drinks. Jerry has become—Christ, it's annoying—Jerry has become the Ear of the Press. My lovely boy, just another reporter now, corrupted by Eggbeater. That whole spring and summer, and a good ways into the fall, he couldn't tear himself away from me—and it got pretty cold in that barn, too, with no clothes on, by the time October and November came around! Now I have to climb onto a chair and scream for him to even notice I'm in the room, much less take the trouble to look me in the eye. His gaze is all for Eggbeater now—Christ, the day Eggbeater has to stand on a chair to get someone to look at *him*! He can get off the ground at a moment's notice, the slime. In the old days at least he didn't do it every single night; it was something a bit special. But not any more. All he needs now is an audience, even an audience of one, and the slightest hint of encouragement. If either of those is lacking, half a glass of booze will do the trick, and if he's had half a glass this morning he's had thirty. Jesus. He must have gotten started in the middle of the night; I caught him fiddling with the sherry decanter just after dawn. I'd been woken up by that damn dog barking again, somewhere out on High St. this time, it sounded like, on the other side of the bridge. Who the hell owns the beast I don't know, but I wish they'd come and take it home, it's been prowling around here a week or more, ruining everyone's sleep in the neighborhood. Huh. Now I think of it, the dog's probably trying to find Eggbeater. I never came across anyone that animals were more attracted to. What they see in him I couldn't tell you, I'm sure, but the fact is, they flock to him and always have—dogs, cats, horses, cattle, too, not to mention other livestock. Birds, rabbits, turtles, even. Not a one of 'em doesn't at the very least turn its head when Eggbeater passes by, and they usually come right up and nuzzle him like a long-lost brother. I bet the fish would, too, if he spent as much time in the water as he does in the air where he doesn't belong. It's a Goddamn embarrassment, that's what it is. I don't know why he didn't go in for veterinary medicine instead of human and be done with it when he was starting out, he would have made ten fortunes by now. Anyway, after that dog I couldn't get back to sleep, so I came downstairs, and there was Eggbeater in the dining room, naked as a jaybird except for the sheet he'd wrapped around himself—like a Roman senator, or an over-fed ghost—with his belly pressed up against the sideboard and his fat, hairy arms reaching out to have another go at the wine. He hadn't seen me come in, so I sneaked up behind him and coughed, really loud. Ha! Caught him completely off guard, it did. He jumped about a foot, lovely, even without levitating! Then he got all huffy and self-righteous. Pretended he was only looking for something—what, he didn't specify—and thought he might have left it behind the decanter. Next, when he saw I didn't believe him, he tried to make a joke out of it, changing to Latin, a Roman senator for fair—"*Gallia est omnis divisa in partes tres*; Carthage must be destroyed!" When he saw I wasn't having any of that either—Grandfather Thaddeus taught me my Caesar before I was five, and I know a damn sight more of it than Eggbeater does, I'll tell you that, dearie, and enough to know that wheeze about Carthage comes from someone else, too—he turned on his heel and walked away. I watched him as he left the room; it was as if he was trying to move through cheese—too drunk to see a hole in a ladder, and the sun hardly up yet. Not that that's anything unusual.

CLKCLKCLKCLKCLK. Well, dearie, I stayed there a while by the sideboard, just to make sure he didn't come back. I mean, *somebody's* got to look out for him, after all. He never knows when he's had enough. He just can't hold it as well as we can, and that's all there is to it. No sense in letting him embarrass us any more than he already has. CLKCLK. But at last I heard him upstairs, snoring his head off. So I went into the cabinet. I'd had that idea, you see, while I was waiting, about what I could do to that adding machine. CLKCLKCLKCLK. But do you know, sweetheart, I don't believe Eggbeater had another drink till Jerry arrived, not even after I left the sideboard. Because I'm pretty sharp, you see—have to be, with someone like Eggbeater around—and before I leave a room I always check the level of drink in any bottle that happens to be there, and—what? Well, of course I do, sweetie, somebody's got to pay attention, the man's a danger to himself and always has been. Anyway, what I was about to tell you was, that when I came back into the sitting room, after Jerry had gotten there and Eggbeater was standing there talking to him, the level of sherry in that decanter hadn't changed one smidgeon. Not long after that, of course, I brought out the champagne punch—had to be hospitable, what the hell—and the old boy made up for his dry hours with a vengeance. The glass was never out of his hand, and he made sure not to stray too far from the punch bowl, either—even took it off the table and down on the floor with him when he decided that big sack of guts he carries around would be more comfortable horizontal than vertical. She giggles. There wasn't even a suggestion of levitation then, I noticed. He got Jerry down there with him, too, didn't he, love, because Jerry is the Ear of the Press now and the business of an Ear is to listen. Christ. That's about the last thing I remember before dropping off, the two of them lying on the carpet with the punch bowl between them, as thick as herrings in a barrel, Eggbeater drinking and working his jawbone and Jerry scribbling away in his notebook as fast as he could, so as not to miss a syllable. Not that he needs a notebook, with that memory of his. Jerry has always remembered *everything* anyone said—just the way they said it—has done for as long as I've known him. Jerry takes his job *so* seriously—which actually, sweetheart, is just what I'd have expected of him, he always was serious, and *thorough*, in everything he did, although how he grew up to be a reporter, is a lot more than I can fathom. But grow up he did, dearie. Just shows what a college education'll do for you, I guess. Why, in the old days, even when he did talk, he would hardly ever raise his voice above a whisper. Who could have imagined him in a job where his daily task was to ask a long string of impertinent questions to famous and influential people and keep right on asking, even after they'd told him to go to hell? My God, just getting him to whisper could be a day's work all by itself. Well, he wasn't whispering this morning, was he, sweet pea? Not by a long stroke he wasn't, with his brand new suit from Fowler Brothers in Boston and his cultured, Harvard-trained voice. He was one of the smoothest-talking, best dressed newspapermen I've ever laid eyes on—not that he'd lay his on me, the ingrate—and in the past five years I've seen more than a couple to compare him with.

She turns her head to the window and chuckles. It doesn't sound as if all that refinement's getting him very far today, though, does it, honey? Harvard College may be good, but it's no match for Eggbeater. The poor lad hadn't a chance to get more than about three and three-quarters questions in edgewise before, with His Highness the German Plagiarist hogging the stage and giving no answers worthy of the name. Ha! Just listen, love—he's hogging it still, wouldn't you say?

"Only a chicken feather, son, only a chicken feather. Nothing exotic, I assure you. Evander's sword is excellent. Caius is slain by Titius, that is, in the respect in which Titius is a slayer, in that respect Caius is slain. Just a common, ordinary chicken feather."

Now, what the hell is Jerry supposed to make of that? *I* don't know what to make of it, and I must have heard it a thousand and fourteen times. Maybe now you can see why I say Eggbeater belongs in an asylum, sweetheart. He *loves* that little sequence, I'm surprised he didn't bring it up earlier. It's his favorite story—yes, dear, that's what he calls it, a *story*, for God's sake, the thrilling tale of Caius and Titius and Evander's truly remarkable pig-sticker! Packed, loaded, cockablock, simply *gravid* with suspense, characterization, intellectual force and high morals, wouldn't you say, peach fuzz? Yes, I knew you'd see the light eventually. He's crazy, that's all, simply out of his mind— alcohol, I suppose. But if you think that's bad, you ought to hear him talk about the piece, the way he builds it up in people's minds before they hear it. Unforgivable, really, it brings discredit onto anyone associated with him. "A great gift from the spirit world," he once called it, "a beautiful and instructive parable." That's what he said to one of the journalists who interviewed us early on, what's-his-name, the one from *Time and Light*—Forbes, that's it—"a beautiful and instructive parable with a moral deeper than the ocean." No, darling, I'm not fooling. He really said that. Yes, about that little sequence, Evander's sword and so on. I *know*, sweetie, that's what I've been trying to *tell* you all this time. Well, I'm not sure, I think there's one in Worcester. No, the one in Boston is just for vagrant children, as far as I know. Don't worry, we'll find something. But, as I was saying, Eggbeater told Forbes all this, and of course Forbes got interested. He's very strong on morals and spiritual uplift and all that sort of thing, and he couldn't wait to hear more. So then Eggbeater told him the story, just the way he did a second ago—even doing that shoddy little trick of his with the chicken feather, that so-called "materialization" which couldn't fool anyone, the purest flapdoodle, although I have to admit I never figured out exactly how it was done myself—and Forbes heard all about how Titius, whoever he is, kills Caius, whoever he is, and how Evander, whoever the Christ *he* is, has an excellent sword. The end. Nothing more, not a crumb. Word for word what you just heard him say to Jerry. Well, that's an insult to anyone's intelligence, let alone a smart man like Forbes, and I don't blame him for writing what he did about us, not one bit. Shit and shallots! If you don't treat people with respect, you can't expect decent treatment in return. If Eggbeater wants beautiful and instructive, let him try this:

"If comets revolve in orbits returning into themselves, the orbits will be ellipses; and their periodic times will be to the periodic times of the planets as the 3/2th {check this} power of their principal axes. And therefore the comets, which for the most part of their course are more remote than the planets, and upon that account describe orbits with greater axes, will require a longer time to finish their revolutions."

Recognize that, darling? 'Course you do. That was Uncle Isaac, sweetie, speaking through me at the very first séance we ever gave, five years ago. And who do you think was there listening, and took it all down, verbatim, in his very own handwriting? My lovely Jerry, that's who! Jerry, before Eggbeater got to him. And I never saw him, didn't even know he was in the room, it was so dark and I was so nervous. They printed it in next day's *Trumpet*, big as life, didn't they, love? I memorized the whole speech right after I read it, I was so excited. You miss most of the fun when you're in trance, you know, or a lot of it anyhow, and I had no idea I'd said all those brilliant things! It was the happiest day of my life. I wrote Jerry right away, to thank him, and to—oh, and to tell him all about myself and what I'd been doing in the years since I'd seen him, when he left Aubrey to go to Harvard. And then, when I finished—it was such a *nice* letter, too, dearie, full of news and good feelings and affection and gratitude and I had such a *lovely* time writing it—when I finished I realized I didn't know where to send it. Jerry had moved away, and his family were all gone, too: Grandfather Welkin had died in '47 and Jerry's parents sold the farm and went south soon after, so there was no one even to ask. I did the only thing I could think of and sent it to him care of the *Trumpet* in Salem. He wrote back—it turned out he was in Beverly, had been there all the time. Very formal and proper he was, but I could still sense the old shyness and innocence underneath the education. Well, I wrote him back, and then he wrote back a second time, and then me again, and he started coming to more of our séances and writing them up in the paper, and so it went, all the way through the last one, before we retired, the Rowley séance. And thank God he did, dearie, because his piece on that session was the only decent one we got! You wouldn't believe it, the things they said, even the spiritualist press who you'd think would have been sympathetic—and all because of a little fire. "Public menaces," they called us! "This time they've gone too far," they said. "Outrageous behavior." "Scandalous." "Teaching bad morals." Compared us to Mr. Melville, they did, and not very favorably at that. As if Uncle Isaac had anything to do with morals in the first place, for the love of God. *Ministers* give sermons, for Christ's sake, why the hell should mediums be expected to? Let the preaching stay in the church where it belongs. I don't know what this world is coming to.

She sighs. Well, dearie, Jerry stuck up for us, as I say, but by that time he was a voice crying in the wilderness. And about a week later I got a letter from him saying he couldn't write about us anymore. But not because he'd gone over to the other side—no, dearie, nothing like that. This was a love letter, the first one, I do believe, that I ever got in my life. Certainly Eggbeater never bothered. Jerry said he was writing in "great distress of mind," or something like that. "I am desolate, I cannot go on this way," I can't remember the words exactly, but you know the sort of thing, sweetheart. He supposes that I "surely cannot be unaware"—or some such laborious way of phrasing it—that at one time his sentiments for me ran deeper than those of "mere friendship"—I remember that, "mere friendship"—and he even dares to believe that my sentiments toward him did as well. But in the fullness of time, he goes on, his feelings changed to the "cooler but no less profound ones"—or words to that effect—of admiration and respect, "mingled, Madam, with not a little awe for the wonderful work you do for the spirit world." But, he is "desolate" to say— poor old Jerry, desolate again!—that of late his original feelings have returned, stronger than ever, "so strong, dear lady, that I am almost ashamed to confess them, even to you, who must recall the—" Edenic? Was that his word, Edenic? I think so, yes—"the innocent and Edenic circumstances in which they were born." Such a mouthful! But pretty, don't you think, dearie? As pretty as you please. And it certainly did take me back—oh, sweetheart, yes it did!

But the rest of the letter—oh, dear, it was sad. "I must not see you again," he says, "no, not even a single séance, not even in a crowd of sitters." The Rowley session, he says, was pure torture. "To have seen you, Madam"—this I remember word for word, dearie—"to have seen you standing there, standing and *growing*, taller and taller, o'ertopping all in your glory, straining—ah, nearly *bursting* your seams, thrusting up and out, up and out—to have seen you so, and to know that you could never be mine, that you have given your heart to another—no, not for all the wealth of all the nations of the world would I repeat such an experience!" So he must bid us adieu, he says, and see us no more. With all fondness he remains, keeping always in his heart the memory of those tremulous afternoons in the Mainwarings' barn so long, long ago, in despair and devotion, my one and only—and so on.

Now, dearie, I ask you—what could I do? I was moved, don't think I wasn't, moved and, well, flattered, and if circumstances had been different I'm not saying what I might have done. But Eggbeater and I were a *team* then—I mean to tell you, sweetie, we were at the top of our powers, and it was still *fun*! I would *never* have considered—*really* considered—I mean, the snake didn't enter the garden, if you follow me, until we'd been retired for a while and he went off on his own hook, started building that Goddamned Oracle. So there was no question of my—well, Jerry in a way was part of my past instead of my present, even if he did do us a powerful lot of good with his articles and all; and anyway, I didn't see how I could be held *responsible* for the way he felt. What the hell. But I wrote him back; I wrote him back a nice long letter, saying I was sorry and so on, and wished we—I said "we"—could continue to see him, but I understood how that wasn't possible, and I wished him well, and added that I enjoyed those memories too. And I didn't tell Eggbeater. As I said, sweetie, Jerry was part of *my* past; I didn't figure my past was any of Eggbeater's business.

So that was that. I didn't hear a word from Jerry, of course, and pretty much forgot about the whole thing, while all of last year happened and everything went to hell. Until this morning, when I came through the curtains out of the cabinet, and there he stood in the middle of the sitting room, talking to Eggbeater! What a beautiful, beautiful sight. And we'd thought they were going to send Forbes!

Gravity Newton:

The Rowley séance was held in the largest room of the "Lyceum," a ramshackle, clapboard building badly in need of repair, which the local Society of Finer Advancement fancied as a center of learning and culture that someday, they hoped, would rival the Lyceum in Gloucester, fifteen miles to the southeast, where the likes of Ralph Waldo Emerson and Henry David Thoreau had lectured. So far the Rowley version had attracted only a Mr. Lox, who painted acorns, and Miss Elvira Jenkins, a harpsichordist from Milford, Connecticut, who was discomfited upon her arrival to find that the Society had forgotten to provide her with a harpsichord and that, except for a violin with two strings missing, there was no other musical instrument in the hall. Her place had been taken by Mr. John Patrick Sheehan of Dublin, who happened to be in town that week visiting his sister and brother-in-law. He spent the evening entertaining the audience with tall tales of his boyhood in County Cork. Afterwards, the gentlemen in the hall retired to the Pig and Bladder Tavern across the street, where the raconteurship became general and continued till closing.

The Cawses' séance was a popular affair, well-advertised and eagerly anticipated. The Rowleyites were anxious to see if these two locals from Aubrey were anywhere near as good as their publicity made them out to be. About seventy-five persons crowded into the lecture hall, which would comfortably have held no more than half that number, the first arrivals seating themselves on the few available chairs, the next ones grabbing the low stools and benches that the Society had scraped together at the last minute, and the late comers squashing together against the walls by the front entrance, sweating, cramped and generally out of sorts. One of these last was Jeremy Welkin, who had written up a number of spiritualist stories in the past and had developed a special interest in the Cawses. Originally squeezed in with the group at the entrance, he managed, with many an "Excuse me, friend of the family, you know" (whatever that might have been expected to mean), to wriggle his way down to the front row, where he sat on the floor in the aisle.

After everyone had gotten in and was, if not settled, at least milling in one place, the Cawses made their entrance through a side door. They were both dressed in black, a departure for Mrs. Caws, who usually wore a rather daring white costume which left her shoulders bare. ("The black showed ectoplasm better," she told me in Wyncote. "I always wore black when I thought there'd be a lot of ectoplasm. I used to have a *feeling* about ectoplasm.") Welkin wrote that she looked "magnificent, tall and stately, her features wonderfully composed, reflecting quiet acceptance of the great and arduous Work that lay before her."

The crowd quieted. Briefly nodding to them, the couple walked quickly to the rear of the hall, where two straight-backed chairs had been set side by side about six feet apart, facing the audience. The Cawses took their seats, folded their hands in their laps and closed their eyes.

There was a pause of about ten seconds. Then—as usual—pandemonium.

It began with Newton. A loud, cracking noise, as of a branch breaking, sounded overhead and an apple fell to the floor beside Mrs. Caws' chair.

Someone snickered. Another apple fell, then another. From above came a peal of thunder. The snickering stopped.

A rough bass voice, shocking in its incongruity, issued from Mrs. Caws' mouth. "Good evening," it rumbled. "I am Sir Isaac Newton."

"Pleased-ta-meetcha!" someone in the back called out. The thunder sounded again.

"I am Sir Isaac Newton," the voice insisted, "and I bid you, I repeat, a very good evening, citizens of Rowley, citizens of Aubrey and any other phaenomena of Nature that may be present, those of you seated in splendid comfort in the front rows, like particles of matter evenly diffused through an infinite space—if I may so express it—and those of you standing squashed in the back, mutually impelled together by some force or forces unknown, making you—may I say—as alike as salt fish in a tin, or peas in a pod or, as Herr Leibniz, the pseudomath on my left might say, identical in your indiscernibility, or indiscernible in your identity, or some such tripe, I apologize in advance for his tediousness. And I thank you for coming. And especially I thank, most, most heartily, my intelligent, my beautiful, my vivacious and my infinitely patient friend Mrs. Caws, through whom I am speaking these words and who is the mistress of this evening's proceedings. Greet the people, my dear."

Mrs. Caws raised her left arm and swept it back and forth in front of her, as if wiping a window. During Sir Isaac's speech, she had slipped down in her chair until she was nearly off the seat, her head resting on her shoulder, with one eye shut and the other staring out above the heads of the crowd. Now a dreamlike, contented smile appeared on her face, and stayed there for the remainder of the séance, unaffected by the disputatiousness of what was spoken through her.

A few more apples dropped in the space between the Cawses and the people in the front row; then Newton got down to the main business of the evening. He reminded his audience that it was he, and he alone, who had discovered the law of universal gravitation, written the *Philosophiae Naturalis Principia Mathematica*, conceived the corpuscular theory of light, invented the reflecting telescope, proved that the force between the earth and the moon is inversely proportional to the square of the distance between them and—his voice shook with emotion—discovered the calculus, an indispensible contribution to modern mathematics, "which I arrived at a full nine years before the upstart Leibniz, that lump sitting to my left who appears to have gone to sleep, stole it from me."

He cleared his throat—or rather, he cleared Mrs. Caws' throat—making a rough hacking sound, like someone with a bad chest cold. The medium smiled on resolutely. "Let me tell you how my discovery came about," Newton resumed, "learned by my own inclination and by my own industry without a teacher—without any teacher at all, do you hear? Good. I would prefer not to have to repeat myself. It all began in the summer of 1663, when I was twenty, at the Sturbridge Fair. I bought a book there on astrology, which, I need scarcely say, I was able to comprehend with no effort at all, except for a figure of the heavens about two-thirds of the way through, that required a knowledge of trigonometry. I therefore bought a book on trigonometry, mastered it in a day or two, went on to study Euclid—whose propositions, frankly, are ridiculously simple—and finally investigated Descartes' *Geometry*. Then, in 1665, when the Plague broke out and I was driven from my College in Cambridge into the country, I made use of my leisure there to work out my method of the calculus—the fluxional method, I call it, a far better term, I think you will agree—computing—you may believe me or not but it is the truth, I swear it—*computing the area of a hyperbola to no less than two and fifty figures!* Let Leibniz "—he hissed the name—"let Leibniz say the same if he can."

He paused. Mrs. Caws' smile broadened. While she had been delivering Newton's speech, ticking off astrology, trigonometry, Euclid and Descartes, small white spots of ectoplasm had blossomed on her clothing. At the mention of Leibniz, a thin, supple length of the substance began to work its way out of her left side, through the black taffeta. Now it slipped down the chair leg to the floor, where it coiled and uncoiled, as if getting its bearings, then slithered across the floor in the direction of the audience. Halfway there, however, it seemed to lose its nerve: it stopped, raised its flat, wedge-shaped head and looked back at its mistress. Receiving no reply, it began to shrivel, its whiteness turning a dirty grey, until, after a few moments, it had vanished entirely.

There was an embarrassed silence while some people in the front row, who had made a beeline for the rear, resumed their seats. Somebody giggled nervously.

"Not even a real snake," another answered in mock disgust.

This produced a real laugh, which broke the tension. "Bring back Pat Sheehan!" A man in the back yelled. Others took up the call: "Pat Sheehan! Pat Sheehan!"

The laughter spread. All at once everyone was enjoying himself.

Including Leibniz: for now Dr. Caws, who so far had sat immobile in his chair, hands on his knees, broke into trills of merriment, throwing his head back violently and striking his palms against his sides. Then, abruptly, he pitched forward, his long black hair falling into his face. "Nonsense," he announced, when he had composed himself and was sitting erect again. "Nonsense." His voice was a pleasant musical tenor, quite different from the doctor's normal gruff baritone. "If A is B and C is D and E is F, then ACE is BDF. Men are writing, that is, Titius is writing, Caius is writing. Titius is a man, Caius is a man. Man is a sentient being. The concept of Adam contains everything that can be attributed to him. $2 = 2 \times 1$ plus 0. Her skin is like milk. Her skin is A. Milk is A. Hand; son; horse; heat; title: who will easily escape from the labyrinth whose unhappy Daedalus is the human mind?"

He stopped, as if expecting an answer. The audience, which had quieted down as soon as Leibniz began speaking, now realized that Dr. Caws' body, though still in a seated posture, had at some point floated out of the chair and shifted several feet to its left. The doctor's feet were now about sixteen inches off the floor.

This changed things considerably. The Rowleyites of 1854 might have been jaded sophisticates so far as falling apples and ectoplasmic snakes were concerned, but their affectations of indifference were no match for the sight of a portly man ensconced unsupported in mid-air, especially since Dr. Caws—keeping the same pose but rising a few inches higher—now began crossing and uncrossing his legs, each time giving a little tug on his trousers to straighten them and flicking invisible specks of dust off his knees with the backs of his fingers. His large dark eyes were wide open, and he beamed at the spectators like a proud parent or a Hindu holy man conferring a blessing. The crowd breathed a low, collective "Oooh!" and gazed in awe. A child pointed, then pulled back its finger as if afraid of being burned. A woman in front sank to her knees in prayer.

Leibniz's displays of anti-gravity always infuriated Newton, making his speech even harsher and more abusive than usual. Sometimes he got so angry that his voice dried up entirely; on these occasions he grew violent. A few weeks earlier, in Philadelphia, at the house of a wealthy matron widely known as a benefactress of the spiritualist movement, he had lifted a tall mahogany chest of drawers (using Mrs. Caws, of course, as his agent) carried it across the drawing room into the dining room and thrown it in a low, wobbling arc (the curve of which he afterwards claimed to have calculated beforehand by his famous fluxional method) through a window onto the street two stories below. Tonight, as soon as Leibniz opened Dr. Caws' mouth, Newton started fuming through Mrs. Caws', and soon a steady stream of ectoplasm, thicker and whiter than before, was flowing from her still-smiling lips. But no one showed any interest. All eyes were on Leibniz. At last, as the latter was fussing with his trousers, Sir Isaac found voice:

"Herr Leibniz will have his little joke, I see, as is common with men of his intellectual stripe, idlers and dilettantes with nothing better to do. I believe some of them are French, and you know that always means Papists. But what

Herr Jokester and his minions do not consider, the swine, is that flying, play though it be to him, is in fact the Devil's own work. For God"—here Mrs. Caws' head fell onto her chest, so that what followed came out as a mumble directed to the floor—"God in the beginning formed matter in solid, massy, hard, *impenetrable* particles, and, that nature may be lasting, Herr Atheist, the changes of corporeal things are to be placed *only in various separations and motions* of these particles. God did not mean man to fly!"

"2 + 2 = 4; 0 − 0 = 0," replied Leibniz, and did a backwards somersault, ending again in the sitting posture. "Peter writes beautifully," he commented. "The sword is Evander's. Evander's sword is excellent." The child who had pointed squealed with delight.

"More! More!" The cries came from all over the room.

Newton responded with a low growl. More ectoplasm, now very thin and wispy, issued from Mrs. Caws' side, flying round her in a spiral before it evaporated, so that briefly she and her chair were encased in a web of luminous, crisscrossing lines. But no one seemed to notice, as Leibniz obliged the crowd by repeating his backwards somersault, this time staying upside down long enough to take a cigar from his inside coat pocket and a penknife from his waistcoat, cut off the end of the cigar, replace the penknife, take out a match, strike it on his heel, light the cigar and drop the match on the floor six feet below. The audience was stamping and cheering.

As the match hit the floor, Newton let out a roar. "More animal than human," wrote Welkin, "it came out of Mrs. Caws' mouth but seemed to have originated somewhere deep in the earth, far below the Lyceum's foundations. At last the crowd gave her its attention. With a jerky motion she pushed down on the arms of her chair and stiffly, as if she had been in the same position for centuries, raised herself to her full height—fuller, for Newton, unable to fly and goaded beyond endurance by an impudent rival, was doing the next best thing: he was commencing his Growing Act."

Even those who, like Welkin, were accustomed to the bizarre doings of the séance room found Newton's Growing Act a marvel. Superficially similar to other elongations of the body in trance, such as were accomplished by a number of medieval saints and later by D. D. Home and other mediums, Newton's version added some impressive personal touches, not the least of which was an element of ferocity and vindictiveness that no other spirit approached or even attempted.

It began with a sudden, dramatic increase in the medium's height, not a gradual elongation but an instantaneous growth of a foot or more. The woman who a moment before had been struggling to get out of her chair now towered over everyone, "Bellona with an Archaic smile," as Welkin apostrophized.

An assistant, a young lad who accompanied the Cawses on their tours and whose role it was to apply various tests that demonstrated the authenticity of Newton's and Leibniz's phenomena, now came down the aisle and—a bit belatedly—knelt in front of Mrs. Caws to hold her feet to the floor. This was a normal procedure, and usually she suffered it gladly, even humming softly to herself to pass the time while the boy went to an adjoining room to fetch a yardstick and step ladder to measure off her height. "But tonight," Welkin wrote, "she, or rather Newton, kicked the assistant away, snarling curses, or what sounded like curses, in Latin, as well, we fear, as some epithets in English which decency shrinks from repeating.

"As she stamped about, her innate modesty and graciousness obliterated for the moment by the strong emotions of Sir Isaac, she swung her foot to land a final blow on the unfortunate youngster's posterior, and for an instant we caught sight of her boot, the laces of which had burst under pressure. The kick delivered, she tottered unsteadily and bent down to grab the chair for support, but before she could do so she elongated again, so that the top of her head nearly brushed against the ceiling. As she stood there, swaying, arms flailing wildly, she seemed a grotesque combination of windmill and caryatid. Such is the sacrifice this gallant lady makes for her Calling."

From his new-found eminence, Newton threw down a challenge:

"How much is 74,368 ½ divided by 19.207693, multiplied by the square root of 18.1 then cubed? How much, eh? How much?"

Leibniz had been smoking contentedly, reclining in the air on one elbow, apparently unaware of Newton's Growing Act. Now he cocked his head upward and met his rival's glare.

"3," he answered affably. "Some laughing man is happy."

"Buffoon," said Newton. "You haven't the faintest idea. Very well: if q = -0.000541708 divided by 11.16196, and r = 0.061, what is $9r$ squared + $13q$?"

"Peter stands handsomely. Man is not stone."

"Idiot. Define 'analysis by infinite equations.'"

"*Nec obstat, quod forte maxima pars eorum in aliis occasionibus typis descripta prostet*, of course. Everyone knows that. Nothing could be simpler. But really," Leibniz continued, rolling over on his back and gazing up at Newton, who was beginning to shake, "why should we waste our time expounding trifles, amusing as they no doubt are for our hearers, when the whole subject can be stated so succinctly and easily in a few basic axioms? For example:

"Every body continues in its state of rest, or of uniform motion in a right line, unless it is compelled to change that state by forces impressed upon it.

"The change of motion is proportional to the motive force impressed; and is made in the direction of the right line in which that force is impressed.

"To every action there is always opposed an equal and opposite reaction: or, the mutual actions of two bodies upon each other are always—"

"Scoundrel! Plagiarist!" Newton shrieked. He turned to the audience. "The swine is using my words! My very words, from my very own *Principia*, fouling them with his filthy tongue. Did I not always say he was a plagiarist? This proves my case—does it not, ladies and gentlemen? You Heavens, I call on you to judge!" Mrs. Caws tried to raise her arms but nearly fell again, only saving herself by backing into a corner.

"Oh, I wouldn't expect too much of the Heavens, you know," said Leibniz, letting his cigar drop and lacing his fingers together behind his head. The Heavens have been very unreliable of late. I have a better idea; you yourself just gave it to me: why not let these good people here help us out?"

In one smooth motion he rolled over again and dropped to the floor, landing lightly on his feet. "My friends," he said, walking back and forth, peering out into the crowd as if to make contact with each onlooker individually, "what you have witnessed this evening, while it seems no doubt extraordinary, even thrilling perhaps, beguiling at the very least but above all, if I do not mistake myself, unique in your experience—what you have witnessed is, to the two of us, mere drudgery, the tedious rote of a debate carried on between us, living and dead, for over a century, with no resolution in sight. We seem at loggerheads in perpetuity. I say Titius is writing, Caius is writing. Sir Isaac denies it. It is obvious to me, indeed I cannot see how anyone in his senses would question it, that her skin is A, that milk is A. Yet he rejects it outright; of her skin and of milk he cares nothing. That there is a possible Adam whose posterity is of a certain sort, and an infinity of possible Adams whose posterity would be otherwise, to me admits of no doubt. But Sir Isaac will have none of it; he insists on his massy, hard, impenetrable particles. And so it goes, my friends, so it goes, through the whole universe of material and immaterial creatures taken together, or taken singly, from the beginning of things till the end, we can find no point of agreement."

He shook his head sadly, and went on.

"You, however, have it in your power to save us. Yes, you, here in this room tonight, can lift this burden from our shoulders. By a simple expedient, brought to glorious fruition by this great republic in which we now find ourselves, you can actually stop fate in its tracks: you can take a vote on it."

The audience murmured uncertainly.

"Yes! Merely by exercising your inalienable democratic rights—and for this special occasion the ladies present may cast their votes as well as the gentlemen—you can put an end to our debate and even—perhaps—give our spirits their freedom. 2 + 2 = 4! The sword is Evander's! Simply indicate by your ballots, or by a voice vote if you like, which one of us you prefer. The concept of Adam contains everything that can be attributed to him. Hail, Adam! We who have died salute you! Our future, ladies and gentlemen, is in your hands. Just remember: a vote for Leibniz is a vote for sanity. *Sympnoia panta.* I thank you."

Abruptly, he turned his back on the audience, went to his chair and sat, hands in lap, eyes closed, just as he had at the start of the séance. Mrs. Caws remained standing, wedged against the wall, a smile still fixed on her face.

Immediately the audience became animated. Small groups gathered, hotly debating the merits of their favorites. "Not even a real snake" … "A double backwards somersault" … "Milk is A" … "Area of a hyperbola" … "Fifty-two figures": these and other cries filled the air. At last a voice vote was taken. The din was deafening for both contestants. Next a show of hands was tried, with Mr. Lox, the acorn painter, deputed to do the counting. The result was a tie. Another vote was taken, and another, but still the tie was unbroken. Finally, paper ballots were employed, and this time Leibniz was determined to have won by a single vote.

Cheers and groans went up in equal measure. Mrs. Caws sank to the floor, her smile transferred to her husband. Someone threw an apple at the doctor. It went wide of the mark, striking Mr. Lox in the back of the head. More apples followed, from all over the room; evidently the Newtonians had come prepared. Enraged, the Leibnizians retorted with a volley of chairs. The Newtonians took to their heels, some running home to get their guns. Others rallied around Jon Patrick Sheehan, who led them across the street to the Pig and Bladder Tavern, where they vowed to hold out till reinforcements came in from outlying districts. Sensing that victory was in its grasp if it acted quickly, the Leibniz faction stormed the tavern, pounding on the door with clubs and chair legs, shouting "Milk is A! Milk is A!" in unison. "Mastered trigonometry in two days!" the Newtonians shouted back, and barred the entry with planks. Someone in the Leibniz camp ran up with a torch, throwing it through an open window at the back of the building. Soon the whole tavern was ablaze. The Newtonians staggered choking into the street, colliding with a cadre of their friends who had come up with rifles to raise the siege.

The Cawses, meanwhile, left alone in the Lyceum, had returned to normal awareness. Mrs. Caws was her usual size again, and stood by her chair exchanging pleasantries with the doctor. They were about to take their leave (they had a carriage waiting for them in the alley behind the hall) when they were distracted by the sight of flames coming from across the street. They went over to the front window to investigate.

"I always loved a good fire," Mrs. Caws confided to me forty-five years later in her Wyncote home. "So did Eggbeater. Especially when we could get close enough to feel the heat of it on our faces. Doesn't it make you turn all to jelly inside, dearie? It always did me."

They stood and watched the blaze for quite some time. Only the sound of rifle fire from the advancing Newtonians roused them from this new trance. Quickly they slipped out the back and made good their escape.

It was only a few miles from the Lyceum to Prospect St. "We didn't waste any time looking at the stars, either," the medium said, "not with all that shooting going on." But the fire had been "wonderful for us," she went on, and not only the fire but "the feeling we both had, deep down inside us," that they themselves must somehow have been the cause of it. There was none of the drained feeling and queasiness that so often overtook them after séances. On the contrary, as they sashayed, arm in arm, across the threshold of Number 18, they felt positively frisky. "'You know, I could do the whole evening over again, right this minute,' Eggbeater told me—which was pretty funny in itself, because he didn't have any better idea than I did what the 'whole evening' would have consisted of. Do you know what he said next, dearie? No, of course you don't. He said, 'By the way, sweetheart, did you hear them shouting "Milk is A! Milk is A!" outside the Bladder? What was that all about, anyway? Dumbest thing I ever heard of, to say at a fire.'

"'Well, you know Rowley,' I said. 'What can you expect?' But I couldn't get that fire out of my mind. 'Wasn't it something, though, Eggbeater, how fast that old building went up? Woosh! Oh, there's nothing like a fire, is there, to put you right with the world.'

"'Nothing, love. Let's have a drink.'

"'Let's have ten drinks!' I shouted. 'Hurrah! Let's have drinks to two and fifty figures!' Now, wasn't that something, dearie? I had no idea what I was saying, but when I read Jerry's article the next day, there it was, big as life. 'Milk is A,' too. Eggbeater and I used to do that all the time—we'd never have known it, either, if it hadn't been for Jerry's pieces. What a memory that boy had. I never saw the like and never expect to. Do you know that once, when we were in Europe, he rattled off every single—What? Oh. Well, as I was saying, I shouted 'Hurrah' and all the rest of it, and went into the pantry to get something to drink, you know, some sherry or something, why not make this special? Why not have one on Papa? Yes, Papa. Remember I told you, dearie, the summer before he died Papa had made some sort of liquor in his laboratory? He called it 'The Elixir,' but it smelled a lot like gin to me. The Aunts and I had taken bottles and bottles of it out to the barn right after he died, along with the rest of his things. I'd forgotten all about that. All right, I thought, we'll have some of Papa's gin. I took a lantern, ran out to the barn, rummaged around and found a bottle, then scampered back to the house as quick as I could. Lord, was I excited!

"'Where've you been all this time, girl?' Eggbeater asked.

"'Sweetheart,' I said, 'I have been out to the barn and—that nature may be lasting—I have brought back a treat.'

"'So I see. What is it?'

"'Papa's gin.'

"'Papa's gi—?'

"'Yes—Papa made it in his laboratory. Remember that laboratory I told you about? Where we have the cabinet now? That's right. Well, I just remembered he made some gin there. And you and I, my love, are going to try it.' I opened the bottle. 'We'll drink to Matter—Matter in massy, hard, impenetrable particles, my Rising Leibniz. And '—and I'm not sure I didn't rub up against him, dearie, in fact I'm sure I did, as I was feeling awfully frisky—'we'll do it by the fluxional method, we will, and afterwards go upstairs and compute the area of a hyperbola! Come on, love! To Matter!' I took a swig and handed him the bottle.

"He was laughing at me so hard he almost dropped it. 'Efficiency,' he said, 'I have to admit—half the time I haven't the ghost of a notion what you're talking about. But what the hell, Milk is A, I always say. And gin is gin. To Matter!' And he knocked back about a quarter of a pint.

"'Say,' he said, when he'd finished choking. 'What is this, anyway?'

"'I told you, love: it's Papa's gin.'

"'Gin? Tastes like Philalethes' Powder to me.'

"'Philalethes' what?'

"'Powder.'

"'What the hell's that?'

"'Oh, nothing. Just an old Elixir I used to know. Here, sweetheart, let me have some more. To Matter!'

"'To Matter!'

"'To Matter!'

"'To Matter!'

"Oh, those were great days, dearie, great, great days!"

The Cry of the Gehirngespinstgemach:

CLKCLKCLKCLKCLKCLKCLKCLKCLKCLKCLKCLK Thelonious Monk will record "Well, You Needn't" in 1954. Miles Davis will record "I Didn't" in 1955. The neurotubules and filaments in the axoplasm of Efficiency's pineal gland go into a dance of ecstasy, as the contents of Sir Isaac's chemical vessel react with each other and the Red Man and his White Wife complete their conjunction. Mercury mixes with salts of Saturn and the Net of Vulcan spreads over all, moisture clouding the surface of the glass. A swollen stream of melatonin courses through the vessel's tubing and debouches into her blood. About to pour another drink, she is overtaken unexpectedly by a deep yawn. The decanter is suddenly too much of a weight; she sets it down again on the floor. You know, sweet, she says, something just occurred to me. I wonder if Jerry has any psychic ability. With those purple eyes, you know, he might very well. Purple is a very *psychic* color, everyone says so. Very spiritual. So *sensitive*, Jerry always seemed to me. That's what people used to mistake for shyness—his sensitivity. And sensitivity is *so* important for psychic work. She yawns again. But even if he doesn't have any—psychic ability, I mean—maybe we—you and I, that is—maybe we could still use him in the act: he could sit beside us, with his notebook, and write down everything Uncle Isaac says. He's really *such* a good reporter, lovey, when he's not being distracted by idiots. So accurate, so *faithful*. And what a memory! Frankly, sweetheart, it begins to look very much as if there will be a place for him in the troupe, because—much as I hate to say it—and you above all people know how I've struggled against admitting it—we're going to have to put Eggbeater away. There. I've said it, it's out in the open now. And a good thing, too. Because it's the truth, the simple truth, and the sooner we—you and I, that is—the sooner we—you and I—the sooner ... Her eyelids flicker and close; her head drops onto her chest.

Newton is there by the furnace. "That's right, my plum pudding," he whispers to her, "that's the way, my kumquat, my orange slice. Now's the time, sweet sister-to-be in the Art, my lovely Soror Mystica of the Champagne and Sherry." He pinches the tubing gently where it attaches to the vessel's spout. "The hour is finally at hand, the hour you've been waiting for—time of uncleane thoughts, words and actions and dreames. He caresses his groin. Go to sleep, sister dearest, and awaken to a radiant new dawn. The air abounds with acid vapors fit to promote fermentations. The ferment consoles bodies, amplifies unions. Let Eggbeater boil in his own cauldron. Come into the laboratory with me, I can show you the Egg of the Philosophers. Let Welkin, too, fall by the wayside; I'll give you Heaven in a Stone. What does either of them know of beauty, of splendor? Have they ever seen the colors of the Peacock's Tail, or watched Mercury grow white in its last sublimations? Have they caught sight of the divine Rebis, or come upon the secret entrance to our Garden of Wisdom, where an apple tree grows with fruits of gold? Do they suspect even one half of one million-millionth of the strength of that unifier of contradictories, the omni-puissant Green Lion, or know what methods to use to hunt Him and run Him to earth? No, my savory snuggle-pet, they do not. They hunt with a bow that has no string. Listen to me, my dovey Diana, listen and turn to me, your sugar-Uncle Isaac, my honeycomb, my rose petal, my fur bush. I can give you an unguent coagulated from a warm and subtle nature. I can make it penetrate from part to part. It is a generating Stone, an aid to the Elixir. It will make you happy beyond your wildest dreams."

"Thank you *ever so much* for dropping by, my dear sir. It was a very great honor, for *both* of us. Be sure to come back tomorrow evening, now, to see the Oracle."

Shit! Efficiency opens her eyes. Shit, piss and cornbread! Eggbeater's out there saying goodbye. Jerry's leaving. God damn it, I've got to see him before he gets away again. Got to talk to him. Jesus, why the hell didn't I do it this morning when I had the chance? Why did I have to be so coy, blowing cigar smoke all over the place like a Goddamn grand duke? And now that I'm going to—now that Jerry and I are going to—oh, Jesus, I've got to get out there right now. She tries to rise, but another yawn cuts her off; she sinks back onto the settee. A soft, greenish light dances in the air around the chemical vessel; slowly it turns pale blue, then citron, then rose, as melatonin continues to rush through the tubing. The itch in her forehead grows worse. Jesus, Mary and God, she says. Jesus, Mary and God.

"Let be, strawberry, let be," Newton whispers. "It's only nature. Nature delights in nature, nature rules over nature, nature subdues nature. I can show you the Sophic Hydrolith, love. It flows like water, but it makes not wet. It is conceived below the earth, born in the earth, quickened in Heaven. It is sweet, beautiful, clear, limpid and brighter than gold, silver, carbuncles or diamonds. It is the fountain of all perfection in the whole world. And it will be yours, dearest sister, yours and mine together. All you need to do is sleep, my lily pad, my lotus, my palm frond, sleep is the road that takes you there. Turn to me, Efficiency, and you will be luminous as a star, fair as the moon with the sun hidden inside her, and our night will be light as the day in its pleasures, yellow and red as the rising dawn. Length of days and health will be in your right hand, and in your left hand glory, my peach, and infinite riches. Your—"

Oh, not now, Uncle Isaac, please, please not now. I've got to get out there to Jerry. Stop it, now, stop it. She tries to rub at her forehead, but her fingers come away thick and numb. She feels the itch widen, it grows warm and strangely comforting.

Her eyes close again, and immediately she is enveloped by a leafy, humid night, smelling of earth and flowers and swamp water. In the darkness she imagines her forehead opening the way the plaster did in her father's ceiling, great jagged cracks to let the apples through. "Yes, my love, you are right," Newton tells her, and now his voice is coming not from inside her head but directly behind her left shoulder, a soft, animal sound, insistent but full of affection, every syllable a love pat in the tropical closeness. "You are right as right can be; your forehead will open, and open wide, to let through the ray of sunshine that will change the world. When Athena breaks out of Jupiter's head, the gold drops into the retort like a rain shower. But before this can happen, dear, you must sleep, sleep in order to awaken. Come to me, sweet, you are almost there. It's only one more turn, my silkskin, my nuzzlefuzz, my doe eyes, my jam jar. The Great Work's here, and we two alone can perform it. Two equal salts carry up Saturn. The eagle carries Jupiter up. Come to me, Efficiency, come to me now, we'll make Jupiter fly on his eagle."

CLKCLK CLKCLK CLKCLK. Outdoors in the sunlight Jeremy Welkin, still dapper despite his morning's carousal, closes the gate to the Caws property behind him and starts off at a brisk pace down Prospect St., his mind on his deadline and on summer afternoons long ago. Watching him leave is Eggbeater, his big oval body bobbing peacefully up and down, at ease in the air about six inches above the walk. He stirs his drink with his chicken feather, comfortably cogitating the immortality of monads, the respect in which Titius is a slayer, and the deeply romantic strain in Miss Nightingale's being. Inside the house, Efficiency Caws has fallen asleep again, this time on the settee instead of under it, breathing quietly, hands folded in her lap, head on her chest, lips slightly parted. The breeze through the window plays with a strand of red-gold hair that has come unpinned and hangs down in front of her face. The decanter on the floor is almost empty. Deep in the inner space behind her eyelids, exploring the nerve fibers and dense-cored vesicles in the soft, spongy flesh of her pineal gland, following the sound of a voice she feels she has known all her life, she stumbles on an entrance into the parenchyma and makes an alarming discovery.

"YOU'RE not Uncle Isaac!" she exclaims.

"NICOLAS FATIO!" Newton fires back. "What are *you* doing here?"

At the corner of Prospect and Main Sts., Jeremy Welkin stops. He goes left, down Main to Washington, then left again, doubling back to the Caws house.

From the bridge out on High St. comes the sound of a dog barking.

The Dog! The Dog! The DOG!

12

OF MATERIAL AND IMMATERIA CREATURES.
CHIMERICAL NOTIONS.

The Encyclopaedia of Reincarnation:

METAKYNOS (also known as Kozei, Sabala, Cynosarges and, since early modern times, *Der Geisthund*), an ancient deity associated with the afterlife, who usually takes the form of some species of canine. Evidence of his worship is found in the myths and artifacts of various civilizations from Greece to the Indus Valley. Vestiges also appear in Siberia, Southeast Asia and parts of North America. His cult was well established in the region around Miletus by the beginning of the first millennium B.C.; Horstmann found theriomorphic statuary of the god while conducting excavations near the temple of Artemis at Didyma, a few miles from Miletus, during the summer of 1903. A shrine belonging to Metakynos has also been uncovered on Samos, not far from the temple of Pythian Apollo. In his cult at Athens, Metakynos was identified with Cynosarges, the mysterious white dog who ran in and stole the first portion of meat sacrificed at the dedication of the new gymnasium just south of the Olympieum, on the left bank of the Ilisus, thereby giving his name not only to the building but also to the Cynic school of philosophy, since the school's founder, Antisthenes, held forth there.

Cuneiform inscriptions from Persepolis, dating from the late Achaemenian period, mention Metakynos and his priests a number of times, most often in connection with the goddess Anahita, one of the primary deities of Mazdaism. In recent years, however, Alex Muschel has contended that worship of the god can be found much farther back, in the Neolithic era. Excavations conducted during the early 1960s by James Mellaart at Çatal Höyük in Anatolia revealed the ruins of a town nearly 9,000 years old, with numerous buildings whose walls were decorated with frescoes of animals. In one room there were also limestone statuettes of male and female deities, including one showing a boy riding a leopard; Mellaart dubbed this figure the "Master of the Animals." Muschel asserts that the boy is, in fact, none other than Metakynos, depicted in human form, and goes on to find other representations of the god in the paintings and sculpture at the site. Metakynos' appearance as a dog, he maintains, is merely "late, and decadent." This view has found favor in some quarters; however, Carlson, Rune-Smith and others have argued tellingly against it, and Muschel has yet to receive wide support. Carlson herself identifies Metakynos with Kozei, the Kamchatkan dog who causes earthquakes. Rune-Smith makes a good *prima facie* case for the red dog sacred to the Kalangs of Java as a manifestation of the god. A confirmed cultural diffusionist, he also finds evidence of the god in myths of the Eskimos and Pottawatomies, as well as the Massachusetts Indians, who tell of a dog that stands guard at the gates of Paradise. Nevertheless, his proposal for the god's place of origin—Stor Oya, a tiny island in the Barents Sea—has found as little support among his colleagues as the theories of Muschel.

Other aspects of Metakynos' lineage are more firmly established. In the *Atharva-Veda* he appears as Sabala, one of the four-eyed dogs of Yama, god of the dead. In the *Avestas* he is a white dog with yellow ears, posted at the head of the Chinvat Bridge, which stretches between this world and the next, who "with his barking drives away the fiend from the souls of the holy ones, lest he should drag them to hell" (Darmesteter, 1895). An older Magian tradition gives Metakynos the same function, but makes him a gigantic angel; eight hundred parasangs tall, with a proud canine head, he stands erect on the bridge, golden light streaming from his fur, his wings reflecting all the colors of the spectrum. His muzzle is yellow and white and his teeth shine like stars. Butter drips constantly from his tongue.

After the sixth century B.C. Metakynos' mythos is usually linked to that of the *Gehirngespinstgemach* (or *apeiron chorion*, as the Milesians call it) and much of the extant literature comes from Greek sources. However, the earliest Ionian texts borrow heavily from the Magian version, especially at the beginning of the story. According to the Magian recension, the *Gehirngespinstgemach* and Metakynos are brothers, emanations of the Voice that is the Creative Logos of Ohrmazd, the Lord of Wisdom. Metakynos is the angel described above. The *Gehirngespinstgemach*, on the other hand, is referred to only as *jism ta'limi*, which Corbin (1977) translates as a "mathematical solid body," dark and dense, of unspecified size and shape. Sworn to do their duty faithfully, the brothers are posted side by side on the Chinvat Bridge, judging the souls of the departed, mixing severity (the sphere of the *Gehirngespinstgemach*) with mercy (the sphere of Metakynos) in proportions suitable to each case. When the catastrophe comes (caused, in the Magian account, by a brief fluctuation in the Voice of Ohrmazd; Greek writers of the Classical period ascribe it to a sudden tremor in the Unmoved Mover), there is a violent shaking all along the bridge as the whole structure rocks on its base. The *Gehirngespinstgemach* loses its balance and falls, plummeting through the ten Intelligences, the eighteen thousand worlds and the seventy thousand veils of light and darkness until it finds itself born into the world of created things as a room without windows. Metakynos, though tossed about, manages to stand fast. But he, too, soon leaves his post, out of compassion, the story goes, for his fallen brother. He dives into the world, in order to find the *Gehirngespinstgemach* and bring him back to the Empyrean. He sees the monad far below, a black dot in a swirl of mist. He watches as the dot falls toward the town of Miletus, and sees Lipnike and Thales there in the well. It is Metakynos' intention to be born from the same womb as the *Gehirngespinstgemach*, to become his earthly twin as well as his heavenly one, and he follows the monad as fast as he can. But the few Empyreal moments that have elapsed between the *Gehirngespinstgemach's* fall and his own make a substantial difference in mundane reckoning: when Metakynos enters Lipnike's womb, sixteen years have gone by, and his father is not Thales but a Thracian mercenary soldier by the name of Gyges. Furthermore, to the angel's chagrin, he emerges into the world not as the splendid, omnipotent creature he had been on the Bridge, but as an unprepossessing, medium-sized yellow and white dog of mixed breed. Thus, despite his considerable intelligence and seemingly limitless zeal, his capacity for influencing events is severely diminished. Undeterred, however, he sets off in search of his erstwhile companion. But he meets with no success, then or later. He is searching for his brother still, the Milesians say. Meanwhile, they add, the Bridge remains unattended, and the world goes from bad to worse.

TRUE TALES OF THE PARANORMAL:

It was three days after Christmas. Fritz Eichhorn had been dead a month. A hospital attendant took Empedocles Schwank his breakfast as usual—seven eggs, scrambled, a bowl of marmalade, and coffee. Schwank was standing beside the bed as he always did, in his zoot suit and red tie. "Very formal he always dressed," the attendant said. "And very nice. Never gave any trouble. Not like some." He put the breakfast tray down on the worktable, beside the metal skull and take-up reel. When he turned back, Schwank had a thick sheaf of papers in his hand. "Ain't no more on that thing," he said, indicating the skull. "Here—give these to Zigzag. Better take the Oracle too." "Zigzag was what he called Dr. Zeisig," the attendant explained. "I did as he asked, skull and all. When I came back later for the breakfast things, he was gone. Hadn't touched his food. Took his typewriter with him. We never saw him again."

The next day, Zeisig got a letter. Typed all in capitals, it read:

DEAR ZIGZAG. JUST COULDN'T MAKE IT HERE ANY LON-GER, BABY. NO OFFENSE, YOU DIG IT, BUT I NEVER SHOULDA FALLEN UP HERE IN THE FIRST PLACE. GOTTA MAKE THE REAL WORLD, GOTTA FIND PREZ. DON'T BOTHER LOOKIN' FOR ME. LATER. –E.

PS: YOU GET THOSE PAPERS ALL RIGHT? BETTER GIVE 'EM TO WHAT'S-HIS-NAME, SQUIRREL MAN'S SHRINK. FIELD MOUSE, I THINK, OR HAZELNUT. AND THAT SKULL, TOO. YEAH. HE WOULDA WANTED IT THAT WAY."

Zeisig did as instructed. "These papers are for you, sir," she wrote Hasel-maus, "along with that awful metal thing. Empedocles asked that they be sent to you, and I do so.

"This is my last official act in this hospital. I am resigning my position, effective today. It would be too painful to stay longer. Empedocles is gone, and nothing can bring him back. The Real World, which he so often spoke of, has marked him for Its own.

"Did you ever meet Empedocles, sir? He was a magnificent being, flawed, as who is not, but magnificent nonetheless. I visited him often here; it was not, strictly speaking, a part of my duties as an epidemiologist, but I took, let us say, an extra interest in his case. I was sure, I still am sure, that he was deeply wounded in some way, far back in his remote past, and that his present confusions were due to a resurgence of that wound, and that I could help him. Did you know, sir, that he claimed to be 335 years old? *That* much past is remote enough for anyone, is it not? –Especially as he did not look a day over sixty, if that, and the hospital could find no records of his existence at all! Even the tests they did on his person registered nothing—heart, lungs, brain, even his height and weight—a complete blank! The egomaniac Eichhorn—please pardon me, sir, I know Eichhorn was your patient, and in any case one should not speak ill of the dead, but I cannot conceal my dislike of that man, so smug, so in love with himself, so pushy—the pathological Eichhorn claimed that Empedocles was an homunculus, as perhaps you already know, which is not only disgusting but even more ridiculous than the notion that he was 335 years old! But to me, good sir, he was simply Empedocles. If he was also psychotic, it was a psychosis made in heaven. I flatter myself that I understood him, at least to some extent, and I think he understood me. He certainly effected a change in me. I used to be very studious, serious—well, I still am, of course, one must be accurate and thorough in my profession, but what I mean is that I was that way all the time, without letup. Empedocles made me see that the lighter side of things has a place, too. It is not just for hare brains. He played his music for me. I pretended to like it, though in truth I could hear nothing in it; it made the most awful racket when it was not plain silly. But what I said about it seemed to please him; he told me I was *Hüfte*. I still don't know what he meant by that, surely not just the laterally projecting prominence of the pelvis? But he said that was what I was, and he laughed, so I told him he was the same, and that a bird lived, which was another thing he said a lot. I keep that as my best remembrance of him, sir, our laughing and being *Hüfte* together."

13

Animal Spirits.
The Moistness and Flexibility of Her Tongue.
Four Miles of Beds.
The Crimea Inches Past Leibniz.

The Cry of the Gehirngespinstgemach:

CHCHJJJCHCHCHJJJJJJJJJJJJJJJJJJJJJJCHCHCHCHCHCHCHCHCH-
CHCHJJJCHCH Images of the divine essence, divine thought and divine
will, continue to dance: Lee Wiley will record "Sugar" in 1940. Bobby Hack-
ett will record "New Orleans" in 1944. CHCHCHCHCHCH The dog continues to bark. "Oh, yes, my dear Eggbeater," says Leibniz, speaking from
his study in the doctor's pineal gland while the doctor himself stands in the
air above the paving stones of his walk, looking absently down on the space
recently vacated by Jeremy Welkin. "Oh, yes, I quite agree with you about
what you call Miss Nightingale's 'romanticism.' It is absolutely fundamental
to her character, *un principe primitif de son être*, and must have been especially
noticeable at the time you knew her, although more recent events have possibly tended to obscure the fact. How old did you say she was then? Seventeen
or so, if I remember rightly. Ah, the idealism of seventeen! The uncorrupted
aspiration! Her face—how did you put it, Eggbeater, when we were talking
the other day? Ah, yes: her whole face, you said, was 'incandescent,' with an

ardency CHCHCHCH with an ardency all the more affecting for the lack of a channel—or 'mission,' to use her word—to give it direction. But there was a wildness in her as well, wasn't there, old friend, a passion that was almost, well, *improper* in its intensity, or that was, at any rate, quite unconventional. 'Animal' is the word that comes to mind; it is not too strong, I think, not too strong at all, ladylike though she usually seemed."

Leibniz grins, and leans back in his chair. "Do you remember the way she behaved that time at the opera, when all her family and friends were giving themselves over so unthinkingly to the gaiety of the occasion? Not, of course, that she wasn't gay herself. But you were struck, weren't you, by the underlying seriousness in her demeanor—the slight impatience she showed, for example, the abrupt shake of her head when declining an offer of refreshment, or the sharp clipped voice she used now and then in answering a question. It didn't require your skill in magnetism to surmise that so far as she was concerned, merry-making was not an end in itself but merely a preliminary phase in the proceedings, a necessary but hardly significant ritual to be gotten through as quickly as possible before the real business at hand commenced. And as soon as the curtain went up, while the others were still gabbling away, she passed into another state entirely—just as if you *had* magnetized her, old boy—completely immersed in the music and in rapt identification with the characters on stage.

"And what a performance it was! *Das Gehirngespinstgemach*, Coturno's revival of old Halbstiefel's warhorse. Think back on it, Eggbeater. A splendid event, was it not? The talk of all Florence that spring, and a far cry, I must say, from the original production, which I happened to see in Nuremberg in a cold and drafty hall, during the autumn of 1666. I don't think there were more than a dozen of us in the audience, and one soon understood why." Leibniz chuckles. "The performance was a shambles. The girl playing Lipnike couldn't sing at all. True, she was pretty enough; in fact, she was enormously attractive, quite stunningly beautiful, so that I, who was just twenty at the time, was completely—did you know that I had a son, Eggbeater? Oh, yes, to be sure, I did, and that lovely girl was his mother, but that is not my point at the moment. My point is the extreme primitiveness of that early production. For not only could the girl not sing, but no one else in the cast could either. The only exception was the bass, who sang the title role, and his acting was abominable—although how an actor, even a good one, should go about playing a room I admit I couldn't say. But what a brilliant transformation Coturno made of the piece, eh? Magnificent. Of course, he did change the plot a good deal. Oh, yes, Eggbeater, it was considerably altered. He made Lipnike, for instance, much more admirable, more *pure* in her motivations. You really ought to look up the original sometime; I doubt if you'd find the libretto, but Acanthus of Rhodes, as I recall, was the author of the text that Halbstiefel worked from. Your wife—that is to say, the excellent-in-some-ways-having-to-do-with-appearance-and-physicality-but-otherwise-coprophagous-Newton—your wife's grandfather began a translation of Acanthus, if I'm not mistaken, although he soon gave it up as too trivial to bother with. Which it certainly was, there can be no question about that. Still, one likes the old stories, trivial or not, and I confess a sentimental attachment to that one.

"But Coturno did a superb job of work. And how Miss Nightingale thrilled to it! Remember the scene on the dock at Miletus, after Lipnike had escaped from the clutches of Thales, only to be parted forever from her new lover Gyges? How the tears welled up in those soulful, grey, seventeen-year-old eyes as the music swelled to a climax and Lipnike sang the great aria, *Mi sento stordito*, from the prow of the merchant ship as it set sail for Samos! How tightly she gripped your arm, right there in the opera box with her family—who were still gibbering nonsense to each other—when Gyges came on a moment later and found the ship gone, and the curtain fell for the end of the act. You turned to her then, you told me; she was staring straight ahead, tears streaming down her face, and she was yipping, yes, *yipping*, emitting little animal noises while the rest of the house burst into applause. She kept hold of your arm for a long time after that, right through the interval. You were not unaffected yourself, as I recall. What a pair of romantics! What a pair of animals!

"But that was nothing new for you, was it, old friend?" Leibniz smiles, and takes a dark German chocolate from the box at his elbow. "Hasn't that always been a characteristic of the women who've attracted you (and whom you've attracted as well, for you've been far from unsuccessful in that respect)—the wildness, I mean, which bursts out unexpectedly from within a decorous exterior? It indicates, at bottom, a connection to the Divine, and a healthy one at that, yet a vulnerability sometimes accompanies it, and a feeling of lostness, both of which are so frequently (inevitably?) the handmaidens of animal spirits in the advanced civilization of your day. I think, for instance, of Frau Hauffe, the Seeress. A simple girl, the daughter of a gamekeeper, conventional in every way, married to a husband she did not love: there must have been thousands like her. But she was also prone to the most remarkable visions, and there were not thousands of women like that. She made the most astounding pronouncements on everything under the sun (on the sun itself, if I remember correctly, and its proper place in the general order of things) and all that she said came straight from the heart of some knowing, some instantaneous perception, far faster than logical thought, and far outside the boundaries of her ordinary, her very ordinary, life. In this she was like a young lady I knew of in Germany, one Rosamunde von der Asseburg, who was in every other respect a sober-minded person, who believed from her childhood that she spoke to Jesus Christ and that she was in fact his wife. The theologians in my country wanted to punish her, though in Spain she would have been another St. Teresa. Perhaps it would have been so with Frau Hauffe.

"But Rosamunde von der Asseburg was in good health; in the Seeress' case her visions were eating her alive. By the time you met her, Eggbeater, she was bedridden, and under a doctor's care. So your courtship, an illicit passion with even more obstacles than usual, as you had not only a husband but a physician to circumvent, called for unprecedented methods of secrecy. And you found them, didn't you, the two of you together? Numbers! Who would have thought it? You whispered sweet nothings—or something's, I suppose one should say, numbers are certainly not nothings—in numbers to each other, for hours at a time. Now, in my opinion that required a cunning deeper than our merely human faculties can manage: only contact with our animal faculties can bring it off. I really must congratulate you both. Though you didn't know me then, Eggbeater, I certainly knew you. I was, and still am one of your most fervent admirers. I don't think I've *ever* heard the Fibonacci series employed with such exquisite eroticism."

Leibniz helps himself to another chocolate. "And that wife of yours," he continues, "so long as we're on the subject, the exasperating and often opprobrious Newton, who holds such seriously mistaken opinions on vortices and vacuums, to cite but two examples among a myriad: granted that conversing in numbers holds little or no interest for her; granted further that her susceptibility to the charms of romantic music and literature appears to be non-existent; but was it not her vitalistic high spirits, the eager canine vivacity in a society of New England primness, that attracted you initially—along, of course, with her auburn hair and other outstanding accomplishments, not to mention quite a nice fortune? Oh, yes, you've been joined to the animals all your life, and they to you. I need not even mention the flock of sheep that followed you out of that village in France. Just look at those squirrels gazing up at you this minute. I do wonder what that dog wants."

The dog continues to bark. Jeremy Welkin, having completed his walk down Washington St., approaches the Caws house from the rear. Pausing only briefly to make sure Eggbeater is still outside, he enters by the back door and proceeds as quickly as he can on tip-toe through the kitchen, pantry and dining room into the sitting room, where he finds Efficiency asleep on the settee. He puts out his hand to touch her, then thinks better of it. He reaches instead into his coat pocket, takes out an envelope and places it on her hands where they lie folded in her lap. He looks down at her a moment, then turns and leaves the way he came.

"A stoop! A STOOP?!" says Sir Isaac in Efficiency's pineal. "I never had a stoop in my life, my dear. On the contrary, my posture has always been excellent. Your father's painting is a forgery. But you, my sweetest one ... " he pulls her to him on the brain sand " ... you really do bear ... only in certain lights, I'm sure, and the light in here is none too reliable ... but you really do bear the most astonishing resemblance to my dear friend Fatio ... " he touches her cheek "... especially around the mouth, I should say, your mouth and, uh, other things. Oh, please do not be offended, my angel. There was something quite feminine about Nicolas, it would have been easy to imagine him—as in fact I once did—in a gown ... or dress ... and possessed of your other, uh, extraordinary attributes. But really, what a piece of luck. Pure delight. More than I ever dared hope for."

"Oh, Uncle Isaac," says Efficiency, and runs her hand over his chest, "what a way you have about you. How could anyone be offended by you? I'm positively flattered. And to think that all these years I was sure you looked—why, you're positively handsome!"

CHCHCHCH. JJJJJ. 121,393 plus 75,025 is 196,418. Leibniz stretches his legs and puts his feet up on a cushioned footstool. He breathes a sigh of contentment. After all, he asks himself, what could be sweeter? Here he is, settled comfortably in his old, much-loved study, with the prospect before him of unlimited, uninterrupted thought and exposition: pure delight. Nor is his pleasure in any way diminished by the fact that the study, and he himself, are situated not where they once were, in the busy city of Hanover where he was Court Counselor to the Dukes of Brunswick, but in the tiny pineal gland of his present interlocutor, Dr. Caws. Why should such a trifle upset him? Leibniz once wrote that the least corpuscle contains a whole world of other creatures; another time, in jest, he allowed as how there might easily be some system similar to our own, which is nothing but the pocket watch of a very great giant. It is true, of course, that in the pineal he will not have the chance to avail himself of the stimulating conversation of his good friends, the Electress Sophie of Hanover and her daughter, Sophie-Charlotte, Queen of Prussia, but neither, on the other hand, will he be importuned by his last employer, the egregious Georg Ludwig, later George I of England. Besides, Dr. Caws has proven himself a more than affable host over the years. It is so gratifying, Leibniz reflects, to have a companion to whom one feels free to say absolutely *anything*! Moreover, he is certain that in this good if slightly bibulous doctor he has at last found the right person, or at least *a* person, to realize his dream, which he never achieved during his lifetime: the completion, in tangible form, of the alphabet of human thought, a universal system capable of defining, analyzing and combining all possible concepts, and, through a new means of calculation, of demonstrating their truth or falsehood with unerring objectivity. Dr. Caws, he is convinced, has the porousness required for such a project, the facility with numbers and—Leibniz hopes—sufficient manual skill to put together the machines that are needed. At this point, with one machine finished, it's largely a matter of pumping enough raw information into his host. Though bright enough in many respects, with a nimble and sometimes penetrating intelligence, Eggbeater is still woefully uneducated. Raw information is absolutely essential, and some knowledge of categories.

Taking his ease like a Turkish pasha or a king in China, Leibniz permits himself a deep, satisfying belch. He is dressed after his own desiring, not after the dictates of fashion—that is, for warmth and comfort, the way he used to receive the elite of Europe in the old days: in an old blue dressing gown lined with fox fur, stockings of the same color, also fur-lined, and a pair of ankle-length socks over the stockings, to favor the gout which he acquired in late middle age which, inexplicably, has not gone away with his death. (There is an open sore on his right leg as well, which still has not healed, after a hundred and fifty years. He treats it only with pieces of blotting paper, as he did of old.)

On his head is a huge, tightly curled black wig, out of fashion even in the early eighteenth century, which reaches down over his shoulders and chest. Before him, in the middle of the study, is a large oaken desk piled high with books and papers, with a number of bones and other curios distributed around them. A good many other books are stacked here and there on the floor. At his elbow is a nightstand, on it a cup of café latte (always about three-quarters full) and a box of dark German chocolates (never more than one-fifth empty). A fine Malacca walking stick leans against the arm of his chair, by his right hand. On the other side of the desk sits a big globe, supported by a stout wooden structure elaborately carved with angels and wind spirits.

Around him the walls of glandular connective tissue are covered with overlapping tapestries hanging in loose folds and decorated with mountains, rivers, oceans and plains, flowers, trees, birds, fish and animals, as well as episodes from history and religious scenes. Leibniz takes a sip of café latte and begins to talk again.

"But it doesn't stop with squirrels, old friend, nor with sheep, not by a turtle's age. As you've long been aware—I hope—thanks to our many conversations over the years, I do not hold with those who, like the estimable but slightly deluded Monsieur Descartes, deny souls to animals. Since no one takes offense at those who speak of permanently subsisting atoms, why should it be found strange that anyone should say the same of souls? Indivisibility, Eggbeater, belongs to souls by their nature, so that by combining the opinion of the Cartesians about substance and the soul with that of the whole world about the souls of beasts, it follows by necessity. It would be very difficult to uproot from the human species the opinion which is accepted at all times and everywhere—a universal opinion if ever there was one—that beasts have feelings.

"Animals and souls, Eggbeater, animals and souls." Leibniz watches a herd of gazelles race across the desert. They disappear into the folds of the tapestry, behind a scene of the Dormition of the Virgin. "All education—and yours, dear friend, is no exception—depends on a right understanding of animals and souls. For they begin only with the world and do not end any more than the world does. And anyone who sees [He fingers one of the curios on his desk, a fragment of mastodon bone he found in a cave in the Harz Mountains] the admirable structure of animals will find himself forced to recognize the wisdom of the author of things. Not only is the soul indestructible, but so is the animal itself, even though its mechanism may often perish in part, and cast off or put on organic coverings. Now you, being a man of science, will have had occasion to look through a microscope—No? You have not? Well, if you had, I'm sure you would have noticed, thanks to your, uh, fair mindedness and respect for objectivity (unlike, *par exemple*, the repellent and possibly Socinian Newton), I'm sure, I say, you would have noticed, as did my great contemporary Leeuwenhoek, whom I visited in Delft in the fall of 1676— You know, Eggbeater, [Leibniz is a little peeved with his student] you really *should* have a look through a microscope sometime, it would do you a world of good, especially considering the kind of medicine you've practiced, I don't mean magnetism, I mean your, uh, other activities—you would notice, as did Leeuwenhoek, the animals in miniature swarming preformed in the spermatic fluid. Preformed, mind you: heads, trunks, limbs and all. Not only was the organic body already present before conception, but there was also a soul in this body. In short, the animal itself was there, and through conception, contrary to what many nowadays think, this animal was merely prepared for a great transformation, in order to become an animal of a different kind. One sees something like this outside generation, as when worms become flies and caterpillars become butterflies."

Leibniz softens his tone. "Now, Eggbeater, please understand me. I don't mean to criticize your activities unduly. I don't mean, in fact, to criticize them at all. For, as the great physician William Harvey observed—he of the circulation of the blood—every child that comes into this world has three, not two parents: its father, its mother and God. And since all God's actions are founded on the principle of the fitness of things, and since he, like a good sculptor, will make from his block of marble only that which he judges to be the best, it follows that when a soul is prevented from entering the world in a body there must be good and sufficient reason for it. Besides, old friend, although since my death I've lost a certain amount of physical mobility (I can no longer travel from Hanover to Rome, say, as in days gone by, unless of course I do it in your company) I've also gained access to a certain amount of information normally concealed from the world of the living. And what I've learned gives me cause not merely to turn a blind eye on your exploits but positively to commend you for them. The dedication and courage you've shown have been exemplary, and under testing conditions to boot.[27]

"Nevertheless, Eggbeater, I think you should avail yourself of the microscope. As my dear friend Francis Mercury van Helmont wrote, 'The beauty of this Living Earth when seen through a microscope will make a man in Love with it.'" Leibniz picks up another bone, a thick, squarish fragment also found in the Harz, which several scientists identified as the back molar of a giant. "It gives you an understanding of scale, as well, and goes to show, if nothing else, the truth of the old Hermetic saying, 'As above, so below.' That is, a correspondence exists, a clear homology, between the largest,

---

[27] Leibniz is perfectly correct. The records of the Empyrean are full of praise for Dr. Caws and his work as an abortionist. Testimonials abound from souls who, but for his intervention, unquestionably would have undergone a further incarnation and thereby caused greater suffering not only to themselves but to an already afflicted planet. Such statements as, "I can never thank Dr. Caws enough, he helped me when I was unable to help myself"; "I can never forget the doctor's kindness, and this to a poor, insignificant foetus he hardly knew"; and "Eggbeater Caws is the finest medical man I never laid eyes on—the world would be a better place if there were more like him" are typical. In the best of all possible worlds he would be another St. Teresa. —*The Encyclopaedia of Reincarnation.*

farthest-reaching phenomena in the universe and the smallest, most localized ones. Indeed, in structure, the two often seem identical. Then, too, the microscope can provide if one chooses, a new and perhaps more enlightened view of human origins. I refer, of course, to the old notion that the testicles of Adam contain all the humans that are ever to come into existence. Now, thanks to the microscope, that can be seen differently—every man his own Adam, eh, Eggbeater? Well, I hardly think it need come to that, and in any case, before we get carried away with ourselves, there is the function of the ovaries to consider, but it certainly does give one to reflect, does it not?" Leibniz smiles indulgently at a woven scene of Caesar crossing the Rubicon.

"Now, Leeuwenhoek, you know, was not the only man to see those creatures in the sperm. There was van Ham, for one, Leeuwenhoek's assistant; he actually saw them first. Then there was Swammerdam, and a host of other microscopists. Some of them discerned such details as hair, teeth and nails. You may not credit this, my jaded sophisticate, but I have even heard of miniature frogs, lizards, and, some say, horses and cows being observed, as well as humans. Dear me, dear me; even Adam could not boast horses." Leibniz helps himself to a chocolate.

"Yes, in my youth there was a remarkable number of scientific investigators, keen attenders to organic phenomena, who made the most startling discoveries. There were Ruysch, Steno, de Graaf, Mentel. And Perrault, of course, Claude Perrault, whom I met in Paris when I was living there in the 'seventies. I'm sure you would have taken to Perrault, Eggbeater, he was a charming, intelligent man with a broad range of interests. I think you'd both have found you had a great deal in common. Your first practice was in Paris, was it not? And you loved the city, I think. Yes. The same as Perrault. The same as me, if it comes to that. What neighborhood did you live in, by the way? The Faubourg St. Germain? Fancy that; I too lived there. Quartier de Luxembourg? No! What street? La Rue Garancière? Oh, my word, my word, Eggbeater, how our paths have crossed! It was not Number 35 that you lived in, by any chance, was it? Amazing. Simply amazing. Do you remember that little bookstall in the Rue du Dragon? No? Oh. Well, that's only to be expected, now that I think about it; a bookstall wouldn't be likely to be there after nearly two hundred years, would it? But that marvelous church, St. Sulpice, they must have finished it by your day, eh? It was barely begun when I lived there. Ah, what a beautiful city, though. What light, what life! There was a city with a *mind*, eh, Eggbeater? Eh?"

Eggbeater is silent. Leibniz falls into a reverie. Paris. The capital of learning—and the city of his youth. He lived there four years, from 1672 to '76. It was there he grew up, intellectually, there he had the chance to test his abilities against the best, and to learn from them too: Huygens, the mathematician and physicist; Arnauld and Malebranche, the philosophers. And then there were the libraries: the knowledge of the ages, available for the asking, and things that could not be found anywhere else—the unpublished papers, for instance, of Pascal and Descartes. And the arts—architecture, the theatre: Leibniz saw Molière on stage once at the Palais Royal, acting in one of his own comedies.

It was in Paris that he finished the first working model of his calculating machine, and invented the differential calculus.

If he'd had his way he would have stayed there forever. But his first patron died, and his efforts to find a position in the city failed. In the end he was obliged to accept the only reasonable alternative, the Counsellorship offered him by Johann Friedrich, Duke of Hanover. Even then, he delayed nine months before leaving the capital, and went to his new post by a roundabout route that included London and the Netherlands!

Leibniz looks around his study, and for the first time since his arrival regards it with something less than enthusiasm. For this room comes not from his Paris days (Bless them!) but from Hanover, and his long immurement there, forty years, from '76 until his death. Did I call Hanover a busy city? Busy village would be more accurate, Leibniz thinks, small not only in size but in mentality, a piffling provincial backwater with nothing to recommend it but the fact that it happened to be the seat for a long line of dukes (three of whom, as it turned out, were his employers). And—aside from the Electress Sophie, and her daughter Sophie-Charlotte, whenever she chanced to pay a visit from Berlin, and the odd visitor such as Leibniz's friend van Helmont— there was practically no one to talk to. "Around here," he wrote in the 1690's, "one is not regarded as a proper courtier if one speaks of learned matters." Blockheads.

And here, in this place, is the conversation any better? Hardly. In fact—Leibniz strikes the desk with his fist—it is far worse. His three friends—and what lovely, lovely, sweet, intelligent humans they were!—are long dead, and the only, the ONLY voice that ever comes through, that ever CAN come through to him, belongs to that lone, unpolished student of his, that Caws—oh, yes, yes, he's promising enough, and porous, yes, no doubt about that, and willing, but oh my God how uneducated he is, how much preliminary, foundational work one has to complete before one can hope to do anything with him—anything that *matters*, that is, and there is so much that matters, that depends, damn it, on him and him alone, for the good, the public good, universal harmony and justice, and today, it would seem, he is not only backward, not only bumbling, but practically monosyllabic in his responses—

Ahhhhhhh! Leibniz struggles to his feet and hobbles about the room. Damn that leg. He goes back for his walking stick. Have a care, have a care, Gottfried Wilhelm, he tells himself. Remember your heart. Remember your own animal spirits, one day they'll get too strong for you. Calm down, now. Nothing can come of this ranting. Where is your famous optimism? Even granted that what you've said is true—which, I must tell you, I do not grant, not without a *great* many qualifications—you still must make the best of things. What prompted this fit, anyway? Paris. Well, Paris was wonderful, of course, but don't forget: even in Paris they rejected you at first, thought you a shallow young upstart from the country—which in some ways you were. You had to prove yourself to them, show yourself willing to learn. And remember one more thing: in Paris you had a backward student, too, the son of your first patron, Boineburg. For sheer recalcitrance no one could touch him. He'd have made Eggbeater look a model of industry. Seventeen and wouldn't do a thing you told him to. Wouldn't learn mathematics. Wouldn't read the Church Fathers. All he wanted to do was waste time with his friends. But in the end, you'll have to admit, he didn't turn out badly. Became an Imperial Privy Counsellor in Vienna, as a matter of fact, and after that an ambassador. So take heart, Gottfried Wilhelm. All may yet be well.

Leibniz sits again at his desk. Caws after all is no *Dummkopf*, he reminds himself. Far from it—why, he put that machine together, didn't he? Yes, he did indeed, and if he wants to call it the Delphic Oracle, well, he's entitled to his own little flourish. Besides, when the two of us are done with it, it *will* be an oracle, and of the greatest good to *all* mankind. Oh, there are deeps in Eggbeater, deeps, make no mistake about it. All he requires is education: keep giving it to him. Progress may be slow, but with you directing matters it will be constant—a perpetual progress, to new pleasures, new perfections! Let's see, now—where did you leave off? Rosamunde von der Asseburg? No. The testicles of Adam? No, not there either. Ah, Perrault. Claude Perrault. "Yes," he says aloud, "I was speaking of Perrault, Eggbeater, and of how much you and he would have had in common. Among his many accomplishments— which included architecture, by the way, as well as mathematics—he was a highly respected anatomist. Now you, when you were a medical student, must have made any number of dissections, and I'm sure that, with your agile and ever-curious intellect, you must have looked not only for—eh? What's that you say—you didn't make dissections? Well, at any rate, you were a medical student, weren't you? Ah. Ah, I see. But then how did you—I mean, when you went to Weinsberg, to treat Frau Hauffe—how did you convince ... ?"

Leibniz's sentence trails off. Everything in him wants to probe, to inter-rogate, to expose, to lay bare, but he opts, just in time, for discretion. Have a care, Gottfried Wilhelm, go gently, he tells himself. Such a passion, in-dulged, could ruin everything. The aim is to educate the man, not convict him as a fraud. After all, he is your only hope. Remember progress, constant if slow. Nature does nothing by leaps: how many times have you said that? All change is gradual. Be calm, be friendly, be constant. "Well," he continues aloud, stuffing several chocolates at once into his mouth, "never mind about that. My only point worth mentioning was that Perrault was an anatomist, and must have carried out hundreds, perhaps thousands, of dissections in his time, on all kinds of creatures too. Why? Animals and souls again, Eggbeat-er, it's as simple as that. Animals and souls and that great abiding question: where is the latter in the former? Perrault had to find out. But for his zeal, I'm afraid, he paid the ultimate price: he died, so they told me, of a disease contracted while dissecting a camel."

Leibniz raises his wig in respect. "However—and this is what I was getting at, old friend—it was Perrault's idea, based, you understand, on direct obser-vation of the innards of countless specimens, that *the soul is in the whole body equally*—equally, Eggbeater—and that sensation occurs in the sensorium it-self, in the eyes, in the feet, the fingers, the toes, the kneecaps, the elbows, the earlobes, the nostrils, the navel. Etcetera. Interesting, don't you think?"

Eggbeater is silent. Leibniz ignores it and goes on. "Well, it *is* interesting, my friend, interesting and provocative, and I can assure you the idea was taken most seriously at the time. But for my own part, and I believe you'll find this pertinent to your own cures by animal magnetism, concerned as you must be with reestablishing an harmonious flow of subtle fluid throughout the patient's body—ah, you *are* concerned with that, aren't you, Eggbeater? Good; good fellow! I was sure you were, never doubted it for an instant, but I wanted to make *absolutely* certain, if you know what I mean, absolutely cer-tain, before embarking ... well, I mean: good fellow!—for my part, as I say, I would have thought that there is a certain liquid, or, if you prefer, an ethereal substance, diffused throughout the whole body and continuous. Through it, the soul perceives: it inflates, contracts, and dilates the nerves. Oh, it *does*, my friend; indeed, indeed it does." Leibniz's face softens. He smiles, as if recalling a fond, long-ago love. "In fact, this liquid—or this Flower of Substance, as I like to call it, in the manner of the old alchemists—subsists perpetually in all changes, and, in a way, contains form alone. Form alone, Eggbeater! Here, let me show you."

In the spell of the Flower of Substance, and forgetting that Dr. Caws can-not see him, Leibniz picks up his walking stick and points it to a section of tapestry. His mind is on the old alchemists, or rather on one alchemist in particular, Maria, she called herself—couldn't sing a note, but then she didn't need to. "Think, for instance, of the shape of that cherry tree," he says aloud, "which is included in the shell of the kernel, or of this wild fruit over here. Add, too, what is said of the Tree of the Philosophers [He moves the stick to another illustration, showing Adam, lying dead on the ground, shot in the breast with an arrow, a thick-trunked flowering tree growing out of his genitals] and also what is said of plastic power [He raises the stick above his head and swings it in wide arcs]—I mean that plastic power is nothing other than an active substance of a certain shape, which increases [He lowers the stick and catches his breath] when it can." And it could, he remembers. It could and could. In a little room in Nuremberg. "Not only that, old friend, it seems to exist before conception, like the animal itself. At conception it is only given the faculty of growth. The soul seems to be firmly planted in this Flower of Substance—a kind of fountain of motion and dilation, as in a burning candle."

Leibniz pulls himself back to the present. To work, Gottfried Wilhelm. There is much to be done. "A burning candle, Eggbeater: once again I think of Miss Nightingale. I can't seem to get her out of my mind." Leibniz smiles. He has plans for the doctor and Miss Nightingale. "I never met her myself, of course, but you have told me so much, so much. And I think of her as she was when you knew her—'incandescent,' you said, bathed in the soft golden light of Tuscany—and as she is now: delirious, burning up with fever, her hair cropped short by her nurses, lying in a hut upon a hill above Balaklava, while the war rages on below." His eye falls on another section of tapestry, just below Caesar crossing the Rubicon, where a large battle is represented. Puffs of smoke, woven in neat white circles, hang over a rolling landscape. Regiments charge and countercharge, colors flying brightly, bayonets fixed, ranks in perfect formation, while officers on horseback shout orders. In the foreground, dead and wounded sprawl in the dirt, uniforms miraculously spotless, their skin a cheerful, unmodulated pink crossed here and there by zigzagging scarlet threads. A wagon stands nearby, ready to cart another load of them away.

Leibniz frowns. He has always hated that scene. The prince who had that woven, he thinks, to memorialize a conquest and heap glory on himself, should have commissioned another—if he had been an honest prince—to stand alongside it, showing nothing but mud and filth and broken bodies ... and *pain*. Now, how might that be represented—pain itself, the core of it, and cruelty, the core of that, not isolated instances? So that all men, seeing that tapestry, should be horrified, and be edified by the horror, and be rid once and for all of the demons of indifference. The artist who could weave that would—No, Gottfried Wilhelm, leave off, you lose your own thread. Such works have been made, by the hundreds, and they have done no good whatsoever. Whereas "Miss Nightingale," he adds aloud, "by acting in the world directly, on her own, with courage and tenaciousness informed by her innate animal spirits transmuted into compassion, has made an immense contribution to the public good, and is destined, I'm convinced, to make a still greater one as soon as she recovers from her present illness. She treated thousands, you know, before she fell sick herself. Often she was on her feet twenty hours at a time, dressing wounds. She received the soldiers' dying words, held their hands till the end, wrote home to their wives and mothers. She stood beside them as they lay on the operating table, gave them strength to endure the suffering in store for them. It was thanks to her that there were tables at all: when she first came to the hospital amputations were carried out on planks laid across two trestles, with no screens to hide the procedure from the other patients. Lice and other vermin were everywhere. The privies overflowed into the wards.

"She went the rounds of the hospital daily, stopping at each bed—there were four miles of beds, Eggbeater!—doing what was needed for each. They used to kiss her shadow on the wall as she passed. And now they grieve, old friend, as for a lost love, each day her recovery remains in doubt. They turn their faces to the wall and weep. Of course you know all this as well as I; you read the newspapers."

Leibniz pauses, to let his words sink in, and to consider his next move. This enterprise is a most delicate one, and so much—indeed everything—may depend on it. He has known for a long time that it is not enough merely to make the alphabet of thought; nor is it enough to educate its maker (even though that is absolutely essential). One must also find the means of putting it to the best possible use—again, for the good, the public good. One must get the alphabet into the world. And to do that ... uh, to do that, he must call on all his old skill as a diplomat, a matchmaker. He must, in a word, be devious. He must find a way to push Eggbeater in the direction he wants, but Eggbeater must be made to feel that he has chosen that direction himself. It is a situation that calls for the *nicest* calculation.

"Now, Eggbeater," he resumes, licking his lips after a sip of café latte, "Let me ask you a question, man to man. I would appreciate your honest—and your expert—opinion of something. Although the present condition of Miss Nightingale's life must unquestionably have been contained in her being as she sat beside you that evening in the opera box (for indeed it had existed even before her conception, if the word of Leeuwenhoek, van Ham and Swammerdam is anything to rely on) did you ever suspect, with your vast experience with matters touching the human soul, up to and very much including the world of the spirit, or at any rate spirits, did you ever suspect even for a moment such a fate for her as the one now working itself out in the Crimea? No? I am not surprised to hear it; I myself would have arrived, I am sure, at exactly the same conclusion. But, knowing your extraordinary prescience in questions of the psyche, especially psyches of the, uh, female persuasion, I wanted to hear it from your own lips." Leibniz smacks his again.

"Now, we both have knocked about the world enough to know that future contingents are certain, since God foresees them, and by this late date it should go without saying that the individual notion of a person involves once and for all everything that will ever happen to him—as I, for one, observed in 1686, and as Xeniades of Croton, for another, is said to have remarked over two thousand years ago in his reputedly excellent but unfortunately lost treatise on the nature of the soul. But, though these future events are known distinctly in the mind of God, we humans must await their unfolding bit by bit, in the fullness of time—a difficult task for all but the most incurious and, for the sensitive soul, a torment. Ah, Eggbeater, if only we could understand the order of the universe well enough, we would find that it surpasses all the desires of the wisest!

"But there it is, my friend, there it is. We *cannot* understand it well enough. Often we cannot understand it at all. The world seems rather a kind of confused chaos than something ordained by a supreme wisdom. The very worst things happen to the best; innocent beings are struck down and killed. And while no one with the slightest knowledge of her could accuse Miss Nightingale of faintheartedness, and no one but an absolutely certified *geistesschwach* could question her fixity of purpose, nevertheless I have no doubt that in the weakened mental state brought on by her present illness she stands sorely in need of friendship as well as a very special kind of support. I don't mean the usual medical care, or the soothing reassurances of bedside visitors. Of those I'm sure she has a sufficiency. No, I refer instead to spiritual guidance, which in her case must come from someone sympathetic to her inner history, and not from a mere purveyor of creedal rote. For Miss Nightingale can fall prey to deepest despair, and is not apt to be taken out of it by homilies. Homilies could only make matters worse. Instead, she needs a friend who is familiar with her past spiritual struggles and at the same time can take—how shall I put it?—the *long* view of her situation, someone who can show it to her in the light of … the light of the *eternal* verities. Someone who might even—if he were *very* successful—make her laugh."

Leibniz takes a deep breath. This is the moment. "Now, Eggbeater," he goes on, "who do you think that 'someone' might be? Who could best serve Miss Nightingale in the capacity I have described? No, not the Archbishop of Canterbury. How could the Archbishop of Canterbury make her laugh— unless, of course, he came to her hut dressed in a clown costume, which I think is highly unlikely. Besides, he knows nothing of her inner history. The Pope? But my dear man, the lady is not even a Roman Catholic, and if the Archbishop of Canterbury would not get into a clown suit to amuse her, why in the world would His Holiness? No, my dear doctor, you must look outside the clergy, I'm afraid. What? *Me?* Why, Eggbeater, you flatter me, and I must say, if I were a hundred and eighty or so years younger I wouldn't mind—but then, of course, there would be other problems as well. Nevertheless, I thank you, and in point of fact you are getting, as they say now, rather warm. Quite warm, I assure you. To be perfectly frank, I can't see how anyone could possibly be warmer. Indeed—what? You say what? *Yes,* my old friend, yes! Yourself! Your very, very own one. I knew you'd think of it sooner or later. You're exactly the right person for it. You'll be—what? You what? Oh, nonsense, Eggbeater, of course you have. Why, good Lord, man, it was spiritual counsel you gave her in Florence, wasn't it? No, not at the opera; what kind of spiritual counsel did you give her at the opera? Letting her grab hold of your arm and hold on to it till the end of the act is not my idea of spiritual counsel, Eggbeater. What I'm referring to is the second interview you had with her—you remember that, don't you? Yes, that's right, when you met the next day."

Leibniz chuckles. "It was even, I believe, a private interview. Now, how in creation did you manage that, you astonishing fellow, with her parents and sister right there with her as the inevitable and adhesive *Anstandsdamen?* It speaks volumes for your ingenuity, and even more for your powers of persuasion. However, that is a side issue. Think back, instead, on the interview itself."

Leibniz leans back in his chair. Things are going well, he tells himself, very well indeed—so far. Soon the Alphabet may have a new home. *Fortune Leading the Chariot of Fate* looks down from the tapestry.

"It took place in the recesses of a chapel, didn't it? The Brancacci Chapel, with the great frescoes by Masaccio. The location was chosen by the young lady. She was pale and drawn; her animation of the previous evening had vanished. Her eyes had a haunted look. It was imperative she see you at once, she said. The refinement and sensibility you had shown at the opera, together with your reputation as a healer and your 'sagacious intellect' (Those were her words, Eggbeater, remember?) had convinced her that the two of you were in some sense twin souls, despite your differences in age, in background and experience, and that therefore you might be able to help her through the trouble that was besetting her. At the very least, she said, even if you could do nothing—and she sadly feared that might very well be the case—she was sure that as a gentleman you would keep in confidence what she was about to relate. (And you did, Eggbeater, didn't you? You've told no one but me all these years.)

"She was in pain, she said, more pain than she had ever thought possible. No, no, it was not physical pain; physical pain she could endure, gladly even, if she knew there was sufficient reason for it (a girl after my own heart, that one!). This pain was of the mind; it attacked her intellect, her emotions and her spirit all at once. Sometimes it was so terrible, it made her want to die. But she had told no one of it till now.

"God had spoken to her. That was the long and short of it. It had happened a little more than a year before, at Embley Park, her family's estate in Hampshire. She was sitting on a bench, between two cedars of Lebanon, her favorite spot for contemplation, when she heard a voice. No, it was not an inner voice. It came from outside herself, as a wholly objective phenomenon. Quite literally, quite audibly, God had spoken to her and called her into his service.

"That was all; and that was what so distressed her. She had no idea what that service was to consist of, eager as she was to serve, and in any way God wanted. She kept waiting for a second message, or some different kind of sign, but none came. It was driving her to distraction. And she asked for your help—not to eradicate her problem, but simply to give her a means of living with it. No, she did not care to be magnetized; the idea—and she meant no offense, she said—the idea was frankly repugnant to her. What she wanted instead was some way of waiting in composure—some method, some technique, something, perhaps, that you had learned in your travels—until her answer came. Something to allay the anguish of not knowing. Some solace for her soul.

"Well, Eggbeater, you answered (rather glibly, I must say, if you'll forgive me, old boy) that she already knew a great deal more than most people, and could take considerable solace from that: she had received indubitable, first-hand confirmation of the existence of God, something which others had to be content to take on faith. She was, you continued, in the rather privileged position of the Old Testament prophets—nay, of Moses himself—for whom the Creator was a living, self-evident reality. Well, old friend, I might have told you that would do no good, not with someone of her character. She had never been seriously in doubt as to God's existence, she said, and the bare confirmation of it hardly came as a surprise. Besides, she was not at all sure that the ordinary person who, faced with the cruelties and injustices of life, nonetheless managed to remain steadfast in his faith, was not far more virtuous, and courageous, than someone like herself who, through no particular effort and certainly no testing of her worthiness, had received revelation *gratis*. She reviled herself for her ingratitude, and for rank cowardice at being unable to live like everyone else, without answers. –What an excellent individual! Really a first-rate heart and mind. And such splendid red hair into the bargain! Did you not find her red hair splendid, Eggbeater, as well as her heart and mind?"

Leibniz grins broadly and fondles the giant's tooth. "Oh, I'm sure you did, old friend. Who would not have? Especially one who already was beginning—correct me if I'm wrong, Eggbeater, but I do believe this to have been the case—who already was beginning to fall under her spell? Yes, just as I thought: your silence speaks volumes.

"But you had the delicacy and good breeding—it goes without saying—to keep those feelings to yourself at the time and to concentrate solely on her problem as she had stated it. Was there nothing, you asked, that brought her any relief? Her family, for instance, the happiness of home life, the sacred bond betwixt mother and daughter? She looked at you as if you had taken leave of your senses. Her home life, you inferred, was less than ideal. Well, then, the opera, you suggested, she had given every indication of enjoying the opera, with its gripping plots and ravishing music? Mere palliatives, she sighed. What about the other arts, in that case? You pointed to the frescoes covering the chapel walls, *Saint Peter Healing the Sick with his Shadow* and of course the great *Expulsion from Paradise* showing Adam and Eve driven out of Eden by the Angel—Adam with his face in his hands, Eve trying to cover her nakedness, head thrown back, howling her grief down the ages—was that not a comfort? No? Well, what was, then, if not that?

"She only shook her head, and remained silent a long time. Numbers, she finally said. Numbers?! You couldn't believe your ears. Yes, she said. Arithmetic. Statistics. Higher mathematics. There was certainty in numbers, she explained, you always knew where you were with them. And she quoted several passages from Plato—with whose name, I believe, you were not yet familiar. But you were familiar with numbers, all right, weren't you, old friend? Backwards and forwards and up and down and sideways you knew them, didn't you? The history of zero, Pascal's triangle—there wasn't anything you hadn't explored. And of course the Fibonacci series. You were a regular veteran of the Fibonacci series—if I may so express it. And you trotted it out for Miss Nightingale again, didn't you, you dog you? Ah, there's nothing like counting, is there, Eggbeater? Eh, Eggbeater? Eh?"

CH CH CH CH CH CH CH CH JJ JJ JJ JJ JJ CH CH CH CH CH CH CH CH CH-CH JJ JJ JJ JJ JJ CH CH CH CJJ CH CH CH JJ CH CH CH CH CH CH CH CH CH *Enfin vous voilà! Enfin vous voilà!* 196,418 plus 121,393 is 317,811. Sonny Rollins will record "I've Told Ev'ry Little Star" in 1958. Lester Young will save the clarinet for his old age. CH CH CH CH CH CH CH CH CH CH CH JJJ JJJJJ How much of Leibniz's talk is Eggbeater hearing? It is hard to say. He stands placidly at his front gate, looking out across Prospect St. at the neighboring houses—the Peters', the McCormacks' and the big new house the Mainwarings recently moved into (he's sure Mrs. Mainwaring insisted on it so she could keep an eye on him). Beyond is the Burying Ground and the South Green. So long as one ignores certain details (for instance, that he is doing his standing about six inches off the ground, treading air with little backwards-and-forwards motions of his feet) the doctor might easily be mistaken for an ordinary, moderately prosperous householder out enjoying his bit of leisure in the clement spring weather. He nods pleasantly to passersby (even though at the moment there are none), he sips his Elixir-and-feather, he smiles at the squirrels. Now and then he repeats to himself selections from his recently concluded conversation with Welkin, speaking softly in a tone of ruminative, almost nostalgic approval.

"Hand," he says. "Ah, hand.

"Son," he adds. "Horse. With heat and title too, who could forget *them*? Not entirely opera-mad, no, never: nothing exotic, only a mission. Caius, you see, is slain by Titius. In the footprints of the Yeti. Come back in 5686, now, to see the Oracle. Come back, Miss Nightingale, come back. Haroop. Here, let me brush the snow off you."

He is, in fact, stewed to the gills, not on gin but on Abimelech Barton's Elixir, which he has been consuming regularly out in his barn throughout the past year and which has recently begun to yield a few of its promised blessings. However, unlike Efficiency, whose alcoholic excesses of the morning have actually broadened the channel already established between herself and her ardent Uncle Isaac, Eggbeater has become increasingly cut off, in the course of the last few drinks, from the cool, reason-loving Leibniz.

Swathed in serotonin, the philosopher's words set out as usual from their source in the doctor's pineal gland, circulate through his subtle body, shoot the rapids of his mesencephalon and fetch up, as they have always done, in the grey matter of his cerebral cortex. But there they languish, as the factors necessary to bring them over into conscious thought are mostly blocked.

Like a blizzard in the Harz Mountains, the Elixir has piled masses of ectoplasm in the ravines and defiles of the cortex, with drifting in places more than a sixteenth of an inch deep.

Cut off by the storm from this part of his brain, Eggbeater does not write the *Discourse on Metaphysics*. He gives himself over instead to Dreames and Revelations, the Apparitions of Angells, visions of the Nature of Man, Beasts, Foules, Fishes; of Trees, Plants, Flowers; Closets, Chambers, Cavernes; Transmutation of Earthy Matter—all accompanied by a feeling of bliss he never thought possible. "Wulfenite is orange," he remarks to no one. "Artichokes are green. The world's smallest mammal is the white-toothed pygmy shrewmouse. Hand; son; horse; heat; title. Haroop. Haroop. Haroop."

This state of affairs is no part of Leibniz's intention. If he knew of it, he would be deeply concerned.

But he does not know of it. Moreover, his teaching has not been entirely obstructed. Every now and then his voice gets through. As we have seen, the doctor has paid lip service, periodically, to his mentor's presence, answering questions if not at length, still as fully as he can. And a complete catalogue of Eggbeater's mental intake over, say, the last ten and a half minutes would include, among the peach trees, grape arbors and Platonic solids, the following items, all showing the unmistakable influence of his master's monologue:

the word "coprophagous";

the word "incandescent";

a warhorse;

a flock of sheep;

Friedericke Hauffe, wrapped in a shawl, lying propped up in bed in her room in Weinsberg, Germany, at the home of Dr. Justinus Kerner in April, 1839, turning away from him to Dr. Caws and whispering the number, "34";

himself replying, "55," "89," and "144," also in a whisper;

Frau Hauffe smiling;

Florence Nightingale in her family's box at the opera in April, 1838, in Florence, just before the beginning of *Das Gehirngespinstgemach*, deep in discussion with Dr. Caws about the immortality of the soul, giving him her whole attention, eyes bright with intelligent interest, turning away just once, and only for an instant, to tell her sister, No, she did not care for an ice just now, dearest, thank you very much;

the unexpected and mildly intriguing strength of Miss Nightingale's hand as she pressed his right arm, her fingers gripping him tighter and tighter while LaBlache, singing Gyges, poured out his despair on the dock at Miletus, just before the end of the first act, her nails digging into the doctor's coat sleeve, so that when he undressed for bed that night he persuaded himself that he saw, by the light of a flickering candle, a little row of new moons indenting the skin of his biceps;

the painted right arm of Eve in Masaccio's fresco in the Brancacci Chapel, her forearm slanting upward to cover her breasts, as she and Adam made their way out of Paradise across a flat surface of lime plaster;

the three-dimensional and by this time quite fascinating form of Miss Nightingale, clad in grey, standing beside him below the fresco, whispering the word "numbers," her lips barely moving, her eyes cast down to the chapel floor;

the Fibonacci number series, discovered in the Middle Ages and borne out in nature by, among other things, the arrangement of the bracts of pinecones and the propagation of rabbits;

the joy with which the doctor employed the series to rouse Miss Nightingale out of her doldrums, as he had done a decade earlier with Frau Hauffe, beginning with the equations 1 plus 0 is 1, 1 plus 1 is 2, 2 plus 1 is 3, 3 plus 2 is 5, and so on;

Frau Hauffe's face lit by a single candle, as she lay in bed in her room a few minutes after midnight on April 21, 1829;

the faint tremor in her lips as she said, almost inaudibly, "28,657" in answer to this, also whispered, question, "What is 17,711 plus 10,946?" their dryness as she and the doctor kissed a moment later, contrasting curiously with the moistness and flexibility of her tongue as she inserted it into his mouth;

the momentarily blinding light, some little time after that, as the bedroom door burst open, revealing Dr. Kerner in the entrance with a lantern;

the term Socinian;

the phrase *par exemple*;

the sound "Delft";

the sound "Leeuwenhoek";

the city of Paris, in particular his old quarters on the Rue Garancière, which contained not only his living quarters but also his consulting room, with its cupboard containing his collection of abortifacients, including marjoram, thyme, root of worm fern, parsley, lavender tea, turpentine, ginger, ammonia, mustard, horseradish, tansy tea, gin with iron filings, a paste of mashed ants, castor oil, rosemary and opium;

his wife Efficiency, and the abortion he performed on her, at her insistence, in August, 1850, shortly after the start of their mediumship;

their mediumship itself, or "the act" as they called it, and the joy it brought them in all its aspects: the fame, the adulation of the crowd, the exercise of animal spirits, the deep, deep pleasure they derived from the public display of undying hatred, the sense of purpose it gave their lives and the gratitude they felt at being thus chosen;

the name Newton, and the poor sportsmanship the doctor believes Sir Isaac and Efficiency exhibited when, after the Cawses' retirement, she objected to his and Leibniz's construction of the Delphic Oracle, going so far as to accuse him of damaging the integrity of the act, the doctor's attitude toward this being "Let them build their own oracle then";

two cedars of Lebanon;

a cherry tree;

a turtle's age, specifically the age of a turtle named Alphonse, whom he met and conversed with in the Luxembourg Gardens from three-fifteen to four o'clock on the afternoon of June 26, 1831, that age being in his estimation about thirty-five or forty;

the slightly deluded Monsieur Descartes;

the testicles of Adam;

the shadow of Miss Nightingale, cast on the hospital wall and kissed by a British soldier, the kiss landing, in the doctor's imagination, midway down her umbral gluteus maximus and leaving for perhaps three and a half seconds an almost-invisible crescent of moisture on the plaster before it vanishes into the Pleroma;

the shadow of St. Peter, falling on the sick and healing them, in the scene painted on the wall behind the altar in the Brancacci Chapel, and Miss Nightingale standing with her back to the fresco, wiping her brow with a handkerchief supplied by the doctor, searching her mind for the number 72,025;

himself as Miss Nightingale's savior, an idea which thrills him, so much so that it immediately produces an image in his mind, fully formed and sharply delineated, of a new fresco entitled *The Order of the Universe Surpassing all the Desires of the Wisest*, covering the space between the *Expulsion from Paradise* and *St. Peter Healing the Sick with his Shadow*, showing a panoramic view of a mountain top in a snowstorm, with the doctor in the center, standing in mid-air in a nimbus, lifting Miss Nightingale out of her hut, her face turned up to him in gratitude, while far below them the Pope and Archbishop of Canterbury, dressed in clown suits, watch helplessly from a ledge and a Yeti runs off in the distance;

the history of zero;
four miles of beds;
the word *Anstandsdamen*;
a man named Perrault;
a camel.

So something has registered, despite Mr. Barton's Elixir. And even if the various units of that something are widely dispersed, separated by a considerable amount of unrelated material—Al Cohn, Zoot Sims and Major Holley will record "Angel Eyes" in 1960, Sascha Feinstein will record "Donna Lee" in 2003—the main thrust of Leibniz's message, that is, the attractions and general worthiness of Miss Nightingale and Eggbeater's potential role in her future, has sunk in. Not only has it sunk in, it has been welcome and gloried in.

But—no. Enough of Eggbeater for now. What about Leibniz? Leibniz, I don't mind saying, worries me—me, the *Gehirngespinstgemach*. I mean Leibniz as he is now, sitting there in the doctor's pineal gland, not Leibniz as he was in the seventeenth century. The seventeenth century Leibniz, the Leibniz of Leibniz's proper lifetime, the Leibniz you'll find in the history books, *that* Leibniz I find no fault in. How should I? Our ideas, our predilections, our appetitions, our very words are so close as at times to be indiscernible from each other. He was the first, after all, to see the true, the metaphysical nature of my being, even if he had no inkling of my fall from it. No, the Leibniz I'm worried about is this Leibniz of the pineal—glandular Leibniz, let's call him—this one sixty-fourth of an inch tall Leibniz with an open sore on his leg, who sits at his desk all day lecturing to Eggbeater, making plans for him, conniving his future. I simply do not understand him.

Where is the old sharpness, the roving intelligence, the eager curiosity about everything under the sun—scientific developments, the arts, medicine, social conditions, events, persons, the rise and fall of nations? A very great deal has happened in all those areas since his death; you'd think he'd at least make an effort to find out about them. But all he does is sit there, telling the same old stories, repeating the same formulas. He practically never asks Eggbeater any questions except rhetorical ones, or to make sure he's listening. Where is there any advance in his knowledge? Oh, I suppose he's learned a little more about the Empyrean than he knew when he was alive, but otherwise I'm afraid he's in a sad state: a most inferior follower of his former self.

And to think he believed in progress, too, the inevitable and continued progress of the human species! This is what I cannot understand—how someone so wise, so secure, so firmly *planted* (to use his expression) in ideas that foster change, development, transmutation, improvement on all fronts, how such a person could seemingly go back on them all, refuse his own vindication, while continuing to pay them lip service. At times his ignorance is breathtaking. And nowhere is this more apparent than in his fixation on Florence Nightingale. How he *insists!* He brings up her name at every turn. "Miss Nightingale this, Miss Nightingale that," Efficiency complains, and I must admit I see her point. Not that Miss Nightingale is not a remarkable person. She's a model of courage and dedication. One can see why Leibniz, even glandular Leibniz, is taken with her. She is doing, and will continue to do, more real good in the world than anyone in her century. I have no quarrel, far from it, with Miss Nightingale herself. But as a match for Eggbeater Caws? *Eggbeater Caws?* This glandular Leibniz has taken leave of his senses!

What in creation possesses him, to imagine that an excellently educated, highly intelligent, upper-class British lady, who has recently become a world-renowned figure—and who has already, by the way, turned down two perfectly acceptable suitors—what possesses him to imagine that she would consider for an instant taking for a husband a very much lower class, miserably educated medium, an American into the bargain, an animal magnetist, sometime abortionist and vagabond of no work who is already married, and whom she met seventeen years ago while on holiday with her parents and whom she has never heard of, or from, since that time? Would she even, for the matter of that, remember him?

There can be but one explanation, I'm afraid: Leibniz is in love. He's in love with Miss Nightingale himself!

TRUE TALES OF THE PARANORMAL:

In the weeks after her resignation from the Helvetius, and without Schwank, Anna Zeisig fell on evil days. She retired to her Zürich apartment, unplugged her phone and shutdown her computer, seeing no one. On the few occasions when she did go out, for food and other necessities, she hurried through the streets, hugging the walls, muttering to herself, a shawl covering her head. At last, in despair, she remembered Dr. Haselmaus and wrote him again:

"My dear, my very much admired Doktor:

I apologize—nay, I abase myself—for trespassing once more on your valuable, in all likelihood priceless, time, but I do venture to trust that by now you have received the material I recently sent you, to wit, Empedocles' many papers, etc., along with his Oracle. I do wonder a little, I must say, that I have not heard from you, at least to acknowledge the receipt of all that, but I confess as well that I have another, and in my esteem more urgent, reason for writing.

"You see, sir, for me just now things are not going so well. In fact, they are going very badly, I cannot imagine them going worse, and I think in order to change their direction I must find out some things about myself. I require, in short, some shrinkage—if that is the proper term for the psychological help you provide—and I require it very soon, indeed immediately. Often these days I want to throw myself in the river. Why I have not already done so is a mystery to me. Every morning I awaken surprised that I am still alive and not at the bottom of the Limmat. Certainly it is not from a lack of desire to be there.

"What is it about me, Herr Doktor, that I always fall in love with men who desert me—or die, which is almost as bad? Empedocles was not the first, by any means, though I mourn his loss more than any. There was Hans, the ethnobotanist, who fell off a ski lift in the Italian Alps and was lost forever, right before my eyes. And Wolfram, the orthodontist, who was taken off by phlebotomus fever, which is not even supposed to be fatal, and all my nursing could not bring him around. And Franz, who ran off to Viterbo and was never seen again, at least not by me. There have been nine of them, I believe, if I have not lost count, as well as three or four others in America, where I passed one of my teenage years. My friend, Anna Sprengel, the famous newspaper columnist, whose fascinating prose you have possibly read, tells me I actually pick them out, knowing in my subconscious mind that they are hopeless, and then throw myself at them, *in order* to be humiliated and abandoned once again. But how can this be? I may be a dedicated epidemiologist, but I am also young and, in my own way, beautiful, sir, even with my glasses on, and with them off I am simply smashing, everyone says so. Nature has been kind to me; I do not need to throw. Men come to me on their own, and in droves.

"Still, I am beginning to wonder after all, whether Anna may be right. Perhaps I have thrown without knowing I was throwing. Perhaps, even, it is I who am the narcissist, and not your erstwhile patient Eichhorn. Great sir, will you help me? I have not a great deal of money, but I have some, and I would crawl to Basel on my hands and knees—willingly, sir, on my hands and knees in this cold, cold winter—to see you. I have heard of your celebrated sleeping cure, and I am eager to avail myself of it. I would give anything for a good night's sleep."

A few days later, Haselmaus wrote back:

"Fraulein:

I am in receipt of the Schwank material. Thank you. As for the rest of your letter, I am officially retired and seeing no patients. However, your suspicion anent your narcissism is perfectly correct. You are also possibly insane. In any case, I will treat you. Never have I encountered such narcissism—I would be a fool to pass it up. My secretary will arrange an appointment.

PS: You do not sleep. *I* sleep. Fraulein Sprengel's prose is disgusting."

"Oh, sir," Zeisig answered, "great magnanimous sir, what joy fills my heart! Such ecstasy! Already I feel restored. What hope you have given me. I come! I come!"

The Cry of the Gehirngespinstgemach:

JJJJJJJJJJJJJJJJJJJCHCHCHCHCHCHCHCHCHCHCHJJJCH-
CHJJJCHJJCHJJ Thelonious Monk will record "I Should Care" in 1948.
Miles Davis will record "So What" in 1959. CHCHCHCHCHJJJJJJJJJJJJ "Eh?
Eh? Eh, Eggbeater?" asks Leibniz again. He is getting a little curious. Not
that he's seriously troubled. Eggbeater's silences have usually been brief—relatively brief—in the past, and in any case it does no good, he reminds himself
now, to fret. Caws is no *Dummkopf*, Caws is no *Dummkopf*, he repeats to
himself. Besides, in his dealings with his protégé the philosopher has always
been blessed with a singular confidence (born, it must be admitted, more of
desperation than of logic, but still, for all of that, born) that the information
he conveys to Caws will not be wholly lost, or even, technically, lost at all,
no matter what the doctor's mental condition when he receives it. During his
lifetime Leibniz worked hard to assert the value of unconscious perceptions,
arguing that far from being negligible they indicate and constitute the individual himself. They make up, he wrote, "that *je ne sais quoi*, those flavors,
those images of sensory qualities, vivid in the aggregate but confused in their
parts, those impressions which are made on us by the bodies around us and
which involve the infinite, that connection each being has with all the rest of
the universe."

Nor have time and the rigors of several further incarnations done anything
to shake Leibniz in these beliefs. On the contrary, he sees (or rather, it must be
confessed, he has no choice but to see) their full and resplendent vindication
in the person—the physical, psychic, etheric and spiritual body—of Eggbeater Caws. For Eggbeater's most striking characteristic, at least for Leibniz's
purposes, is his enormous receptivity to just such unconscious perceptions.
He not only takes them in, like anyone else, but his body seems positively
greedy for them. This is what Leibniz means by his porousness. In fact, the
philosopher has the impression—although he has no way of verifying it, confined as he is to his host's pineal gland—that Eggbeater has been growing a
good deal over the last few months, since about the time he began working,
under Leibniz's direction, on the calculator. Leibniz attributes this expansion

(assuming it is true) to the greatly increased dosage of minute, unconscious perceptions which he has been feeding the medium. And not only have these been introduced into Caws' body, they have also (the philosopher trusts) been retained there, and will reappear (he hopes against hope) fresh as paint, when the time is right.

And the time *is* right, Leibniz mutters to himself, the time has been right for quite a while now. Where is he, anyway? Miss Nightingale and I can't wait forever. Grunting, he crosses his legs, leans forward in his chair, pulls the ankle-length sock off his right foot, then does the same with his fur-lined blue stocking. He peels the blotting paper off the sore on his leg, wincing slightly at the pain, then applies a new piece. One always knew, he says to himself, that some things never change. One was prepared for that. But why must one of them be *this* thing? He props the leg up on the footstool.

"Eggbeater," he begins again. "Eggbeater? I do hate to bother you, old boy, but it certainly would be nice if you let me know you're here. Well, of course, I *know* you're here, how could you be elsewhere, but I mean it would be nice if you could give me—if it's not too much trouble, that is—some little sign that you hear me and understand what I've been telling you. Almost anything would do. It wouldn't even have to be words. A whistle would be all right. A grunt, a belch even. A fart, if you like. Oh, a good, well-rounded fart would be perfectly acceptable, I assure you. Or a little sputtery one if you prefer. But, you see, it's rather important that you do *something*, and quite soon—important not just to me, old friend, I hardly count in this at all, important, instead, to Miss Nightingale. *Miss Nightingale*—did you hear, Eggbeater? I do hope so, because they're bringing in more wounded, even as I speak, up the hill, past her hut, to the hospital, on mule-litters, on stretchers, in wagons. And the sick! A steady stream of them—there is typhus, cholera, dysentery, erysipelas, rheumatic fever, scurvy, diarrhoea, gangrene. Amputated limbs float in the harbor. And look," he adds, forgetting again that he cannot be seen, "just look at this leg!" He points. "I, too, Eggbeater, I too am wounded. And I bleed, my friend, I bleed in my heart—for myself, for Miss Nightingale, for you, for all of us. Go to Miss Nightingale, Eggbeater, you can save her, *we* can save her, together we can do anything. Eggbeater, I beg of you—go to her, friend, go."

"Miss Nightingale! Miss Nightingale!" Eggbeater shouts it from the center of his nimbus. She raises her face to his as he takes hold of her arms. The snow swirls around them in the wind. The Yeti howls in the distance. The dog barks on the other side of the bridge.

"Miss Nightingale! Miss Nightingale!" Eggbeater's voice resounds in the pineal. Hurrah! Hurrah! Leibniz claps his little hands in glee. "Ah, Eggbeater, Eggbeater! I knew you were listening! Good man, good man, sturdy, solid, dependable Eggbeater."

In a single swift movement he knocks back the café latte and throws the empty cup at the tapestry. It strikes the top of the globe, disappearing into the Barents Sea. "Oh, my dear man," he says, "my dear, delightful responsive human. I feel like a lad of twenty again. Hurrah! Hurrah!" He throws his sock after the café cup. It sinks off Novaya Zemlyia without a trace.

"Wonderful. Simply wonderful." Leibniz pulls on his fur-lined stocking. "Do you know, Eggbeater," he continues, "I have to admit I'm a little bit envious of you, going off to see Miss Nightingale like this. Oh, I know, I'll be with you, too, and the Oracle of course as well. We couldn't forget the Oracle, could we now? Of course not. But you'll be the one in control, you'll be doing the talking, the consoling, the counseling—perhaps even the wooing, eh? And you know, my friend, you are nothing short of hypnotic when you go to work on people, when you really take it into your head to go to work on them. I wish I had your skill. You make contact with something truly deep in people; lesser lights lose their grip entirely. Not that Miss Nightingale is a lesser light. Far from it. But she is human, and [Leibniz works his index finger into the curls of his wig] every kind of gyration seems to be performed in the human brain, as the soul observes its own vortex. *Every* kind of gyration, and Miss Nightingale is no exception. Good Lord, man, species—whole species, Eggbeater—are nothing but undulations of a liquid that is subject to pressure. Imagine, then, the effect on a sensitive, well-bred but highly ... highly ... well, highly *compassionate* young lady like Miss Nightingale when—well, when I say that every undulation is preserved for eternity even if, when put together with others, it becomes imperceptible, I think you'll know what I mean. Eh, you sly dog? Eh?"

He smiles. "But that the soul agitates a vortex—on top of all that, the soul itself—that is wonderful. And it does, my friend, it does, for you and me and Miss Nightingale too, because [Leibniz leans forward in his chair, his voice growing urgent, his blue eyes as bright as Miss Nightingale's grey ones] because we do not act as a simple machine, but out of *reflection*, that is, *out of action on ourselves*. And consider this, please, dear doctor, you who still live in the world of men and events, of striving and suffering: perhaps the whole vortex of the great globe [he reaches across the desk to his globe and gives the Altai Mountains a shove with the heel of his hand] is vivified by a soul of the same kind [he hits the globe again to make it go faster; Urgench and Tiflis pass by in a blur] which is the reason why the laws of the system are observed, and all things are compensated. All things, Eggbeater, all things!" He sits back, grinning from ear to ear. "Caius *is* slain by Titius. Peter *is* handsome insofar as he is standing. The whole world is one vortex for God!"

"Wonderful! Simply wonderful!" The cry erupts from Eggbeater's common bile duct, echoing through the duodenum and crashing into the cerebral cortex just below the peak of the Brocken. Eggbeater, now locked in an embrace with Miss Nightingale, their nakedness covered by the thickening mists of his nimbus, repeats the words aloud, slurring them. He disengages himself for a moment, takes the feather out of his Elixir and waves it in front of him like a conductor's baton. He feels his body jerk upward an inch or so and then, to his surprise, the scene changes; he feels himself rising, alone, through the warm spring air of Aubrey. In the pineal gland Sinope, Constantinople, Olympus and Corfu pass before Leibniz, closely followed by Tarentum, Naples, the Tyrrhenian Sea.

The philosopher raises his wig again in tribute. His bald head glows softly in the green-grey light. He gives the globe another smack and presses the wig to his heart. Malaga, the Pillars of Hercules, the Azores, Guadeloupe, the Gulf of Mexico speed by. A low purring sound, as of smooth-running machinery or a cat, issues from somewhere inside the globe. The squirrels out by the front gate prick up their ears. The dog barks. Eggbeater continues to rise, going past his second storey and up over the roof. Isla Clarion, the Society Islands, the Caroline Islands, Chungking.

Down in his hippocampus, on the surface of the Ocean of Memory Selection, there is a disturbance in the undulation of a liquid subject to pressure. Two images appear on the horizon, riding toward the shore on bucking sea horses and clamoring for their host's attention. It is the doctor himself as he looked seventeen years before, accompanied by a prim young Englishwoman, and as they dismount in the brain sand and speak their lines, the words conjure up an interior that Eggbeater remembers well: a Florentine chapel lit by flickering candles and the slanting afternoon sun, with Renaissance frescoes covering the walls. The doctor and his companion stand side by side under the paintings, he wearing his usual rumpled black suit, she in a stylish grey dress with an elegant cloak to match. Lhasa, Lake Van, Izmir, Ifni. The Bahamas, Acapulco, Hawaii.

DR. CAWS: Oh, yes, Miss Nightingale, I agree with you entirely. It gives me joy, in fact, to hear you express yourself in this manner. In numbers there is indeed certainty—eternal certainty, I would even venture to say—far beyond the reach of doubt or opinion, and even further removed from the frivolities of fashion.

FLORENCE NIGHTINGALE (*sadly*): One sees so much frivolity nowadays, too. (*Ruefully she fingers the black and silver threads on the trim of her cloak.*) I often reproach myself for it.

DR. CAWS: Let me hasten to assure you, my dear Miss Nightingale, I meant to cast no aspersion—

FLORENCE NIGHTINGALE: Nor did I infer one, dear Doctor. (*She smiles wanly.*) If any aspersions are to be cast, they will come only from myself and be intended for me alone. And they will always hit their mark. (*She sighs.*) But let us, with your permission, leave such dismal topics. For as I intimated at the outset of this interview, I long for some relief from them. And, unless I have wholly mistaken your meaning, your recent words lead me to hope that you, too, hold numbers in more than customary esteem.

DR. CAWS: I do, dear lady, I do. Frankly, it could be said I hold nothing in higher—save, of course for the sacred spiritual verities.

FLORENCE NIGHTINGALE: I am happy to hear you say it, Sir; there are not many like us, I fear. But, Doctor, your two passions, as you have just described them, may be more intimately connected than you realize, for Plato says—

DR. CAWS: Who?

FLORENCE NIGHTINGALE: Plato.

DR. CAWS: Ah, Plato. I, uh, thought you said someone else. Yes. Plato. Just so.

FLORENCE NIGHTINGALE: Yes. Well, Plato says that the practice of arithmetic compels the soul to reason, and that with numbers it is even possible to lay hold of true being.

DR. CAWS: Does he, then? How nicely Plato puts things. And he could not be more correct, of course. Now, along those same lines, my dear lady, I was just about to observe—to take only a single case in point among quite a few others—that 1—if you follow me—always is 1.

FLORENCE NIGHTINGALE (*nonplussed*): Oh. I see. Why, that is … that is … Well, I must say, Doctor, that is really quite cleverly put—although I confess I cannot precisely grasp, at least not at the moment, all the subtleties your statement undoubtedly contains. But it is, uh, remarkable nonetheless, so succinct and, uh, exclusive. (*Brightening.*) Yes, exclusive—I mean that, naturally, in Thomas Taylor's sense of privation of multitude, associated of old with the god Apollo, with Apollo in this case as the original monad. 1 *cannot*, in fact, be anything else, can it?

DR. CAWS: Not anything, my dear Miss Nightingale, not anything. It is inconceivable that such a monstrosity should occur. (*He smiles.*) I thank you for your kind words and shall endeavor to live up to the sentiments from which they spring. Permit me to add, *im Vorbeige-hen* as it were, that 1 plus 1 always is….

FLORENCE NIGHTINGALE: Why, 2, of course. That's really quite simple, isn't it?

DR. CAWS: Simplicity itself. Or rather, that is, herself—for I always think of Simplicity as one of the Muses, left out of the original eight.

FLORENCE NIGHTINGALE: Nine, you mean.

DR. CAWS: Oh, nine, of course, nine. How very silly of me. How very doltish indeed. Please forgive me, Miss Nightingale. Nine it is. However, to return to our business, 2 plus 1—

FLORENCE NIGHTINGALE: Why would simplicity be one of the

Muses?

DR. CAWS: Er ... What?

FLORENCE NIGHTINGALE (*more sharply*): Why would simplicity be one of the Muses?

DR. CAWS (*at a loss*): Why? Oh, no reason ... That is, I simply ... I mean I *merely* ... considered ... that is, if such a fancy is even worthy of being called a consideration, it's a mere bagatelle, no more. To consider it a consideration would be ... er ... considerably....

FLORENCE NIGHTINGALE (*coming to his rescue; she cannot say exactly why, but she finds this person really quite refreshing and would hate to hurt his feelings, even if he turns out not to possess the great wisdom she at first ascribed to him. Already she feels rather buoyed by his presence.*): Please don't give it another thought, dear Doctor. It was my fault entirely for bringing it up. I think, actually, upon con—upon reflection, that is—that Simplicity would have made a very fine Muse. She probably would have had good common sense, and kept the others in line. But to return to our numbers. You were saying, before I interrupted you ... ?

DR. CAWS: You, interrupt *me*, Miss Nightingale? I assure you, nothing that you ever conceivably might say could be consid—could be construed as—an interruption, not by any furthest known latitude of the expression, and certainly not by me. But, as to your question, I did presume to mention, a little while back, that 2 plus 1—

FLORENCE NIGHTINGALE (*warming to the game*): Ah, Dr. Caws. 2 plus 1!

DR. CAWS: —Always is 3.

FLORENCE NIGHTINGALE: It is very true.

DR. CAWS: And very beautiful, if I may so. (*He regards her.*) Very beautiful indeed. Now, to continue this train of thought for a moment—I hope I take no liberty, Miss Nightingale—

FLORENCE NIGHTINGALE: Oh, no, no, no, no, no, none at all, Doctor, no liberty in all the world. On the contrary, your voice cheers me strangely—to say nothing of your numbers. Please proceed with what you were about to impart.

DR. CAWS: Thank you, my dear Miss Nightingale. I am profoundly gratified if my poor offices have been of benefit to you. I was only about to observe that 3 plus 2 is 5.

FLORENCE NIGHTINGALE: There is much in what you say, Doctor. In fact (*she giggles girlishly*) there is 5 in it.

DR. CAWS: And more where that came from, Miss Nightingale, more where that came from. For 5 came from 3 and 5 plus 3 is 8.

FLORENCE NIGHTINGALE (*enthusiastically*): Oh, so it is! So it is! (*Recovering her poise*) Although, on the face of it, Doctor, that is—naturally—quite obvious. Any child would know it instantly. But ... I must ... at the same time I must acknowledge ... that there *is* something—most uncanny—about that equation ... something about it that beckons one ... uh ... (*She lowers her eyes; a blush appears on her cheek.*)

DR. CAWS: Deeper?

FLORENCE NIGHTINGALE: Yes! Deeper! The very word. How kind of you, dear Doctor, to supply it, just when my own poor vocabulary—

DR. CAWS: It was nothing, dear lady—

FLORENCE NIGHTINGALE: Ah, no, dear friend—for I think I may call you that—

DR. CAWS: But of course, dear Miss Nightingale—

FLORENCE NIGHTINGALE: It was certainly not nothing, it was a very great deal, for you not only supplied a word, you indicated—and bravely, so bravely, I shall never forget it—a *direction*: viz., downward, into ... (*she passes her hand over her brow*) you must excuse me, Sir, my brain is reeling with it ... down into the very heart of the number itself. For 8—that is to say, 8 1's or 4 2's—is also, as your sequence shows, made up of a 3 added to a 5, both of which numbers proceed ineluctably from a 2 and a 1, with, in each case, the adjacent previous number coupled with the present one to produce the next, that next being, as it were, their offspring. And this offspring in its turn unites with—oh, Doctor, I hardly dare say it, a thrill of fear runs through me and I feel I am trespassing on holy, forbidden ground, where the innermost secrets of generation lie hidden, in all their incestuous coilings, but it must follow, as the night the day—

DR. CAWS: Or as the day the night, dear Miss Nightingale—

FLORENCE NIGHTINGALE: Or as the day the night, just as you say, dear friend, it *must* follow—oh, it must, it must—

DR. CAWS: With sweet ineluction—

FLORENCE NIGHTINGALE: Smoothly—

DR. CAWS: Adroitly—

FLORENCE NIGHTINGALE: Fondly—

DR. CAWS: *Sans* friction—

FLORENCE NIGHTINGALE: And with silky tenderness, Doctor. (*Smiling broadly*) We must not leave out silky tenderness.

DR. CAWS: Verily we must not, dear lady. And with ardor aforethought as well, may we add?

FLORENCE NIGHTINGALE: With ardor aforethought indeed, dear friend. It must follow, therefore, with all these qualities, that 8 plus 5—

DR. CAWS: 8 plus 5—

BOTH: 8 plus 5 is 13! (*Miss Nightingale squeals with delight.*)

The Sea of Japan, Ankuang, Ulaanbaatar, Ust' Kamenogorsk. Alga, Odessa, Prague. Toulouse, the Bay of Biscay. Cap Raz, Gloucester. Mackinac Island, the lands of the Essanape, the Wichita, the Apache. Drake's Bay. Leibniz watches them, spellbound, his wig still pressed to his heart. It is his daily devotion. "*Vera origo atque intima aeternitatis natura est ipsa existendi necessitas,*" he intones, "*quae nullam per se dicit successionem, etsi fiat ut omnibus coexistat, quod aeternum est. Sympnoia panta, sympnoia panta, sympnoia panta.*"

Eggbeater floats to the top of the elm tree at the corner of Prospect and High Sts. Smoothly, adroitly, he reflects. 8 plus 5 is 13. His head disappears in the leaves.

In his hippocampus the sea horses of memory gallop ahead an hour. When they come to a halt Miss Nightingale is standing with her back to *Saint Peter Healing the Sick with his Shadow*, wiping her brow with a handkerchief. Dr. Caws is beside her, talking.

DR. CAWS: (*earnestly*): Yes, yes, it *is* hard, Miss Nightingale, but certainly it is not impossible. You can do it, I know you can.

FLORENCE NIGHTINGALE: Oh, I am so *tired*, Doctor, so *very* much exhausted. The numbers are swimming before my eyes.

DR. CAWS: Ah, yes, it is often thus. Rather like a pond full of fish, is it not, as seen from a distance?

FLORENCE NIGHTINGALE: Ye-es....

DR. CAWS: You can only see some confused movement, a heaving, so to speak?

FLORENCE NIGHTINGALE: Just so, Doctor, a heaving ... oh, dear ...

DR. CAWS: But you can't make out the fish themselves?

FLORENCE NIGHTINGALE: No ... In fact, one does not want to think of fish. One is slightly—not to put too fine a point on it—nauseated.

DR. CAWS: But my dear, dear young lady, there is no need to be stopped by a mere temporary queasiness. Take no notice of it. You only have to achieve a more distinct, sharper-edged vision and all will be well. Concentrate! 121,393 plus ... plus what, Miss Nightingale?

FLORENCE NIGHTINGALE: Oh, please, Doctor, I can't, I've lost track. (*She takes a step backward, inadvertently brushing against a leper waiting to be healed.*)

DR. CAWS: No, you haven't, not a bit of it, Miss Nightingale. Here—come away from that painting, you'll catch something. Your vision is only a trifle blurred. And no wonder, my dear, no wonder, after what you've been through—a message from God, after all, God himself, no less, in the flesh. Really, now, what could anyone expect? But look—do look—into the pond again, I pray you, sweet friend, look closer. Breathe deeply, that will help. And close your eyes, my dear, if you like. It often works better if you close your eyes. (*She closes her eyes.*) There. Try it now. 121,393 plus what—what?

FLORENCE NIGHTINGALE: Ah! AH! Seventy-five thousand, and then a zero ...

DR. CAWS: Yes, Miss Nightingale, yes! Go on.

FLORENCE NIGHTINGALE: 75,025! Ah, now I see them, plain as day. They line up like soldiers on parade. 121,393 plus 75,025 is (*triumphantly*) 196,418!

DR. CAWS: Yes, it is, Miss Nightingale. My congratulations. And 196,418 plus 121,393?

FLORENCE NIGHTINGALE: Why, it's ... oh, my dear, my dearest Doctor! It's 317,811!

DR. CAWS: Precisely, dear friend, precisely. It is, it was and it always will be.

FLORENCE NIGHTINGALE: And 317,811 plus 196,418 is ... is ... 514,229!

DR. CAWS: But of course.

FLORENCE NIGHTINGALE: And 514,229 plus 317,811 is 832,040. And 832,040 plus 514,229 is 1,346,269. And 1,346,269 plus ... plus ... oh, dear friend, please, you must forgive me, everything's swimming again.

DR. CAWS: Please don't concern yourself, dear lady, I beg of you. Don't give it a second thought. Let the numbers swim a little now, if they want to. They've earned it, and so have you. Merely for the record, 1,346,269 plus 832,040 is 2,178,309. But you've done wonderfully well. It must be nearly time for you to return to your family in any case; we've been here quite a while, you know. So, in a few moments—whenever you feel yourself quite composed—you may safely open your eyes. You will, of course, find yourself back in this inspiring chapel, with its gorgeous collection of, uh, Masaccios. Indeed, my dear young friend, you have never left it. And—*il va sans dire*—you need not trouble yourself to remember anything of what has passed.

Magdagachi, Gusinoozersk, Ulaan Goom. The spinning globe loses speed. Karaganda, Chelkar, Kulsary. Astrakhan. Elista. Tikhoretsk. The sea horses prance a few minutes' worth. When they stop, Florence Nightingale and Dr. Caws are just leaving the church of

Santa Maria del Carmine, in which the Brancacci Chapel is situated, coming out into the busy daylight world of the Via Santa Monaca. Miss Nightingale is talking excitedly to her somewhat bewildered companion.

FLORENCE NIGHTINGALE: ... and all in linear perspective, with natural light and shadow, too! Oh, it may not seem so startling today, Doctor, especially not to you, familiar as you must be with the most advanced art of Paris—Picot, Vernet, Delacroix, to say nothing of Monsieur Ingres, of whom one hears so much—but in Masaccio's time—he began painting the frescoes about 1425, I think—it was a radical innovation, not only in Florence but in all of Western art. Why, it was as if the viewer were suddenly transported, beyond the chapel interior, into a wholly real world—as real as the one you and I now find ourselves in, here in this street. Oh, do be careful, Doctor. Keep an eye out for traffic. (*They press up against a building as a troop of horsemen clatters by.*) And this innovation was not merely a technical feat—no, there was a profound intent behind it: in these sacred scenes Masaccio wanted to show the spiritual existing in *this* world, the real physical space in which each of us lives, not the world of heaven or the hereafter. It was a time, you know, when the spiritual and the temporal—the down-to-earth—mixed freely together; that's what I love about the period. Have a care, Doctor, watch out for that pushcart. And there was even, I've read somewhere, a political message in those frescoes—all the heads, you know, are portraits of important people of Masaccio's day—promoting a movement to reunite all the city states of Italy into a single nation, in an order akin to the ancient Roman Empire. The idea was that the papacy should help to effect this change. Isn't that fascinating? Oh, I know what you're going to say, Doctor, with your aesthetic sophistication: you're going to demur. Such interpretations may be perfectly sound in their way, you'll say, but the proportions of his figures are derived not from rule but merely from observed experience. Adam's arms, for instance, are too short, his feet too big. And you'll be absolutely right, from the standpoint of strict academic correctness. But for expressive power, for plastically convincing volume and for the strength of individual characterization (just think of that head of Saint Peter healing, or the stricken face of Eve!) there is almost no one to equal Masaccio. And those who did equal him, learned from him! Why, Michelangelo himself came to the chapel, to copy those figures. And—just think— Masaccio was only twenty-six when he died—poisoned, some would have it, perhaps by a jealous rival, or even at the behest of some churchmen who objected to the papacy having to share power with a united—Oh! (*She breaks off, stopping suddenly in the middle of the street, and turns to Dr. Caws. They are on the Via Romana now, headed toward the Ponte Vecchio. Miss Nightingale has been striding purposefully ahead, and the doctor, struggling to catch up, almost bumps into her.*) I'm so sorry, Doctor; I feel such a fool. I've just realized—I've been doing all this chattering, on and on, and never even took notice of how lighthearted I've become—really *lighthearted*—for the first time in I don't know how long! I haven't the faintest idea what caused it, I only know that in some way you are responsible. How ever can I thank you?

DR. CAWS: My dear, dear Miss Nightingale, no thanks are necessary. I have all the gratification I could possibly want in your animation, your brilliant and edifying discourse, your manifestly rejuvenated spirit. You are too kind when you hint that I played a significant role in your transformation. You yourself are its cause, dear friend, you yourself and no one else. I only allowed greater freedom to what was already there in your being. I perhaps helped to remove an obstruction, shall we say. Do you remember last night, at the opera—it was just before the curtain rose, I think—we were conversing of this and that, and you happened to remark that doctors, well-meaning though they are, often cause disease in a patient, simply by the act of diagnosis? (*She nods.*) Well, it can be the same, exactly the same, my dear, with God.

FLORENCE NIGHTINGALE (*laughing winsomely*): Oh, Dr. Caws, you really are too amusing!

"And what do you think?" asks Eggbeater, addressing an elm leaf that has called itself to his attention, dancing in the breeze an inch or so away from his nose. "It turned out the girl hadn't even bothered to make up an excuse to give her family when she went off that day to see me. That's right; nothing whatever. Well, *I* couldn't believe it either, when she told me, but it was abso—Haroop!—absolutely true; her sister c'rob'rated it later. Miss Nightingale just marched into the drawing room, in the suite they were renting, and announced that she was leaving for the afternoon and wouldn't be back till dinner time. And then she left! Turned on her heel and walked out, without so much as a goodbye to any of 'em. And no one dared say anything—'magine that! Well, she certainly did have an *effect* on people, I can tes'fy to that if anybody's interested. I never met anyone more *determined* in my life. And I'll bet if you asked the British War Office about her, it would say just the same thing today!"

Krasnodar. Krymsk. Temryuk. Taman. The globe turns ever more slowly. The Crimea inches past Leibniz: Kerch. Feodosia. Koktebel. Sudak. Alushta. But the philosopher does not see them. He has dropped off to sleep, snoring gently, his wig fallen into his lap. He dreams of tangents, cosines and surds, of the alphabet of human thought, brass wheels spinning within brass wheels, marked with letters, numbers, hieroglyphs. A girl turns towards him in bed, her skin gold ochre in the light. "Lyebanists," she whispers. "Sweet Lyebanists!" He pulls her against his chest. Gurzuf. Yalta. Balaklava. The globe comes full stop.

Across Prospect St. Mrs. Mainwaring stands at her second storey window. "Calvin," she calls. "Calvin, come look! Dr. Caws is up in the tree again!"

Mr. Mainwaring joins her at the window. "Where?" he asks.

"Up there, near the top. In among the leaves." She points.

"Don't be stupid, Alice. That's only a big crow."

"No, it's not, either, it's the doctor. What you think is a crow is his coattails. You never get anything right, Calvin. Last time, you thought he was a vulture. The time before, a dress. Well, this time I *saw* him go up there. He was standing down by his front gate, after that man, that what's-his-name, that writer, had gone away, he was just standing there, and all of a sudden—Whoosh!—he rose straight up in the air and floated across the street and into the tree. He's up there now, talking to himself, something about the British War Office. Do crows talk about the British War Office? Do they, Calvin?"

"So now you're hearing things, too," says Mr. Mainwaring. "I knew we never should have bought this house." He turns away from the window.

"Philistine!" she shouts after him. "Pharisee! Lout! Newtonian!"

14

INTERMEZZI

1. The Dream.

The Cry of the Gehirngespinstgemach:

> The brass wheels go round,
> hieroglyphs flicker as they pass.
> "Lyebanists, sweet Lyebanists"—
> the gold-ochre girl turns to him in bed.

While Eggbeater talks to the elm leaves, in his pineal gland Leibniz sleeps on. In his dream he is twenty again, and the bed he and the girl are lying in is an old four-poster, with canopy, in his room on the *Fruchtgartenstrasse* in Nuremberg, just as it was, and they were, in waking life in early November, 1666.

Leibniz was finishing up his studies at the University of Altdorf, a *wunderkind* admired by all. He had just published his *Dissertation on the Art of Combination*, the treatise I mentioned a while back which Bach would later admire. Also, looking to deepen his knowledge beyond what the university offered, he had just joined a society whose members were dedicated to the transmutation of metals. He had straightway been made their secretary, and thus had access to the records they'd made of their experiments. "Pale and sweating," one of them read, "my nose pressed against the bowl of the glass, I saw them, if only for the blink of an eye. A tiny man and woman—or were they children? It was impossible to tell—were swimming near the bottom, joined in a lover's embrace. His skin—if it was skin, and not merely a

244

dark streak in the bloody broth of the waters—was a deep brown red, and hers—surely hers must have been that little smear of white which at first gla-ce seemed only a splotch of loppered milk. But no—there they were again, arms and legs wrapped round each other, the Red Man and the White Wife, going at it for fair! The Kingly Child—they were making the Kingly Child, I swear it, just as the old books promised! But even as I formed the thought, the vapours in the glass flew out in a great whirling cloud, by turns green, blue, black and yellow. The stopper blew off the mouth of the vessel. I staggered backward, my hair and eyebrows all singed. When I recovered myself I saw the work was ruined; nothing left of it but a layer of hardened slime stuck to the bottom of the glass."

Leibniz met the girl at the opera about a week after he joined the society. In fact, it could be said that the girl *was* the opera. Her name was—possibly—Maria; at least that was what she consistently called herself, though the titles she attached to it were plainly absurd, like those that appeared on the leaflet he had been handed as he was taking his seat, just before the start of the performance: "Tonight the role of Lipnike will be sung by the enchanting, the exotic, the gracile and *famous* MARIA PROPHETISSA, the Queen of the South, toast of two Continents and seven Seas, fresh from a tour of France, the Low Countries and the British Isles. She appears on our stage for this per-formance, AND FOR THIS PERFORMANCE ONLY, by the benevolent permission of His Grace, Lionel of Antwerp, first Duke of Clarence; Jobst, Margrave of Moravia; and Their Supreme Aurifacient Glories, Fu and Mu, Emperor and Empress of China, Afghanistan, Egypt and India."

"Not a word of truth in it," the gentleman sitting next to Leibniz assured him in a fatherly tone. "Lionel of Antwerp's been dead for centuries, you know. Halbstiefel found the girl only last month, in a tavern in Heidelberg. Can't be a day over twenty, if that. And," he added, as the orchestra, such as it was, shambled on stage with a few horns and a bass drum, " she sings the role every day, too. Friend of mine saw the piece yesterday, and there she was."

Leibniz had no need to be told. The claims made in the leaflet were man-ifestly fraudulent, blatant lies of the type he most detested, as they not only sought to deceive but to insult his intelligence into the bargain. Maria Pro-phetissa was a legendary alchemist, who lived—if she lived at all, which he seriously doubted—about the year 200. Jobst was long dead, too. Leibniz began to regret he'd ever come. He'd only done it in the first place to ingratiate himself with some people from the alchemical society, who had begged for the pleasure of his company that evening and who, he noticed, were now nowhere to be seen. He was on the point of leaving, and would have done so, except that his seat happened to be in the front row, and his departure, down the full length of the castle's hall, would have made him more conspicuous than he cared to be in a public place. So he stayed where he was, fuming. But all that changed when, a moment or two later, the orchestra struck up a ragged overture, the curtain was drawn back, and the girl came on for the first scene.

It was not—Lord knows it was not—her singing that took his fancy. Her voice was at best barely adequate, at worst embarrassing. There were odd misplacements of stress and intonation, so that the very meaning of some of the lyrics was thrown into question. He even doubted whether she knew the German language. No, it was her body that fascinated him, a supple, compact little body with an animal eagerness which spoke to him in every move she made. There was a vitality in her impossible to resist. Nor did he want to resist it. Even when she was standing still, her costume, an old, not very white sheet that made do for an ancient Greek slave girl's outfit, breathed with her, commanding his attention in a way that surpassed all his previous imaginings. Her skin as well had a mystery of its own; he never quite managed to classify her complexion—now a very light tan, now deep gold, now almost an olive shade, then copper flushed with pink. Abundant black hair, untied and falling loosely down her back. Soft black eyes, the lids painted with kohl. Leibniz could not take his eyes off her.

He went back to the opera, night after night, for the entire week remaining in its run, arriving well ahead of time to be sure of getting a front row seat, taking no chances despite the steadily diminishing attendance (for in truth the work was a miserable effort), always beaming with what he hoped was obvious delight when the girl entered and applauding loudly after her exits. For the plot of the piece he cared nothing; for the rest of the cast, some of whom sang even worse than she did, he had only contempt. His devotion was to her and her alone. But it was only after the final performance (at which he had been the sole spectator), when the curtain closed for the last time and the orchestra began to pack its gear, that he summoned the courage to venture backstage and talk to her. After all, he told himself, it was now or never. Besides, how formidable could she be? The gentleman who had sat next to him the first night had been right, she was only about twenty, his own age, probably less. And a tavern singer. He, on the other hand, was a university graduate, a doctor of law, an author. Also, he had thought up a couple of approaches to her that might at least seem passable, even though they did sound pretty stilted now as he ran them over in his mind. In any case, he had nothing to lose.

As it turned out, though, the girl saved him the trouble. For as he left his seat to make his way over to the curtain, she came out from behind it and walked straight up to him, a great welcoming smile on her face. "Aha! How de-lye-de-ful finally to meet you, Hair ... er ... Lyebanists, iss id nod?" She spoke in English—at least he thought it was English, but with a thick accent he had never heard before. "I ham Maria Prophetissa, lade-e-lly from London, where I was 'sociated wit tee great Philalethes—praps you haff glan-ced at his work—but before tat I ham from Egypp hand udder places. I ham also called, ass is 'scribed on tat paper in your hand, tee Queen of tee South, ass well ass udder tinjes nod mentioned there: Maria tee Jewess, Mary tee Copt, tee Queen of Sheba, tee Queen of Angkor Thom, tee Daughter of Pluto, *und so weiter*. But I ham above all, *mein* dear, *mein* dearest Sir, tee frand of him who iss lon-e-lly. Hand I ham so plea-sed to see you. *Enfin vous voilà! Guten Abend*, dear frand, *guten Abend*."

She executed a quick curtsy, then, seeing he was nonplussed (and not only on account of her accent, for English was not a tongue he was fluent in and he had to struggle to keep up), she reached out tentatively, as if with sudden shyness, to stroke the lace on his coatsleeve. "Ahh, Hair Lyebanists," she purred, "your honner will, I hop, podden my fo'wadnesses, but I haff heard so mush 'bout you, hand haff been so dezirrus of makinj tee acquainnance of sush a 'lustriuss gennelman, tee auffer of tat splennid work, *Tee Heart of Commonayshins*. I ham so—how you say?—*dankbar*? *Reconnaissant*? *Grato*? Tankful, tat iss tee word, I ham so tankful for your innrest—nide after nide, *mon Dieu*, hand always in tee front row—in our poor play. I would kiss your feets, ride now, here on tiss bare stage, I wood jet down flat on tee floor hand kiss your feets—excepp, I notiss, you are wearinj boots."

Leibniz stood there speechless. He could not believe his luck. The girl came closer and sighed, eyes cast down, her golden face suddenly flushed. Her fingers moved up his arm. "But oh, oh, I ham so sorry, Hair Lyebanists. Pleass b'leef me, I ham. Praps you do not care to haff your feets kissed. Praps you wood prefurr I kissed you elsewharr. Wharrever id iss, dearest Sir, Maria iss add your surface." She looked up at him and lowered her voice. "I hask only one thinj, although, Jod help me, I hoddly dare menshin id. I haff so mush wann-ed, for sush a lonj time now, sentries and sentries id seems, to fine tee ride man to do somethinj vey vey imporden wit me, and you, sweet purrson, are b'yon henny douts him. Cood you spayr me, do you tink, some liddel time—nod *vey* mush time really, juss seffenteen days, you will neffer miss id owd of your life, to make the Kinjly Child wit me? I do *so* mush hop you says yess. I worship you, Hair Lyebanists, I worship you."

Before Leibniz had a chance to respond, the curtain, the stage and the castle hall vanished, and, as he later recalled it, he and Maria were suddenly ensconced in her coach, driven by (as she called them) her "phil-soff-cull horses," riding at top speed across the city to the hotel where he was staying. The opera company were disbanding, she confided, leaning against him on the narrow seat and whispering in his ear, after this last and—"excepp for your own incompabull pressins"—completely unsuccessful performance. They were cancelling all future engagements, she had nowhere to go. And so she stayed with him—him of all people, university graduate, doctor of law!— secretly in his rooms: for exactly seventeen days she was his and his alone, and he was hers. They closed up the shutters, barred the door, let nothing and no one in. They would make the Kingly Child, she said. Leibniz protested that he had no vessels or other laboratory equipment, but she only laughed at him. "Oh, Lyebanists, Lyebanists, I luff you vey mush, but sometimes you are slidely silly. Id iss true tat in my time I haff made use of labtoy 'quipmens, in fack I haff invenn-ed a jood deal of jlassware, but for tiss we do not need tem, tey wood only be in tee way. *We* are tee vessels, Lyebanists, you hand me. Juss tee too of us. We take off our cloth-es, ride now. Comm!"

"And then, the morning of the eighteenth day, I woke up and she was gone. The shutters were open, the bar off the door. She'd vanished without a trace—except for a long black hair and a smudge of kohl on the pillow. Now, tell me, old man, could all that *really* have happened like that?" Leibniz asked, when he told his friend van Helmont the story years afterward. Could it, for that matter, have happened at all? The more he thought about it, and he thought about it a great deal in his later years, the whole thing seemed impossible, more a piece of wishful fantasy or fairy tale than an actual event. Perhaps it had simply been a dream, brought on by a too-close reading of his alchemical colleagues' experiments, late at night, with only a candle for company. But his memory, his stubborn memory, fought back, insisting that what had taken place had been no dream but a series of concrete, tactile actions in which he had physically participated—enjoying every minute of it, too. Seventeen days, after all, was a long, long time for a dream. Not since the fabled sleep of Epimenides—and it *was* a fable, without any doubt—had there been anything to match it. And how could he explain that black hair? And the kohl?

Van Helmont, who knew about such things, was inclined to agree. He did not for a minute consider the wishful fantasy or long dream hypotheses. He spoke instead of sylphs and sirens, dybbuks, mermaids and melusinae not as mythical creatures but as living entities who had their origin not only in the outer world but in the human soul as well, and who therefore could assume—often spontaneously—an infinite number of seductive, convincing and entirely palpable forms. If one of them took it into her head to appear as Maria Prophetissa, and, for that matter, add a whole opera, audience and castle hall into the bargain, van Helmont had no doubt she could do so. But if, on the other hand, the girl Leibniz had encountered actually *was* Maria Prophetissa, in her latest, present-day incarnation—well, *that* was a different matter entirely, different and far more mysterious. And the Kingly Child! The Kingly Child himself! Leibniz had read Philalethes, had he not? Of course he had. And he remembered that Philalethes specified that the Child takes exactly seventeen days to produce. And had not Maria told him that she was "lad-e-lly from London," where she had known Philalethes himself? "And I don't need to remind you," van Helmont added, "do I, old friend, that her statement, 'I am the friend of him who is lonely' is a famous one ascribed to Hermes Trismegistus—an even greater and more ancient figure than Maria?

"It seems to me, in fact, that you have been uncommonly blessed, singled out in a way that no one in our times can claim for himself. That opera, I hope you realize, was staged entirely for your benefit. Why else would they have put on such a dreadful performance if not to guarantee a smaller and smaller audience, night after night, and finally an audience of yourself alone? Maria, of course, knew you wouldn't leave: she saw to that, didn't she? I really do think," van Helmont concluded, "that you would have no trouble understanding any of these things had they happened to someone else, and not to your good and entirely worthy self. Even after all these years, you are still too close to these events: you are, if I may so express it, *inside them* in a way that keeps your understanding from operating properly—all it can do is make up absurdities such as 'fairy tales' and 'wishful fantasies.' All this is much realer than you have any idea.

"Let me put it this way: you are inside the events, but they are inside you as well. You are, as it were, like the mother who is sealed in the belly of her infant. You'll find that in Philalethes, too."

Leibniz listened, but he remained unconvinced. Until—fifteen years after the conversation with van Helmont and forty-five years after the girl herself—the Kingly Child himself appeared on his doorstep!

2. The Man I Love.

From *Jazz Me Blues: Further Computations of the Soul,* by Seneca Kirk (New York: Randolph and Wing, 2001).

It was Miles' session, he was the leader: "Miles Davis and the Modern Jazz Giants," recorded December 24, 1954. What a great record! Giant they were, all right, every one of them: Milt Jackson on vibes, Thelonious Monk on piano, Percy Heath on bass, Kenny Clarke on drums and Miles, of course, on trumpet. Some of the best musicians around, then or ever. The supreme wisdom had found the means, as Leibniz might have quipped. And Miles was the youngest of them, not that that mattered, musically speaking. He was the leader for that session, and what he said went. So when he told Monk to lay out during his solos—not play, that is, while Miles was improvising—Monk, even though he was nine years older and had a lot more experience, still had no choice but to do it. Now, here you need to understand something. Miles loved Monk; Monk had been one of his teachers. He used to go over to Monk's apartment all the time, like so many others did, to hear new chord changes, learn how to use space, how to get more freedom in his playing. So why tell him to lay out now? Ingratitude? "Killing the father"—some Freudian thing? No, nothing like that, nothing like that at all. Here's what he told Nat Hentoff in 1958: "I love the way Monk plays and writes, but I can't stand him behind me. He doesn't give you any support." Was that the whole story, though? I've heard it said, more than once, that what Miles really wanted was someone to shine his shoes, make him sound extra good. And Monk wasn't about to do that, not for Miles, not for anyone. As far as Monk was concerned, you had to be good on your own, or you shouldn't have been up there in the first place. Goodness is perfection of the will, baby, every time. But to be fair to Miles, Monk's comping could pose a player some serious challenges. I remember Sascha Feinstein telling me years ago, "Nobody—but *nobody*—ever comped for a soloist the way Monk did." And Don Cooper said, listening to one of his records, "You never know where he's going to go harmonically." But all that aside, when Miles told him to lay out, Monk was *pissed*. He hadn't come all the way from West 63rd St. to Hackensack, New Jersey on a Christmas Eve just to sit there and do nothing while Miles strutted his stuff. He played his ass off on his own solos, all right, and when he was comping behind Bags—"Bags" was Milt Jackson. But when Miles came on he had to lay out, and he was pissed.

He got even, though. When they were rehearsing "Bags' Groove" and Miles had begun his solo, Monk got up from the piano bench and went over and stood beside him—just *stood* there—while he was playing. Now, Monk was a huge man, and Miles was little, and anyhow he was sitting down, so Monk really towered over him. Wouldn't that have made you nervous, if it had happened to you? Well, it sure did Miles. He was spooked, and when the number was over he asked Monk why he'd done that. "I don't have to sit down to lay out," was all Monk said!

Then there was the famous argument on the first take of "The Man I Love," busting up the beginning of the piece. You can hear the voices on the record—Miles asked the engineer, Rudy Van Gelder, to keep it in and he did. But Monk got his best revenge in his solo on the second take of that tune— his own solo, mind you. Halfway through it he stopped, stopped cold. He was laying out on himself! Listen to it on the record, it's wild: first you're following Monk, digging what he's doing, waiting to hear what's coming next, and all of a sudden you realize *nothing's* coming next! There's no more piano, just Percy and Klook, bar after bar, bass and drums walking, keeping time. Finally Miles couldn't stand it. He came in—into what was still Monk's solo space, even if he wasn't using it—with a het-up little phrase, telling Monk on his trumpet to get out there and play. Well, as soon as he did that, man, Monk POUNCED! A jet spray of notes—"Get the fuck out of my space!" He'd been waiting for him, man, just waiting for him!

15

Asparagus Mazarin.
The Topsoil Purrs In Delight.
Alice Mainwaring Shakes Her Butt.

The Cry of the Gehirngespinstgemach:

May 28, 1855—

The day advances. In some parts of the world it is already drawing to a close. The long, well-ordered dream casts its net. Look!

Eggbeater Caws has fallen! He lies unconscious in the late afternoon sun, at the foot of the elm tree across the street from his house, his face buried in the grass. A North American grey squirrel stands guard a few inches from his nose.

"2222222222222222222," the dream tells Eggbeater. "2222222222222222. 6. 28. 496." Its voice is low and cultured, like Miss Nightingale's.

"Help," the squirrel tells himself, contemplating his fallen hero. "Needs help. Animals, come."

22222222222222222222222. On the hillside above Balaklava, in her hut under the stars, Florence Nightingale turns in her sleep. The moon is in Scorpio. Since Lord Raglan's visit—a dear man, a charming man, reminiscent (how?) of someone she knew long ago—her fever has been steadily diminishing. The Persian gentleman—finally!—has gone away, the multitudes have been fed and provided for, she can rest. She is a girl of seventeen again, the long, well-ordered dream tells her, mad only for opera, back in Florence in the Brancacci Chapel in front of *Saint Peter Healing the Sick with his Shadow*. Years seem to pass, a century, an aeon, continents are molded, minerals grow in the earth, granite, feldspar, gypsum, hematite, and still she is a girl of seventeen, gazing at the fresco. But at last there sounds a fanfare of trumpets; an unruly, laughing crowd bursts into the chapel. It is the cast of *Das Gehirngespinstgemach*, Thales, Lipnike, Gyges and the Dog. Splendid in their costumes, they cavort around her bed. Eggbeater Caws comes out from behind the altar, grinning obsequiously, his moustache curling up over his cheeks. A grey squirrel sits on his left shoulder; in his arms he cradles a package wrapped in grey paper. "Ah, Miss Nightingale," he says. "My dear, dear, dear, dear young lady, I thought I should find you here. Florence is simply too charming at this time of year, is it not? 222222222222222." He starts to undo the package. "Permit me to present you with some small—oh, very small, but conceivably amusing—tokens of my esteem." He takes out an object and holds it up. It looks like a zucchini. "Miss Nightingale, I give you the number 6!" He holds up a rutabaga. "And the number 28!" He holds up a carrot, then a bunch of radishes. "496! 8,128 as well!" He approaches the bed. "A bouquet of perfect numbers, my dear young lady, perfect numbers chockablock with their aliquots, perfect numbers for a perfect soul—if I may so express myself without overstepping … without seeming to overstep … the bounds of … the bonds … without seeming, that is, to break free of, I mean, the trammels of … the trammels of … good and proper breeding, everything we hold sacred and, er, profane. Ah! Ah!" He flings aside his vegetables and paces back and forth histrionically in front of the fresco, head thrown back, hand pressed to his forehead. "This breeding, Miss Nightingale, this breeding will be the death of me, I swear. Try as I may I cannot stop it. 33,550,336! There, you see? It's happened again." He drops to his knees before her. "What more can I say, my dear young lady, what more can I say?"

"Why, 8,589,869,056," she answers, smiling. "8,589,869,056, to be sure, my dear doctor. 137,438,691,328," she adds, winking at the squirrel, who has just jumped up onto her pillow. "All the aliquots you could possibly desire."

King Squirrel I, his one-and-a-half inch tall porcelain body glowing softly in the starlight, surveys his domain from the heights of the dresser in the bedroom in Naumburg, Germany. Below him, on the window sill, the table, the floor, miniature soldiers are deployed, French, Russian and English, all made of lead, gathering in raiding parties, crouching in trenches, behind earthworks, in craters imagined by their young general, Friedrich Nietzsche, the King's master. The boy sleeps soundly, in his bed on the other side of the room, the long, well-ordered dream deflected away from him. For some time now, since the disturbing dreams he experienced after the death of his father a few years ago, young Nietzsche has made a point, every night before bedtime, of instructing the Squirrel to do his dreaming for him. The King is well-equipped to comply. Molded a century ago by the ceramist J. J. Kaendler out of kaolin and alabaster, treated with Philosophers' Wool, Butter of Antimony, Butter of Tin, the Doves of Diana, the Eagles of Jupiter, the Stone Serpents, the Philosophical Fish, the Green Lion, the Red Lion, the Red Man and his White Wife—all strictly in accordance with the specifications the mad alchemist Böttger scrawled on a bit of paper just days before his death—and fired in a kiln at 1450 degrees centigrade, King Squirrel I is endowed with faculties far outstripping those of ordinary chinaware. He can count up to 2, for instance, and hear things taking place miles away. He can see and even speak after a fashion, but only very softly and only to his master. Placed in a solution of rainwater and toad's urine, he releases a substance that cures catarrh, hives, ringworm, jaundice, scrofula, pox, constipation, diarrhoea, ulcers, gout, yaws, grinder's rot, the French Disease, the English Disease, the Italian Disease, the Swiss Disease, the Spanish Disease, the Dutch Disease, the Flemish Disease, the German Disease, the Polish Disease, the Danish Disease, the Swedish Disease, the Norse Disease, the Finnish Disease, the Russian Disease, the Portuguese Disease, the Turkish Disease, the Greek Disease, the American Disease, kidney troubles, bladder infections, red-water, pink-eye, bluetongue—a panacea that would have been the envy of Eirenaeus Philalethes or young Newton's Mr. Clark. Dreaming is nothing for him. He closes the eyes installed behind his painted ones, descends through his inner world of feldspar and gypsum, and begins.

2222222222222222222222222. In the Rue de Lille in Paris, in the apartment he and his wife share, Monsieur Jean-Auguste-Dominique Ingres, portly, seventy-four and the first painter of Europe, prepares to retire, having earlier in the evening attended a banquet at the Salle Montesquieu, where the menu included four soups (turtle, cold chicken *velouté*, purée of barley and carrot, and sturgeon), six kinds of fish (trout, turbot, sole, whiting, salmon and carp), roast chicken with truffles, chicken fried in batter with bread crumbs and eggs, stuffed chicken with béchamel sauce, calf's sweetbreads, lambs' testicles, pheasant, duck, partridges in aspic, braised goose, roast larks in a pastry, potted pigeons, quail with grapes, lobster au gratin, jugged hare, roast venison, saddle of lamb, rack of lamb, roast pig, beef with glazed onions, round of veal, rump of veal, oysters, sea urchins, *langoustines*, snails, pike fillets, mussels, squid, apricot fritters, artichoke hearts, asparagus, Mazarin, *pommes à l'huile*, cauliflower Bragelonne, peas à l'anglaise, salad à l'Alsacienne, caviar, cantaloupe, peaches Varenne, cheese brioche, nougat, chocolate soufflé, vanilla custard, Italian ices and seventeen kinds of cheese, all washed down with plentiful quantities of Beaujolais, Bordeaux, Chablis, Burgundy, Rhone wines, champagne, marc, cognac and Armagnac. Taking off his shirt, the artist recalls the famous passage in Plotinus on the enforced transmigration of sinful human souls into the bodies of animals, and speculates idly on what the great Neo-Platonist might make of the moral failings which, according to his theory, now drift to and fro in the painter's digestive system. On the whole, however, when he considers the manifest beauty and sweetness of so many animals he has known, especially the cats he used to feed at the Villa Medici in Rome, Monsieur Ingres is inclined to prefer the counter-theory of Valerius Turpens, which he came across one day in the Villa's library, that animals do penance—voluntarily and for the sins of the whole world—by suffering reincarnation as humans. "*Quel sacrifice!*" He sighs, thinking of the bloated face of one of his fellow diners, the contemptible Monsieur X, whose excesses have scandalized even the Paris of the Second Empire. "*Et quel gaspillage en sus.*"

2222222222222222222222222. Sarah Maloney and Charity Foxcroft, late of New York and Philadelphia, dead by their own hands no more than a day, have crossed the River Styx. Never having met in life, they nonetheless have disembarked together from Charon's boat and walked side by side across the scorching Plain of Lethe. Now, as Monsieur Ingres delivers himself of a long, pleasurable belch and King Squirrel dreams porcelain pigs, beavers, frogs, chickens, cats and elephants, they reach the River Lethe and throw themselves, panting, down on its bank to drink from the Waters of Forgetfulness, cupping their hands in the stream. With each swallow a portion of their lives is wiped out. They drink and drink and drink, tasting contentment they never dreamed possible. Cleansed! Cleansed! They dunk their heads in the water, then plunge in all the way. Behind them a new contingent lines up, souls of the creatures killed to make the banquet at the Salle Montesquieu. They cluck and chirr, growl, twitter and moan, impatiently waiting their turn. The women stand in the river and sing. Monsieur Ingres, himself a former West African bush pig although he naturally is unaware of the fact, snuffs out his candle and gives himself to sleep.

His dream will return again and again in coming months, nightly companion of his spring and summer. He finds himself deep in the ground, under the city of Paris, making his way carefully along a narrow passage through abandoned mines and catacombs cut into gypsum beds in the sedimentary rock, keeping an appointment with Monsieur X. How could he have allowed this to happen? He asks himself. It all comes of not being able to say no. He passes a low-ceilinged chamber where a madman, held on a long chain attached to the wall, molds animals out of clay and casts them into a furnace. In another chamber Paganini is playing violin. In the third, a disused graveyard with broken monuments and headstones, Monsieur X is waiting for him. Obese, oily as ever, he wears a thick new moustache with its ends curling up, making him even more repulsive than usual. Smirking, he explains that this will be the artist's new studio; he indicates paints and an easel set up in a corner of the cemetery. Monsieur X has paid for everything, he assures him, and will continue to pay, "*généreusement, généreusement, cher maître,*" until the commission for which he has engaged the painter is finished. This is to be a portrait of a young lady, "*une protégée*" of his; he pronounces the word slowly, with long, loving attention to its vowels. The lady's name, he continues, need not concern the artist, indeed it must not on any account be spoken, not even in a whisper: to do so could only profane it. It will suffice to understand that she is a person of enormous wealth and beauty, whose charms are given added piquancy by the slight whiff—the tiniest *soupçon*—of *notoriété*, not to say *scandale,* that surrounds her. He smacks his lips. She is possessed of those classic unforgettable features which Monsieur Ingres has painted a hundred times, and to which he alone can *fait honneur*, do justice. "*Seulement vous, seulement vous,*" Monsieur X repeats, leering. "*Vous êtes unique du monde.*" He chuckles, as if at some private joke, then bows himself out of the chamber with perfunctory phrases of admiration slurred together, expressing appreciation in advance for the work the painter will do. The lady, he adds, will arrive momentarily.

Not much gratified by the interview—the man was insincere to the point of insult—Monsieur Ingres nevertheless decides to make the best of things. He hates to do portraits, they usually make for nothing but aggravation, but he seems to be stuck with this job and the sooner he can finish it the better. He starts looking through the broken monuments and other rubble for inspiration, muttering "*honneur … honneur*" to himself. Perhaps he will paint her as the Roman goddess of justice, scandal or no, as Bona Dea, seated on a throne. But wait! Monsieur X said young. Young! His mood brightens. Justice, indeed! Who gives a fig for it? If she is young he must make her a Kore. Yes! The spirit of spring, of nature startled anew into life. The painter's heart goes out to such freshness, such innocence—all the more poignant because so short-lived, so fragile. Ah, such good fortune, to be given the opportunity to recapture it! He will paint her as he did Mademoiselle Rivière half a century ago, in a pure white dress, with a great white ermine boa, stuffed with swans' down—ah, the lovely, the tragic Mademoiselle Rivière, dead at only fifteen, not a year after the painting was completed—

A blast of trumpets brings him out of his reverie. It seems to come from one of the rooms behind him, probably the cell where the madman is working. A fanfare! Yes! She is coming, she is coming. He hears a rustle, as of skirts, moving along the passageway outside. Ah—and what is that other sound, that ever-so-soft whisper, a brushing, a brushing, could it be fur against cloth? Could it be—is it too much to hope for—an ermine boa stuffed with swans' down, keeping pace with its mistress, dancing, frolicking, coiling itself round her body? Is its mistress Mademoiselle Rivière herself, back from the dead, a ravishing Persephone? Ah! AH! The rustling grows louder, any moment now she will enter, whoever she is. Monsieur Ingres feels like a lad of twenty-five again. Of twenty! Of eighteen! Of—But there, on that *of*, it all ends. He wakes with a grunt in his bedroom, Madame Ingres asleep by his side. Somewhere, behind the wall or maybe inside it, through hundreds of miniscule cracks in the plaster, babies are talking.

2222222222222222. King Squirrel counts in his sleep. The porcelain animals pair off, pigs and beavers first, elephants bringing up the rear. The Red Man and his White Wife lead the dance, a blanket hornpipe. Out, in, in, out, inside, upside, outside, down. 2222222222222222.

In her sitting room in Aubrey, Efficiency Caws' body lies unconscious on the settee. But her soul is wide awake in her pineal gland, where she and Isaac Newton are hard at work. They lie together naked beside Newton's alchemical furnace, curled up in a nest they have constructed out of interstitial tribecular tubing, swans' feathers and Philosophers' Wool. "Goo, goo, goo-goo-goo, goo," she whispers to him. "Coo, coo, coo," he answers. "Coo-goo, coo-goo, coo, goo, goo." They rub each other with clarified Butter of Antimony. The Kingly Child gestates in the retort.

Light! Light! Let there be Light! Outside on the grass a Son of Light, Eggbeater Caws—Royal Arch Mason of Batavia, New York, knower of the secret name of God; Rising Leibniz of Aubrey, Massachusetts; builder of the Delphic Oracle; animal magnetist and healer of Paris, London and Florence; defender of the Unborn where ever he goes—opens an eye. Two eyes. Green. Green. Nothing but green; smell of sod and meadow-grass. Who is he, where is he. Killing headache, thirst. Somewhere a dog barks. Christ. Have to find a drink. Christ! Can I even move? He shuts his eyes again.

Brother Chaos, you are in the dark.

Brother Chaos, you are in the dark.

Is there no help, no help for the widow's son?

In the blackness behind his eyes aeons pass in an instant. A fiery globe appears, its crust a glowing red-orange; flames leap up through fissures in the rock. The fire subsides, the globe turns grey, then blue, then green. A mist rises from its surface; lightning flashes in the heavens. Rain pours down, a great wind rises. The sea surges over the land. Cities and empires are swept away, fishbones cast up on the mountains, the British War Office in a treetop. A thousand yetis dance in the Harz on the head of a pin, stuck like a piton into the peak of the Brocken. "*Metoh-kangmi, metoh-kangmi, metoh-kangmi,*" they sing, shrieking over the noise of the storm. The rain turns to snow. It is the last week of January again, all the passes are blocked. Leibniz composes the *Discourse on Metaphysics* in a mountain cabin, with werecats and kobolds howling at the door. The continual action of God upon us. One of the worst winters on record. My dear, dear young lady. Aaaaaaaaaggggggh.

Is there no help for the widow's son?

Far below the doctor's brain, deep in the great adductor muscle of his right leg, Thelonious Monk lifts his hands over the keyboard. They hover there, set to descend. With a groan the doctor rolls over, onto his side. The tenor saxophone is here to stay. You can watch anything, you can watch rabbits. He opens his eyes. AAAAAAGH!

The grey squirrel is sitting there, less than a foot away, staring at him with grave, worried eyes.

Oh. Oh. It's Squirrel, he tells himself. Good old Squirrel. Thought for a minute I was seeing things again. Remember those hippopotami last year? A brace of them, sashaying down Prospect Street, cool as you please. Made the turn together into the Burying Ground, right through the front gate, in perfect step with each other, and disappeared into thin air. Somewhere around the Exhumation Sweet monument, or the Mallard family. Prancing along one second without a care in the world, the next second—poof! He shudders. That's what comes of drink. Or the lack of it. Just goes to show you. Better get some, Eggbeater, if you know what's good for you. Now.

He tries to move, fails. Monk's hands stay poised in the air.

Imagine it. You can do it if you imagine it. Maybe. Imagine it.

The doctor does. He imagines raising his torso, using his forearms, flat on the ground, as a brace, getting himself on all fours, resting a moment, breathing deeply, then, in a single effort, so smooth it seems no effort at all, rising gracefully to his feet, straightening his clothes, looking around, orienting himself (he *thinks* he is across the street from his house, under the big elm tree, but it will do no harm, and possibly a great deal of good, to be sure), then walking, even flying perhaps, or skimming (a thing that gives him great joy), the soles of his boots just brushing the tips of the grass, across the street, through (or over) his front gate, and quickly down the path, past his house, to the barn behind it, without being seen, and inside where, he is certain if he is certain of anything, a bottle—two bottles, maybe even three!—wait patiently for him, snuggled safe beneath a length of sailcloth, against the wall under old man Barton's worktable. Or simply running, getting somehow to his feet and running, bent over, head down, stumbling, across the street, pulling the damn gate off its hinges if he has to, then down the path any old way so long as it's fast, even rolling, what the hell does he care who sees him, just so he gets to the barn and in, in, in at last, ahhhhhhhhh.

He imagines all this, he strains to put it into action, but it does not take place. Nothing takes place but the thought. Then the thought that nothing takes place. Nothing at all, no matter how hard he tries. Mind and body have parted company. The harmony is disestablished. Monk drops his hands to his side. Oh, dear. Oh, dear.

Ben Webster will record "Easy to Love" in 1965.

Joe Albany will record "Little Suede Shoes" in 1966.

Hampton Hawes will record "Crazeology" in 1958.

Charles Mingus will record "The Shoes of the Fisherman's Wife Are Some Jive Ass Slippers" in 1971.

But in 1855, in Aubrey, lying paralyzed on the ground in broad daylight, what is to be done? Is there really no help, no help for the widow's son?

("Help," says the squirrel. "Animals, help.")

Lie here, Eggbeater tells himself. Stop struggling. Lie here till it passes. *If* it passes. *If*, Brother Chaos. And if not? Oh, dear. Oh, dear.

Silence. For the first time (in how long?) the doctor becomes aware of a silence. Not in the world outside; he still hears the birds in the trees, the rustle of leaves, and that damn dog barking—won't it ever stop?—well enough. No, this silence is inside himself, where most people never hear anything, their whole lives, but where he, for years now, has been getting—Oh, no. NO. This is serious.

Leibniz. Leibniz. What has happened to Leibniz? His inspiration, his mentor, his companion, his friend, his guide. That voice, sympathetic, even-tempered, inexhaustibly intelligent, a little bit reedy but rich, rich and vibrant, like that invention of Adolphe Sax's the doctor first heard in Belgium, witty, quizzical, serious, intimate, revelatory, a balm and an instigator, confessor, instructor, entertainer, homilizer, sometimes loud, sometimes soft, sometimes quiet as snowfall but never, never, entirely absent—that great voice, suddenly stilled. And in its place? Nothing. Cold, empty nothing. Drafty nothing, shivery nothing. Silent nothing. Is this what it was like *before* Leibniz came? Eggbeater wonders. He can't believe it. Surely he didn't live, couldn't have lived, forty-five years this way, his whole life, until that day five years ago when he and Efficiency, after having been driven practically out of their minds ... Yet it must have been like this, it must. Only the voice made a difference, the voice made everything possible, and there was never a voice before Leibniz. No wonder he made such a mess of things. Heart in the right place, of course, whose isn't, but otherwise? My God. Eggbeater feels as if he could wander for centuries—if he were still capable of wandering, that is—through the corridors and anterooms and closets of himself and could never come across one scrap of evidence of human habitation. Just a cold, cold wind. Brain a blank, unused—he whose mind bubbled with the voice, right up through this very morning, ideas vaulting, piggyback, one over the other, then all down together in a tumble, and up again eager for more. Up, up, up again. Up.

And now?

And now?

Well, you have to make allowances, even for Eggbeater. How did anyone live before *jazz*? That's what I don't understand. Heart in the right place, of course, but otherwise? You have to make allowances:

Sonny Stitt will record "At Last," but in 1982.

Harry Edison will record "Blues for Bill Basie," but in 1957.

Harold Ashby will record "Just Squeeze Me," but in 1992.

Sheila Jordan will record "Baltimore Oriole," but in 1962.

Hampton Hawes; Charlie Parker; Art Tatum and Ben Webster; and Bud Powell and Don Byas will record "All the Things You Are," but in 1955, 1945, 1956 and 1961 respectively.

Charles Mingus will record "All the Things You Could Be by Now if Sigmund Freud's Wife Was Your Mother," but in 1960.

And this afternoon in 1855 ...

A good thing I laid in a stock of wigs, anyway, the doctor says to himself. And dresses, and gauze for ectoplasm. Efficiency always made fun of me for that, back when we were just starting out. "What have we got to worry about?" she said one time. "We're not like those other mediums, the Spitz brothers, and Kranck up in New Hampshire, or that assistant of Hobart's down in Braintree who got caught last week sending his master prearranged hand signals. Our ghosts are *real*. They're real and they do things nobody else can—and *we* couldn't either, if we tried to fake it. What good would a few wigs and a change of clothes do, if Newton and Leibniz ever left us? But they're not going to leave. Can't you feel it, Eggbeater? I can. They *like* us, and they're here to stay! Remember what Uncle Isaac said last night, at the séance in Gloucester? 'Bodies will pass through uniform Mediums in right Lines without bending into the Shadow,' he said. Sweetheart, I ask you: do our Lines look bent to you? Of course they don't, they're as straight as straight can be. This act will go on forever." Sweetheart, I ask you. Hah. I wonder how long *she'll* last. She certainly didn't look any too chipper this morning, crawling under the settee. Stayed there, too, the whole time what's his name—Welkin—and I were talking. Probably still there, sleeping it off. Terrible thing, drink; she never could handle it, really. Worse and worse these days. Go on forever—pooh. Well, at least one of us had some foresight. We can limp along for a while, I suppose. I used to be able to manage some fairly quick costume changes on the Continent, in the days I was on the run, and as long as we stop doing séances in broad daylight and keep the curtains drawn I ought to—Oh, what in the name of God are you talking about, Eggbeater? You can't even move, let alone change your clothes. And even if you could, who's going to want to come and see Leibniz stumbling around the room in a borrowed frock? It's Leibniz *rising* they want, rising and scoring off Newton and rolling around on the ceiling and smoking cigars up there and making eyes at the ladies and generally lending the proceedings some *tone*. You couldn't lend tone in your present condition to the ground you're lying on. Face it, Eggbeater. The act is finished. You are finished. You'll probably never walk again, or even crawl, much less fly. Acute, irreversible ascending paralysis is what you've got, or I'm no doctor. Pott's paraplegia, too. Cerebellar atrophy, in all likelihood, into the bargain. Tick paralysis. Lambing disease. Milk leg. Oh, God, I need a drink.

"Dr. Caws? Oh, Dr. Caws!"

The voice comes from somewhere above him, behind him and to his right, floating down through the spring sunshine. A voice full of concern and sympathetic interest: Mrs. Mainwaring. Of course, the doctor thinks, might have known it. Leave it to her to find me out. Why else did she make her husband buy that house, anyhow, right across from ours, except to keep an eye on me and contrive occasions for us to meet. Completely dotty, and a busybody to boot. She adores me, damn it. Can't let her see me like this; I'd better—you idiot, Eggbeater, in the name of God what are you saying? She *has* seen you like this, would she have called out like that if she hadn't? You really *are* losing your mind, old man: cerebellar atrophy for certain. Aaaaaaaaaggggggggghhhh-hhh! Move, God damn it, try at least to move. Move, body, move.

"Dr. Caws! Are you all right?"

He strains again within himself, wills one long wrenching twist, and—a miracle!—actually turns over on his other side, so that his gaze is directed upward, at the second storey window of the Mainwaring house, where, sure enough, Mrs. Mainwaring is looking down at him, eyebrows furrowed with care. Big, florid face, as usual, light grey hair, almost white, piled on her head in layers, like a cake. Twenty years ago it would have been blond, he thinks. Or not. Does it matter? "Guuughhghssshhhhhh?" he asks aloud.

"Are you all right, Dr. Caws?"

Well, at least I have a voice. Of sorts. Go on, now. Make words with it.

Quickly he summons what faculties he has left, what fragments of vocabulary (Leibniz, Leibniz—where in the world is Leibniz?) to deal with, to stave off, to placate (Oh, God, please let me placate!) this dreadful woman until I … Until you what? *What?* Never mind that now, Eggbeater, can't you see you have to say something quick? Talk, damn it, *talk.*

"Oh," he manages, after what seems an hour. "Oh … uh … yes, Mrs. Mainwaring, perf … perf … perfectly all right, thank you for so much asking. That is, I mean, thank you so much for … for, uh … for that. Yes.

Good afternoon, by the way," he ventures. "It is—er—it is still afternoon, is it not?"

"Why of course it is, doctor, of course it is, latish, I admit, but definitely afternoon. What an, uh, amusing question to ask." She smiles indulgently. "You are so delightfully unpredictable, Dr. Caws. Uh ... are you *quite* certain that you're ... "

"Oh, yes, thank you, madam. Quite, quite, quite certain. Quite. Only a slight ... uh ... syncope." (There. That ought to hold her.)

"But you were all the way up at the top of that tree."

"Oh, well ... " (Was I? Damn.)

"I was watching you."

"Oh yes?" (She would be, the pry.)

"And I turned away from the window—just for a second, I swear—to fetch something for Calvin—for Mr. Mainwaring, that is—but what Mr. Mainwaring wanted wasn't where I thought it was, and it took me, oh, just a moment or two longer than I thought it would, but no appreciable time, doctor, no *appreciable* time at all ... "

"Ah ... yes. No appreciable time. Mr. Mainwaring, yes. I see." (What the hell is she getting at? My head is killing me.)

"And then I came right back, right back I promise you, and there you were flat on the ground." A note of aggrievedness comes into her voice, as if she had been denied a treat and the doctor owes her an explanation.

"Well, yes, uh, yes," he begins. His memory of the afternoon is nearly a blank. He recalls Welkin leaving, late in the morning, he thinks, but as for what happened after that he has little to contribute, beyond a feeling that a substantial amount of time definitely passed. He thinks he had a conversation with a leaf, followed by a floating sensation, then a gradual descent. But whether this happened this afternoon, or several days ago, or even last year and to someone else, is a mystery to him. Nor does it seem of the slightest importance. But placate, placate. He manages to sit up, his head reeling.

"Yes, as you say, madam, yes, indeed, dear lady, flat. Flat as a ... uh ... [Quick: the epitome of flat, what is it? Flat as a what—Horse? Hand? Newel-post? Where is Leibniz? Leibniz would know that right off.] ... As flat as flat can be," he finishes lamely. "As I say, a slight syncope." He makes a final effort.

"Surely you, dear lady, with your, uh, spiritually ... spiritually *advanced* sensibility, surely you can understand. Syncope or ... or lipothymy, yes, one might equally say lipothymy. Or catabasis, dear lady, assuredly one could go that far. Cataplasia, even. Much the same thing, really. In the East it is called ... [What the hell *is* it called in the East? Yeti? No, not yeti. It isn't called anything in the East. Why in the name of God did you start that sentence, Eggbeater? Madness, sheer madness.]

He gropes for a word. Any word. "Aliquots!" he finally shouts." (Now, whatever made me say "aliquots?" I haven't thought of aliquots for years. And why does it remind me of Miss Nightingale?)

"Oh, doctor, your vocabulary is such a wonderful thing." Mrs. Mainwaring seems mollified. She beams down at him from the window. "Words, words, beautiful words—I've never seen you at a loss for them. I always say to Calvi—to Mr. Mainwaring, that is—'What a vocabulary that Dr. Caws has! I wish you could be more like him.' Of course ... " she leans over the sill and lowers her voice to a stage whisper " ... Mr. Mainwaring is a *Newtonian*." She sighs, and raises her eyes to heaven. All the sorrows of the world have come upon her. "Oh, I'm sure it comes as no surprise to you, doctor; I've no doubt it's general knowledge by now, the way stories spread in this town. I'm not proud of it, Heaven knows—some days I think I must die of the shame. Some days I can't even bring myself to leave the house, I just stay here at the window, looking, looking, and thinking—ah, thinking of happier times, when the world was young and all of us were gay. Little did we know, ah, little, so little, did we know." She wipes away a tear and tucks an imaginary wisp of hair back into the layer cake. "Still, there it is, dear doctor. One must face facts. One cannot give way entirely to grief, nor can one live wholly in the past, as much as—I don't mind admitting—as much as one sometimes would like to. Each of us has a cross to bear, I'm sure you have yours as well, dear sir, and one must simply go ahead and make the best of things, day by day. Mr. Mainwaring is a Newtonian. That is a fact, and one must face it, repulsive as it is. I, on the other hand, am a Leibnizian, and I say it with pride, sir, the name Leibniz is my banner, by blazon, my gonfalon, my faith. I draw my every strength from it, my strength to go on. But oh, it is hard, hard." An impulse seizes her. "Dear sir, dear doctor, I wonder if you could—I would be so grateful if you could suggest—Dr. Caws! What are you doing?"

"What? Oh. Er, yes, Mrs. Mainwaring." During the preceding, the doctor had spied his feather and glass on the ground about twenty feet away, pitched himself forwards, raising himself to a kneeling position, dropped on all fours and crawled over to retrieve them. When Mrs. Mainwaring calls his name, he is licking the inside of the glass for traces of alcohol. "Yes, dear lady. My apologies. I was merely ... uh, merely ... uh, merely ... yes. My feather, you know." He holds it up to her. "Feather. Old friend. Old ... friend. Oh, please do not think," he adds hastily, noticing her frown, "please do not think for an instant, dear lady, my dear, dear Mrs. Mainwaring, that I was not taking in, taking in and digesting, digesting and absorbing, even, if I may coin a ... coin a ... word ... osmosing, yes, osmosing, everything you were good enough to be saying. [What *was* she saying? Catabasis? Yeti? No, that was me. Oh, yes: Newtonian. Her husband. Shame of it.] You are quite correct, and your attitude is no less admirable, not to say heroic, no less heroic for being ... for being

... [For being what? For being *what*? I've got to get to the barn.] ... for being the only possible one to take and still remain ... ['still remain'—what a miserable construction; Leibniz would never have stooped to that.] ... still remain ... uh, sane. Yes. Still remain sane. Yes. Still remain sane. Yes. Still remain sane. Sane." He throws the glass away, having found it worse than useless, a mere tease, but puts the feather carefully in his vest pocket. He starts crawling toward his front gate, which he sees waiting—faithfully!—across the street. "Sane," he repeats in a whisper. "Sane. Sane. Sane."

"But, doctor ... " she calls after him. "Dr. Caws!"

Keep going, keep going, he tells himself. Tactical retreat. "Good day, Mrs. Mainwaring," he mumbles. "Pressing business, you know. Extremely pressing. Must attend to." Sane, sane, sane, he adds silently. Gate, gate. Get to the gate. You can do it. Then the barn. Barn. Barn. Barn.

"Doctor! I beg of you!" Her voice rises to a shriek. "Whatever am I to *do*? I am practically beside myself with worry. Oh, the shame, the shame!" She rips and tugs at her hair, ruining the layer cake.

The doctor stops. Damn. Have to humor the woman. She'll have the whole town here if she keeps that up. So much for tactical retreat. Damn.

"Forgive me, dear lady, I beseech you," he begins. "My behavior was quite inexcusable." While he is not yet by any stretch of the imagination old, commanding Caws-Leibniz of the séance room, his voice at least has regained a touch of its former suavity. The realization that he is actually capable of sustained motion, even if it be on all fours, and that his barn is therefore an attainable goal in this lifetime, not a mocking will-o-the-wisp, has quickened him. "I must apologize for my manner of, uh, peripatesis. I make small doubt it must have seemed odd, even, perhaps, wholly original, but in point of fact it forms an essential part of an old, if little-known regimen, originated by, uh, originated by someone. It does wonders for the, uh, popliteal region—ham of the knee, to the lay person. But then I ask myself, as we all must in the end, what is one popliteal region more or less, when Newtonians appear on the scene? I quite understand your distress. Tell me, dear Mrs. Mainwaring, if I may be so bold as to enquire, how does Mr. M. manifest his Newtonianism?"

"Oh, in any number of ways, doctor, any number of ways. It is so hard." Now that she has his attention again, her manner is more subdued. She chokes back her tears and begins patting her hair into place.

"Be as specific as you care to, dear lady, although I realize, of course, that one cannot recite ... even in confidence, to a trusted physician ... all the ... that is to say, I would deeply sympathize with your position if you preferred to keep ... But often such revelations are, uh, good for the soul."

"We-ll ... a great heaviness has overtaken him of late."

"Heaviness."

"Yes. He mopes and skulks about the house. Nothing suits him."

"Ah."

"He has no levity in his being."

"No levity. Oh, dear."

"He is obsessed with gravity."

"Oh? In what way?"

"It seems always to be on his mind: he says 'down' all the time."

"'Down'?"

"Yes. As in: 'Alice, quiet *down*.' He—oh, I wonder if you knew, doctor," (she smiles winningly) "that my first name is Alice?" She giggles.

"Yes, dear lady, I, uh, believe I had heard something to that effect, now you mention it."

"You had? Oh, I'm so glad." She blushes. "Anyway, he says it all the time."

"'Alice'?"

"No, '*down.*' Of *course* he says 'Alice.' Oh. Oh, I see. You will have your little joke, won't you, doctor? Ha-ha. Levity. Yes, levity—oh, I miss it so!"

"Ah, yes. Levity is the soul of wit. But tell me, dear lady, he does not by any chance—forgive me if I appear to be taking a liberty—but he does not by any chance happen to, uh, *elongate*, does he?"

"You mean, get taller?"

"Yes."

"Like Mrs. Caws?"

"Precisely."

"Why, no. Not *precisely*. I don't think he ... he might be an inch or so taller in his new boots. But nothing like Mrs. Caws, no." She looks at him with new sympathy. "Ah, my dear sir, I should have remembered. My sorrow cannot compare to your own." Her eyes fill with tears again.

"Still, as you say, madam, we all have a cross to bear." He sighs. "My heart goes out to you, Mrs. Mainwaring, as a fellow sufferer. However, given that there seems to be no, or little, elongation in the stature of Mr. M, and given that what little there is may well have a natural explanation, I would say you have no reason—yet—to be excessively alarmed. Indeed, you may never have. You may be able to take comfort in the thought—as I once did, in the early days—that as a Leibnizian you have at least a worthy opponent, in fact the only true opponent possible for you in the struggle of life—for life *is* a struggle, dear lady, and an unending one, as I'm sure I don't have to tell you. After all, the hidden harmony is better than the obvious, as Hercu ... as Herac ... as Harry ... [Harry who? Harry *who*? He is beginning to tire again. If only Leibniz would come back! If only that dog would stop barking. Oh, my head.] ... well, as a philosopher I know once said. Of course, such thoughts may not be the sort of thing that brings you comfort at all. That's as may be. I must say, I find them rather thin myself at present. But at least—at the very least, dear lady—you may reflect that the world has enough Newtonians in it to make it certain that they constitute no aberration or sport of nature, but are part, inevitably, of a Divine plan. Therefore, their presence ultimately must be all for the best, even if it is so in ways we cannot readily—or at all—conceive. Oh, I will not dissemble, I will not hide from you the fact that I, sometimes, find it as difficult as you do. Gravity, gravity: it is a terrible thing for the likes of us. We groan under its weight. We writhe. Indeed, it often boggles the mind—does it not, Mrs. Mainwaring?—that such persons as Newtonians [A fragment of Leibniz's comes back to him, he grabs for it—] should have been admitted to existence at all, preferably to other persons, not unlike … not unlike … [The quotation floats off again, leaving him suddenly empty, conscious only of a great exhaustion] … not unlike, uh, the question of … the sin of … Who was that fellow in the Bible, dear lady … you know the one … betrayed what's his name … ?"

"Judas?"

"Judas! Just so. The very same. Judas, a carrot. [Why did I say that?, he asks himself. That can't be right. Well, what is it, then, if you know so much? Zucchini? Radish? Rutabaga? Judas, a rutabaga—does that sound any better? Ah! I have it—] Iscariot! Iscariot I meant, of course. Judas Iscariot. What an amusing contretemps. Thank you, Mrs. Mainwaring, thank you, dear friend. And yet, I think, you are even more than a friend, you are a Daniel, a Daniel come to … [Come to what? Where? Dinner? Bethlehem? Aaaaaagggh.] Well, you are, let us simply say, a Daniel. Thank you, Daniel."

"Alice," she corrects him gently. "Alice, dear Egg—dear sir. Oh, you are most, most welcome, most welcome indeed." Mrs. Mainwaring is in heaven. "I am only too glad, glad and privileged, to help you in any small way I can. Iscariot! Your erudition is simply amazing, doctor, I have always worshipped it. Oh, from afar, from afar, but worshipped nevertheless, in the … in the secret places of my heart. I don't mind saying, sir, your erudition makes me go all—" She blushes again. "Oh, dear, oh, dear, what a silly goose you must think me!"

"Goose? Nothing of the sort, my dear lady. Never a goose. The idea is preposterous. I think of you … I think of you … as a Leibnizian, rather, a true and faithful Leibnizian. We Leibnizians, you know, must stick together!" He stretches a hand toward her, and falls flat on his face.

"Oh, my dear doctor! You *are* unwell. And so brave—just think—concealing it all this time. Such stoicism! And all for the sake of one little conversation with me! Don't think I'm unmindful of such things, my swee—my dear doctor. I'll come right down and help you into your house." She makes to leave the window.

"No! No!"

"But I can so easily—"

"No!"

"But I *want* to, oh, I so much want—"

"NO, dear lady, *please*. [That's all I need, to have her in the house. Never get her out. She'd go through everything: kitchen, sitting room, bedroom, all. Force of nature. Couldn't stop her. The Oracle, too—she'd find that right off: "Oh, Dr. Caws, whatever have you got behind that curtain? I do *so* love mysteries." "Mrs. Mainwaring, I must insist—" "Oh, doctor, what a charming little, uh, stock room. How clever of you to put it right off the sitting room. And what a curious little machine. However does it work? Oh, I *do* hope I haven't hurt it." And Efficiency. Wouldn't *she* have something to say! "Bringing your harem into the house, are you now? Is that how they do things in Paris?" I'd never hear the end of it.] Please, madam. I'm quite all right, I assure you. Never better. Only a momentary tipsiness—or rather, of course, a tippiness, a tipping, like a table, ha-ha. A tipicity, as it were. No need to worry. And your visage, dear lady, there at your window, like … well, like some ladies, your visage restores me enormously. Stay just like that, pray, exactly as you are, the spit of—"

"Spit?"

"Pardon me, madam, please, that was most infelicitous. I meant to say, of course, the spit and image of … of la belle … yes, of La Belle, in the famous portrait by Masaccio! You will do me, I swear, a great service, if only you will stay there."

"Well, if you really think I can be of more use … "

"Madam, I ham cerdain ubbid—of it, that is, cerdain as aliquots. I shall be forever gradevllull—grateful, I mean—hiff you stay there and speeegg—speak—to me. Yes. Do. Continue our … our … "

Our what? The word, a short one and very common, in clodhoppers and gingham, dances briefly before him, the way Leibniz's images of the divine essence, divine thought and divine will did earlier in the day, then disappears into the void. No other word takes its place. A long, struggling silence ensues. Thelonious Monk falls asleep over his keyboard. The void itself yawns.

"Our ... " The doctor gives up. "What do you call that, dear lady," he finally asks, "when two people ... uh ... [he opens and closes his mouth in pantomime] ... to each other?"

"You mean, 'talk,' doctor?"

"'Talk!' Yes, 'talk!' The very word. Ow prilllliand. Tang you once more, dear friend." It is in fact the word he was groping for, but she could have said practically anything and it would have done as well. Words for Eggbeater are coming unstuck from their meanings, taking on lives of their own. Their sounds rever their sounds rever their sounds reverberate in ways that perplex him. Talk? Talk? What is that? he asks himself. Tawwww? Tawwww-ulk? Uuuuuulk. Lllllllkkk. Kkkkkkgggg. Ggggg. What is that? He gathers his will to say,

"Tawg, madam. Tawg to me, bleeeeese."

"But what shall I talk about, dear doctor?" She sighs. "I am so uneducated compared to someone like yourself. My experience of the world is so narrow. What could I possibly touch on that would be of any interest to you?"

There she has him. The doctor cannot really think of anything. He rolls over on his belly. "Thgggrrsssssss," he mutters to the earth.

"Uuuuuuooooeeeeiiiaauuauauau," the earth replies. It is a deep rumble in *Natur-Sprache*, the Ur-language of Adam, pulsing up from the ground vowel by vowel into the doctor's solar plexus.

"Whad?!" he asks.

"Uuuuuuooooeeeeiiiaauuauauau," the earth repeats. "Whelllcomm, Edjbeader, whelllcomm. *Enfin vous voilà*. Id's bin a lonj time, *mein* Lyebanists."

"What did you say, doctor?" Mrs. Mainwaring wants to know. "'Thuggr ... ?'"

"Gararara ... " Eggbeater essays, and gives up in despair.

"Oooooooeeeaiii," the earth interposes, whispering her message through the convoluted ducts of his left epididymis. "Don't worry abowd her, Lyebanists. Juss jet rid huff her. Comm! I'll show you how. Aoaoaoaoaoaoaoao." The sound runs through his vas deferens, stirring up the fluid in his seminal vesticle.

"Grass." Suddenly the doctor finds his voice again. "Green, monocotyle-donous herbage. Growing all around us. Hair of the earth," he expands, rolling onto his back, face turned up to the sky. "Glowds—clouds, I mean. Hills. Drees." He starts to tire. "Birruds. Bumplepees. Plackperry pushes, prample-pushes, priors, tickets. Danlions. Pflaoaoaoaoaoaowers. Whadhefferyoo lige, Mrs. Hem." He waves a hand weakly in a gesture of permission, then turns over again on his stomach. "Nayyyshr," he mumbles to the monocotyledons.

"Iiiiiiiiyyyyikkyikkyikky!" the monocotyledons answer. "Well done, Egg-beater! Our hero!"

"Ooooyooo ooooyooo," agrees the earth. "Nayyyshr, indeed, Edjbeader, nayyyshr, sweet Lyebanists. Comm down hand join us. You've hearnnd a hrest."

"Did you say 'nature,' doctor?" asks Mrs. Mainwaring. "Is that what you want me to talk about?"

"Say yes, Edjbeader. Make her feel useful, so she woan bodder hus. Uuuuuuuyaa." She exhales into his vas deferens.

"Yes!" The doctor cries, his face still in the grass. "Yes, Mrs. Mainwaring, you've hit the mark. How prilliant—brilliant. Nature! The very word."

"But what shall I say about it, dear doctor? The topic is so large, so"—she looks around her—"encompassing, and I so small, so uninformed. Alas, I fear I shall only disappoint. Oh, dear sir, dear, dear, *dear* Dr. Caws, I could not bear to disappoint!"

"Fiddle-faddle, Mrs. M! You, disappoint? Himpawssibyl. Simbly say whaddever comes into your mind, and everythinj will be fine. All you haff to do is put yourself in trance."

"Trance? Like a medium? Like you, dear doctor?"

"Yes. Preciiiiyyyii—precisely." He turns his face up to her. "Simbly say to yourself, '1 is 1.'"

"1 is 1."

"And, '2 is 2.'"

"2 is 2."

"Good. Then, '3 is … uh … 3 is … Whadd iss tree, dear leddy, if you happen to know?"

"Why, 3, I suppose. What else would it be? That's right, isn't it, doctor?

There's no trick to that, is there? No hidden meaning? Oh, please, sir, please, tell me there isn't. Oh, there *is*, I know there is, there must be! Alas, I am lost! Oh, 3, 3, the hidden meanings of 3!" She tears at the layer cake again.

"But my dear leddy! Calmb yourselb, there's no trig, no hidden meaninjes. Neffer such a thinj—thing. Never. 3 is exactly what 3 is. You couldn't have been more ride. Correct, that is. You haff bractically ruin-ed your hair, and for noffing. Your monocotyledons must be fuming."

"Oh, are they? I am so sorry, dear doctor. I have—ah!—such an impulsive temperament. I must look a sight."

"Nod ad hall, Mrs. Hem, you loog charmin—charming—has heffer. Now, hin order to go hinto drance, simbly rebeat to yourselb, hover and hover, '1 his 1, 2 his 2, 3 his 3. Do id for aboud, oh, for aboud ten minuds. Then speag."

"On nature?"

"Yisssss."

She starts to count. Eggbeater, exhausted, buries his face in the grass. The earth returns to his solar plexus. "Jood, Lyebanists, very jood," the earth says. "You harr drooly a master. Now comm, han join us hall down here. Comm han join, comm han join."

"Come join," agree the earthworms.

"Come down," say the wood ants.

"Come home," say the burying beetles. "You've been gone too long, too long."

"Loose yourself, Edjbeader," murmurs the earth, "loose yourself with us. Led yurr hans jo, yurr feed. Yurr harms, yurr ledjes. Yurr hair, yurr neck, yurr bij roun belly. Dissolve, sweet Lyebanists. Dissolve in me. You remember, doan you, yurr own Maria? Comm home, Lyebanists, home."

The doctor closes his eyes. He feels the pulsing all through his body.

"Yippeeeeyeyeyeye—yippeeeeye!" shouts the topsoil. "Eggbeater is coming! Eggbeater is coming!"

"IjjjyIjjjyIjjjy!" answer the rhizomes, twisting their roots in ecstasy. "He's on his way. Oh, didn't he ramble!"

"Didn't he ramble!" they all shout back.

"He rambled all around

In and out the town,

Rambled till the butchers cut him down!"

1 is 1; 2 is 2; 3 is 3. Mrs. Mainwaring counts on. Dr. Caws feels his body enlarging, spreading out over the grass, its underside merging with the ground beneath him. His head, he is certain, has grown immense, swollen almost to the bursting point as the grey matter in his brain uncoils—he can feel it unfolding, millimeter by millimeter—to open to the world like a flower. Pflaoaoaower. Danlion. Whadhefferyoo lige, Mrs. Hem. Ticket.

1 is 1; 2 is 2; 3 is 3. 14,930,352 plus 9,227,465 is 24,157,817. Mose Allison will record "The Earth Wants You" in 1994.

Coleman Hawkins will record "Goin' Down Home" in 1954. Wulfenite is orange. Talc is greasy. A well-fed black-and-grey-striped tiger. The lingering effects of a head cold. Demonstration of the Existence of God. Only quick action on Bach's part saved the score from serious damage.

Kgjd1234ghhgff5654321? dhfgrh! GNHJJ! Suddenly it dawns on the doctor that he is dying. Well, why not? he thinks. Bound to happen sometime, why not now? All for the best, probably—what the hell, as Efficiency says. I'd never make it to the barn anyway; that woman will finish her counting in a minute and then I'll be in the soup again. Leibniz is gone for good; the act is dead. Die with it, then—point of honor, really. Like a captain and his ship. Go down with it, down, sink into the ground—at least *it* wants me—sink and disappear. Somebody can come along in a couple of weeks, dig me up and bury me proper. Or not. Better not, on second thought—all that fuss and stink. Especially stink. Better leave me there, with the worms. Let me rot. What a story I'll make: Annals of Disintegration. "Medium Molders." Let What's-his-name—that man from the *Trumpet*—Welkin—write it up: "Dr Eggbeater Caws, the celebrated animal magnetist and Rising Leibniz of Aubrey Massachusetts, expired late yesterday afternoon, on the eve"—no, approaching the eve, got to be accurate about these things—"approaching the eve of what would have been his greatest triumph, the unveiling of the Delphic Oracle"—dear Oracle! The only thing I'll miss—"struck down in his prime by a barrage of impertinence, truckling, and meddlesome false kindnesses fired at close range by Mrs. Calvin Mainwaring, the well known nightmare and pest. The police have Mrs. Mainwaring in custody; she will be hanged at dawn for high treason. The doctor sank into the ground without a trace, unable, despite Herculean exertions and the patience of a Job, to traverse even by crawling the last few feet remaining between himself and his barn, where life-restoring spirits, a balm of Gilead, awaited him—him for whom ceilings were once a dancing floor, and treetops but stairways to the open sky. As the doctor sank, the Subterranean Tabernacle Choir, Sweet Singers of the Pit, sang his praises, welcoming him to his new home. Their voices were heard clearly as far away as the Kidney, and are reported to have carried across the Bay to the settlements on Pig Island. Beaten in body but not in spirit, Dr. Caws accomplished his descent with his usual aplomb, waving a final, plucky farewell to the universe of sunlight and gladness that he loved so ardently and celebrated in thought, word, deed and séance room." Or words to that effect. Not bad, really. Wish Welkin was here with his notebook, I'd dictate it to him. If I could remember it, that is. If I could talk. If, if. I, the one now speaking. You, the one now listening. Pasta, Lablache ... not a dry eye in the house. Only a chicken feather. Hand; son; horse; heat ... not *entirely* opera-mad ... title; predicate. Her skin is *A*. Milk is *A*. Rectify them, Eggbeater, rectify them! Dampen the old moustache again, what? Put things right in a minute, eh? Part; effect; possession; accident ... a very great honor. *Termino.*

Kgjd1234ghhg ... *sympnoiapantasympnoiapantasympnoapanta*. Dave McKenna and Zoot Sims will record "Grooveyard" in 1974. ghhgghhg. In the hut above Balaklava, her temperature returning to normal, Florence Nightingale walks with Lord Raglan over the blood-soaked ground of a dream battlefield. They stop to dig graves for the corpses. A large pepper-and-salt moustache floats down out of the night sky. It lands on the rim of one of the graves, stays there a moment flapping its hairy wings, then drops out of sight.

The moustache travels northwest, going underground on fast-moving telluric currents, and reappears almost instantaneously in Naumburg, on the dresser in young Nietzsche's bedroom. Waking suddenly out of a dreamless sleep, the lad sees it hovering there and reaches out to it in fascination. King Squirrel I, dreaming inside his porcelain shell, hears a cry from far away, "Help, animals, help."

In Paris, on the Quai Voltaire, Monsieur Ingres, having at last gotten back to sleep, wakes again in anguish. He has just seen his portrait of Mademoiselle Rivière desecrated by a shaggy, drooping pepper-and-salt moustache, painted like a crude number 3 turned on its side.

" ... is 3." Mrs. Mainwaring finishes her counting. She opens her eyes, leans out from the window and looks down at the doctor on the grass. A week from now she will say in court,

"I knew he was not long for this world. One look at him and I knew. He'd been stumbling around for the longest time, couldn't even walk properly. Down on his hands and knees mostly. But he was proud, oh, so proud, and brave, brave as always. He pretended nothing was wrong, passed it off as ... catabasis, I think he said, yes, a touch of catabasis, that was it. Wanted to set my mind at rest. Absolutely *insisted* on talking to me, passing the time of day as if nothing was wrong. Seemed to think he owed it to me, as a matter of politeness. Such manners he had! A perfect gentleman, from head to toe. But I knew. Deep in my heart I knew. And when at last he collapsed, and lay there barely breathing, face buried in the grass—well, who *wouldn't* have known then?"

But today her outlook is different. It has never occurred to her, not for a moment, that Dr. Caws is near death. She sees him instead as one afflicted by ungodly spirits, one whose constant converse with the world beyond the senses has left him open to their machinations and brought him—but only temporarily—low. Far from feeling that he is beyond help, she is convinced that all he really needs is the aid and comfort of a sympathetic fellow being, a person attuned to the finer workings of his psychical nature—in a word, herself. She has seen this happen before, to other mediums. O, it is a sad, sad thing, Lord knows, but it seems to be a disorder intrinsic to the calling, and can even prove, with proper guidance, to be but a prologue to a glorious resurgence. Now, gazing down at the doctor not only from a physical elevation but from the heights of intensified spiritual awareness which, she is sure, she has just induced in herself, she thinks she has found a way to assist the object of her infatuation and to advance her own cause into the bargain. If only she can give her mediumistic abilities free rein (and she knows she has them, of that she makes no doubt whatsoever, having heard the Fox sisters,

Miss Sprague, Mrs. Hatch, Miss Love and Mr. Davis as well as the Cawses in a hundred séances in ten cities, seven years and three states) she is confident that she can spiritualize with the best of them, and that the spirit world must inevitably provide those few well-chosen phrases that will give Dr. Caws surcease from his pain and at the same time show him a side of herself that he has never seen, perhaps never even suspected, before: a person of power and decisiveness, a trance medium in her own right, a force to be reckoned with in the spiritualist movement. A serious, reliable medium, with a healthy message, a message of Love and Devotion and Harmony—not like that Efficiency he's married to, that changeable, pesky Newton. She always was a flighty, shallow-brained thing, Mrs. Mainwaring remembers, even as a girl. Not a serious thought in her head. Never would look you in the eye, either; you just knew she was up to no good, even if you couldn't catch her at anything. Spent most of her time skulking around Calvin's father's barn, her and that boy Welkin, the writer that came to see them today. Humpf. Spoiled, too, and lazy. Wouldn't do a lick of work. Thought herself too good for it, I suppose, what with that wealthy father and her Aubrey Female Academy manners and the notions they put in her head. Didn't want to ruin those soft white hands, or disarrange her pretty red curls. And didn't the boys love them, too, those curls! And that shapely young figure she never minded showing off. Still doesn't—those bare shoulders—the idea!—brazen. That's how she caught Dr. Caws, curse her, when he came to town, that and all the money she'd inherited by then. I used to think it was weak of him, weak and shallow—but how could he have helped it, even without all the money? He was only a man after all, poor thing, and no man could have resisted that girl once she'd set her cap for him, curse her a second time. Humpf!

It makes Mrs. Mainwaring's blood boil. In her opinion Efficiency Barton is responsible for practically all of the good doctor's troubles, hazards of the calling or no, the most ungodly spirit of any. Sir Isaac Newton! Doesn't that name, all by itself, conjure up everything that is gross, materialistic, greedy, mean-minded, venomous, false and finally *dirty* in the world? 'Course it does, she answers herself. The worst possible influence on a man as sensitive, as true, as fine, as *elevated* as Leibniz. As the doctor. All that beauty, all that grace, all that penetration of intellect, all that *cigar*, all that sympathetic brown eyes when they look at you it seems they've known the whole world and its sorrow, all that manly carriage, that suppleness of limbs, that free, floating rotation of the hips in mid air, all that frisky little shake of the shoulders he gives as he turns upside down, all that *moustache*—ah, all that!—to be blocked, barred, impeded, denied, spurned, derided, forbidden, encumbered, forbidden, checked, forbidden, hobbled, forbidden, dragged down, forbidden, forbidden, forbidden … O! It is sinful! Ugly! A stain of vileness discolors the world. But not for long—no, not for long! Mrs. Mainwaring will oppose the she-devil, armed with Truth and Love she will oppose, and conquer! Nay, even (dare she think it? Yes!) *supplant*! After all, Love is invincible. Love—how does the poet put it? Well, Mrs. Mainwaring forgets at the moment, but what does that matter at a time like this? The spirits will supply all speech that's needed, when it's needed, and the spirits are working through her already, she can feel them. The brain grows light, the heart beats faster, the throat muscles loosen. She cannot act save with perfect harmony. All she has to do is open her mouth and speak—or speag, as the doctor seems to prefer. Very well, then, she tells herself, sleag. Speag, Alice, speag!

"OOOOOOOOOooooooooOOOOOOOOOooooooooOOOOOOOOOoooo oooOOOOOOOoooo!" It is a deep, rich, long drawn moan that shakes her shoulders and hips as it comes, breaking out like theophany into the Aubrey air. The world sits up and listens. The burying beetles pause on their rounds, the Subterranean Tabernacle Choir breaks off its song. Thelonious Monk wakes with a start, catching Dr. Caws in mid *termino*. The topsoil purrs in delight. "Tell it, sister!" squeal the rhizomes.

Mrs. Mainwaring does not hear them. She is deep inside her sound, one she never knew she could make; indeed, she has never heard anything like it. She marvels at the spirits who must have produced it. It comes, however, not from spirits at all but the as-yet-unborn Gertrude Malissa Pridgett, better known as Ma Rainey, Mother of the Blues (1886–1939), resplendent in diamonds, fringed headband and feather boa, who belts it out from her seat in Alice's white bottom, with Thomas A. ("Georgia Tom") Dorsey on piano and Tampa Red on kazoo. Her voice vibrates through the fibers of Mrs. Mainwaring's gluteus maximus, flattens Martin Luther where he cowers in the anal column, travels up her etheric spinal cord, circulates through her shoulders and chest, brushing past Louis XIV in the sternum, and enters Alice's vocal cords in the region of her throat chakra.

"OOOOOOOAYAYAYAYAYooooooohhhhhhhhhooooooooahhhhhhhhhh-hoooom," she moans. "*L'Etat, c'est moi*! An indulgence can never remit guilt! Hear me talkin' to ya! I don't bite my tongue! OOOOOOOooooooooeeeeeeeeaaaaaaah-hhhmmmmm mmmmmmmmMMMMMMMMmmmmmmmm."

All over Aubrey the monads light up. All souls of a sudden know their own nature, awaken from their state of stupor. Salts, metals, plants, animals—images of the universe shimmy in the sun.

Mrs. Mainwaring's throat chakra glows softly, the color of smoke. Its petals open and vibrate, their deep red surfaces dancing with vowels like the numbers in Dr. Caws' dream. The doctor's leg keeps time to the music as Monk hits the keys and goes into a sprightly version of "Nice Work If You Can Get It," with Gene Ramey on bass and Art Blakey on drums.

"OOOOOOOAYAYAYAYAYooooooohhhhhhhhhooooooooahhhhhhhhhh-hoooom." The sound goes through subtle bodies like jism, quickening the souls preformed there and predisposed to assume one day the human shape. Miles Davis, sipping a drink between sets at the Showboat Lounge in Philadelphia, modeled in ectoplasm in the vestibular fold of Efficiency Caws' larynx, nods his approval and speaks a twelve-letter word to his scotch and milk. It resonates through Efficiency's vocal cords as she presses against Newton in her pineal gland.

"Do you think so, love?" asks Sir Isaac, running his hands down her back. "Well, you may be right." He laughs. "Certainly the Mother sealed in her Infant's belly swells and is purified." He kisses her earlobe. "Ye brother and sister too become fruitful, don't they, sweetheart? Both are perpetual workers, eh? Both have a *prodigious* active principle. No heat is so pleasant, is it, lovey? No spirit searches bodies so subtly and swiftly. Coo, coo. Coo, coo, coo." He pulls the Philosopher's Wool around them again.

"Dig," answers Miles. He finishes his drink and gets back on the bandstand. Coltrane is already there with his horn, with Red Garland on piano, Paul Chambers on bass and Philly Joe Jones on drums. The rhythm section goes into the opening bars of "Blues by Five." Miles comes in, playing with his back to the audience.

"M M M M M m m m m m m m m m m m m m h e y h e y h e y y y h e y m - mmmMMMmmmmhhhh." Effects follow their causes determinately, in spite of contingency and even of freedom. Alice Mainwaring, who longs to speak of Nature, its immense variety and its *ad infinitum* division of bodies, shakes her butt. Like mirrors endowed with an internal action, the 7,889 sequins on Ma Rainey's dress wink and sparkle as she sashays down to the footlights at the Bed of Roses Musical Theater of Valdosta, Georgia, a gaudy two-storey structure nestled comfortably in Mrs. Mainwaring's ample posterior.

"Ceeeeee Ceeeeee rider," Mrs. M sings, starting a slow, ageless blues that will be sung by practically everybody—Bessie Smith, Leadbelly, Lightnin' Hopkins, John Lee Hooker, Ida Cox, Alberta Hunter, Ray Charles, Chippie Hill, Blind Lemon Jefferson and a thousand others, souls who, like the song, have been in the seed, and in their progenitors as far back as Adam.

Dr. Caws struggles to his feet.

"Cee Cee rider, see what you done done.

Cee Cee rider, see what you done done.

Made me love you,

Now your gal done come."

I, the one now speaking. You, the one now listening. Music is the concealed art of computation for a soul unaware of its counting. Mrs. Mainwaring sings it, but at the back of her mind she is starting to fret. Her fascination with this new voice that has taken possession of her is wearing thin. These harsh, guttural sounds, this growling: what is this spirit possessing her? German? Pennsylvania Dutch? This is disgusting, she tells herself. I must do better.

She looks around for Doctor Caws, to see how he is taking it all, but finds that he is gone—back across the street, heading toward his barn, stumbling to be sure, but definitely in motion, and definitely homing in on his objective. He has taken advantage of Mrs. Mainwaring's trance to make his escape. "Dr. Caws! Dr. Caws!" She calls, but gets no response. The barn door pulls shut behind him. The squirrels, having followed him, stand waiting outside.

True Tales of the Paranormal:

Anna Zeisig was feeling her oats. She had arrived in Basel in high spirits, the day before her appointment with Haselmaus. The train ride from Zürich had soothed her nerves, and done much to ease the pain caused by what she thought of as Schwank's desertion. She was dressed stylishly, in a black suit by Cavallini. She could feel the other passengers' admiration in the quick glances they directed at her from time to time. Here was a successful professional woman, she could feel them thinking. Beautiful, too, absolutely drop-dead gorgeous, in the American argot. *Hüfte*, into the bargain. And modest. Why was she traveling by herself, then? Because there was no one quite good enough to sit beside her, of course.

What *was* her profession, they must have been wondering? Was she a lawyer, perhaps, another Portia, stepped out of *The Merchant of Milan*, if that was the name of the play? Or a doctor, conceivably? —Yes! She had wanted to cry out, a doctor! A doctor! I know everything there is to know about epidemics. Influenza, bubonic plague, scarlet fever—whatever you like. Come and talk to me! But just in time she realized that would have ruined the effect, and forced herself to be silent. Silent and *mysterious*. Yes.

"It really was the most pleasant experience, that trip," she told Anna Sprengel when she phoned her from the train station. "Like being on holiday. I just had to tell you all about it, dearest." Freed from her job at the Helvetius ("I never did like it there, nothing but sick people, day in day out") she could do anything she wanted to, stay in Basel as long as she liked, maybe even move there permanently, who knew? "She was in Heaven," Sprengel said later.

Zeisig had realized something else on the train as well. Her appointment with Haselmaus, far from being a slightly embarrassing—even, to some people, she supposed, degrading—admission of illness and need of help, took on a certain cachet all by itself. Haselmaus was *famous*, for Heaven's sake. Properly explained, her appointment gave her status. She made a point of mentioning it several times, therefore, while she was checking in at the Basilisk, the hotel recommended by Haselmaus' secretary, buttonholing people in the lobby and dropping psychological terms like *Oberbewusstsein* and *Unterbewusstsein*, dementia praecox and organ inferiority. She said she had suffered from all of them at one time or another, and without question "they all had something to recommend them." Her "first love," however, was "good, old fashioned narcissism. You know where you are with narcissism," she explained.

Over dinner, which she had at *Das Fresser* with a man she had met on the train, she pronounced the food delicious, consuming three entrees and five desserts, washing them all down with several bottles of expensive red wine. "I really don't know what's come over me," she told her companion, batting her eyes. "Normally I eat like a bird. But one feels so free in Basel. *Hüfte*, if you know what I mean. *Ein Vogel lebst.*"

After dinner she felt unwell, and asked her escort to take her back to her hotel instead of going on to the opera as planned. At ten o'clock she phoned down to the desk clerk and asked in a weak voice to have a doctor sent up. When the doctor arrived a few minutes later, he found her soaked in sweat, incoherent and running a high fever. She claimed a huge eye was staring at her from across the room, and grew angry when the doctor could not see it. He applied ice packs, gave her aspirin and sedatives and a cold sponge bath, but nothing helped. Her complaints turned to moans and uncontrollable shaking. She thrashed about in the bed. A little before midnight she died.

That was not entirely the end of her, though. There were the ghosts, who began to appear almost immediately after she gave up hers. About a week later, in early February, 2003, a dozen or more witnesses watched a black Cavallini suit, surmounted by a head of flowing black hair, glide across the lobby of the Basilisk Hotel, pass through several patrons and disappear into the back wall. A few months later there was another apparition, a few feet above the waiting platform at the Basel train station. The suit trembled a moment in a sudden cloud of steam and was gone. And that fall, in the dining room of *Das Fresser*, Anna Zeisig herself appeared, filling out the suit as alluringly as ever she had in life. Sparkles of silver played round her hair, and as she drifted slowly from table to table, many diners swore she had a white feather in her mouth.

16

THE DEATH OF THE ORACLE

The Cry of the Gehirngespinstgemach:

" ... Oh, formidable, indeed, Eggbeater, formidable and inescapable. But what would we do without 'em, eh, old friend? What could we possibly do without 'em? Your own, as you call it, 'act,' to take an instance at random: without those two, it would be seriously hampered, not to say extinguished." Leibniz chuckles, savoring the thought. He touches the Temple of Anaitis in Pontus with the end of his stick, turning the globe idly from east to west and back again, throwing the goddess' worshipers into confusion. "I speak, of course, of Love and Strife, those two great originating forces which, as Empedocles pointed out—Empedocles of Acragas, that is—more than two thousand years ago, govern all mortal things on this earth, with Love joining them together in one grand cycle and Strife tearing them apart in the next. Or words to that effect, my memory at the moment is a trifle, uh, blurred." He closes his eyes and leans back in his chair. His stick slides down through Antioch and Damascus, cutting a line through the sands of Nabatea before it drops off the globe entirely and breaks its fall on the edge of the philosopher's desk. "A remarkable man, Empedocles," Leibniz goes on. "He held a number of other views, especially concerning the transmigration of souls, which I used to find rather odd. For example, he alleged that he had once been a bird, at another time a bush, and at still another a fish in the sea. During my lifetime I rejected such statements out of hand, although my peregrinations since then have obliged me to admit that there may be more than a grain of truth in what he says. Did you know, by the way, that my son was named Empedocles? Yes, indeed he was, though he was born, I believe, in North America, not Acragas. His mother named him, of course. I had nothing to do with it. Had it been left up to me I should have chosen another name entirely. Do not misunderstand me, old friend, I admire the Acragan enormously, but I should definitely have picked someone closer to my own time to commemorate, one whose achievements were of a more contemporary and consequently more, uh"—Leibniz passes a hand over his brow—"comprehensive, yes, that's it, one whose achievements were of a more comprehensive nature. A name such as my own, for example: Gottfried Wilhelm."

It is eleven o'clock at night. Eggbeater is sitting in the barn, sipping away at Mr. Barton's Elixir, exactly as he has been doing since late afternoon, when he escaped from Mrs. Mainwaring and what seemed the certainty of an early death, fetching up at last at this table, with this glass and this bottle and this juniper-oiled comfort. The dim light and the cool of the barn were heaven at five in the afternoon. Now, with the room still cooler and a single candle to give no more than the necessary illumination, he feels he has found true home, true center, his blessed island of safety and fulfillment, reward for a well-spent life.

Leibniz's voice came back shortly after he gained the barn, within the first few swallows of Elixir in fact, apologizing profusely for having dropped off to sleep—"Inexcusable, dear boy, quite inexcusable, in the middle of my afternoon prayers to boot." He has been babbling happily ever since, although Eggbeater thinks he notices a falling off in quality, a slight vagueness from time to time, a tendency to wander from his subject and to repeat himself, as if he were not yet fully awake or simply a very old man.

Both of these speculations are true, but what is remarkable is not their correctness but the fact that the doctor is capable of making them at all, he having up until now accepted uncritically everything Leibniz has said. Indeed, Eggbeater has grown sharper and sharper in his thinking in the last few minutes. Perhaps his recent brush with death, and Mrs. Mainwaring's voice, have affected him; or (more likely) Mr. Barton's Elixir has begun to take hold, after six hours of uninterrupted ingestion. The Elixir, be it known, is no simple gin; it contains a number of secret ingredients whose powers Dr. Barton himself may not have understood.

In any case, Eggbeater has managed a feat which is often spoken of but very rarely accomplished: he has actually drunk himself sober.

"The name Schwank was a joke, of course," Leibniz continues, "or it should have been." He straightens his wig. "He was no more a Schwank than I am. But that was the name of his mother's 'protector,' or whatever you want to call him, the head of the opera company, I think it was, with whom she came to America, God in Heaven knows why. I knew nothing of any of that business then, and little enough now. I was even unaware of the boy's existence, until the day he turned up, unannounced, on my doorstep—in *1711*, if you can credit that, and he forty-five years old by then! He had with him a letter of introduction, written to me years before by his mother to prove his identity. And a good thing she did, too, I'd never have believed him otherwise. He looked horrible, Eggbeater, in dirty clothes, a torn coat. Even his shoes didn't match! And there was a tinge of the criminal about him, too: dark, sun burnt skin, as if he'd been on the run for a good long time, and little shifty eyes that never stayed still and never would look straight at you. A Colonel he called himself, though I never found out what army he'd served in. An explorer, too, though he couldn't give much account of where he'd been, beyond saying he'd spent time in the wilds with various bands of red Indians and used to know some Ottawa hunters at a place called Mackinac. Said he'd been jailed later for no reason—likely story!—in Newfoundland, managed somehow to escape, bribed his way onto a fishing boat, which took him to Portugal. At last he arrived in Hanover, having walked most of the way from Lisbon. No money in his pockets, of course. Nothing but that letter.

"Well, I took him in hand, didn't I?" Leibniz pounds his stick on the floor. "It turned out he *was* a thief. Appearances in this instance did not deceive; he tried to make off with a gold case he found in my rooms. But I lectured him up and down, put the fear of God in him, taught him how to behave in the presence of his betters. Made certain he did some lessons, too, basic readings and arithmetic, the man was woefully ignorant. And blessings be, Eggbeater, within a week—just one week, mind you—that scoundrel was transformed. You could trust him with anything—jewels, money, even information. I found out, too, that he actually had some military talent after all, a real feeling for tactics. He'd even saved his village on one occasion, when it was being attacked on all sides. I was able to introduce him to some of our finest generals; they found his ideas extremely useful. And his *manners*, Eggbeater! He developed such beautiful manners, such suavity; I used to take him with me on my diplomatic missions. Everyone we met was *so* impressed."

Leibniz pauses. "Or perhaps ... perhaps not." He sighs. "Ah, Eggbeater, there's no good in pretending. Finally, there is no good." He shakes his head. "His mother could do nothing with him and neither could I. By the time he got to me, he'd acquired every bad habit you can think of, but one wonders— it is a hard thing to say, old friend, but one wonders—whether there was not something evil in his makeup from the very start, something no amount of training, no effort of good will and understanding, could eradicate. He stole repeatedly, anything he could get his hands on. When he was caught—and he always was getting caught, he was really rather inept, I'm afraid; one could at least have had a certain admiration for a successful thief—he would always abase himself, burst into tears, curse himself for an ingrate, promise to do better. And then, of course, go back on his word. And his morals! He acquired a nickname, 'Father of Bastards,' among the retainers at court. It was well-deserved, I assure you! It took all my skills in diplomacy, as well as a good deal of money, to keep him out of prison. And the devil of the thing was, he looked exactly like me! People must have guessed who he was, although nobody said anything to my face. Nevertheless, son or no son, I'd have sent him away— many times over I'd have kicked him out, and with joy in my heart!—but that letter always stopped me. Gave him into my charge, she did. *She* did. Eventually he ran off on his own and I never saw him again." He shakes his head. "He was never meant to be in the first place, Eggbeater. Never meant to be."

He fishes in his coat pocket, pulls out a folded, crumbling piece of paper, opens it tenderly and reads: "'Never was the Kingly Child meant to be born on the physical level, my sweet.'" He smiles. "She would have pronounced it 'Kinjly.' Yes. Our secretions were to have been transmuted, by a secret method which she alone knew. 'Trust me, Lyebanists,' she had said. She called me 'Lyebanists.' 'The Great Work's here, in this little room. We'll make Jupiter fly on his eagle! Athena will burst out of Zeus' forehead.'

"But something—she never understood what—went wrong, and instead of Athena, *him*. And I never knew it, not for forty-five years. How could I not keep him, Eggbeater? How could I not?" Leibniz falls silent, staring at the letter.

He might stay that way for hours, or days, or an entire incarnation. Left to his own devices, he probably would: who shall escape, he once wrote, from the labyrinth whose unhappy Daedalus is the human mind? But suddenly, in a breath, he does: out of the night of the long, well-ordered dream an image comes to him, unbidden—a high hill under the stars, a tiny hut near the top of the hill, and inside the hut, inside the hut—

My God, he asks himself, what have you been doing these last few hours, prattling away to no purpose, dredging up old miseries, old mud? One has one's failures, after all, one is only human. But the life, the urgency, the springtime *possibilities*—your hopes, dreams, desires, *appetites*—are sitting in front of you, right in front of you, Gottfried Wilhelm, HERE! He pokes his stick across the desk directly at Balaklava.

Miss Nightingale! The delicious, the splendid Miss Nightingale. You must push this thing along. Pick up with Eggbeater where you left off, in the Brancacci Chapel. He seemed to take to that well enough. Pick up with him there. But push it, take it just a little further—then further still, until—Ah, Gottfried Wilhelm, until, *until*!

"Eggbeater," he calls out. "Oh, Eggbeater! What an old fool you must think me, what a dodderer." That's it, he tells himself, grovel a bit. Never hurts. "Here I've been, jabbering away all this time, with never a thought for the wishes, the predilections, the entire glorious future, indeed, of your patient and worthy self. Pray allow me to redress that wrong, while you're still in attendance. Er—you are in attendance, aren't you? Good. Now, as to your future: we were speaking, some little while back, before I dropped off—unconscionably, unconscionably, I confess it—to sleep, of our mutual friend, Miss Nightingale. (I've never met the lady in, as they say, the flesh, of course, but I venture, from the warmth of your descriptions of her, to call her friend, just as you do.) Specifically, we were discussing (although 'discussing' is such a cold word, is it not, I would say instead we were reliving, you through your recollected experience and I through you) those tremulous moments you shared with her in the Brancacci Chapel in Florence. Ah, those dear, dear long gone moments, they envelop one in a haze, do they not, a haze moreover of radiance, not fog, a soft golden glory that lends magic to all it suffuses. As well it should, dear friend, for the glory emanates from Miss Nightingale's deepest being, her true and imperishable essence—the *Luz* of the Rabbis, my friend van Helmont tells me. But I would ask you to consider the lady from a slightly different, a more, shall I say, practical perspective than the rather elevated and mystical one I have just alluded to. I have already, I think, spoken of the usefulness of your going to her, comforting her in her present distress in the war-torn Crimea. I now ask that, in making your journey, you also consider her as a possible helpmeet and life-partner. Oh, I can fully understand your anxiety on such a head, dear boy, if any chance should exist. For seven—is it? Yes, I think it must be fully seven—long years you have been subjected to the vagaries, to call them kindly, of the *merde*facient Newton, and the very term "helpmeet," not to say "life-partner," must fill you with bitterness. But I think I can put your mind to rest on that subject, and convince you that Miss Nightingale, as you have described her and I, uh, have imagined her (all notions of extension, after all, involve *something* imaginary) is the perfect mate for you. And my proof, dear friend, is to be found not in some clever casuistry of my fabrication, but in your own direct experience of the lady.

"Cast your mind, if you will, back to that delectable moment in the Brancacci Chapel, when Miss Nightingale cried out in delight—in chorus, as you told me, with your good self—that 8 plus 5 was 13. Well, it was, of course, and still is and always will be, but that is not my point. My point has to do with the unfeigned glee in her voice, the free and open expression of it, sure sign of the very great pleasure she took in collaborating with you—with *you*, Eggbeater—chorically. And as she ran through the next equations—13 plus 8, 21 plus 13, 34 plus 21 *und so weiter*—did her face, that lovely, smooth seventeen-year-old face, not betray an expression of deepening understanding and satisfaction? And when she finally began to master the more difficult equations—after a moment or two of entirely excusable, in fact fully-to-be-expected and in its own way quite charming nausea—did not her sparkling grey eyes and her smiling mouth, that small but delicate, ever-so beautifully formed mouth, so plastic—nay, so esemplastic!—in its articulation, did not those features hint at feelings more fervent than friendship? I think they surely did, Eggbeater, else all these years have led me far, far astray."

Leibniz fondles the head of his stick, a rough-cut icosahedron of reindeer bone carved with an image of Pan, given him by van Helmont back in the 1690's. He falls silent again, letting his imagination stray as much as it likes this time, to Miss Nightingale's neck, its whiteness, and to the perfect, ever-so gradual, breathtakingly sinuous curve it must have described on that spring day in Florence, starting behind her sweet, nuzzleable ear lobes and descending to her exquisite shoulders. He plants kisses over its entire length and breadth, front and back, not neglecting the underside of her chin, which she obligingly lifts to allow him easier access, and the cavity just below her Adam's apple. Then, gently but insistently, he runs his finger underneath her—What *are* women wearing nowadays, he wonders? He really must confess he has no idea. Are bodices still cut low, are they stiff or smocked, the shoulders bare or partly covered? Are there still hooped petticoats, flounced underskirts and overskirts, ribbons, lace, long full sleeves turned up to the elbow, loose gowns, rich colors, maroons, yellows and greens? No, Eggbeater said grey. But grey what, grey what, and how are they fitted? How much of that matchless bosom is visible? Leibniz is sure it must be matchless, the breasts full but firm, the nipples erect as they press lightly against her undergarment. Is her waist tightly cinched? Do her hips—no, how could they, hidden, as they must be, under an armature of hoops? But if they are not? What then? Ah, there is so much he does not know, so much he has never even considered. Really, Gottfried Wilhelm, he tells himself, your laxness is inexcusable.

Suddenly it strikes him that he does not even know what the Crimean War is about, nor which nations, exactly, are fighting it. Presumably one of them is England, else why would Miss Nightingale be doing her nursing over there and how could a British soldier be kissing her shadow? But what other nation, or nations, are involved? Portugal? Spain? Germany? France, the Netherlands, Russia, Turkey, Rome, Venice, the Duchy of Modena? Leibniz is slightly abashed that he has never bothered to find out. Certainly he could have done so without any trouble: even Eggbeater must know that much.

On the other hand, he reminds himself for the second time this evening, one is only human. No one can think of everything. He glances with not a little satisfaction at the tomes on his desk: Plato, Aristotle, the Pre-Socratics, the Church Fathers, Messieurs Descartes, Arnauld, Malebranche, Pascal,

Gassendi, the works of More, Conway, Hobbes, Spinoza and, stacked all over the floor, volume upon volume of history books, mathematical texts, works on anatomy, mining, engineering, physics, alchemy, mystical tracts—the *Kabbalah Denudata* of von Rosenroth, the works of van Helmont, Paracelsus, Ramon Llull—books of law by Thomasius and Pufendorf and hundreds of other volumes on as many subjects, ranging across the whole knowledge of the world and its history up to 1716. There are even one or two works by the uliginous Newton. Not to mention Leibniz's own *Theodicy* and his ocean of unpublished manuscripts, along with his correspondence—over 15,000 letters, copies of his own and letters from persons all over the world, on everything from coach design to the hexagrams of the *I Ching*, stored behind his chair in cabinets, chests, boxes and folders reaching up to the grey-pink flesh of the ceiling. Eggbeater's pineal gland is a monument to learning.

Admittedly, Leibniz's understanding of developments since 1716 is more than a bit sketchy; he would be the first to admit to that. But, he would add, there are also more than a few mitigating factors here; even his harshest critics, taking a look at his present position, would have to confess that he is up against some troubling obstacles. He'd like to see how Descartes would fare, trying to get his work done under such conditions, not to speak of Malebranche or Hobbes or even the feculent Sir Isaac, having Eggbeater Caws as their sole source of news from the outside world, and their sole means of responding to it as well. Besides—Leibniz returns to his theme—even in the best of all possible worlds, no one can think of everything. And what good would it do, in the last analysis, what ultimate good, what public good would it do for him to know which nations are at each other's throat this time? Those details can easily be supplied later on. The Alphabet of Thought will sort it all out anyhow; the reasons men go to war change little over the centuries. Servile greed, impulses of hatred and revenge, dreams of personal glory—would the results be any different if the combatants were different, if the Chinese, for instance, were storming the heights above Balaklava, loosing a hail of hexagrams against the foe, or if a crack troop of Ottawa hunters led by his renegade son the Colonel, fresh in unmatching shoes from the wilds of North America, were marching to the relief of the Hottentots down in the valley?

Leibniz laughs at the image, a rich, full belly laugh which echoes and re-echoes through the pineal gland. How free he feels! How adventurous and unrestrained! The spirit of Miss Nightingale, the very thought of her, has brought a lightness into his life, a buoyancy—nay, a kind of mental levitation, to match Eggbeater's physical one—that he never supposed existed in this world, save in the minds of Enthusiasts or cretins. Ah, Miss Nightingale! He imagines her again, standing in front of *St. Peter Healing*, her eyes closed in concentration, rapt in the magic of numbers … 75,025 … 196,418 … 317,811 … Leibniz basks in the confidence that he will soon be with her, for surely his exhortation to Eggbeater has had its effect.

Of course, he reminds himself, she will not be seventeen any more. By now she must be—assuming, that is, that the year really is 1855, as Eggbeater says it is—by now she must be thirty-five, with a great many more things to wrinkle her brow, Gottfried Wilhelm, than the numbers of the Fibonacci series. But in my experience a certain amount of age and responsibility brings only wisdom, and an even deeper beauty, to women of Miss Nightingale's intelligence and, how shall I put it, great-heartedness. Yes, maturity only increases their thirst for the eternal truths. And let us not forget that from the time of Pythagoras people have been persuaded that enormous mysteries lie hidden in numbers. Nor let us forget my own discovery of binary arithmetic, which shows, bless its heart, how all numbers are expressed by means of Unity and Nothing. Of course, as she will instantly comprehend once I—or rather Eggbeater—show her, God alone is the primary Unity, of which all created or derivative monads are products. This secret ordering of things makes it evident how everything is derived from pure being and nothingness. 1001, for example. 10100. I wonder if nurses' uniforms have smocked bodices.

Probably what wakes Efficiency is the Dog (the Dog!) barking. He has been at it all day and through the evening, too, but now the sound seems closer. Or it may have been a breath of night air, through the open window, or a spirit borne on that breath, caressing her cheek. In any case she turns on the settee and opens her eyes to the night. Somewhere far away, perhaps even in the center of her head, she hears Uncle Isaac softly cooing, and her own voice cooing back. Oh, yes, she remembers, butter of antimony. Dear Uncle Isaac. I wonder if I look any younger.

She notices that for the first time in a long time she has no hangover. She feels, on the contrary, quite refreshed. She moves to get up, and something brushes against her hands. Looking down, she sees a small squarish envelope. She takes it to the window, tears it open, and reads by the light of the moon. Herb Pomeroy and Donna Byrne will record "No More" in 1996.

Gravity Newton:

"Oh, it was a beautiful letter," Mrs. Caws told me, "the most precious letter I ever got in my life. Full to the brim with fine phrases, and a desperate, desperate longing. Jerry was always such a romantic.

"He said he'd tried to stay away from me, tried his very best, but it was no good, he was losing his mind. I haunted his dreams and consumed his every waking thought. He was writing at dawn, he said, and he was coming to interview us that morning. He'd put in especially for the assignment, not only because he had to see me ('I burn, I burn,' he wrote) but to give me the letter. Somehow he would manage it without 'that clod' (Eggbeater, of course) noticing. He wanted me to run away with him, that very night, he couldn't live like this any longer. He said he would be waiting with a horse and carriage at midnight, on the Aubrey side of the High St. Bridge. If I wanted to go with him I should be there then. If I didn't come—well, he would know I didn't care about him any more and he couldn't say what he would do. Whether he lived or died, it wouldn't matter, his life would be over either way. Now, wasn't that a nice sentiment, sweetheart? Who could have resisted it? Not me, anyhow. I went right upstairs to pack, and that letter was the first thing I put in my bag."

Where was the letter now, I asked. Could one see it?

"Not a chance, dearie. I threw it down the sewer, one day when I was mad at him."

The Cry of the Gehirngespinstgemach:

"Leibniz!" Eggbeater calls, his voice full of concern. He has just realized he's heard nothing from the philosopher for some time. Exactly how long he can't say, as he was only partly listening before. He was thinking over something Leibniz said a while back, which made quite an impression on him—something about Love and Strife, and how important they were to the act. He said some Greek was responsible for the idea. What was his name again? Pedocles? Something like that. Yes. Well, Leibniz got that one right tonight, if nothing else. Love and Strife were the meat and potatoes of the act, no doubt about it. Eggbeater thinks he and Efficiency should probably do more with the idea; maybe they could get old Pedocles' spirit to come through. Wouldn't that be something, now? A brand new spirit! Wouldn't that just be something? I wonder what Leibniz would think. Better not mention it yet.

It was then that Eggbeater realized his mentor had gone silent again.

"Leibniz!" He calls a second time. "What are you doing? You haven't fallen asleep again, have you?"

"What?" Leibniz shakes himself out of his reverie. "Oh, no, my dear fellow, not at all. Never asleep. I was merely experiencing, uh, a multiplicity of minute perceptions, quite a large multiplicity, actually, involving for the most part our friend Miss Nightingale, her many attractivenesses, and the philosophical questions rising therefrom. The question of being, for example."

"Being?"

"Yes. And nothingness."

"Ah. Then you must have been reflecting on your binary arithmetic."

"Yes, indeed, old friend. The model of creation I discovered: 'One is enough — '"

"'—for deriving everything from nothing.'"

"'For deriving everything from nothing.' Exactly. My, but you are on top of things this evening. It is still evening, isn't it?"

"Yes. Quite late in it, actually."

"I thought so. You positively sparkle tonight, Eggbeater."

"Thank you, *cher maître*. I have to confess I've noticed it myself. It's this Elixir, I think."

"Elixir? Oh, yes, I believe you mentioned something about an elixir once. Mr. Barton's Elixir, I believe you called it. I'm bound so say it concerned me a bit at the time. Such nostrums are rarely reliable. And this one had been produced by the father of the execrable Newton; that made it even more suspect."

"Yes, but don't forget we used some of his equipment to make the Oracle."

"I wish you wouldn't call it that."

"Well, that's what it is, though."

"No, it isn't, Eggbeater. It's a calculator. A key to the Alphabet of Thought."

"Well, have it your way. Still, we used some of his equipment to make it."

"No, we didn't. That's preposterous. What equipment?"

"A lot of the metal things lying around here in the barn."

"Oh, those. The raw materials. But the plans, the ideas—those were ours. Or mine, really. Forgive me for making a point of it, dear boy, but the ideas did come from me."

"Oh, yes, most of them. No question about it."

"What do you mean, 'most of them?'"

"Well, there was one thing."

"'One thing,' he says! What 'one thing,' I'd like to know."

"Automatic carrying."

"Automatic carrying! Eggbeater, are you going to stand there—if you are standing—and tell me that that … that … that unspeakable person's father was responsible for automatic carrying?"

"I'm afraid so. And actually I'm sitting. Right here at Mr. Barton's desk."

"Good God. And what was wrong with the method I dictated to you?"

"Well, you know, *cher maître*, you always did have trouble with it."

"Always had trouble, did I? Humph. Some people are getting *too* smart. And where, may I enquire, did you find the solution? In this Barton's papers?"

"Yes. It's still in the top drawer here, I think. I can read it out to you if you like. It was one of the few things in all his papers that I could understand. Most of what he wrote seemed to be in some sort of code."

"Code! What sort of person was this Barton?"

"Well, I don't really know. He was Efficiency's father, of course. Banker. Had some scientific interests. Stank up the house with his chemicals, I think. Kept to himself a lot of the time. Efficiency didn't like him much."

"And he made a calculator, too?"

"Well, not exactly. But something he wrote gave me an idea how I—I mean we—might solve the problem."

"How *you*—! What was it he wrote?"

"It must have been a note for some machine he was making. He wrote, 'Sprockets longer.' That was all, and that was the only thing on the page you could decipher. The rest was all letters and numbers."

"Sprockets! The stepped reckoner, it must have been. Did you change the stepped reckoner, Eggbeater?"

"Oh, I just made a couple of adjustments … "

Amazing, says Leibniz to himself. I never could get that right, and this *Hanswurst* comes along and … Then, aloud: "Well, Eggbeater, I must, uh, congratulate you. And this Barton too, I suppose, although he seems to have played a very minor part in the affair. The creative work, it seems to me, was all yours. As for the code, this is not the first time I've encountered that sort of thing from his family. The graveolent Newton, I recall, employed a code in the only letter he ever bothered to write me. That was in the days when we were at least feigning politeness. The code was a tease. He never thought I would solve it. I did, of course, without the slightest trouble. Not surprisingly, it turned out to be something I already knew. Typical of the scoundrel; I'm sure Barton was no different. Still, Eggbeater, I think we would be remiss not to have a closer look at his papers. You never know, eh, what might turn out to be useful. You'd better gather them up, and we'll take them with us when we leave tonight for the Crimea. Take along some of that Elixir, too, dear boy, if it pleases you."

"Wait. What did you just say? 'When we leave tonight for the *Crimea*?'"

"Certainly. Not this instant, of course. We should take time to pack properly. But sometime before daybreak, without fail. We ought to get an early start."

"But, Leibniz, that's—"

"Yes, Eggbeater?"

"That's *crazy*. We can't—"

"Of course we can. Those plans are as much ours as anyone's. Certainly Newton—that is, Efficiency—has no claim to them. I doubt she even glanced at them after the man's death. Didn't you tell me she simply chucked every-thing of his into the barn? Yes, those plans are ours, my lad, codes and all. My Lord, I doubt there's anyone alive who could decipher them, besides me—and you, of course, Eggbeater, and you."

"But, Leibniz, what makes you think we could ever—"

"Ah! I see what you mean, and I confess I hadn't considered it. The fervor of the moment, the itch to be gone, after all these years, the animal spirits coming at last into their own—really, old friend, you must forgive me. You are quite correct; it would be the utmost in folly to fly like thieves in the night without proper preparation, with no ready money for the journey, except whatever you may have on your person at the moment, with no prospect of procuring more when we need it. Good Lord, in my excitement I had quite forgotten those details—although 'details' is hardly the word, considering that they provide the very foundation of all successful motion, that is to say mo-tion which achieves its desired end with as little interference as possible. After all, one is not twenty anymore. At the age of fifty, and at the age of—well, let us simply say at the extraordinarily advanced age which I seem somehow, will I, nil I, to have attained—one wants to travel in comfort. Besides, there is no *absolute* need for haste. Yes, Eggbeater, on reflection I think it will be best to proceed with deliberation and to delay our departure until ... well, until after tomorrow evening's unveiling of the, as you call it, Oracle. The publicity we receive from that assuredly sterling event can in no way do us harm, and may even reach the ears of Miss Nightingale, assuming of course that her fever has abated and that newspapers are available over there, which I have little doubt is the case. Tomorrow you can spend the day making arrangements for our various modes of transportation and withdrawing sufficient funds from the bank—sufficient, I would say, for quite an extended stay on the Continent. What a pleasure it is to think that the source of those funds is that scapegrace's inheritance. In fact, you may as well clean out the account entirely. As for transport, your Masonic connections, as I recall, helped you out on your pre-vious emigration some years ago; surely they can still be of assistance. I pre-sume you remember your secret pass-grips? But I needn't ask, of course you do: once a Mason, always a Mason." Leibniz puts his feet up on the footstool. "Ah, what a joy it will be, the adventure of it, the open road again, just the two of us, like the old days—my old days, but yours, too, Eggbeater—living by our wits, the *only* way to live, really. Did I ever tell you about the time I escaped an assassination attempt, all by myself, in a storm on the Adriatic?"

"Yes, many times. But—"

"It was in the fall of 1688. I had taken a small bark in Venice, traveling south along the Italian coastline. A beautiful coastline it is, too, especially the lagoons and marshes around the Foci del Po. I was the only passenger, and the crew was not what I would call entirely trustworthy. They had, all of them, a kind of *sidelong* expression in their eyes (I would see that expression again, in the eyes of my son). But I thought nothing of it until suddenly, just after we had left the Gulf of Venice, a storm blew up, one of those squalls from the northeast which are such a danger to navigation in that sea. Well, the going became quite rough, and—would you believe it?—I overheard the crew openly discussing, with no sign of compunction, the idea of throwing 'the heretic'—namely, myself—overboard and dividing my money and other possessions among themselves. They assumed, of course, that a German Protestant would have no knowledge of their language. Well, as you know, Eggbeater, I am nothing if not ecumenical, and although I had no intention of risking the fate of Valens Acidalius, who reputedly died of brain fever after embracing the Roman Catholic Church, I did happen to have on my person a string of rosary beads. These I now took out and, kneeling down on the deck, mumbled various nonsense syllables over them, affecting to be saying my prayers, pleading for rescue from the storm—upon which, one of the ruffians declared to his comrades that I was a true Catholic after all, and he could not take my life. So the others desisted as well, and, the storm having blown itself out, I disembarked at Mesola.

"Now, naturally, old friend, I don't expect our crossing of the Atlantic to be fraught with scalawags like the aforementioned, and, thanks to all the money you're going to get tomorrow, we'll be traveling on land most of the time in considerable comfort, but nevertheless we may find ourselves in situations where quick thinking is called for. Do not worry, Eggbeater. It will only lend greater zest to the proceedings. Remember, too, that Miss Nightingale has herself undergone considerable danger; we could hardly consider ourselves worthy of her if we were to shun it. By the way, dear boy, perhaps you can enlighten me: do nurses' uniforms have smocked bodices these days?"

On the point of interrupting and putting a stop to this drivel, Eggbeater is momentarily taken aback. "Smocked bodices?" He answers. "Oh, I shouldn't think so. They all button right up to the neck, so far as I know. But, Leibniz, this has nothing to do with—"

"No? All the way up to the neck, you think? To the cavity below the Adam's apple? What a pity. But on the other hand, nothing lasts. Fashions may suddenly change. We can but hope." He stretches. "Ah, but I feel so expansive! So sanguine! So pregnant, if you will, with the future. Never have my animal spirits been so exercised. They prance, they leap, they fly through the—"

"LEIBNIZ!" The doctor shouts. The sound reverberates through the barn. Outside, by the door, the squirrels snap to attention. Even the Dog (the Dog!) leaves off his barking for a moment. The flow of melatonin slows in the pineal. Leibniz raises an eyebrow.

"Yes, Eggbeater? What is it? No need to shout."

"Yes, there IS a need to shout! You're not making the slightest bit of sense, and haven't been for the last—oh, for I don't know how long. What in the world makes you think the ... how could you expect me to ... where would we find ... I don't even know where to begin. What's gotten into you, anyway? Don't you remember—just to start somewhere—don't you remember there's a war going on over there? The British and French and Turks and Russians are all in it. Sevastopol is under siege, casualties are mounting by the hour—you said as much yourself this afternoon. I'm as likely as not to get shot before we get within a mile—within ten miles—of Miss Nightingale, and if I get shot what will become of you, not to mention the Delphic Oracle? You're not—"

"Aha! The British and French, you say? And the Turks and Russians too? I wondered about that. Well, that will be very nice. Really, Eggbeater, we couldn't ask for anything better. The French, of course, I know well; so do you. The Turks ... well, the Turks. But the Russians! This is a real piece of luck. I knew the Tsar—Peter the Great, that is—met with him a number of times when he visited Germany. A remarkably energetic and intelligent man he was, too, most interested in applying scientific advances to the betterment of his country. I gave him a model of my calculator; he seemed most impressed. Wait until he sees the Alphabet of Thought! But there, there, what am I saying? He must be dead, too, by now. But his spirit, I'm sure, was

Russian to the core—to the *Luz*, in fact—and that lives on in the soldiers. Don't fret, Eggbeater, the Russians will present no difficulty."

"But—"

"Now, as for being shot, surely, old friend, you don't think I had neglected such a possibility? I had not, I warrant you. In fact, I must say that, given our unfamiliarity with the terrain around Sebastopol, the generality of the conflict and the natural inclination of military men to shoot anything that moves, it is more than a possibility, it is a distinct likelihood. But don't you see the beauty of it? By the time we get over there, what with the uncertainties of any sea journey—even if we are not set on by assassins—and the unavoidable rigors of overland travel, not to mention, now that I think of it, another sea journey through the Straits of the Bosporus into the Black Sea, Miss Nightingale will undoubtedly have recovered from her fever and be back at work in the hospital, where she will be sure to visit you. She never misses a single patient, you know. She will recognize you (how could she forget?) and unquestionably her heart will melt, especially when you start to work your magic on her. The old 8 plus 5, eh, Eggbeater? Yes, by all means you should arrange matters so that you get yourself shot. It is by far the best thing that could happen."

He pauses. Eggbeater takes another swallow of Elixir. He feels his mind getting clearer and clearer. "Leibniz," he says quietly, trying to regain his calm, "you're beginning to worry me, you know. Are you absolutely certain that you're feeling all right? You talk—forgive me, *cher maître*—but you talk like a man who's gotten a touch of the sun, although I don't see how you could have, considering where you are. Get myself shot?! On *purpose*? I never heard of such a thing."

"But my boy, we must be prepared to make sacrifices. Miss Nightingale is making them all the time. What better way to show her your great love, your grand passion?"

"Great love? Grand passion? What in the world—?"

"Certainly, Eggbeater. I'm surprised at you. Miss Nightingale is a person of refinement, of sensitivity. You can't expect to drag her off like a sack of potatoes, without at least a few *pour parler*s. Where are your manners, old friend? You must *woo* her, man, by deed as well as word. How else can you expect to win her hand? If you know a surer way, I should like to hear it."

"Win her hand?" Eggbeater feels he is dealing with a lunatic. "What about Efficiency?"

"The superfluous Newton? Why, to hell with her, of course."

Eggbeater explodes. "Superfluous! What the hell are you talking about? Efficiency is part of the act! There wouldn't *be* any act without her. How long do you think people would listen to you babbling away, on and on, my God I never heard such tripe, if you want to know the truth—how long do you think people would stand for it, without someone to break up the monotony at least?"

He starts pacing around the room. "Why do you think I levitate, if it comes to that? Or the Oracle—why do you think I spent all those hours carrying out your instructions—and pretty vague instructions they were, too, let me tell you—except to make something that would spice the act up a bit. And at that I had to supply a few details of my own, and Mr. Barton's, to make the thing work properly. Besides, what's wrong with Efficiency, anyway? She's only a little jealous now, because we're working on the Oracle without her, that's all. When she sees what it does for the act she'll come round all right. *Her* attitude is at least understandable. Yours isn't. You really expect me to give up everything here—and this is a nice life, Leibniz, I don't know if you've noticed, blathering all your blather—and go gallivanting across the world? Well, I've *gone* gallivanting across the world, more than once or twice, with the police after me half the time and not a penny in my pocket, and let me tell you, it wasn't enjoyable. Spirit of adventure! Ha! There was no spirit in it at all, and there wouldn't be this time either. Miss Nightingale was seventeen when I knew her, for the love of God. She wouldn't even remember me, and why should she? And even if she did, what could she do for the act? Answer me that one, you're so smart. WHAT COULD SHE DO FOR THE ACT? She probably couldn't even elongate."

"But, Eggbeater," Leibniz whines, "Peter writes beautifully ... "

"Don't change the subject."

"Evander's sword is excellent, excellent, that is, insofar as—"

"And DON'T you give me that Evander's sword wheeze, I've heard it so many times—SAID it so many times, God damn it—I'm sick of it. What the hell do you mean by it, anyhow? I've asked you I don't know how many times and all you tell me is, it's very important. From your 'logical papers,' you say.

Well, the hell *with* it, as Efficiency says! I'm sick of that story and I'm sick of you, too. I've a good mind to give you up and go out on my own. Don't think I couldn't, either. I know your damn speeches by heart now—Christ, I ought to, the number of times I've had to say them. And don't forget: I can levitate! *That's* what brings the crowds, brother, not your God damned speeches."

"But Eggbeater—please ... What about the public good ... the glory of God...."

"No. Not another word. I'm finished with you!"

"Eggbeater ... I feel my leg acting up again ... "

Eggbeater storms out of the barn.

F H S J K F H F H S K J F J R E I T Y O Y P N N B M M K S H-W H G D F J S K D H S S S S S S S S S S S J J J J J J J J S J F U T J K ############################### Thelonious Monk will record "Friday the Thirteenth" in 1953. Miles Davis will record "Something I Dreamed Last Night" in 1956. XVXCVXBFGDHCMSJFHBSSNFHFH-GFHSNM The Moon is in Scorpio. Amazonite is green. Eggbeater makes his way across the field carrying a lantern, heading back to the house. The squirrels follow after.

It is nearly midnight.

Metals grow like trees under the earth in the Harz Mountains. Under the hills around Balaklava, where the image of the squirrel god lies buried, silver whispers to stibnite, gypsum to iron.

King Squirrel turns in his sleep in Naumburg.

"'The public good! The glory of God!'" Eggbeater fumes. "I'll glory of God him. From now on, we're on our own, just me and Efficiency. And Newton. *That'll* fix Leibniz. Fix him good. I'll just levitate, and say whatever of his I happen to remember, or anything else that seems good. Why should I keep to his script anyway? 'We have in our souls ideas of everything only because of the continual action of God upon us'—what kind of garbage is that? 'All substances sympathize with one another and receive some proportional change corresponding to the slightest motion in the whole universe'—I never heard such claptrap. No wonder Forbes can't stand us. I'm really better off making up my own material. Like ... um

... um ... well, I'll think of something when the time comes. Just let it flow, you know. Maybe add another spirit to the act, too, like that what's-his-name—Pedocles. Right. Good old Love and Strife Pedocles. One thing's for sure, though. I'm finished with Leibniz for good. He can talk all he wants, I'm not going to listen. And tomorrow night, when I unveil the Oracle, I'll say Leibniz didn't really make it. I'll say it in Leibniz's voice, too! I can do Leibniz's voice all right without Leibniz, my God, after all these years it'd be a minor miracle if I couldn't! I'll levitate, then I'll confess, in that funny voice, that I—or he—stole the whole thing, the same way I—or he—stole Newton's calculus. Hah! That *will* get him! Now, let's see, who shall I say he stole the Oracle from? Wish I could remember more names. Who was that philosopher Miss Nightingale liked to quote? Some ancient Greek ... No, not Pedocles ... Masaccio? ... No, he was the one who made the paintings ... Plato! That's right—I'll say Leibniz stole the Oracle from Plato!"

Eggbeater reaches the house, still mumbling. His mind has never felt so clear.

In the doctor's great adductor muscle, Monk flats a fifth.

In his cerebral cortex, the metal trees on the Brocken sprout fruit from their branches.

The ermine boa dances in the sleep of Monsieur Ingres.

"Good," mutters Eggbeater, opening the back door and going down the hall. "It'll be *Plato* and Newton from now on, with a little of the Love and Strife man on the side. Plato and Newton and the Delphic Oracle! I can see the newspaper headlines, after the séance tomorrow. 'CAWSES BACK! LEIBNIZ RECANTS! PLATO TRUE AUTHOR!' That'll make him—"

"Eggbeater."

"—sit up and take—"

"Eggbeater!"

"—notice all right."

"EGGBEATER!"

Monk flats another fifth. Eggbeater blinks and looks up. In front of him is Efficiency, standing at the bottom of the stairs. She wears a dark cloak over the white dress and carries a traveling bag.

"Oh, hello, 'Fishiency.'" He holds the lantern up to her face. "I was just looking for you. Had a new idea for the act. You going out? Pretty late to be going out, isn't it?"

"Eggbeater, hear this and hear it well—and get that light out of my face, for Christ's sake. The act is finished. Some unctuous and sulphureous bodies refract more than others, and that's all there is to it. Uncle Isaac and I are leaving you. For good."

"What!?" He lowers the lantern and staggers back.

"I said, Uncle Isaac and I are leaving you. The act is over."

"Leaving? LEAVING? You can't leave now! Where are you going?"

Oranges and grapefruit, suddenly ripe, hang from the boughs in Eggbeater's cerebral cortex. Peach trees flower on the Brocken. The yeti in the valley stops howling. He pulls a mango off a tree and bites into it. The Pope and the Archbishop of Canterbury sit cross-legged on their ledge, munching bananas.

"Never mind where I'm going. None of your business. Uncle Isaac and I know what we're doing."

The Archbishop of Canterbury turns to the Pope.

"Say, Mr. Pope," he asks, "did you hear the one about Evander's sword?"

"You mean the sword that is property insofar as Evander is owner?" The Pope answers.

"That's right," says the Archbishop. "Did you hear the one about it?"

"No," says the Pope. "Tell me."

"Well, the sword is excellent, of course, everyone knows that, but if it is acted upon when Evander acts, Evander is to that extent just!"

The Pope collapses in laughter, pounding the ground with his fists.

"You're crazy. You'll never make it on your own."

Efficiency bridles. In the vestibular fold of her larynx, Miles Davis turns to glare at his audience. "*I'm* crazy?" She says. "I like that. You, Eggbeater, have been out of your mind for years. How Uncle Isaac and I put up with it all this time I can't imagine. You're not fit to live without a keeper. You really belong in some sort of home, not that any self respecting asylum would have you. Why don't you try one of those cathouses in Paris? Or that highfalutin' English girl—that Miss Nightingale you're always going on about—maybe she would take you in." She sweeps past him and out the front door.

Cantaloupes and honeydew melons fill the *couloirs* in Eggbeater's Harz Mountains. On the ledge, the Pope recovers his composure.

"Did you know that Peter writes beautifully?" He asks the Archbishop, wiping his eyes.

"You mean, that is, that Peter writes something beautiful?" The primate answers, peeling another banana.

"Yes, to be sure," says the Pope, "but Peter—you won't believe this—Peter is also handsome insofar as he is standing!"

The Archbishop throws back his head and roars.

Eggbeater watches her go, too stunned to move, too stunned, even, to stop the Leibniz voice that wells up unbidden in his throat. "Everywhere there are substances actually separated from each other by their own actions!" He yells at her. "Why do you want to be one of the crowd?"

"Oh, go to hell, Eggbeater!" Efficiency yells back from the gate. Across the street, the Mainwarings' second storey window opens. "Suppose an obstacle is interposed to hinder the meeting of any two bodies A, B, attracting one the other: then if either body, as A, is more attracted towards the other body B, than that other body B is towards the first body A, the obstacle will be more strongly urged by the pressure of the body A than by the pressure of the body B, and therefore will not remain in equilibrium! So you go straight to hell, you and your God damned Leibniz, and take that stupid Delphic Oracle with you. And don't think I don't know about *that* little bit of skullduggery, you and Leibniz out there in the barn, pawing through Papa's papers till you found what you needed to make that contraption. You'd never have done it by yourselves, that's for sure. Oh, I'm on to you, Eggbeater, I've been on to you for a long, long time. Stealing Papa's ideas, stealing Uncle Isaac's ideas, and

God knows who else's, that's all you do and have ever done. Get away from me, God damn it!" She kicks at the squirrels, who have begun to gather in the yard in greater and greater numbers. "The only thing I'll miss about you, Eggbeater, is not seeing the stupid look on your face when you and Leibniz unveil that thing tomorrow night and ask it the first question. Oh, what a sight that will be!"

"Efficiency, you don't know the first thing about it!" Stung at last into motion, Eggbeater has advanced to the doorway. He shouts across the space between them. Monk plays a D-flat triad. "The characters that express all our thoughts will constitute a new language! There will be no equivocations or amphibolies, everything which—"

"Amphibolies, my latus rectum! They're the last things you'll have to worry about. Silence will be your problem, Eggbeater. Silence and more silence. The audience is going to walk out on you in the first five minutes. They won't even wait to see you levitate. Face it: without me and Uncle Isaac, you and Leibniz'll be finished on the circuit. You'll be playing the cathouses, and count yourselves lucky to get them. Unless, of course, your fancy friend Miss Nightingale can get you an audience with the Queen." She laughs. "Say, there's an idea, Eggbeater. Why don't you go back to Europe, you and Leibniz, and show that machine to Miss Nightingale? Who knows, she might even fall for it, she's dumb enough—can't even elongate, from what I hear. You two are probably made for each other. But just remember one thing, Eggbeater: second inventors count for nothing. Nothing! The axes of the planets are less than the diameters drawn perpendicular to the axes, and don't you ever forget it!"

She is gone. In her larynx, Miles Davis leaves the Showboat Lounge, gets into his white Mercedes-Benz where it sits parked on Lombard St. and heads out of town, hitting a hundred and ten miles per hour on the Ben Franklin Bridge.

"All right, damn you, I will!" Eggbeater screams into the night. "I'll go to Miss Nightingale. For the public good. For the justice of wise charity! Wisdom is the science of felicity, you know! To love is to find pleasure in the perfection of another, in case you've forgotten! You'll see, Efficiency! Just wait, you'll see!" He goes back in the house and slams the door.

The Dog (that Dog!) continues to bark.

"Some dog is not a man," says the Archbishop of Canterbury sadly.

"*No* dog is a man," laments the Pope. They are sitting in a strawberry patch which has sprung up suddenly on their ledge. "No not-man is a man," he adds, "if it comes to that. No stone, no cloud, no horse, no title, no heat. No squirrel. And Caius is slain by Titius. What does it matter that Evander's sword is excellent? What avails it that Peter writes beautifully?" He hangs his head.

"But on the other hand ... " ventures the Archbishop. He fingers the pom-poms on his clown suit. A letter A on his hat distinguishes him from his companion.

"Yes?"

"Well, on the other hand, every man *is* an animal."

"True." The Pope brightens. "An animal of some sort, in any case. A poor thing, perhaps, but an animal nonetheless."

"Exactly. Man A is an animal, man B is an animal, man C is an animal."

"Yes ... "

"And ... Do you know what, Mr. Pope?"

"What?"

"*Some* man is a laugher."

"No!" The Pope cannot believe his ears. He touches the P on his hat to make sure he is not dreaming.

"Oh, definitely, Mr. Pope. There can be no doubt of it whatsoever. Per-pend: every laugher is a laugher. Is this not so?"

"Certainly."

"And every laugher is a man. Correct?"

"I suppose so. For the purposes of argument."

"Therefore—therefore, my good Pontiff—some man is a laugher."

"Oh, no." The Pope makes a gesture of dismissal. "Very clever, Mr. Archbish-op, very clever to be sure, but can you seriously expect me to agree? From what you say it does not follow that there really is some man who is now actually laughing. It does not follow at all. Why, 'now actually laughing' is not even an entity! And what of all the other creatures who laugh? What of stones, what of mountains, what of rivers, clouds, trees? What of dogs? What of the strawberries under our arses? Can you not hear them? They are laughing fit to bust a gut. The whole of creation is laughing, all except some man. You have gotten my hopes up for nothing." He bites into a strawberry, which screams at him.

"Well ... " The Archbishop shrugs. "You can't say I didn't try. But tell me, Mr. Pope." He pokes his companion in the ribs. "Did you hear the one about the man called Greenhill?"

"Greenhill? No. Tell it me."

"With pleasure." The Archbishop clears his throat. "There once was a man called Greenhill. A friend says to him, 'It would be enough if you were called "Hill."' 'Why?' He replies. 'Do you think that all hills are green?' 'Yes—now at any rate,' says the friend. For it was SUMMER!"

"Summer?"

"Summer."

"Summer!" The Pope chuckles. Then he laughs outright. Then he guffaws, clapping the Archbishop on the back. "Summer! Summer!" He shouts in his glee.

"Laughers are now laughing! Laughers are now actually laughing!" The Archbishop answers. They toss their hats in the air, rolling over and over in the fruit.

Eggbeater Caws does not hear them. Nor does he laugh. Leibniz was right, Leibniz was right all along, he tells himself as he goes down the dark hall, footsteps echoing in the empty house. Damn the woman! Of all the impudence! And after all I've done for her. Cathouses, eh? I'll cathouse her! Miss Nightingale, we're on our way! Leibniz and I and the Oracle. For the public good! For the science of felicity. For a fountain of motion and dilation, as in a burning candle! For the—but wait. He stops at the door to the sitting room. What about Leibniz? Will he go along with it now? Will he forgive me after what I said to him? Is he even speaking to me? Oh, God, what an idiot I was. "Leibniz!" He calls aloud. "Leibniz? Are you there?"

"Why, hello, Eggbeater." The voice comes through smooth as silk. "How nice of you to communicate with me. Yes, I'm here, dear boy, at your service as always."

"Oh, Leibniz, I'm so terribly sorry I—"

"Now, now, Eggbeater, there's no need to apologize. We all of us lose our tempers every once in a while." The philosopher glances down at his books, lying on the floor where they fell when he swept them off his desk a few minutes ago. "Anger is nothing more than a violent effort to rid oneself of an evil. And what, in this instance, could have been more appropriate? For whatever else has taken place in the last half hour, we have certainly been rid of an evil, have we not?" He smiles broadly. "Oh, yes, my friend, I overheard everything. The woman has a carrying voice. She behaved abominably, of course, but that was only to be expected, considering the pestilence at her core. Really, one's faith in the ultimate salvation of all beings is sometimes strained to the breaking point. The everlasting fires of Hell seem a piffling chastisement, a merely token reproof, in the face of such wickedness." He bends down, picks up the tome containing the writings of the Church Fathers, and replaces it on the desk. "But that is a side issue. The important thing, my good old Eggbeater, is that at last we are free, you after a heptad of years, I after what feels like aeons, to pursue our own goals, to bring our long-balked projects—banausic, metaphysical and, uh, amatory—to a successful conclusion." He goes on returning books to his desk. "By the way, I thought you were magnificent just now. You responded to that creature's tirade with composure and dignity, yet at the same time with eloquence, with passion. 'Science of felicity' is a wonderful phrase, is it not? Wasted on her, naturally. But not on me, old friend, I assure you."

He retrieves the footstool from the other side of the room, where he had kicked it, and sets it again beside his chair. "I was especially pleased to hear you speak with such zeal of Miss Nightingale, and to declare (so *forcefully*, Eggbeater, your resolve was truly statesmanlike, you reminded me of Louis XIV, or perhaps even a duke of Hanover) your intention to go to her. By far the best course, in my opinion, and one which will be all the easier to put in train, now that we have the house to ourselves and that Gorgon is out of our lives for good. I suggest we get started immediately."

"Then you're really not angry with me?"

"Angry? *Angry?* What a ridiculous idea." He massages the cover of the *Kabbala Denudata* where he struck it with his walking stick. "How could anyone be angry at such intrepid behavior? Entirely the wrong response. You were a tiger, a lion, a Defender of the Faith, a veritable Mars Christianissimus. The way you stood up for the public good, for the charity of the wise, all Christian virtues in the truest sense! I found you positively inspiring. It will be nothing less than a joy for me, a joy and a deep, deep privilege, to accompany you back to Europe. Ah, Europe! My leg feels better already." He flexes it, wincing. "The exercise will do it a world of good, and sharpen our wits as well. Did I ever tell you about the time I escaped an assassination attempt, in the middle of a storm on the Adriatic?"

"Well, er ... "

"Ah, yes, I *did* mention that, didn't I, just a few minutes ago, in fact. Forgive me. A momentary lapse. In any case, this is no time for reminiscence. We must bestir ourselves. We should certainly ransack the house, in case that scoundrel has left behind something of value—stolen jewels, perhaps, precious metals, cash, some of her mathematical papers. A person of her stripe would have found a thousand places to hide things in a house this size, places, Eggbeater, that even your penetrating gaze may not have suspected. I think the best room to start in is the space you call the spirit cabinet (quaint term, that) where the Alphabet of Tho—that is, where the Oracle as you call it, is kept. It doubles, as I recall, as a species of storeroom. She's undoubtedly secreted all manner of treasure there, under the mattresses, in the crannies formed between the pieces of piled up furniture, behind the things on the shelves, behind the shelves themselves even. The swine worked for years at the Mint, you know, and unquestionably robbed it blind. There must be enough gold in that room to ransom an army." He strikes his forehead. "By God, Eggbeater! Do you realize, we *could* ransom an army, or at least bribe a few regiments, once we get over there. If reason won't convince people, money usually will. The Turks ... well, the Turks. As for the French, Louis XIV has never been known to turn down large supplies of cash, especially if it comes from British coffers, and he's not about to start now. By Heaven, we could even change the course of the war, perhaps put a stop to it entirely. Hurry, Eggbeater, hurry, there's not a moment to spare!"

Eggbeater does not need to be told twice. He passes quickly through the sitting room, his lantern held high, his reason awash in thoughts of riches and reprisals. Just you wait, Efficiency, just you wait, he says to himself, as Leibniz slavers in the pineal gland, rubbing his palms together, and alligator pears, apricots, persimmons, ugli fruit, sugar apples, rose apples, sour apples, sweetsops, raisins, figs, tamarinds, jujubes, kumquats, Jaffa oranges, tangerines, raspberries, blueberries, dewberries, blackberries, elderberries, huckleberries, hagberries, gooseberries, lingonberries, loganberries, red currants, plums, passion fruit, plantains and muskmelons cover the slopes of the Brocken.

Monk gets up from the piano and begins to dance, moving in a shuffle step through Eggbeater's adductor muscle. The bass and drums continue without him. Charlie Rouse starts a solo on tenor saxophone.

Nietzsche's squirrel taps porcelain toes in his sleep.

Efficiency reaches the High Street Bridge and looks around for Welkin. The town clock strikes twelve. She taps her foot impatiently. Miles Davis, the New Jersey Turnpike long behind him, enters the Lincoln Tunnel.

Welkin, late as usual, urges his horses through Ipswich and out onto the Aubrey Road.

The Dog stops barking. He comes to a halt (Oh, no!) about half a mile short of the High St. Bridge.

Eggbeater reaches the curtain, pulls it back and steps inside me. He sweeps the lantern back and forth; lights and shadows dance across the room. Where would she put it, where would she put it, he wants to know, not even asking himself what "it" might look like. Treasure, that's all. Treasure, riches, GOLD! His mind has never been so clear. Ah! He sees the mattresses. Yes, of course! Find a knife, slit them open. Where knife?

His eye falls on the Oracle, sitting on its table. No knife there. He is about to pass it by, but—

"LEIBNIZ!"

"Yes, Eggbeater? Find something already?" The philosopher smacks his lips.

"Leibniz, it's all—"

"Yes? Yes? All over the room, you say? Imagine—the scoundrel didn't even bother to hide it. What insolence! But typical, typical. I remember one occasion when—"

"No, Leibniz! Would you please listen for once? It's the Oracle!"

"The Oracle?! What about it?"

"It's all wrecked! The wires have been twisted."

"What!"

"The magnets are out of place—"

"No!"

"The zinc and copper plates have been pulled every which way. And the automatic carrying mechanism is bent. It's been shoved up against the crank. The crank is turning all by itself! How in hell can that have happened? Must be the magnets. Or the wires. Most asinine thing I ever saw. Completely useless. Oh, damn! This must have been what she meant when she said the audience would walk out on us! My God, Leibniz, this is unspeakable, a deliberate, malicious destruction of everything we've—I'll kill her. Yes, I will! I'll kill her dead." He starts out of the room.

BDJGKSJDSKHNMGUCFNEHSGAWWWWWWWN. 24,157,817 plus 14,930,352 is 39,088,169. Thelonious Monk will record "Off Minor" in Paris in 1966, with Charlie Rouse on tenor saxophone, Larry Gales on bass and Ben Riley on drums. But why wait? They're playing it tonight in Eggbeater, and Monk is dancing. As Rouse begins his eighteenth chorus and Riley, playing in between the beats, nudges Gales' walking bass, Thelonious starts to rotate. He spins counterclockwise, in small circles at first, then in an ever-widening spiral, his feet maintaining the shuffle step, body twitching, eyes half closed. Midway though the chorus, Riley hits a rim shot. Monk turns to him, calls "You got it!," walks backwards down the steps of the bandstand and, still dancing, disappears into a fold in the adductor, moving in the direction of the iliotibial ligament.

The Dog lifts his head and sniffs the air. Horses. Somewhere behind him. He feels the beating of their hooves through the calluses on his paws, and the turning of wheels. He trots back (OH, NO! NO! NO! NO!) in the direction of Ipswich.

THE DOG! THE DOG HAS TURNED AWAY!
IS THERE NO HELP,
NO HELP FOR A LIVING MIRROR OF THE UNIVERSE?
BROTHER CHAOS, I AM IN THE DARK!
BROTHER CHAOS, I AM IN THE DARK!

MGHSKFJTNMVKSJJFJJJJJJJMMMFNSHFSPPFFFT. On the Aubrey side of the bridge, Efficiency gives up on Welkin. She starts back towards the house, fuming.

"Oh, Eggbeater … Eggbeater, dear boy?" Leibniz purrs as the doctor puts his hand on the curtain. "So sorry to bother you at a time like this, but might I have a word?"

"A *word?* Leibniz, I'm in a hurry."

"I know you are, old friend, and I fully sympathize. I'm as disturbed as you are, really I am. And in complete agreement. Kill her dead by all means, Eggbeater. Wring her neck. The jury will never convict you."

"What!?"

"You'll get off without so much as a reprimand. I'm convinced of it. I myself will conduct your defense. I have considerable experience as a jurist, as you surely must know—you have often quoted from my excellent dissertation, *De Casibus Perplexis in Iure.* I think we will plead *un crime passionnel*, that should fit the facts nicely. Bedeviled for years, almost beyond endurance, by a froward and frightful creature whom at bottom you wished only to raise up and enlighten—chafed, clawed, lancinated, stung by a thousand indignities—at last you discovered a betrayal so base, so wanton, that her malefactions could no longer be ignored. You lashed out, you—what, Eggbeater? You what? But my dear man, of *course* there will be a trial. How could there not be? Unless, that is, you have the presence of mind to kill her in such a way that you are not suspected, which in your present state I very much doubt. You are, shall we say, considerably overwrought. Oh, with cause, with cause,

I certainly don't deny that. I am scarcely underwrought, myself. But my God, man, you seem to have abandoned all your powers of reflection. You are on your way out the door, are you not? Are you proposing to kill her on the high road? Yes, I do believe you are. Eggbeater, Eggbeater, have you not given thought to witnesses? Dead of night though it may be, you're sure to make some noise. Indeed, you have already made a good deal of noise, the two of you, screaming at each other in front of the house. Some of the neighbors must infallibly have been awakened. The ever-vigilant Mrs. Mainwaring, for instance—she must be leaning out her window even as we speak, hoping for more. I know she is a Leibnizian; the fact does her credit, of course. But would her loyalty extend so far as concealment of a homicide? I can't say conclusively, old friend, you know her better than I, but I'd hate to have my life depending on the answer.

"And even if there are no witnesses, if—miracle of miracles—Mrs. Mainwaring suffers a stroke, or simply falls asleep at her post, or if you somehow manage to drag Newton noiselessly off the road and do her in behind a bush, what about the body? Are you in any state to dispose of it properly, that is to say completely, as if the quantity Newton had been (would it were so!) subtracted from the universe, or at least North America? No, I'm afraid you are not. The body will be discovered, and people—you can hardly blame them—will talk. Questions will be asked. Fingers will be pointed. At best, it will be a nuisance. At worst … ? uh, at worst."

"Hmmm."

"Hmmm, indeed, dear boy. In fact, thinking things over, might you not find it a better course to wait a while before you kill her? Until you're calmer and can form a plan. Or even—because no plan is perfect, not even the best of all possible plans, there always remains some crevice of uncertainty through which the demons may rush and bring down the most splendid of constructs—simply leave foul enough alone? Not kill her at all, I mean. Now, now, Eggbeater, before you erupt like Vesuvius, just listen a moment. Don't lose sight of the main thing. I mean, of course, our freedom, our *present* freedom, present and palpable, right here, just as we are, in this place or any other we choose to occupy. We can change the world with it, Eggbeater, effect wonderful things in nature, the purification of souls, their gradual improvement and elevation, a perpetual increase in joy, the rejuvenation, need I mention, of Miss Nightingale, the proliferation, even, of smocked bodices, but only so long as we have our freedom. Kill Newton and—irony of ironies!—we lose it. Contingencies pile up, our movements are circumscribed, we are tethered, hemmed in, fate overpowers wisdom. We—"

"But Leibniz! She wrecked the Oracle. How can we let—"

"Precisely, dear boy. How can we let her get away with it? I know. The deed is despicable, repulsive; it cries out for redress. But look at it another way: she ruined the Oracle, yes. Therefore, how can we not repair it? A functioning Oracle is a necessity, revenge a mere luxury, and a fatal one at that. How could we fix the Oracle distracted by the rigors of a murder trial, you languishing in prison and I searching through my law books for precedents, exceptions, technicalities and such? Whereas, if we stay here and leave the wretch to her own devices, no such problems present themselves. You—"

"But how can I fix—"

"My dear friend, nothing could be simpler. In your passion you forget your own abilities. You put the machine together, did you not? Oh, the specifications were mine, *ça va sans dire*, but you carried out the construction. Piece by piece, you brought it into being. Therefore, you can bring it back."

"Bring it back?"

"Oh, yes, Eggbeater, I'm certain of it. Nothing done by a Newton, even such a Newton as she, can be irreparable. Why, just now you enumerated the atrocities she committed, did you not, and in perfectly clear language as I recall. The magnets were out of place, you said. That would suggest you remember where you put them originally. Do you?"

"Well, yes ... "

"Excellent. Then put them back. Same thing for the wires. If they're twisted, untangle them. As for the zinc and copper plates and the automatic carrying mechanism, they may take a little longer, but the same principle applies. Get to work, dear boy, get to work. You'll have your Oracle back, good as new, before you know it."

"Well, I suppose I might be able to ... "

"Don't suppose, Eggbeater. Do it! Take one of the wires. Hold it between your fingers. Now, give a little tug."

OH!

33333333333333333333333333333ghfjtkdnkllklklkkthe orbital period of Jupiter is 11.86 years. The world's smallest mammal is the white-toothed pygmy shrew- mouse333333333333333333333333

"There! Well done, old friend. Now go on to the others."

NO! LEIBNIZ, EGGBEATER, STOP IT!

22 years, 7 months and 26 days old. The upper back portion of her left rear leg was Ururururururur. Ururururururur stood to name a star 3333333333333333 eyes the color of graphite clkclkclkclk

Deep in the iliotibial ligament, Monk comes upon an abandoned celeste. He leans over it and plays the opening bars of "Pannonica."

Racing towards the High St. Bridge, Welkin sees a yellow-and-white Dog coming at him in the moonlight. His horses rear and shy as (*NO!*) the animal passes. It takes all his strength to keep them from bolting.

Efficiency reaches the front gate. God-damned Jerry, she says to herself. Just like him, too. Never on time in his life. What the hell kind of lover does he think he is, anyway? Expects me to *wait* for him, for Christ's sake. That's the story of my life, God damn it, the story of my life.

"Excellent, Eggbeater! One more wire and you can start on the magnets."

Eye of the Gorgon Eye of the Gorgon Mary Walsh and Nikola Tesla will receive messages from Mars over Cincinnati, Ohio. The first British Ladies' Golf Championship was signed in 1648, the Magna Carta in Hanover fur stockings. Molybdenite attempted to reconcile the Protestant and Roman faiths. EyeoftheGorgonEyeoftheGorgon33333333333333333333333333333

STOP IT, YOU IDIOTS! STOP!

"Do you know, Leibniz, I think this is actually going to work. All I really have to do to free the magnets is ... "

EYEOFTHEGORGONEYEOFTHEGORGON Artichokes are green. The cranial capacity of Lady

" ... unbend the automatic carrying mechanism, and I—"

Margaret Scott will marry Urururururururur's fossilized brain case in Blessed Germaine Cousin Nicolas Fatio de Duillier M. L. Bryan of New York J. J. Kaendler of Miessen the Reverend H. B. Jeffries Johann Friedrich Böttger ductile steel the Green Lion Hyatt's Life Balsam the age-old theater of transmutation Hackensack, New Jersey the speed of light squared the above-mentioned gravy stain a circular black spot

Efficiency opens the front door and walks down the hall. Have to make up with him, I suppose. Of all the rotten luck. She passes through the sitting room and into GHDNFHGFJGJSDKFGJDFGUSSUSUUUUUUUIIIIII-IAAAAAAAAAOOOOOOOOOOEEEEEE

King Squirrel awakens in Naumburg. He whispers his dream to the still-sleeping Nietzsche. The little philosopher half-opens his SHSHVGDGFKDKD-KDKL and DJGKFSGYYYYYYYYYDHFKSLAAAAH

first balloon wedding   the Giant's Shoulder   external as well
as internal male and female reproductive organs
the sun is in a dog suit

LEIBNIZ! EGGBEATER!

Mary Walsh and Nikola Tesla Mary Walsh and Nikola Tesla Mary Walsh and Nikola Tesla Mary Walsh and Nikola Tesla Mary Walsh and Nikola Tesla Mary Walsh and

"There! I think that's got it. Now to—"

Efficiency opens the curtain.

"Eggbeater?" She asks quietly. "I just wanted to—"

"You! YOU! How DARE you come in here? I'm going to XHGKSBVH-FNSK   XHXHXSKKKKSJJJJJJJJJJ3333333333333333333xxxxxxxxxxxm-mmmmmmmmmmmmmmmmmmmmmmmmmmmmmmmmmmmmmmmmmmm
mmmmmmmmmmmmmmmmmmmmmmmmmmmmmmmmmmmmmmmmmmmm
mmmmmmm mmmmmmmmmmmmmmmmmmmmmmmmm
mmmmmmmmmmmmmmmmmmm
mmmmmmmmmmmm
mmmmm
mm
m

BOOK 3

17

BUT WHO IS TO BLAME?
CAN THE SOUL COMPLAIN ABOUT ANYTHING
OTHER THAN ITSELF?
(YES.)

Gravity Newton:

"No, it wasn't, either! *She* did it! She killed him, same as she did her father. I saw her!"

Alice Mainwaring's voice rang out in the crowded courtroom, rousing the spectators from their stupor. Having piled into the chamber at the crack of dawn, anxious not to miss a minute of what promised to be the most exciting inquest in the town's history, by mid-morning the Aubreyites had been lulled almost to insensibility by the medical examiner's relentlessly detailed description of Dr. Caws' insides and outsides, capped by his assertion that there had been nothing unusual about either (apart from the feather in the mouth, which seemed harmless enough) and that, so far as he could tell, the deceased had met his end because his heart had stopped beating. The medical examiner was followed on the witness stand by Calvin Mainwaring, who had discovered the body shortly after midnight on the morning of May 29. He, too, spoke at length and, according to a number of newspaper reports, quite slowly, so that it was some time before the fact that he had found Dr. Caws lying on his back by the side of the road with his coat open was communicated to the Court. After what seemed an interminable pause, he added that the deceased's cravat was askew and that he smelt strongly of alcohol. "Gin ...

probably. Didn't sur ... prise me much." Then, after what the correspondent for the Boston *Sentinel* called "a lithifaction of waiting," he opined, "Reckon that's what ... killed 'im." It was then that his wife interrupted, causing spectators to cheer and the Court to lodge a stern protest.

Mr. Mainwaring added his voice to the Court's. "You wait your turn, Alice. I ain't ... done yet."

"Oh, shut up, Calvin," she answered. "Nobody wants to hear any more out of you. Mr. Mainwaring is a Newtonian," she explained to the spectators, who had turned to stare at her as she stood in the back row. "No, Calvin, don't try to deny it," she warned as her husband opened his mouth. "You always have been and you always will be. Not that that excuses you. But it takes a Leibnizian to tell the truth."

At this point, the correspondent from the Philadelphia *Mercury-Leader* noted, "Some considerable disturbance broke out." "Most regrettable," commented the Cleveland *Courier*.

And so it very likely was. The Cawses were nothing if not controversial, and, once delivered from their lethargy, the townsfolk cheerfully and boisterously took sides, just as they had in days gone by, despite repeated warnings that the courtroom would be cleared and the more flagrant offenders held in contempt. But in fact Mrs. Mainwaring's assertions cannot have come as a surprise; they included nothing that she had not been saying ever since the tragedy to anyone who would listen, and nothing, for that matter, that most people had not been thinking on their own, even if none of them could claim to have witnessed the event.

And who could have blamed them? The circumstances surrounding the doctor's death were suggestive enough to excite suspicions in the most phlegmatic individuals, and the Aubreyites, with the possible exception of Mr. Mainwaring, were hardly phlegmatic. First, a nationally known medium had been found lying dead in the road, with not a mark on him and a white feather sticking out of his mouth. Second, the door to his house, only a few yards away, had been left standing open. Third, his wife, an equally well-known medium, was missing. Fourth, a prominent feature of the couple's séances, repeated over and over in the cities in which they gave exhibitions, had been undisguised rivalry and implacable strife. Fifth, the journalist who had interviewed the pair on the morning before the husband's death, was also missing. And sixth, reports had been received of the medium's wife having been seen the next day in Boston, in the company of the journalist who, it was rumored, had been her close friend since childhood.

Little wonder, then, that the courtroom was jammed, or that the press was giving the matter its closest attention. The mysterious death of an already-mysterious person; the open question of murder, possibly committed by the deceased's wife, and conceivably by occult means; the open question of sex, specifically an illicit affair, perhaps as motive for murder but certainly as a leitmotif—these were the makings of a genuine, juicy, long-lasting scandal of much more than local interest. There was even a correspondent in Court who represented a journal in Paris, where Dr. Caws was said to have lived at one time.

Mrs. Mainwaring took the stand directly after her husband, whose testimony concluded ("mercifully," according to the *Sentinel*) shortly after her outburst. As she took the oath, she seemed to the *Courier's* reporter to be "in an elevated state." Her face was flushed, and her eyes shone "with an unnatural brilliance. She had every appearance of one infused with a sense of mission." She was dressed "rather ostentatiously" in mourning, the only person in the room thus attired.

Asked by the Coroner to describe the events which led her to awaken her husband on the night of Dr. Caws' death, and to send him out into the road to investigate, she begged leave of the Court to "begin at the beginning." Advised that that was always the best way, she commenced a stirring redaction of Leibniz's *Monadology*, explaining that Monads, the true atoms of nature, were simple substances—"'simple' meaning without parts"—and that they and none other were the irreducible units of reality, from which all "composites" were formed. They were also, she alleged, "souls," and as such could never perish. "They can begin only by creation and end only by annihilation," she said, "unlike composites, which begin and end part by part. Oh, how sad it all seems now!" She lifted her eyes to Heaven.

Here the Court intervened, raising Its voice to be heard above the Newtonians caviling in the front rows, and directed Mrs. Mainwaring to come to the point.

"Certainly," she replied, according to the Ottawa *Spirit-Intelligencer*, "if your Honor wishes it. But I had understood you to permit me to begin at the beginning. Surely a brief excursus on the simple and indivisible substances which comprise the ultimate and sole realities of the whole of Creation would fall under that heading."

Told to confine herself to May 28 and the events she witnessed leading up to the death of Dr. Caws, she sniffed, but answered, "Very well, your Honor. I am, of course, at your command. All matter is interconnected in any case."

She testified that late in the afternoon of the date specified, "happening to be standing at window," she saw the doctor lying on the ground at the foot of the elm tree which stood across the street from his house. "He must have fallen out of it," she said. "Just a minute or two before, he had been up in its top-most branches and—Oh, I suppose I should have mentioned that at first. He had flown up there earlier in the day. Certainly I saw him, your Honor. Didn't I say I was at my window? But it was nothing so terribly unusual, you know, not where the doctor was concerned. He often flew up there. It was *his* tree," she explained. "Not legally, no, sir. Legally, I suppose, it was ours, Mr. Mainwaring's and mine; it was on our property. But spiritually it belonged to Dr. Caws. He used it for meditation, for self-renewal. He bathed in the etheric currents, communed with heavenly beings. Ah, ah, what mortal can say what truly took place at the top of that tree, what sacred conversations, what flights of the spirit?"

Here the Court broke in again, warning her to confine herself to what she, personally, had seen or heard. That, his Honor added, seemed sufficiently extraordinary in itself without further embellishment. The *Spirit-Intelligencer* reported that he stressed the word "further," much to the delight of the Newtonians in the front rows.

Chastened but, in the words of the *Courier*, "determined to tell her story," Mrs. Mainwaring accepted the rebuke, although she insisted that she had in fact seen the doctor fly to the top of the tree. "Many times," she said. "Plain as day. Anyone would have, who had been there."

However, she admitted, she had not actually seen him fall. She had turned away from the window for a moment, "a moment I shall rue all my days," and when she turned back Dr. Caws was "lying there, flat on the ground." She was sure he could not have climbed down the tree. "It is a tall, tall tree, and there simply wasn't time." Besides, she said, he was hurt. "He could hardly move at first, when I called out to him. And then, later, it was an effort for him even to crawl. His speech was thick and slow. Oh, he tried to put a bold face on it, that was always the good doctor's way. He said he had only suffered a slight 'catabasis.' He had such a wonderful vocabulary. 'Catabasis!' What a beautiful, beautiful word. An inflammation of the lungs, it means. In the East they call it 'aliquots.'"

The doctor finally pulled himself together, she testified. He got across the street and through his front gate, stumbling off in the direction of his barn. "But I knew in my heart it was no catabasis that was troubling him. He was deeply hurt, hurt in soul as well as body. Oh, forgive me, your Honor, but the thought came into my mind that there had been a spell put on him. Yes, your Honor, a spell! Oh, I knew then that he was not long for this world. One look at him and I knew. The squirrels knew, too. I could tell from the way they followed him."

"Squirrels?" asked the Court.

"Yes, your Honor, squirrels. Did I not mention them before? It was remiss of me. There were squirrels under the tree. They gathered there during our conversation. Squirrels were the doctor's special animals. Oh, he loved all animals, of course, and they him, they followed him everywhere. But squirrels were his special friends."

"Ah," said the Court.

The next time Mrs. Mainwaring saw the doctor was late that night, "getting on for midnight." She was preparing to retire, when she heard a commotion across the street, "voices arguing," first inside the Caws house and then in the yard. She went to the window and opened it. "I thought perhaps there was something I could do to help, one never knows, does one, and I wanted to hear better—just in case the doctor called out to me. Oh, she said some terrible things to him, I don't like to repeat them." Told that she must do so, she squirmed in her chair, according to the *Spirit-Intelligencer*, raised her eyes to Heaven according to the *Courtier*, and began.

"She—that would be Mrs. Caws—screamed at him that one body was more attracted to another body than that body was to the first, and that an obstacle (that was her word, 'obstacle') would come and the pressures of the bodies—oh, Heaven forgive me for saying it—the pressures of the bodies would not keep them in equilibrium. And as if that weren't bad enough, she told him to go to H___ and made fun of amphiboles. And all Dr. Caws would say, bless his heart, he was always so meek and mild, all the good doctor would say was to remind her that to love is to find pleasure in the perfection of another—which it is, of course. And then she left him, walking up Prospect St. towards the bridge, swinging the traveling bag she held in her hand. The doctor went back in the house."

Mrs. Mainwaring testified that she remained at the window "transfixed" (according to the *Mercury-Leader*), "in a kind of trance" (according to the *Sentinel*), "like a helpless witness to some impending, inevitable horror" (according to the *Courtier*). A short time later, she saw Mrs. Caws return, "clomping down the street muttering to herself, mad as anything," and go back in the house. Then, almost immediately, "the door flew open and the both of them rushed out, her in the lead, still carrying her bag, him running after her and shouting, 'My Oracle! My Oracle!' They went through the gate and out into the street."

At this point, the correspondent for the *Spirit-Intelligencer* wrote, Mrs. Mainwaring paused dramatically. She rose up in the witness box, staring out over the crowd, "her eyes fixed, as it seemed, on some vision above our heads, as if she were reliving her experience, not merely recounting it. Her voice took on a depth and resonance we had not previously suspected. The room quieted down. Even the Newtonians fell silent, as Mrs. Mainwaring narrated the final act of the tragedy.

She told, the correspondent continued, how the doctor finally caught up with Mrs. Caws in the street. He reached out to touch her, grabbing at the traveling bag in her hand. But she broke away, and turned to face him. Then, without warning, she grew in height, towering over him and hissing "like a serpent. The doctor, God rest his soul," the witness went on, "took a step backwards, like a fencer, and that little feather of his materialized in his hand. He twirled it, and on the instant he shot up in the air, twenty or thirty feet, and he was *laughing*, yes, God bless his precious heart, he was laughing at her.

'Look,' he shouted, 'just look at this! Your gravitation of matter toward matter is a fool's dream. Action at a distance is an illusion! You're finished, Efficiency!' And he laughed and laughed. And then ... and then ... "

Mrs. Mainwaring's face reddened. She herself appeared to grow taller in the witness box. She raised her arms above her head; her voice deepened even further as she intoned her testimony. "And then I, Alice—I, Alice—saw the heavens open, and the sky turn bright as day, and I heard the thunder roll. And I saw *her*, far below him, staring up at him with hate—oh, such hate!—in her eyes. And she pointed a finger at him where he stood in the air, and she *jabbed* the finger and screeched, '*I'll* give you action at a distance!' And oh, my blessed Lord, a hundred cantaloupes materialized in the sky, and then another hundred, and another after that, and another after that, and so on up to seven hundred cantaloupes hanging in the sky, far above the dear doctor's head, and there was a crack of thunder, and the cantaloupes fell and struck the doctor, one after another they struck him, to the number of seven hundred, and his body went limp and *he* fell, oh, he fell and fell, all that awful way straight down. And he hit the ground with a terrible, sickening thud and lay still. And she, the strumpet, just stood there, looking down at him with a self-satisfied smile on her face. 'The hypothesis of vortices is done for, Eggbeater,' she said. 'You should have known that a long time ago. You have no one to blame but yourself.' And she picked up her traveling bag, cool as you please, and turned on her heel, and went off again toward the High St. Bridge. But then, Oh! Such a howling rose up from the earth! It was the squirrels at first, but then the grass and the rocks took up the cry, and finally his tree, his dear tree, joined in as well. The whole of Creation poured out its grief, till at last the heavens closed and it was night again. And I, Alice, I alone have escaped to tell thee."

The *Courier*, the *Sentinel* and the *Mercury-Leader* gave similar accounts of the testimony. The latter paper added that it was delivered in an "embarrassingly" dramatic fashion, full of exaggerated gestures and sudden changes of pose accompanied by low, inarticulate moans. The *Sentinel* mentioned frequent wringing of the hands and discerned an overall effect of artifice. The Parisian paper, *L'Esprit*, whose dispatches were published a full month after the event, also took a dim view of the performance in a scathing, though admittedly humorous piece, "*Les cantaloupes du ciel: l'apocalypse selon Ste. Alice.*"

The Aubreyites' reactions were more complex. On the one hand, spectators in the courtroom were put off by Mrs. Mainwaring's histrionics. Not just the Newtonians but also a fair number of Leibnizians, who initially had been disposed to believe her account, felt she was merely trying to make a name for herself and that everything she said was, in the words of one, "tainted by spleen." "She always was jealous of Efficiency, even as a girl," said another. But there were also those who wondered if the witness could have made it *all* up; it was generally agreed that she hadn't the imagination. Her testimony might have been embellished, and her manner of giving it unfortunate, but the circumstances surrounding the doctor's death remained highly suspicious. Mrs. Caws had disappeared, probably in the company of the writer, Welkin. They had been seen together in Boston, or so it was rumored, the next day. Some said that they were sighted in the act of boarding a train, perhaps for New York. Others said it was a ship, and they were on their way to Europe. Newtonians, however, dismissed these reports as unconfirmed and insisted that Mrs. Caws should not be judged too harshly, even assuming some core of truth in Mrs. Mainwaring's story. "She should get another chance," one of them said. "She probably didn't know what she was doing. Who are we to judge?"

The jury, who did have to judge, had the same questions and concerns as the spectators but also a much greater responsibility, a fact they bemoaned as they discussed the case over their midday meal. Or course, as jurors at an inquest, it was not their duty to determine innocence or affix guilt, nor even to level an accusation, but they knew that if they brought in a finding that the deceased, himself a well-known medium, had met his death by supernatural or occult means, there was only one person who could conceivably have been the wielder of such means, even if they chose to discount the most damaging parts of Mrs. Mainwaring's testimony. And if that person were arrested and tried and found guilty, or even found guilty *in absentia*, might not Aubrey become known as another Salem? Might not the affair even start a rash of prosecutions of mediums nationwide? It seemed very likely. On the other hand, to reject Mrs. Mainwaring's testimony entirely, in effect to brand her a liar, would satisfy no one: present suspicions would linger, questions would still be asked, and more insistently than before.

But even more vexing than these considerations, serious as they were, was the jury's abiding sense that the whole business was at bottom a family affair, their own special affair as Aubreyites, and that courts, judges, coroners and medical examiners had no right to meddle in it. After all, Efficiency Caws traced her lineage all the way back to the first settlers. Her husband might have come from elsewhere, but he had quickly made himself one of them, not only by his personal charm but by the obvious fact, which radiated from him like a sun, that, like them, he did not fit in anywhere else. If this husband and wife, exemplary in so many ways, happened to have a little dispute (and what husband and wife did not?) and if the dispute happened to get out of hand, with one or two unfortunate consequences, whose business was that? Whose but the Aubreyites', who knew the couple best? The "damn Law," as one of them called it, which in their view was made and executed by outsiders, "should damn well stay out of it."

The jurors fumed at their predicament. The blood of Notwithstanding Mallard and Exhumation Sweet, of Colonel Schwank and the other heroes of the Ipswich-Rowley Wars flowed in their veins. Their great great great great grandfathers had fought Indians, Puritans and Royalists alike with equal fierceness, had brawled, bickered and wrangled, stolen, cheated and lied, turned friends into foes without a moment's hesitation, all to preserve their way of life. And now they had to truckle to the Law, dance to the tune of some circuit judge from Salem, scrape to the county coroner. Confound Alice Mainwaring anyhow. If only she'd kept her mouth shut!

Happily, the testimony of Justinian Forbes, which followed Mrs. Mainwaring's in the afternoon session, resolved the jurors' dilemma, or at least offered them an acceptable way out. Mr. Forbes was called, of course, not as an eyewitness but as an acknowledged expert on spiritualism and psychic phenomena, who could provide an objective assessment of the evidence in the case. He stated categorically that Mrs. Caws could not possibly have killed her husband, "by cantaloupe or any other occult means" according to the *Spirit-Intelligencer*, simply because she didn't have the power to do so. Both husband and wife were frauds, he asserted, and had been since the beginning of their career. In support of his statement, he cited his numerous articles on the couple, published in *Time and Light*, as well as long passages from the works of Leibniz and Newton which the pair had "obviously committed to memory and shamelessly repeated verbatim." He also read at length from Welkin's interview with the Cawses, published by the Salem *Trumpet* the day after Dr. Caws' death. (The *Trumpet*, deprived of Welkin's services, sent a part-time replacement to cover the inquest; he contributed little or nothing that the other journals did not do better, and left out quotations entirely.)

Mr. Forbes remarked as well on the wigs, false beards, gauze and various costumes discovered in the Cawses' house after the tragedy, making special mention of "the utter lack of moral teaching or spiritual uplift in the couple's séances. Indeed," he said, "they positively encouraged discord and internecine strife."

That the mechanisms responsible for the Cawses' "supposed" feats of levitation and elongation had not been discovered was no proof, he continued, that such mechanisms did not exist; it merely indicated the couple's "admittedly impressive ingenuity." The doctor, he noted, had been known to be clever with gadgets and machines. As for the "alleged coincidence" that Mrs. Caws' father had also been killed by a falling cantaloupe (an event witnessed by numerous persons, many of whom were still alive) the witness delivered a lengthy and, all the newspaper accounts agreed, erudite lecture on the phenomenon he called "collective hallucination," replete with examples from ancient times up to the present day. He then seized on the cantaloupe "story," as he called it, to suggest it as a source for "some of the undoubtedly sincere but, shall we say, vividly imagined" elements in Mrs. Mainwaring's testimony, adding pointedly that no cantaloupes, nor any trace of cantaloupes, were found on the ground the next day. Careful to emphasize that he in no way wished to impugn the lady's honesty, "insofar as honesty is a factor here," Mr. Forbes nonetheless suggested that hallucination "or even, conceivably, wishful thinking" could have played a substantial role in what Dr. Caws' neighbor "thought she saw." He added that the fact that there were no other witnesses to either corroborate or contest Mrs. Mainwaring's statements (her house, bordering the Burying Ground, being the only home within earshot) "must be counted a misfortune, but, I fear, an unavoidable one."

(He neglected to mention—as did the Court—that several other villagers had reported falling cantaloupes that night, though not to the number of seven hundred.)

Asked if he found the white feather sticking out of the dead man's mouth in any way significant, since this detail had become the object of not a little lurid speculation, Mr. Forbes delivered himself of another lecture, expatiating on the symbolic meanings attached to feathers throughout the ages, beginning with the Chaldeans and ancient Egyptians and continuing through the Greeks, the Romans, the Persians and St. Gregory of Nysa. He spoke of air, thought, the wind, the soul, as well as faith and contemplation, particularly when combined with white, the color of purity and spiritual illumination. But white also signified death, he asserted, which fact suggested obvious connections to the condition in which the doctor found himself in the early morning of the 29th. And, it went without saying, there was another significant emblem, the white feather of cowardice, which, Mr. Forbes implied, many observers might find more pertinent than any of the aforementioned meanings (although he did not say exactly why).

On the whole, though, the witness doubted that any of those meanings was truly pertinent to the case. For the feather in question had been nothing more than "a cheap trick," a distraction the deceased habitually employed to divert the viewer's attention while he put into action the real mechanism—"whatever that may have been"—that produced the illusion of flying. Mr. Forbes added that in this respect he could not forbear mentioning the Biblical example of Simon Magus, arch fraud, heretic and necromancer, "who in the first century of our era produced notorious illusions of flying but was finally brought low by the prayers and pure heart of St. Peter."

In closing, the witness asked the Court if he might be permitted a few remarks on an aspect of the case not strictly within his area of expertise but nevertheless related to those parts of his testimony that touched on "the character of the deceased." Begged by all means to proceed, he referred to Dr. Caws' "known intemperate habits" and mentioned the strong odor of alcohol which Mr. Mainwaring, "a steady, reliable individual," had smelled on the body. Furthermore, Mr. Forbes understood from the medical examiner's testimony, as well as previously published reports in the press, that there were no signs of violence on the body, not even a single bruise, which one would have expected had the deceased fallen "from a great, or even a small, height." In fact, the doctor's heart seemed simply to have stopped beating on its own. "Is it too much to suppose," he asked, "that it was no external cause, occult or otherwise, that precipitated this man's death, but the accumulated and pernicious abuse of his system practiced, no doubt, over a period of many years, beginning long before he arrived in Aubrey?"

Now, Justinian Forbes was not popular in Aubrey. Most of the townsfolk considered him a spoil-sport on account of his long-standing rejection of the Cawses' mediumship, and they found his moral pronouncements, a regular feature in each issue of *Time and Light*, repugnant. The over-ripe tomato which flew out of the back row of benches in the middle of his testimony was not an *apport*. And the fact that the hurler (the "old codger" quoted by Welkin in his final piece for the *Trumpet*) was quickly identified and ejected from the chamber did not lessen the general hostility to the publisher. But while the jurors fully concurred with the popular sentiment, they also recognized in his testimony a heaven-sent opportunity to resolve the case with a minimum of embarrassment. Efficiency Caws had not killed her husband: Mr. Forbes swore she was incapable of it, and Mr. Forbes should know. The doctor had not died violently, but of natural causes: once again, Mr. Forbes was the authority, supported this time by the medical examiner. And Alice Mainwaring had not committed perjury, even if everything that came out of her mouth was as false as wooden teeth: Mr. Forbes had explained her story as "hallucination." Of course, all this meant that they were publicly accepting the word of a man they detested, admitting his authority and tacitly giving him leave to pass judgment on them and their doings. It was a bitter pill, but they had to swallow it. "That's all right, though," they told each other. "We'll get even with him later."[28]

---

[28] They never did. Three years after the inquest, Mr. Forbes sold *Time and Light* and acquired a controlling interest in *The Cross*, an evangelical publishing empire with offices in New York, London, Cairo, Benares and Katmandu. Thanks to this enterprise, as well as the income from a string of brothels he set up in those cities, he became immensely wealthy, gaining universal recognition along the way as an influential arbiter

The jury brought in a verdict of death by natural causes, to wit, stoppage of the heart. Legally the matter was at an end.

For the first few months of our acquaintance (and a short enough time it was, all told, from the first week of March till the end of October) Mrs. Caws refused to say anything about her husband's death and the circumstances immediately surrounding it. If I asked a question that seemed to her to come too close to those events, she would immediately change the subject, politely but with a warning tone in her voice all the same. Indeed, she did not really care to discuss Dr. Caws at all. She much preferred reminiscing about her theatrical career and her many artistic friends in Paris during the 'fifties and 'sixties. "Monsieur Ingres" was her particular favorite. In choosing her as a model (for a religious picture, the famous *Ste. Germaine of Pibrac*, finished in 1856) the painter had evidently made a lasting impression on her. "What an eye for beauty that man had," she said. "He told me I was 'a dream come true.' His very words. 'Course he was speaking in French, but you know what I mean. I happened to be wearing an ermine boa that day, which somebody had given me—not Jerry, that's for certain—and it sent Monsieur Ingres into ecstasies. But when all's said and done, dearie, who could blame him? I looked wonderful. Degas used to brag that when he was young, he'd once held Ingres in his arms. But I, *I*—oh, dearie, I could a tale unfold."

---

of public and private morality. Upon his death in 1879, he was reincarnated, in quick succession, as a Moroccan side-striped jackal (1880–1883); an angel shark in the Sea of Japan (1884–1888); and an American white-tailed kite (1889–1892). Then for a longer period (1892–1931) he was a liquid manure spreader in Flanders, with a pipe and sprinkler arrangement attached to a tank strapped to the operator's back. In 2003, as Marcion John Knox, the CEO of AL-FAN, a multi-national holding company, he was indicted for misappropriation of company funds, extortion, securities fraud, evasion of taxes, bigamy, conspiracy to obstruct justice, subornation of perjury, child molestation, corrupting the morals of a minor and the attempted overthrow of a foreign power without obtaining prior security clearance. Convicted on all counts, he was fined $115 and ordered to perform two weeks of community service. He is now raising funds to mount a campaign for the Presidency of the United States. –*The Encyclopaedia of Reincarnation*

Curious as I was about Dr. Caws' demise (for I suspected, from several hints she let fall, that there was some scandal connected with it) I was far too bashful to persist with my questions. I feared, too, that it might endanger a growing friendship, for the existence of which I felt only gratitude. After all, Mrs. Caws and I had not met on account of any special talent or achievement of mine, but only because I was a near neighbor and had helped her one afternoon to carry some packages into her house. That she had asked me, a person of no distinction half a century her junior, to stay to tea, speaking to me from the start as if we had known each other for decades, that she had then invited me back and, finally, had asked me to make my visits regular—all this was flattering almost beyond words. The gifts of fruit and sweets I always brought her, along with the occasional bottle of sherry, were, I considered, poor recompense for the joy I felt in her presence. If she held unorthodox opinions and was sometimes colorful in her speech, what of it? She had a vast experience of famous people and faraway places, and she introduced me to a world of culture and sophistication beyond anything I had ever known in Quaker-grey Philadelphia. The thought that I might one day write the story of her life never, at this stage, entered my mind.

Indeed, this book might have remained unwritten had it not been for the fact that, after summer had come and gone and the first chill of fall was in the air, Dr. Caws' name began to appear in her conversation, first in widely spaced instances, then with increasing frequency. Casual references to their joint mediumship abounded, and once she even favored me with a snippet of their courtship. "Do you know what he told me, sweetie? No, of course you don't. He said that weeks before he met me, as he was crossing the Atlantic, he heard a voice calling out to him, as if from beyond the sea. 'Come to me, Eggbeater, come!' it said. 'Quickly, quickly! Now, now!' And when he finally got to Aubrey and heard me speak, he recognized the voice as mine. Now, wasn't that something, dearie? Eggbeater might have been a—well, he might not have been so acceptable in some ways, but he could be awfully nice when he wanted to be."

Still, I kept my questions about the doctor's death to myself. Then one morning, around the beginning of October (she had only a month to live, although I had no inkling of it, as she seemed in perfect health and her youthful appearance was unchanged) I came into her parlor as usual, to find her on the couch with an album open on her lap, looking through some old newspaper clippings. A glance at the headlines ("NEIGHBOR TESTIFIES AT INQUEST," "EXPERT TAKES STAND IN MEDIUM'S DEATH") told me that these pieces concerned the one subject she would not talk about. As tactfully as I could, I asked her whether she would mind if I looked at them.

"What? These?" she answered. "Humph. Go ahead, dearie, if you want to, help yourself. Not that you're going to learn much." She seemed a bit out of sorts.

I sat down beside her immediately, and read the clippings straight through, from beginning to end, fascinated. I had been led to expect some little scandal, but was entirely unprepared for publicity of national, even international, scope, complete with allegations of murder and adultery, not to mention witchcraft. The first and last charges had been rejected, and the second, apparently, never proven. But wronged or not wronged, innocent victim or fugitive from justice, my benefactress had obviously been a person of highly conspicuous notoriety. The air of mystery which had also surrounded her in my thoughts thickened considerably, not unmixed with a certain awe.

"Amazing," I said, as I put down the last clipping. "Simply amazing. I had no idea."

"No idea of what?" she snorted. "Lies—that's all there is in there. Lies. Even worse than I remembered. That Justinian Forbes—the gall of him!"

"But ... "

"I know what you're going to say: it was his testimony that got me off. Well, I don't care." She took a generous drink from the bottle of sherry I'd brought. "I don't care one crumb. He did it with nothing but lies. 'Mechanisms!' 'Tricks!' What the H_____." She took another drink, this time not bothering with the glass. "Eggbeater and I never gave one dishonest séance in our lives. We didn't have to! You don't, you know, when you have *real* power. That's what sludge-eaters like Forbes will never understand, the hopeless dummies. Everything Eggbeater and I did in the act was straight and true, it was—what's that, sweetie? Well, of *course* he could levitate. And of *course* I got taller. And no 'mechanisms,' either. Oh, that brassbound liar! It makes me so mad I could spit."

335

"Then Mrs. Mainwaring's testimony was true after all?"

"Hah. Alice Mainwaring never knew her _____ from her _____, honey. She fancied herself a medium, but she hadn't any more talent for it than she had for anything else. That's not surprising, though." She tapped one of the clippings. "All she really wanted was Eggbeater. Naturally, she hated me. She'd have stopped at nothing to do me a hurt."

"But did she make everything up? Was the testimony at all accurate?"

"You can't really talk about 'accurate' with a woman like Alice, sweetheart. Accuracy doesn't come into the picture at all. What she never mentioned— she wouldn't have, but then nobody else has ever mentioned it either, in all the years since it happened—was the self-defense aspect. Yes, dearie, self-defense. H___, I didn't wish Eggbeater any *harm*. Well, not much harm, anyhow. I just didn't want him to kill me. I've got a right not to let somebody kill me, I hope. 'Course I do. I just never thought he'd fall so *hard*. But was I about to wait around and try to make people believe that? Especially people in Aubrey. They didn't think much of me to begin with, most of them—just jealous, you know—and there I was, out in the road at midnight with a dead husband and a traveling bag, and Jerry—that's right, Jerry Welkin, sweetheart, one and the same—likely to arrive any minute, which he did finally, about twenty minutes late as usual—well, honey, how the H____ could I have explained all that away?"

Mrs. Caws continued to insist that the doctor had tried to kill her. "Oh, I never saw him so mad. He had a look in his eye, so *mean*, I never would have thought him capable of it. I had to do *something*, didn't I?"

She paused a moment, then suddenly grinned at me, her head cocked to one side. "Besides, dearie, just between the two of us, I wanted to prove a point."

"Prove a point?" I was incredulous. "At a time like that?"

She took a sip of sherry and giggled. Her fury had become a thing of the past. "It must sound strange, I admit, honey, but you wouldn't think so if you'd known Eggbeater. I mean, if you'd had to live with him." She drank again. "You see, Eggbeater always claimed that action at a distance was impossible. You know what I mean by that: one thing happens here, and that makes something else happen a mile away. Or even two miles, what the H____. Or what the moon does, controlling the tides. Eggbeater said none of that was true. I don't know why—some dumb idea of Leibniz's, I guess. He also said there was no such thing as empty space. Can you imagine? He insisted that there were only *things*, be they ever so small, invisible even with a microscope, and that those things had to collide, actually hit, in order to affect each other. So naturally that meant there was something wrong with Uncle Isaac's law of gravity. I know it's hard to believe, sweetie, but that's just the sort of thing Eggbeater *would* have said. He was never really happy unless he was fighting with Uncle Isaac. He claimed Uncle Isaac never bothered (that was his word, 'bothered') to find out the *cause* of gravity, and that in reality (imagine *Eggbeater* talking about reality!) everything was controlled by vortices, swirling around in big masses of ether. That used to get on my nerves. I mean, everybody else just *knows* about gravity, all you have to do is look around you. And if you want to see empty space, you just look up at the sky. Action at a distance? Well, it just *happens*, that's all. What do you think warmth from the sunshine is? It's all so obvious, nobody in his right mind would ever question it. But it wasn't good enough for Eggbeater, oh no. Eggbeater had to be different. He had to have his vortices. No empty space for him. No action at a distance. Well, I guess I showed him, didn't I, love?" And she laughed her girlish laugh.

18

Salad Days

Roy K. Williams, *The Thracian Histories of Acanthus of Rhodes*, Introduction:

The final book of Acanthus' *Histories*, in which he recounts the later years and death of Lipnike and Thales, survives only in fragments. Fortunately, however, much of his tale can be pieced together from other sources.

Most authors agree that after Lipnike and Gyges escaped from Miletus they sailed north to Samos where, after the birth of Metakynos, Gyges abandoned her. He went north again alone, through the Straits of the Bosporus and into the Black Sea. After many adventures, he reached the Tauric Chersonese (the Crimea) where he went ashore at what is now Balaklava and was killed by a volley of arrows from the temple of Artemis.[29]

On Samos, Lipnike was befriended by the wealthy merchant Mnesarchus, who was also the father of Pythagoras. Impressed by her many abilities, especially her gift of prophecy, Mnesarchus took her to Delphi, where she was eventually installed as Pythia.

This appointment does not seem to have satisfied her, however, despite the veneration in which she was held. In one fragment, Acanthus writes: "Lipnike died at Delphi oversoon, worn out, unhappy with her lot. She wrote Mnesarchus, complaining that although she had received the gift of prophecy

---

[29] Myron of Lemnos, *Gygiad*, II, IV, V. Euphoron of Corinth, fr. 7. Teisias of Himera, frs. 22, 30. Only Ephemeron of Cos (fr. 19) maintains that Lipnike never went to Samos, and that Artemis spirited her away to Crete, leaving a phantom, formed from clouds, in the ship with Gyges in her stead.

she had no opportunity to exercise it properly. 'They come in their hundreds, but only to ask single questions: whether to wage a war, or to take so-and-so's daughter to wife, or some other foolishness. Mere pieces. What can you say about mere pieces? Nobody wants to know ... " Acanthus' text breaks off here, but a similar statement, attributed to Myson of Etis, may complete it: "Nobody wants to know his own future."[30]

Another fragment of Acanthus' reads: "Now, Thales lived to a great age, although he, too ... " Pseudo-Pausanias, however, in the *Peripatetics*, tells us:

"Thales, nearing the end of his life, became obsessed, like many old men, with youth. He who had once held that everything possessed soul now felt his own slipping away from him, and he longed to recover his former vigor. Therefore, he surrounded himself with young folk: pupils, flute girls, wrestlers, runners, hoping their liveliness would call forth a similar response in himself. But it was all to no avail: he only felt older and weaker.

"At last, on the advice of his pupil, Anaximenes, who had come to minister to the old man in Anaximander's absence, Thales repaired to the *apeiron chorion*, the existence of which he had almost forgotten, in order to find some way out of his predicament. He spent day after day there, in the underground chamber, until finally he heard a woman's voice, faint at first, then louder and more urgent, calling to him out of the darkness. 'Lipnike,' it said. 'Lipnike, Lipnike. Bring her back to Miletus. Let all be as of old between you.'"[31]

Gravity Newton:

Mrs. Caws died in her sleep sometime during the night of October 30–31, 1899, at her home in Wyncote. Her housekeeper found her body the next morning: "She was layin' there just like always, with the covers pulled up to her chin and her eyes closed. The only thing different was the little smile on her face."

---

[30] Hegesander of Sigeum, fr. 6.

[31] Pseudo-P. *Peri.*, II, v, 38-40.

I had seen her the previous afternoon. It happened to have been her seventy-second birthday, and she insisted I share the sherry and angel food cake with which she was regaling herself. She seemed in excellent health and looked, as always, radiantly beautiful. As usual, she offered me a cigar. I marveled for the hundredth time on her amazing youthfulness; she could easily have passed for someone half her age or even younger. What was her secret, I wanted to know?

She burst into laughter. "Oh, dearie, dearie, dearie! Haven't you guessed that by now?"

I shook my head.

"Why, it's Uncle Isaac, of course."

"Uncle Isaac?" I got out my notebook. She waited patiently, keeping silent till I'd found a pencil.

We were quite comfortably used to each other by now, well settled into our respective roles as author and subject. It had been a full month since she had accepted my proposal to write her life, a proposal stammered out shyly and without much hope after reading the newspaper clippings of the inquest following Dr. Caws' death. "Why, of *course*, sweetheart, I'd be delighted," she had answered, to my astonishment. "My life *is* fascinating, isn't it? I've thought for years that somebody ought to write it up. And naturally the best thing is to do it while I'm still around to help out. Because when I say I could a tale unfold, sweetie, I mean I could a tale unfold. You won't find it anywhere else, darling, no matter who you talk to. What's that, love? Mediumship? Why, certainly we can talk about mediumship. Yes, and Eggbeater, too, whatever made you think we couldn't? –*What*? 'Close-mouthed?' Now, that's the first time I've ever been called *that*, I should think. I wasn't being close-mouthed a bit, honey, I just didn't want to go into a lot of … I mean I'd hardly even *met* you, and I did enjoy your company, and … well, things like that aren't everybody's glass of whiskey, if you'll pardon the expression. But now that you're going to do a *book*—well, we'll just talk about *all* of it, won't we? We'll talk it up, down, sideways and backwards. It's high time the record was set straight. A book—just think of it. A *book*!" From then on, she had been an active, enthusiastic participant in the project, eager to speak at length but at the same time solicitous of my note-taking, concerned that I'd manage to get it all down.

"Of course it'd be Uncle Isaac," she repeated now, when I was ready with my pencil. "It was all part of his ... well, I suppose you'd call it his inducement to me ... along with the prospect of undreamt-of attainments and revelations of the spirit and all that. *Youth*, sweetie, that's what he offered. 'You will never grow old,' he said. No more fear of old age. Not that he really cared about me, of course. He was in it strictly—but *strictly*, honeybunch—for himself. All he wanted from me was ... well, never you mind about that just now, dearie, maybe I'll tell you later. Just suffice it right this minute to say that once he'd gotten it, Uncle Isaac lost interest. Just like any other man, if you know what I mean. Oh, he came through once or twice later on, when I was in Europe, but only to make excuses. Too busy, he said. Or he didn't feel well. Ha! Uncle Isaac was never sick a day in his life, the pig. But I will say this: from that day in his laboratory right up to this minute, I've never aged. Not a hair, love. That's the one promise he kept, the old lecher. Unless—" She paused a moment, seeming to consider something. "Unless it was Papa's Elixir."

Her eyes opened wide. "My Lord, I never thought of that before! What if it was Papa's Elixir? Nothing to do with Uncle Isaac at all! Oh, my Heavenly Lord—what if it was Papa's Elixir!" And she started to laugh.

Roy K. Williams:
Pseudo-Pausanias continues:

"Now, Thales was more than willing to carry out the wishes of the voice, but he had no idea where Lipnike could be after all these years. (It never seems to have occurred to him that she might be dead, as in fact she was.) Superstitious as ever, he made a little image, a human figure of flattened lead, and scratched Lipnike's name on it. Then he put it in a wooden box together with a strip of papyrus, on which he wrote, 'Great Goddess, direct this image to the bed of Lipnike of Thrace. Take sleep away from her, bind her soul to me, Thales, son of Examyas, make her burn with lust for me, give her body no rest till she comes to me, quickly, quickly, immediately, immediately, now, now.' To make the charm perfect he should have bound the message to the image with a strand of Lipnike's hair, but that was not possible. Instead, he pricked his finger and smeared both papyrus and figurine with his blood.

Then he sealed the box tight and, because Lipnike and Gyges had escaped by water, sailed out of the Lion Harbor and threw it into the sea.

"Months went by with no answer. At his wits' end, Thales went to Delphi and sought the counsel of the Pythia (Lipnike's successor, though he did not know she had ever been there at all.)

"'Thales, son of Examyas: take heart,' was the Oracle's reply. 'Stop grieving. Go home, live your life again. One day all will be as you wish.'

"Thales returned to Miletus, back to his wrestlers and runners, full of joy. He began to take pleasure in the things of the world again: sunlight, flute girls, the night sky."

Gravity Newton:

The light was fading now in the sitting room, but she made no move to put on a lamp. "Yes, sweetie," she said with a grin, "there's an awful lot to be said in favor of perpetual youth, and I must admit I've had quite a good time out of it. You seem pretty smart, so I won't try to convince you I've always had the best judgment in the world, but I guess that goes with being young. 'My salad days, when I was green in judgment,' Cleopatra says! Everything comes at a price, I suppose. But it could be much, much worse. Imagine if you'd been given perpetual *judgment*—and nothing else!" She leaned forward, and added in a conspiratorial whisper, "All the judgment there is in the universe won't get you *men*, honey. If you haven't found that out already, you will. Men could not care less about your judgment. And let me tell you, love, [she moved even closer, so that her face was only an inch or two from mine] Uncle Isaac might have lost interest in me, but he was just about the only one!" She threw her head back and laughed. "That's what Jerry couldn't stand, you know. It used to make him crazy, and without any good reason, most of the time." She sipped her drink. "I mean, to be jealous of Monsieur Ingres! The idea. My Lord, the man was in his seventies. But Jerry went green, absolutely green, the moment he heard Monsieur Ingres pay me a compliment, the night he first saw me, at that reception in Paris. And it wasn't as if we were off in a corner by ourselves, there were about four hundred other people in that room. But that was Jerry, through and through. He was all right when it was just the two of us in that carriage, making our getaway, him and me against the world and all that, but once we got over to Europe and—at last!—some real *society*, well, it was a different story. Jerry really wasn't comfortable, I found out, with the better class of people. That may sound harsh, sweetie, but facts are facts and they have to be faced. Those people brought out the scared little boy in him. Not that they meant to, of course, they had nothing to do with it, it was all in Jerry's mind, one look at Countess this or Baron that and he turned into a ten year old ragamuffin. And when they started paying me attention, well, look out! I thought he'd bust a blood vessel when Monsieur Ingres asked me to pose for him. And when I *accepted*—Oh! The things he said to me! 'Don't you realize only *whores* pose for artists? What kind of reputation are you going to get?' On and on like that for hours. Naturally I told him my reputation was my business, and if I didn't care why should he, unless his real worry was that he'd be thought a procurer. Somehow, I don't think that helped much."

She giggled, and helped herself to more sherry. "Yes, lovey, that was quite a scene. But it was nothing to what he did when I wore the ermine boa. He was white with fury. First off, he had no idea who'd given it to me (I can't remember myself now) and he was too proud to ask. Not that I'd have told him. None of his d____ business. Anyway, when I left the hotel, he followed me—can you believe it?—he actually followed me to Monsieur Ingres' studio, ducking behind carriages and vegetable stalls and such so I wouldn't (he thought!) catch sight of him. Then he barged in, just as *cher maître*—that's what we called him, honey, *cher maître*—was telling me I was a dream come true, and a ravishing Persephone, if I remember right, and, oh, one or two other nice things that only the French can think up. A something to spring-time, I think. Ode. It's the same word in French, dearie: *ode*. And *cher maître* said it so beautifully, too, spreading his arms wide to welcome me into his studio. *Ode. Une ode!* Well, just then Jerry barged in, and he made such a scene. Insisted I come back to the hotel immediately, shouting at the top of his lungs. Called me the most dreadful names, picking up where he'd left off the night before. Except he wouldn't say 'whore,' I noticed, not in front of *cher maître*, even though he was speaking English (Jerry never would learn French). 'Harlot,' yes, 'streetwalker,' definitely, 'woman of the town dressed

343

for business,' but not 'whore.' Probably thought it wasn't refined enough. That boy certainly had some strange manners.

"Well, I stood up for myself, just as you'd expect, sweetheart. Told him he had no G__ d_____d right, the little s____, to use language like that in front of the greatest artist in Europe, and to order me around, and criticize my ermine boa. Told him he could get the H____ out of there and go back to the hotel by himself, and if I never saw him again I wouldn't mind it a bit and he could thank his lucky stars Eggbeater wasn't alive because Eggbeater would have thrashed him within an inch of his G__ d_____d life. And do you know what, sweetie? He took it! Took it without a word. He huffed and puffed a little, as if he was trying to get something out and couldn't, then turned on his heel and marched out. Typical of him, really. Jerry never did know how to stand up for himself.

"When I got back to the hotel after posing—oh, yes, I stayed and posed, dearie, it was my first session with *cher maître* and I wasn't going to let it slip by (and *cher maître* was such a gentleman about the whole thing, though I do imagine he must have been a *little* surprised to hear words like that out of a lady's mouth—even if he couldn't understand me it was pretty obvious what *kind* of thing I was saying—and I was supposed to be posing as a saint!) But when I got back to the hotel I found Jerry had left. He'd taken all his things and gone, not even leaving a note. That was when I threw his letter down the sewer.[32]

---

[32] After considerable research (which included, I am sorry to say, extended trips down several blind alleys) I was able to establish a few facts about the later career of this elusive person. Jeremy Welkin left Paris abruptly in October, 1855 and passed several years in Spain and Italy, working as a journalist for a series of short-lived radical newspapers. He was evidently furious with Mrs. Caws and wanted to "show her." In 1859 he joined the Alpine infantry under Garibaldi, and was wounded in the arm at Casale. By March, 1871, he was back in Paris, where he joined the Communards and participated in the May uprising which saw the destruction of many prestigious buildings, including the Palais des Tuilleries and the Hotel de Ville, which houses Ingres' *Apotheosis of Napoleon I.* Welkin was arrested during the street fighting, and executed along with his fellow Communards at dawn on May 28, in the Père Lachaise Cemetery. (Note: May 28, 1871 was Welkin's forty-third birthday. By a curious coincidence I was also born on May 28, exactly one year later.) –E. M. S.

"Hmm? No, love, I never saw him again. Haven't the faintest idea what became of him. Never really cared to find out, if you want to know the truth. I simply will not tolerate rudeness. Are you *sure* you don't want a cigar, sweetie? Oh, well, suit yourself."

She refilled her glass. "And then there was Narbot," she sighed. "Not that Narbot was much better. You remember Narbot, don't you, honey? One of *cher maître*'s assistants? Yes. Naturally, a busy man like *cher maître*—so many commissions he had, I don't see how he kept track of them all—a busy man like him couldn't have been expected to paint *all* of that great, big picture by himself. He just painted the important parts, my face and hands—and what a beautiful job of them he made, sweetheart, so *sensitive!*—and had his assistants finish off the rest. And naturally one of them, Narbot, fell in love with me, seeing me pose day after day, and then *he* caused a stir—threatened to shoot himself and all that, unless I ran away with him, or at least ... well, you know, honey. And him a married man with Lord knows how many children! But I've told you all that before, haven't I? What I haven't told you, though—and it made me so mad at the time, dearie, almost as mad as I was at Jerry—was what Narbot did to my *feet*. That's right, my feet. No, in the painting, I mean, sweetie, my feet in the painting. You see, Narbot wasn't really a very good painter. I suppose he was a nice enough person in his own way, as long as he kept his hands to himself, but—again—facts are facts and you have to face them: Narbot wasn't a very good painter. He couldn't manage to paint my feet so they stayed flat on the ground. In the finished picture I look as if I'm about to levitate—just like Eggbeater, G__ d____ it. Go see that painting sometime if you get a chance, dearie, you'll see what I mean. D____ it, d____ it, d____ it! I tried and tried all those years in the séance room and couldn't do it, and then this Frenchman, claiming to be in love with me, came along and by *mistake*—Ugh! Not only that, he put a flock of sheep in the background, and one of them has lifted his head and is staring right at me. Again, it was just as if I were Eggbeater, with animals following me everywhere! Now, Narbot didn't have any idea that Eggbeater used to—Wait a minute." She paused and leaned back. "What if he did? That story was in the Paris papers. They published plenty of background tripe on Eggbeater. What if Narbot read it, and ... Do you know what I think, sweetheart? This never crossed my mind before. I think maybe Narbot was not such a bad painter, after all. I think maybe he did it out of spite, just because I turned him down!"

She drained her glass and filled it again. It was getting quite dark now; soon I would have trouble writing. But for once Mrs. Caws seemed to take no notice. She knew I was there, of course, and knew she was speaking for my benefit, but sometimes she seemed just as much to be speaking to herself. More and more pauses crept into her speech, unexplained and longer than usual.

"Eggbeater," she said after a silence. "Eggbeater follows me everywhere I go. Not animals. Eggbeater. Lately he's been in my dreams ... Always shows up where he's least ... expected. Last night it was Paris, in Madame de Rillon's drawing room. Great hostess, dearie, don't think I've mentioned her before. Used to attend all her salons, once Jerry had left ... Well, last night—in my dream—Degas was there, with Baudelaire and Manet, and Papa. And *cher maître*, it goes without saying. I *always* dream of *cher maître*. But last night I was in my ghost costume, reciting *Hamlet* to them—unfolding a tale for fair, dearie, wild and whirling words!—when all of a sudden there was Eggbeater, up on the ceiling, smiling down at me and signaling me to join him. 'But I can't,' I called, 'I don't know how to levitate, Eggbeater, you know that.' Well, he just kept smiling and crooked his finger again. His lips never moved, but it was as if I could hear him saying, 'Don't worry, 'Fishency, don't worry. You can do it, it's easy.'

"Humph. Easy for *him*. But then a lot of things *were* easy for him. I mean, he just knew how to do things, beforehand-like, even if he'd never done them before ... Oh, it wasn't knowing with his brain, it wasn't *thinking*—Eggbeater was a little bit stupid, if you want to know the truth—it was more like knowing with his body, with his fingertips or the soles of his feet, or knowing from inside his belly. I don't think he could have told you himself where it came from. But he knew, all right. 'Always know,' he used to say." She drank and reflected, looking down at the floor. After a long pause she raised her head again.

"'Always know,'" she repeated. "Always. I've never told anyone this before, sweetheart, I surely wouldn't have admitted it when Eggbeater was alive, but deep down I always thought he could do anything. I never got over that, either. I've missed it ever since, too, not having someone like that around, someone I could feel like that about. You can *play* when you've got that kind of person on your side, dearie, you can really play. Play *up* to him, too— 'Look what I can do, Eggbeater, look what I can do!' And he would *look*, too, he would really look ... until he stopped looking, and started building that G__ d_____d Oracle. That was during our retirement. The dumbest thing we ever did was retire ...

"But that doesn't matter anymore, all that Oracle business, it's over and done with ages ago—just like everything else. There was nothing to be done about it then and there's nothing to be done about it now. What matters is, what happened after."

Another long pause. "Or what *didn't* happen." She emptied the bottle into her glass. "That time at the Salpêtrière, for instance, long after Eggbeater died. I was giving that séance in front of Charcot and his students. Charcot, the great neurologist. They wanted to see what I was made of. Everybody was staring at me. I was sitting all by myself, in my white dress, on a little stool in the middle of the room. And nothing happened. Absolutely nothing. It went on for hours, at least it felt like hours. I couldn't do anything. Couldn't even elongate. And Uncle Isaac, the _____, didn't even bother to say he wasn't feeling well. Oh, sweetheart, it was so humiliating! And I just sat there, wanting to disappear. But afterwards, sweetie, afterwards, all I could think was that Eggbeater would have known exactly what to do. And he would have, too, honey, he'd have known in half a second! Eggbeater would have *made* something happen. He'd have twirled that little chicken feather of his and— whoosh! The spell would have been broken. *He'd* have shown them what we were made of! Whoosh! Whoosh! Whoosh! WHOOSH!" She jumped to her feet, waving her arms about. "*Apports!* Dinner plates! Sideboards! Apples!"

She sat down again, a little short of breath. "Oh, dear, oh, dearie me," she sighed. "Wouldn't we have had some fun, though. Neurology (is that what you call it, honey, have I got the name right?) neurology would never have been the same."

I noticed that somehow, in the last few moments, another sherry bottle had materialized in the shadows beside the empty one. She opened it and poured. "You know, it's funny," she went on, "Eggbeater was the one who used to worry that someday we'd lose our powers. I never thought much about it one way or the other. But he kept those wigs and things around just in case. He never would have needed them, though, never. No matter what he may have thought. That was just his *brain* thinking, anyway, sweetie, and Eggbeater's brain didn't have a lot of confidence in him. But as soon as he had an audience in front of him, that brain got shut off, and he was absolutely in command. All Eggbeater needed was an audience. He just had bad luck, that was all."

"Bad luck?"

"That's right. What else would you call it—I ask you, sweetheart, as one intelligent being to another—what else *could* you call it, for a natural medium like that to get stuck with a spirit as dumb as Leibniz? Dumber than Eggbeater, you ask? S____ and shallots! Dumber than Eggbeater by *far*, dearie, and Eggbeater didn't deserve it, having to say all those things night after night and sometimes in two and even three shows, day *and* night—how Evander's sword is so G__ d_____d excellent, and how Milk is A (whatever that means) and vortices are the best things ever, and there's no such thing as action at a distance. That s____ always used to make me mad, sometimes so mad I was half crazy with it, but I've been thinking the past day or two, honey, and I've come to understand something: you really can't blame Eggbeater for *any* of that nonsense. It just wasn't his fault, he had absolutely no control over it. It was all that stupid Leibniz. Uncle Isaac may have been a pig, but at least he made sense every once in a while."

She leaned towards me in the dark. I was writing almost without sight of the page now, praying my notes would be legible. "There's something else I have to say," she whispered, "and I don't like to admit it, sweetheart, but now that we're ... well, now that we're where we are, I guess I have to. I was *never* in Eggbeater's class as a medium. Even in my prime, even with Uncle Isaac still going strong, I was mostly ... mostly just his foil, what we call in the theatre a feeder. I gave him material to play off of. Oh, I'm not saying I was any kind of slouch, I could do a thing or two, there wasn't any *other* medium in the world who could touch me when I was in form, but when all was said and done I just didn't have Eggbeater's genius. He made it all work—the act, I mean. He made it *go*. I just helped out. He was the star."

She fell silent again, drinking her sherry. Her hand went up to her face, and it seemed to me she wiped away a tear. "Remember that séance in Row-ley I told you about, sweetheart?" she asked. "When Leibniz called for an election, and Eggbeater won the audience's approval by a single vote? Well, it should have been a thousand, dearie, it should have been a thousand."

19

EPILOGUE:
HASELMAUS THE DREAMER.
THE OLD BASIE BAND.
AS FREE AS IT IS POSSIBLE TO GET
IN THIS WORLD.
THE DAY IN QUESTION.

TRUE TALES OF THE PARANORMAL:

"An homunculus!?" Dr. Haselmaus exclaimed. "Did I understand you to say 'homunculus,' my dear sir?"

I allowed that such had been the case.

He regarded me sternly from behind his desk. "May I remind you, young man, that we are not in the editorial offices of *Der Guckkasten*, or some other scandal sheet? We are in *my* office, in the Basel Psychiatric Institute, one of the most prestigious institutions of its kind anywhere, in a city renowned for its learning and standards of academic excellence, with a history of cultural pre-eminence dating back to the fourth century. And you have the *Unverschämtheit*—nay, the *chutzpah*—to come in here and ask me if Dr. Eichhorn—Dr. Fritz Eichhorn, my former protégé and, until his tragic downfall, a brilliant psychoanalyst in his own right—to ask me if Dr. Eichhorn 'ever really made an homunculus.' I never heard such effrontery."

I started to stammer out an apology. There had been so many rumors, I explained, circulating since Dr. Eichhorn's death; Dr. Haselmaus could not be unaware of them. Surely it was time to lay them to rest once and for all. An unequivocal denial from a recognized authority such as himself could—

I stopped. Dr. Haselmaus had produced a water pistol and was squirting water at the ceiling. He turned to me, grinning from ear to ear.

"Please. My dear sir—Mr. Tiflis, as you like to call yourself. Enough with the rumors. No explanations are needed. I was only joking. I must have my little joke now and then. Did you not note the twinkle in my eye? I am not nearly as stuffy as people think. I am not stuffy at all, as a matter of fact. I am quite a jolly fellow. But your question deserves an answer, and a serious one."

He spread his arms wide. "Of *course* Dr. Eichhorn made an homunculus! And what a magnificent thing it was. Empedocles Schwank, late of the Helvetius Psychiatric Clinic in Zürich, a fully functioning, life size homunculus indistinguishable in appearance from an ordinary human, but with an intelligence and understanding far superior to ours and a will—a *free* will, it is worth pointing out—all his own: the first viable homunculus of modern times, and possibly the first free will ever, in anyone. And all this the doctor accomplished as a mere child, not yet fourteen years of age. It was a stupendous achievement. And right up your alley, sir, if I may say so."

It was indeed. This was much more like it. "I'd like to meet this homunculus," I said. "Where is he now?"

"Ah, young man, if only I knew!" He put down the water pistol. His voice, high-pitched and a little hoarse, suddenly shook with emotion. "If I did I wouldn't be sitting here, I can tell you that! He disappeared, sir, into thin air. An attendant at the Helvetius had come into his room to give him his breakfast. Schwank was standing by his bed. The attendant put his tray on the table, and when he came back a little later—there was nobody there! He looked in the bathroom: empty. Out in the hall: same thing. He summoned help. The whole building was searched, the grounds, the streets, the entire city. Nothing."

"Remarkable. There was no mention of it in the papers."

"Certainly not. The clinic kept it quiet. No police or anything like that. Fear of scandal. It would have been too much, coming as it did a mere month after Dr. Eichhorn's demise. Besides, the Helvetius takes care of its own, you know."

"So I've heard."

"Yes, sir. But it was a deeply troubling event, all the same. It was as if … please forgive me, sir, you may think this a mere flight of senile fancy, but it was as if the homunculus, in some paroxysm of intuitive certainty, felt his creator's passing and chose, then and there, to follow him. Such was the loyalty Dr. Eichhorn could inspire."

His eyes filled with tears. "He was a very great man, Mr. so-called Tiflis, a very great man indeed. I flatter myself that I knew him better than anyone, better even—better by far!—than his own mother. He was no saint, I admit, but he was something infinitely finer: a hero. A striver in the cause of truth, who dared to enter the unknown, to embrace the irrational, to close with it lovingly, no matter what the cost. He was struck down by a force over which he had no control, but that does not lessen his greatness one iota. No one has any control over *that* force. They say it was madness that brought Fritz Eichhorn low. Madness, indeed! They know nothing, nothing of his demise and nothing, believe me, of his glories either. And they call themselves students of the psyche! Rationalists, the lot of them, mere rationalists. Dr. Eichhorn was the most misunderstood man of our time. Yet there is hope—yes, sir, verily there is hope. I look at you, sitting across from me with your notebook and your pencil poised, and I see it: you have it in your power to put all that injustice to rights. Yes, you, young man, and no one else! That is why I invited you here. Have some cheese." He lifted the lid of the big silver platter on his desk.

It was a meeting I never thought would take place. For weeks I'd been stewing, trying to come up with some way to approach him. Dr. Haselmaus had information vital to my book, but he was an august and forbidding personage, "Haselmaus the Dreamer," the "Epimenides of Basel," who had long since removed himself from worldly affairs and social interactions. He had not been seen in public for years. In his published work nothing had been more obvious than his disdain for the popular, the fashionable, the exoteric—in psychology, in writing, in practically any field you could name. And he re-served a special contempt for that brand of literature that was my own stock in trade, the popularized treatment of so-called "occult" subjects. "Soiling the sacred," he called it, "mocking the mysteries."

I didn't like to think what he'd make of me, who'd been soiling the sacred professionally for years. I'd dabbled in hauntings, psychokinesis, soul retriev-al and other aspects of shamanism, with only moderate success. Finally, I'd settled on homunculi, and homunculi had not disappointed me. I'd become a rather well recognized authority on the subject, giving lectures and continu-ing education courses, I'd even been interviewed on national television.

I was sure that Haselmaus would disapprove. The fact that in my spare time I was also an amateur jazz musician wouldn't help either.

There was an even greater obstacle. It was said that Haselmaus spent most of his life these days asleep, perfecting, so his followers claimed, the technique that had made him famous. (It was a deceptively simple analytical maneuver, which had earned him much praise from the cognoscenti, along with, it must be said, quite a bit of ridicule. While the analysand sat in a chair and spoke to him, the doctor would lie on the couch and go to sleep, entering, as he put it, "the exfoliating Dream of the Cosmos," taking the patient's situation with him as a question for those he called "the Higher-Ups.") Now, in retirement, he chose to live in dream as much as possible, no longer consulting with "Higher-Ups" but with a mysterious figure he called simply "the Oracle," a not-very-veiled reference, his detractors said, to himself. He still kept his office at the Institute, but used it only to sleep in.

Eichhorn had been his last patient. Haselmaus had been profoundly af-fected by his death, falling into a deep depression on account of it. I was told that even his physical appearance had changed radically, and that the "tone" of his dreaming was different as well, although what this expression meant I could not fathom, and my source, a prominent neurosurgeon, could not or would not elaborate.

For all these reasons an interview seemed out of the question. So I could not believe my luck when the phone rang one morning in my Zürich apart-ment, while I was tuning my double bass, and the voice on the other end identified itself as Dr. Haselmaus' secretary, one Georg C. Dietz. Herr Dietz was formal to say the least; my old aunt Sonia would have said he talked as if he had a mouth full of mush. Was my name really Llanvair K. Tiflis, he wanted to know. I assured him it was.

"Tiflis?" he repeated. "That was a city in Georgia. Now called Tbilsi."

"Actually, it's a pen name," I said, and went on to explain that my ancestors were Armenian and Tiflis—or Tbilsi, if he preferred—had a large Armenian quarter.

"Formerly in the Soviet Union," he persisted.

"Oh, my people were long gone by the time the Soviet Union got started. Driven out en masse, decades before. A pogrom. They ended up in Wales."

"Hence the Llanvair?"

"You got it," I said. I didn't add that I was born in Lichfield, a small town in northern New Jersey, and that I'd never been anywhere near Georgia, even the American one, in my life. I didn't think it was any of his business. I was getting a little hot under the collar. Much as I wanted to meet Haselmaus, I'd have been just as glad to hang up on the bastard and go back to my bass. Dietz was probably a fascist anyhow, and if he thought he was going to worm any more of my genealogy out of me, not to mention my real name, he was crazy.

He was not crazy. He professed himself satisfied and merely desired to know if it was true, as he had heard, that I was writing a book about the, uh, paranormal. I was? Good. In that case, it was imperative that I see the doctor at once on a matter of considerable urgency. Did I have a car? Better and better. Dietz had been instructed to set up an audience (he actually used that word) in the doctor's Basel office that very afternoon, if possible. It was possible? How convenient. Dr. Haselmaus would be awake by 2:00; that should give me plenty of time. And one more thing: I should plan on a stay of several days. Dietz would make a reservation for me at a local hotel. The Basilisk should do nicely; their rooms were quite comfortable. No, I needn't trouble myself; Dietz would take care of everything. He and the doctor would see me at 2:00. The connection went.

Haselmaus turned out to be shorter than I'd expected, a good deal shorter, in fact. Only his head and shoulders were visible behind his desk. He wore a pair of brilliant magenta pajamas, the lapels of which peeked out from under a plain grey dressing gown that matched his thinning hair and patchy chin whiskers. He surprised me in other ways, too. After his first response to my opening question—the stern gaze, the high and mighty tone—there was no trace of austerity or remoteness. Everything about him was animated. His tiny black eyes darted from point to point around the room; his hands continually popped up over the desk top, to emphasize some phrase, or to play with his water pistol, or, as often as not, just to wave back and forth, as if he were conducting a piece of music he alone could hear.

He repeated his offer of cheese, pushing the platter towards me across the desk. I thanked him, though cheese was not exactly my favorite food. "I'd like to know more about the homunculus," I added. "Much more. Tell me, how did Dr. Eichhorn manage to—"

He held up his hand. "All in good time, sir, all in good time. We mustn't neglect our stomachs. There's quite a nice selection here, as you can see. Backstein and Fontainebleau, for instance. Västerbottensost. Slipcote. And Swiss, of course. But one gets tired of Swiss." He cut off a large chunk of it, nevertheless, using the breadknife on the platter, and nibbled away contentedly.

"Mmm. You really should try some. I find it a wonderful aid to concentration. Binding, too. The crackers are also quite tasty. Zwieback, with beet green and celery. I have them made specially; Herr Dietz sees to it. They're mostly for visitors, though. I rarely bother with crackers, myself. Go on, sir, don't be shy. Have some cheese. Do." For sociability's sake I took a piece.

"Ah, the Slipcote." He smiled. "Moist and mellow. You couldn't have chosen better. It's one of my favorites as well. Yes, we're going to get along beautifully, I can feel it in my bones. Would you care for something to wash it down with? Vodka, gin, Scotch, bourbon? A rye highball, a champagne cocktail? Lager? Can I tempt you with a martini? A Kubla Khan? An Ockham's Razor? Plain seltzer, you say? Certainly. I will buzz Herr Dietz."

He pressed a button on his desk. Dietz came in at once. I'd seen him a few minutes before, at his desk in the waiting room, a slender, late middle-aged man in a well-tailored grey suit, with blond hair and a carefully trimmed moustache. He looked as if he'd never cracked a smile in his life. "Ah, Georg," said Haselmaus. "A glass of seltzer for Mr. Tiflis, if you would, please. Nothing for me, thanks." Dietz retired silently and returned a moment later with my drink, which he set in front of me on the desk, together with a cocktail napkin.

"Cheese, yes," the doctor continued, as Dietz completed his butling and went out. "From the Latin *caseus*, I seem to recall. Related, curiously enough, to the Welsh *caws*. But, just between us, I prefer the alternate derivation, from the Urdu *chiz*, meaning 'the thing.' As in, you dig it, 'the coming thing,' 'the big thing.' The big cheese. A nice sound, too, *chiz*, short and crisp, like a sock cymbal—*chiz, chiz, chiz*." He tapped his fingers on the desk. "No matter, I like it in all etymologies, never can seem to get enough." He cut off another slab, from, I thought, the Backstein. "Probably not good for me in such quantities, but who cares? Life's a many-splendored gig, as Herb What's-his-name used to say. Cha-cha-cha."

Sock symbol? Herb What's-his-name? So Haselmaus was a jazz fan! The last thing I'd have expected. This might turn out to be easier than I'd thought.

"Pomeroy," I reminded him. "Herb Pomeroy." I wanted him to know I was up to speed, on this subject at least. "'Life is a many-splendored gig'—that's the name of his record. I agree—he's terrific. I've heard that band several times. But about Dr. Eichhorn: how did he manage—"

"Isn't he, though? The band swings beautifully. Did you know Jaki Byard played tenor in that band? —What? Oh, to be sure. You were asking about Eichhorn. Of course. A great man, as I've said, even though he never had much truck with jazz. Something to do with his father, I think. Or cheese. With him it was nuts, all kinds of nuts. Even used them in his Nietzsche paper—just look at the title. Never without a few in his pockets. It got a bit excessive towards the end, I'm afraid. By then it was acorns. I heard he used to gather them in the yard at the Helvetius. After he died, they found them all over his room, in the dresser drawers, under the rug, everywhere. Poor Eichhorn! What a loss to mankind." He conducted some music, using the cheese as a baton.

"He thought he was a squirrel by then, didn't he?" I asked. "Not just gathering nuts in the yard but climbing the trees. That's what the papers said, anyway."

"Oh, yes. The papers would jump on that. Meat and drink to them. But at the same time, you know, he was absolutely right: *Eichhorn* means squirrel. Perhaps he was having his own little joke."

Yes, I thought, and *Haselmaus* means dormouse. But I kept it to myself. "I understand Herr Dietz found his body," I said aloud.

"Yes. He had gone to Zürich at my bidding, to observe Dr. Eichhorn's condition for himself and report back to me. Travel is no longer easy for me, more's the pity."

"I've heard the doctor had a white feather in his mouth."

Haselmaus stopped conducting music and leaned forward, his little hands flat on the desk. "Mr. Tiflis. Please. Let us not worry about feathers for the moment. Nor even squirrels. Let us be round with one another. You are writing a book about the paranormal, correct?"

"Correct."

"And you wish to include a section on Dr. Eichhorn, yes?"

"Yes. And his homunculus. Homunculi are kind of my thing, frankly. And it's more than a section. It's the heart of the book. To be perfectly straight with you, sir, the play the story got in the papers made it irresistible."

"I shouldn't wonder. The Eichhorn case is about as sensational as it gets, isn't it, especially when reported by the likes of Anna Sprengel and the other vultures of her calling. A mad psychoanalyst, an homunculus subjected to sexual abuse—mercy me! Who could blame you for wanting to feature it, and feature it to a fare-thee-well? But: to do so you require my help. Also correct?"

"Yes. And I would be most, most grateful if—"

"Please, sir. There's no need to implore me. Let me set your mind at rest. You need my help. I intend to give it, freely and with no strings attached. How could I not, after all? Anyone who's heard Herb Pomeru—"

"Pomeroy."

"Pomery, of course. Stupid of me. Anyone who's heard Herb Pomery deserves the best of everything. But—I must confess it—there's another reason as well. You see, sir, by a delicious synchronicity, our interests converge. You want to tell the story, and I would like nothing better than to get it out—the *whole* story, told properly for once—in order to honor Dr. Eichhorn's memory and to rehabilitate him, at least in the eyes of those few who are capable of seeing anything clearly. My problem is that my usual channels, the academic publications—many of which, by the way, I helped to found—are closed to me. The swine who now edit them refuse to touch the subject. Too lurid, they say.

'Not our sort of thing at all,' one of them wrote me. 'Please recall that we are a serious organ.' *Canailles. Schweine.* When it was my reputation that started those 'serious organs' in the first place! The analytical community today, Mr. Tiflis, is just as hidebound, just as ossified, as any other conventional, bourgeois, backward-looking, anal retentive—Gah! It is disgusting, sir, it is nothing short of vomitous. Eichhorn to them is only a lunatic, someone they'd rather forget about. Do you know, I think they even regard *me* as a little touched by now. Well, let them!" He picked up the water pistol and started squirting at invisible targets. "We'll show them, Mr. Tiflis, you and I together! We'll show them a thing or two—or three. Or four, five, or six. Or seven. Or eight. Or nine. Or—"

He was interrupted by Dietz, who came in bearing a tray with a glass on it filled with a brownish liquid. "I beg your pardon, Herr Doktor," he murmured. "Time for your, uh, tonic."

"Ah!" Haselmaus put down the pistol. "Thank you, Georg. Don't know what I'd do without you. It had clean slipped my mind. How time does fly— whether or not one is having fun. But in this case, of course [he nodded in my direction] sheer delight. 'Our Delight'—eh, Mr. Tiflis? Tadd Beiderbecke."

It was Tadd Dameron, of course, but I let it go. The doctor took the glass from the tray, downed the contents in a gulp and handed it back. Dietz withdrew silently.

"My Elixir," Haselmaus explained. "Philalethes' Powder, they call it. Perhaps you've heard of it, in your embrushments with the occult? No? No matter. I take it in whortleberry juice. Terrible tasting stuff, but it keeps me alive—that old black magic, ha-ha. I was four hundred and eight last January, you know." He tipped me a wink and burst into laughter.

I joined in to be polite, although I didn't think his remark was terribly funny. Anyway, I was more interested in the effect the drink was having. Whatever was in it certainly was not a tonic. The doctor sank back in his chair. His movements slowed down, becoming almost normal. There was a long pause.

"My apologies, sir," he whispered at last, reaching up and getting some more cheese. "I sometimes let my ... " His voice trailed off. He conducted for a few measures, then resumed, apparently in the middle of another sentence: " ... all occupational hazards, I suppose, for those of us who ... " He yawned. Another silence ensued.

Suddenly he roused himself and stood up. "But apologies again, Mr. Tiflis," he said, pacing back and forth between his desk and the door," and abject ones at that." He waved his arms about, all motion once again. "There is so much to tell you, and so little time to tell it. The Elixir is starting to work, and here I have been, wasting precious seconds. Suffice it, for now, to say, and quickly, the things you *must* hear. I have at last been driven, much against my principles, nay, against my instincts, to seek an outlet for publication in the popular sector. It was Herr Dietz, as a matter of fact, who suggested your name. He did some research into the work of the various authors who might conceivably be suitable for the project, and he settled on you. He said you were the best of a bad—that is, he recommended you highly. Please do not be offended, sir. I meant nothing personal. What in ordinary circumstances would have made your work, uh, questionable in my eyes is actually in this instance a virtue. Simply put, sir, your books *sell*. And you do like homunculi, don't you? *Vampire Homunculi, The Invisible Homunculi of Gorakhpur, Homunculi of the Haunted Toilets*—all these were immensely successful. That last achieved a kind of cult status, did it not? Inspired a line of outhouses, Georg tells me—the celebrated Tiflis Potties, with copies of your book inside. My God, man, people actually *read* you—an almost unheard-of phenomenon in my own literary experience and therefore, I must confess, a slightly suspect one. Nevertheless, in this case, it is the very thing that is wanted."

He went back to his desk, waving his arms and humming to himself. He pulled open a drawer, took out a bulky package wrapped in brown paper and placed it in front of me beside the cheese.

"There! This, Mr. Tiflis, should answer all your questions." He undid the wrapping, revealing two cardboard boxes about the size that typing paper comes in. "Now, you may or may not know this, but while he was confined in the Clinic, Dr. Eichhorn kept a journal—kept it, that is, until the force, the profundity I should say, of his discoveries removed the possibility of writing. This box, the one marked 'E,' contains that journal, along with some other pertinent material: letters, newspaper clippings and such. This other box, marked 'S,' contains the transcriptions made by the homunculus Schwank, of the so-called Delphic Oracle material, the voice—'the Cry,' I call it—of the *Gehirngespinstgemach*. Are you aware of the *Gehirngespinstgemach*, Herr Tiflis?

Well, you soon will be. The *Gehirngespinstgemach* knows everything. *Everything*. These are only photocopies, of course. The originals are in my vault." He wrapped the package up again and handed it to me. "I want you to take these documents, sir, and read them. Read them posthaste! Then come back here and tell me if you can use them. At this time tomorrow, shall we say?"

"Why, yes—yes, of course," I answered, trying to hold back the big grin I felt welling up inside me. "I'm—well, I'm honored. You've been more than helpful, Doctor. You've been positively splendid." I picked up the packages and rose to go. "I'll certainly come back tomorrow, at 2:00 PM sharp. And I think I can confidently say this is just the beginning of a long and fruitful association."

At the door I turned. "I wonder, sir, could you tell me one thing before I leave?"

"With pleasure, if I can."

"When you wave your arms about, as you did just now, are you hearing music?"

"Of course. I would have thought that was obvious. Did you not hear it, too?"

"No."

"What a shame. Perhaps you should have your hearing tested. You're missing something really extraordinary. It fills my old German soul with joy. It just might fill your Welsh-Georgian one likewise."

"Welsh-Armenian, actually. There was a large Armenian population in Tiflis. I bet I'd like the music, though. What is it?"

"Duke."

"Duke!" Ellington was one of my favorites.

"Yes! Wellington himself! Wellington indeed and forever! 1941. 'I Got It Bad and That Ain't Good.' With Ivie Anderson singing. I find it intensely beautiful. Now—no more questions, my dear sir. Not till you've read the documents." He yawned. "Please forgive me, sir. I would love to discuss music with you—our tastes seem to run along the same lines—but perhaps we can do so tomorrow. Now it really is time for sleep. My afternoon *Schläfchen*. At my age I can't do without it. Not that it rests me, you understand. On the contrary: it rouses me, it vitalizes me, it makes the blood race and the heart go pit-a-pat. The only time I can relax is when I'm awake." He picked up the water pistol and waved it, rather weakly, I thought. "Sleep is *work* for me," he went on. "I live for it, but it's positively exhausting. The things I see there! The things the Oracle sees! Oh, I could a tale unfold, as What's-her-name liked to say." He yawned again. "Enough. Read the documents, sir, read and learn. And come back tomorrow. *Chiz.*"

In the matter of hotels, Dietz was as discriminating and sensible as could be. Despite its name, which at first caused me some uneasiness, the Basilisk proved to be a thoroughly hospitable place, its staff courteous and welcoming, its rates reasonable, its rooms "comfortable and well-appointed, their design executed [according to the brochure on the desk] in obedience to the rules of Feng Shui." That was all to the good, I supposed, and I appreciated Dietz's thoughtfulness, but Feng Shui was about the last thing on my mind just then. Neat and clean would have been more than adequate, and this room was both. I plunked my suitcase down on the bed, and myself in the easy chair, and soon was deep in the material Haselmaus had given me.

Now, I am not a superstitious person. Well, maybe that's an exaggeration. Let's just say I'm no more superstitious than I need to be to practice my profession, nor am I likely to accept whole hog every high-flown piece of mysticism that comes my way. But as I read and reread those pages, I slowly became convinced that forces larger than I could imagine were at work on me, and that whatever had placed me in that specific hotel room, with those specific writings, had done so with a purpose. That may sound pretentious, but you weren't in that room. I felt I was reading part of my own life story, even though I didn't actually appear in it anywhere.

Consider: someone, possibly Haselmaus himself, possibly another physician at the Clinic, had typed up a brief biographical sketch of Eichhorn and appended it to his narrative. In it I discovered that his mother was Mary Gwynn, the noted Philadelphia painter.

Well, Mary Gwynn was also a distant cousin of mine. I had never met her. She was a good deal older than I, and her parents had left Lichfield for Philadelphia some years before I was born. Still, she had been an important figure for me; her accomplishments were legendary in the family. I remembered my other cousin, Jane, telling me when I was little that Mary was the only one of our whole clan who ever did anything unusual with her life. Everyone else was just like everyone else, she said. That statement depressed me. It suggested that the rest of us were nothing but carbon copies of each other, doomed to perpetual nonentity. I promised myself then and there that when I grew up I would become, if not the first, at least the second person in the family to achieve something worth talking about.

However, beyond her name and legend, I knew almost nothing about Cousin Mary. I didn't recall having seen any of her work, even in reproduction, had never read anything about her, and certainly had never made an attempt to meet her. I really wasn't interested. I knew only what I'd been told, years before, that she had defied her parents' conformist expectations, gone to art school against their wishes, and had become a fairly well known artist. That she had also become Fritz Eichhorn's mother was something I was completely unprepared for.

Just as surprising was the discovery that, as a child, Mary had been friendly with Ethel Mammon Striker, the author of *Gravity Newton: The Life and Legend of Efficiency Caws.* How remarkable! *Gravity Newton* was the book that first piqued my interest in the paranormal, back when I was a teenager and found a copy, covered with dust and unshelved, in the back room of the Lichfield Public Library. They'd probably meant to discard it and forgotten. Well, thank God they did, for it set in motion the chain of events, too long (and, I'm afraid, too boring) to recount here, that determined my entire professional life. And to think that Cousin Mary had actually known the author! *That* was a synchronicity if ever there was one. I couldn't wait to tell Haselmaus the next day.

As I read on, though, I found I'd have much more to tell him, although I doubted he'd believe it. I had trouble believing it myself.

The "it" was Anna Zeisig.

You see, I knew her, too. We went to high school together for about a year, while her parents were here in the States on business. We became good friends. We even—well, we dated some. We dated quite a lot, actually. "Siskin," I used to call her. But I was just one of quite a few other guys. That girl was really something. She didn't look the type at first, with those thick, horn-rimmed glasses and the studious, slightly superior expression she usually wore, with her nose always in some medical book—even then she knew what she wanted to do for a career, and was as likely as not to give you a detailed lecture on pustules and scar formation, right in the middle of the cafeteria, in her perfect English with just the smallest hint of a German accent—but when she took off those glasses and let her long black hair down, watch out! She was a whole new person. And boy, did she get around. I guess I had a little crush on her for a while, and I think she did on me, too, but she never could stay with one guy for very long. Looking back on it now, I'm grateful to her for that, because, deep down, I probably wouldn't have wanted it to go on much longer myself. Not to the point of being really "committed," as they say. I mean, there was plenty of passion, but it wasn't exactly what you'd call a *grand* one, on either side. We were sixteen, for God's sake.

But now here was her name in the material Haselmaus had given me. There were even letters of hers, written to him. Incredible. It had to be the same person, too. How many Anna Zeisigs were there in the world, anyway, who also were devoted to medicine? Who also were short, with long black hair? Yeah, hair could be dyed, sure, but these resemblances were too close. Epidemics were her thing, as well. I used to think she lived for them.

Anna Zeisig! And, according to one of the newspaper clippings, she died at thirty-two, in the same hotel I was staying in. Maybe even the same room. And to think she'd been living in Zürich all the time I was there, into the bargain. We could have passed each other on the street, hundreds of times—why didn't we?

If only I'd known! I could have tried to—anything might have happened! Even—

I thought I heard her voice, calling my name—"Johnny, Johnny," in a little whisper, the way she used to do—and looked up. There was nobody there, of course, but for the first time I realized that the comfortable, well-appointed, supposedly Feng Shui-ed room the Basilisk had given me had no windows.

I stayed up all night reading, finishing everything a little after sunup. I knew I had my book, its liver and lights. *True Tales of the Paranormal*, I'd call it—the homunculus book of a lifetime! I felt tremendously keyed up, but thought I'd better at least try to catch a few hours' sleep before my appointment.

It was no good, though. I kept being awakened by an onslaught of vividly colored, overlapping dreams, a mix of real life and shards of what I'd just read. No sooner would I get back to sleep than they returned to the charge, clamoring, it seemed, to be heeded. The number seven, girt with ravens, took wings and swooped down over the Winthrops, father and son, who were walking in Zürichhorn Park. Thales of Miletus chased the French Universal Exposition around the Grossmunster.

Images of the divine essence, I suppose Eggbeater Caws would have called them. Their little toes atwinkle. Hah.

The last dream—I think it was the last, before I gave up and got out of bed—took place in Lichfield, outside the house where I grew up, on the corner of Madison and Highland Avenues. It was May Day. A parade was due to pass by. Swiss guards lined the sidewalks, waiting. Cousin Jane was standing beside me. She said to be sure not to miss Mary Gwynn, who would be riding on one of the floats as the Homecoming Queen. Music sounded, with deafening brass, the lead trumpet playing way up in the stratosphere. Maynard Ferguson all the way. Marchers appeared in the distance, followed by a float painted all black and draped in mourning, drawn by six black horses. Riding on it was a tall woman in shrouds, her face hidden by a hood. As she passed, she turned in my direction, raising her arms in a welcoming gesture. I turned away to speak to Jane, but found that Anna Zeisig had taken her place.

Anna pulled me away into a doorway. "Oh, Johnny," she whispered, "sweet Johnny K_____, how gaseous to see you again. It has been *so* much too long. 'Herr Tiflis,' they call you now, do they not, but that is a silly name and we both know it. You are still sweet Johnny to me, cha-cha-cha." She planted a kiss on my forehead, another on my lips. "I have read all your books, Johnny," she said, "you have such a funk on your shoes now, you are so *hüfte*. You know the score, cha-cha-cha, you know the score." She pressed herself against me, and slipped her hand inside my shirt. "*Graben, graben*," she breathed. "I may be dead, beautiful Johnny, but I am still in love with you. We should—how do you say it—*split*, should we not? Let us go inside, eh? I will pay you such rabbit. I promise! Come."

Haselmaus was not in his office when I got there, a few minutes before two, although the outside door was open. Dietz had taken his place in the sanctum, sitting at his master's desk. He looked a little more human than he had the day before. There was something careworn about the man.

Dr. Haselmaus would not be able to see me today, he said. "He was called away suddenly, I'm afraid. On urgent business." Dietz passed a hand over his brow.

"What a drag. I was looking forward to seeing him. When will he be back? Tomorrow?"

"I really couldn't say for certain, sir. The doctor left somewhat precipitously. But probably not tomorrow. Nor the day after. I wish I could be more precise."

"So do I. This is, well, a little unsettling. Dr. Haselmaus was expecting me. He *wanted* to see me."

"About the manuscripts."

"Yes. The two boxes he gave me. The 'documents,' he called them. I have them here, in this traveling bag."

"Mmmm. I rather thought you did, sir. That padlock on the handle with the chain going round your waist suggests as much."

"Damn right. Nobody gets this away from me."

"Just so. One cannot be too careful these days. But as to your meeting with the doctor, sir, you may set your mind at rest. Dr. Haselmaus left me specific instructions on that score. About the only instructions he did leave," he added under his breath. Then, in his normal voice: "I take it you have read the material?"

I assured him I had, both boxes, every word. It was the most amazing thing I had ever come across, I told him. It was absolutely priceless. I could not imagine my book without it. The effect would be stupendous! The academics would rage, but let them—they'd raged before. The public, on the other hand—and they were the ones that mattered—would see Eichhorn as a pioneer, a tragic hero, a quester probing at the outermost reaches of science, the no-man's land where science and psyche meet, the danger zone where the universe—

"Yes, yes, Mr. Tiflis." Dietz cut me off. "That is, uh, wonderful news." He suppressed a frown. "The doctor would appreciate your enthusiasm, were he here, and doubtless would join you in it."

"I'm sure he would," I said. "And that worries me some—his absence, I mean. From what he said yesterday, the way he carried on, I would have thought ... Whatever is keeping him away must be awfully important."

"Yes, it is—apparently. But you need not fret, sir. The doctor anticipated your reaction to the documents. He has given me *carte blanche*, a power of attorney if you like, to act for him in this matter and assist you in any way needful."

"That's good. I'm obliged to you. But I'm concerned about the doctor all the same. He didn't strike me as someone who should be out on his own very much. He's pretty old. And he needs his tonic."

"He certainly does," Dietz agreed. "Mixed daily, by me, to his own specifications, with the hardest-to-come-by ingredients. The doctor must have his sleep. Especially at his age. Not that he's nearly as old as what he may have told you, of course. He likes to pretend that he is a contemporary of the great adepts. But he certainly is no spring chicken. I'd say, if I had to, that he's about a hundred and ten—at the outside. I reminded him today, as his hand was on the doorknob, I called out to him, 'Your Elixir, Herr Doktor! What about your Elixir?' 'God will provide,' he answered, barely turning his head. Smugly he said it, patting the side of his suitcase! Then he left, and not a word of farewell."

"Oh, brother. Where was he off to, anyway? If you don't mind my asking."

Dietz squirmed in his chair. "Oh, sir, it is not for me to mind or not to mind. I freely admit, however, that if it were left up to me, I would keep silent. Not from any lack of candor, you understand, or love of mystification— actually, I hate such an attitude—but simply because in learning the answer you might form a wrong, even a frivolous, idea of the doctor's, uh, mental state. Of his seriousness, that is. But none of that matters, for Dr. Haselmaus wanted me to tell you. In fact, he explicitly directed me to do so. Very well. I tell you." He sat up straight and squared his shoulders. "It would seem that he has gone to a jazz concert."

"A jazz concert!"

"Yes, sir, a jazz concert. I beg you not to take it amiss. He was convinced, I am afraid, that the homun—that is, the psychotic Schwank, whom he insists on calling the homunculus—would be present, since it had been announced that the musician called 'Prez' would be playing. The event is to be held—please understand, sir, that I am merely repeating what the doctor told me this morning—the event is to be held in 'the land of the Hyperboreans, beyond the North Wind.' His very words. Of course, as you know, Hyperborea is a mythical place, completely without factual basis, one of the many 'paradises' humanity has invented for itself in order to compensate, I suppose, for the persistent distresses of our actual life. But to some people, including, I am sorry to say, Dr. Haselmaus, it is entirely real. It is the abode, allegedly, of the Blessed, a land of peace and abundance, celebrated in fable for thousands of years. Herodotus situates it in the farthest north."

"Yeah. I know about this place. Schwank claimed to have been there. There's music connected with it, too."

"Yes. The god Apollo is honored there with music and song."

"And white feathers fall from the sky, right?"

"Yes, sir. So the fantasy runs."

"But, you know, Herr Dietz—and I'm as skeptical as the next guy, don't think I'm not—some of the things I've read about Hyperborea since I've been in this line of work make me think there may be more than fantasy operating here. Sure, it all sounds like pie in the sky, but then so did Atlantis, and it's been shown that the Atlantis story has a solid historical grounding. Lots of scholars, from Jane Harrison to Cyrus Gordon and John Michell, believe such a place really existed, and they make excellent cases for it, too. Now, as far as Hyperborea is concerned, who knows what really goes on that far north? You can't just say 'Eskimos' and leave it at that. Peary and the other explorers didn't cover all that territory, either, not by a long shot. White feathers falling from the sky does sound a bit much, I'll admit, but—say! Eichhorn had a white feather in his mouth when you found him, didn't he? Just like Eggbeater Caws and just like—well, just like a friend of mine, too. Her ghost, that is," I finished lamely.

"Her ghost?" Dietz raised an eyebrow. "Well, well. That is, I suppose, extraordinary. But to return to Dr. Eichhorn for a moment, it is true that there was a feather in his mouth when I discovered his body. And it was, indeed, white. However, that does not change the fact—indeed, it has no bearing at all on the fact so far as I can see—that there is no such place as Hyperborea and there never has been. You know that perfectly well, sir, when you are not being engulfed by your enthusiasms. At some level of his being, Dr. Haselmaus must know it, too." He sighed. "Even the doctor. But this morning he could not, or would not, take time for reflection. He said he had to get an early start. He had gotten word of the concert only last night, in his sleep. Apparently, the event is to feature something he called 'the old Basie band.'"

Dietz took a crumpled scrap of paper from his jacket pocket, smoothed it out on the desk and read from it: "'With Buck Clayton, Harry Edison, Benny Morton, Eddie Durham, Dicky Wells, Earle Warren, Herschel Evans, Prez, Jack Washington, Freddie Green, Walter Page, Jo Jones, Billie Holiday, Helen Humes, Jimmy Rushing. And Basie, of course. And Desi Arnaz.'"

"Desi Arnaz!?"

"Yes, sir."

"Let me see that thing." Dietz handed me the paper. I stared at it, and handed it back. "Incredible. The old Basie band—with Desi Arnaz. Jesus Christ."

"Was Desi Arnaz not in the old Basie band, sir?"

"No, he was not. Nor any of the other Basie bands, either. Not in a million years. The doctor is as full of shit as the Christmas goose."

He frowned. I was afraid I might have gone too far. "Sorry. That just slipped out. It's an expression a friend of mine uses a lot. Lowell Cohn. Sorry."

"Lowell Cohn. And who is he?"

"Well, he's an advertising executive, actually. But he's a pretty decent tenor player, too."

"Tenor?"

"Tenor saxophone."

"Ah. You seem to know a good deal about the subject, sir."

"Yeah, some. Well, quite a lot, I guess. I've been a jazz fan since I was a kid. Bought a Thelonious Monk record at fifteen and never looked back. I play a little, too. Acoustic bass. On the side, of course. But there's something else that worries me about that list. Everybody on it is dead."

"Indeed, sir? I confess I am not surprised. The doctor is often, uh, cavalier in his disregard of such details. Of course, he may also presume that in a place like Hyperborea, death will present no obstacle to musicianship." He sniffed.

"Yeah. You could be right. It certainly doesn't seem to have stood in his way any—if that's what you mean by cavalier. He heard about this concert in his sleep, you say?"

"Yes." Dietz made a face. "That is where he gets most of his information now."

"Well, he always did, didn't he? 'Haselmaus the Dreamer,' right?"

"Yes, Mr. Tiflis, but that, as you say, was *Dreaming*. With a capital D, if you like: magnificent. But he no longer dreams that way. Even his Elixir does not help. It puts him to sleep, yes, it keeps his body alive, but it no longer has any effect on his dreaming. Everything comes out twisted, now. It comes not from the Dream, but from what he calls [Dietz shook his head] the Oracle."

"Yeah, he did mention an oracle. Is that the same thing as the—?"

"Yes, it is, sir. The 'Delphic Oracle,' so-called, made by Eggbeater Caws back in the nineteenth century and stolen out of a museum in the United States a few years ago. Stolen, one has every reason to believe, by the psychotic Schwank. At any rate, Schwank was carrying it when he made his first appearance in front of Jung's house in Küsnacht and started all this trouble. Dr. Haselmaus is devoted to it. He takes it to bed with him, he hugs it like a teddy bear. He never dreams now when he sleeps, he listens—so he says—to the Oracle. 'So much more accurate,' he says. Hah! He had it with him today when he left. He opened his suitcase and showed it to me, in with his socks and pajamas. A miserable, dented chunk of metal, like a shrunken head.

"The museum got wind of the fact that the doctor had it, by the way, and asked for it back. He made me write them and say it had disappeared, along with Schwank. To my everlasting shame, I did so."

Dietz put his head in his hands. When he looked up again his eyes were moist with tears.

"It is a pity, sir, a very great pity, that you never met the doctor in his prime. He was an extraordinary man, a true healer, with the sharpest intellect and the greatest capacity for empathy of anyone I have ever known. And, it goes without saying, he was an amazing dreamer. But ever since Dr. Eichhorn's death he has, to a considerable extent, lost touch with reality."

"He did seem a trifle … "

"Yes? Please be honest."

"Well … elevated."

"Precisely. As if he were Eggbeater Caws, for instance. Who, of course, he is not." He loosened his necktie. "It is all so very sad. I hope you can appreciate that, sir. Dr. Haselmaus has been a great friend to me, a friend and a mentor. I owe him more than I can ever repay; I do believe I owe him my sanity. Many years ago, he rescued me from a disastrous analysis with Stachelschwein, who was, without doubt, completely around the bend. You say Dr. Haselmaus was elevated. Well, you should have seen Stachelschwein! I bear the scars to this day. I could not have recovered at all, I am sure, without the doctor's care and attention. It hurts me deeply, therefore, to have to criticize him in any way, especially when it comes to his own mental balance. But I see no way to avoid it. You, as the chronicler of these unhappy events, have a right to know—not only a right, but a positive need. Besides, I'm confident that you will treat the revelations I'm about to make with delicacy and fairness. I did more research into your professional record than Dr. Haselmaus' comments yesterday may have suggested, and—although I seem to have missed your, uh, musical proclivities—I know you have a reputation for honesty and responsible workmanship, even if you do sometimes pander to popular taste. Also, you should know that the doctor liked you. After you left, he was even good enough to compliment me on having chosen you. He added, I'm afraid, that the Oracle too had expressed its satisfaction with the arrangement.

"Very well. I think we can now proceed. First, it is important that you be told some things about the doctor as he used to be, before … before all this Schwank nonsense.

"He was a rather large man, it may surprise you to learn, not a giant by any means but taller than he is now by fully a foot, with a barrel chest and a deep, resonant voice. He would have made a marvelous radio announcer. In school, and later at the University, he was an outstanding scholar. His undergraduate paper on the Island of Rügen and its mythological and spiritual significance for the German people, was a brilliant piece of work which was passed from hand to hand among the faculty and earned him many admirers. His first book, on the dreams of the pantheist Kosegarten, was a classic of its kind.

He was a good athlete as well, running, rowing and boxing with enthusiasm and skill. He showed me his trophies once; he was quite proud of them. He used to work out in the gymnasium here, when he was not seeing patients, or dreaming, or writing his poem. Oh, yes, sir, his poem. He took that nickname of his, 'the Epimenides of Basel,' very seriously. Epimenides, you know, not only slept for fifty-two years, he also wrote poetry. I sometimes wonder whether Dr. Haselmaus did not plant that name on himself; he certainly approved of it. In any case, he was writing a cosmogony, just as Epimenides did, in hexameters. It was to have been an epic in the antique style, recounting the generation of the cosmos out of Chaos and Night, Erebos and Tartaros. Unfortunately, he did not get as far with it as one would have hoped. It broke off in the middle of a stirring passage in which Night had Tartaros by the throat. It is a great shame he never managed to bring the work to completion. Even as it stands, however, it is an exceptional thing—a fragment, but an heroic one, like a broken column."

"So what kept him from finishing it?"

"Eichhorn's breakdown. It put a stop to all the doctor's creativity. Eichhorn, it distresses me to say, had been like a son to Dr. Haselmaus, and to see him brought low, in such a public and humiliating fashion, was a great shock. Even worse were those final weeks at the Helvetius, when Eichhorn was physically present but mentally God knows where. He no longer recognized anyone. He did nothing but write his narrative, which itself soon degenerated, as you have seen, into illegible scrawls and squiggles, just as his speech reverted to grunts and gurgles and inarticulate shouts. Dr. Haselmaus could not stand his own helplessness in the situation. He could not even bear to see his protégé like that. At last he sent me in his place. It was dreadful, sir, and much harder, in my opinion, for the doctor than for his patient. The doctor felt everything much more keenly; Eichhorn was merely making noise. I know that sounds harsh, but *conscious* suffering is so much more painful than the other kind, is it not? I believe, too, that it was the doctor's first real failure as a healer.

"After Eichhorn died, Dr. Haselmaus forgot all about his other projects. He threw himself into a misguided attempt to rehabilitate him in the eyes of the world, first by the printed word and second—incredibly—by validating that creature, Schwank, as a genuine homunculus, Schwank who (it goes without saying) was no more an homunculus than you or me. You are fidgeting, Mr. Tiflis. Are you all right? Would you like some more seltzer?"

I was all right, and told him so. But I didn't like the turn the conversation was taking. Since finishing those documents, I'd put my skepticism on hold. There was something compelling about this story—much more compelling, I had to admit, than the stories in my other books, which I'd been able to treat lightheartedly. There was humanity in this piece as well as weirdness. But the homunculus element was still at the center of it: no homunculus, no story. I was pretty sure my public would agree with me, too.

As for my fidgeting, it had nothing to do with what Dietz had been saying. For the past few minutes I'd been experiencing a curious sensation. Something—it felt like a hand—had been stroking my chest under my shirt. I remembered my dream of the night before, and then Anna herself, years ago in Lichfield, on my parents' couch, her body against me.

Dietz continued. "You see, sir, the doctor had been obsessed with homunculi for many years. Yes, obsessed: the word is not too strong. He often told me, long before he met Eichhorn, that he thought it might be possible to make one. He said he had been a dedicated Paracelsian—those were his very words, sir, 'dedicated Paracelsan,'—from his earliest youth. To be perfectly frank, I always thought Dr. Haselmaus, much as I revered him, had a little screw loose when it came to homunculi—begging your pardon, sir, I know they are your specialty as well. But yours is a literary involvement, very different from the doctor's. All his rational thought processes, his usual capacity for discrimination and judgment, seemed to desert him when the subject was broached. He took all the lore literally, like a fundamentalist with the Bible. So you can easily see why he was devastated when, on top of Eichhorn's death, the psychotic Schwank vanished as well. The doctor behaved, I have to say, like a crazy person. He hired private detectives. He consulted a medium, Gretchen N., who had been a friend of Eichhorn's. He began to listen to jazz, in which he'd never shown the slightest interest—and of which, as you yourself have demonstrated, he never acquired much real understanding—hoping it might somehow attract his quarry.

"He thought he'd struck gold one day when he got a letter (you have a copy of it in the material the doctor gave you) from a woman who claimed to have known Schwank. I think you'll agree that from what she said and the way she said it, she appeared to have been in love with him. She also appeared, quite obviously it seemed to me, to have been a borderline case herself, teetering on the edge of some serious mental disturbance. She enclosed a good many things that, she alleged, Schwank had directed her to send him. But, since the doctor almost never deigns to answer his mail, he did not acknowledge receipt of the material. However, it did occur to him that she might know something that would provide a clue to Schwank's whereabouts, and after a second letter from her in which she revealed that she was contemplating suicide, he decided to take her on as a patient. He wrote her a reply (rather an abrupt one, I thought) and had me set up an appointment for her. Sad to say, though, she died suddenly, as you've read in the newspaper clippings, the night before she was to see him.

"Dr. Haselmaus was as frustrated and angry as I can remember. He cursed what he called the 'bad luck' (how distressing that an analyst of his experience should have descended to such a commonplace!) that had thwarted their meeting. He began sleeping with the Oracle beside him. And he began, almost imperceptibly at first and then quite noticeably and rapidly, to shrink.

"It was an alarming thing to watch. It must have worried the doctor, too—how could it not?—but he pretended not to care, even to welcome it. He said he was getting down to his 'fighting weight.'

"All his attempts to find Schwank came to nothing—needless to say. As, it would seem, my attempt has as well. For I must own, Mr. Tiflis, that I picked your name out of scores of others primarily because I hoped that your treatment of homunculi—breezy, slightly cynical perhaps, even dismissive on occasion but, at bottom, good-natured, might rub off on the doctor and jar him out of his mania. And indeed it could have done so, especially since I chose better than I knew on account of your ... musical involvements. But it was useless, all useless, for now he is gone. On an errand not even a fool would accept. For—please understand, sir, if you take nothing else away from this interview, please understand: there *is* no homunculus. There never *was* any homunculus, never at all."

This was really bad. My story was on the ropes. It didn't make me feel any better, either, to hear my Anna (as I now thought of her) described as a borderline case—even if she had been. Where the hell did he get off, talking like that?

"Never at *all*? I shot back. "Come on, Herr Dietz, get a grip on yourself. Think back a bit, man. What about that thing Eichhorn made when he was a kid? What about that, eh? You may not remember—I don't know how long it's been since you read his narrative—but he says specifically, specifically and unequivocally, Herr Dietz, that he did make an ho—"

"Calm yourself, Mr. Tiflis! Please. Take it a little easy. No one is calling you a liar. Nor was Eichhorn a liar, either—not entirely so at any rate. There *was* something at the bottom of that Mason jar, I'm sure, even if it was only a wish. Or a fantasy. And I have no doubt the boy masturbated: as you see, I recall the narrative quite well. But (and I'm sorry to have to tell you this, sir) the truth was nothing like what Eichhorn describes. His mother, you see, told us all about it, Dr. Haselmaus and myself, when she was in Basel last April for an exhibition of her paintings. Mary Gwynn." Dietz smiled. "A very beautiful and cultured lady—and such a contrast to her offspring. An Abstract Expressionist—a dying breed, they say, but you would never know it from her work. I purchased several of the smaller pictures myself (there were a few in the show that were huge, ten or more feet long). There are no recognizable images in her paintings, but they are richly evocative of natural process." Dietz warmed to his theme. "One thinks, perhaps, of the James Brooks of the 1950's, or the feeling of atmosphere and weather that Hyde Solomon gets in the same decade, but her work has felicities all its own. The color, the lines, the forms, even the textures, pulsate with feeling and intelligence."

"That's nice to know. She's a distant cousin of mine, incidentally. But back to that homunculus: I don't see how you can say—"

"A cousin of yours! Indeed. You are a most fortunate young man. She is a great artist. You saw the exhibit, then?"

"No. Unfortunately. I was in Winnipeg at the time, lecturing on toilets."

"What a shame. But then you must have her work in your home. A constant presence, an Agatha-Daimon, as it were. A good angel. She happens to be in Basel again, by the way, for a short visit. Perhaps you can see her before you leave? She is staying at the *Bildungszentrum* 21. Oh, I quite understand, sir; time and publishers wait for no one. You must forgive my maundering.

I get carried away sometimes. Many years ago, in the old pre-Stachelschwein days, I was an art student. The appreciation lingers, if not the skill.

"Now, as to Eichhorn's alleged homunculus: according to his mother, the whole business got started after the boy's father left them. Oh, yes, sir, he left them. Eichhorn doesn't mention that in his narrative, does he? No, he most assuredly does not; he paints an idyllic picture of his home life. Such was hardly the case. As you know, the father was a musician, playing jazz for a living. He is rather well known, I believe—Eichhorn mentions him in his narrative. Do you know him, sir?"

"Squirrel Eichhorn? I've never met him, no, but I've heard the music."

"And what, if I may ask, do you think of it?"

"Not too much, if you want to know the truth. Too commercial for me. Practically Muzak."

"I see. Well, I can't say I'm surprised to hear that. I had formed the same opinion myself. People stand in line for hours to hear him play, though—stupefying. But all that aside, when Eichhorn was a boy, the father spent a good deal of time on the road, as I'm told the expression is, and was away from home for long stretches. Young Fritz resented this, and resented jazz as well, which was keeping his father from him. Finally, Eichhorn Senior left for good; he went off on a tour and never came back. He sent money home at first, but less and less as time went on, and at wider and wider intervals. At last the checks ceased altogether. Word came, through friends, that he was not on the road at all but living in Helsinki with a teenage mistress. So that was that. Fortunately, Mar—Ms. Gwynn—had an income of her own, or God knows how they would have managed.

"Fritz's resentment turned to hatred. He had always had a vindictive streak, his mother said, and he was not one to take a grievance lightly, especially a grievance as weighty as this one. (He never changed, by the way. I remember he once told Dr. Haselmaus and me that he had a highly developed sense of 'abstract justice,' which, as he practiced it, amounted to much the same thing.) He told his mother he was going to get even; moreover, he knew just how to do it. He had seen a book in the Swedenborg section of the town library (Bryn Athyn was a Swedenborgian center, remember), a volume of Paracelsus' alchemical writings, in which it was explained, step by step, how to make an homunculus. An homunculus, Fritz said excitedly, could do anything you wanted. All you had to do was give the order. He was going to make this creature, train it up and send it off to do ill turns to his father, ruin his love life, wreck his career, make him play wrong notes at concerts, fall down the stairs, lose his hair, his teeth, his girl friend, his mind. The boy's eyes gleamed with malice.

"Strange to say, his mother was not particularly shocked by this. She had no illusions, she told us, about her son's capacity for mischief. She had seen him play too many practical jokes, none of them amusing, all of them involving some degree of physical discomfort for the victim. But, she said, she was a bit put off by the, uh, necromantic strangeness of the project. On reflection, though, she decided not to stop him. She thought it might be good therapeutically for him to work out his anger this way, and much less dangerous than plenty of other things he might think of—he was nothing if not inventive. I dare say, also, knowing her as I do, that the project secretly pleased her in a way. Surely she too had been imagining some sort of comeuppance for her husband—with perfect justification, of course.

"In any case, she gave her approval, and Fritz went to work in the basement. He went down there every day before and after school for about a week, his mother recalled, and then he stopped. When she asked him how his homunculus was coming, he only turned his face away and muttered, 'Not so good.' He refused to say any more about it, so the next day, while the boy was at school, she went down into the cellar to see for herself. All she found was a Mason jar broken into three pieces, with a little congealed slime clinging to what had been the bottom. So much for the boy Faustus, the master magician."

This was a setback, no doubt about it. Why couldn't Cousin Mary have minded her own business that morning—done a painting or something? What the hell.

"Disappointing," I admitted. "From my point of view, that is. But [I saw a possible bright spot] what about your point of view, Herr Dietz? You didn't care much for Eichhorn, did you?"

"No, sir, I did not." The question didn't daunt him. "I found him odious. A narcissistic, self-promoting careerist, with grandiose notions about his own importance and a fixed determination that everyone else share them. Brilliant, perhaps. A healer, sometimes. But he only healed for the glory it brought him. He cared nothing for other people, he only used them. That medium, for instance, Gretchen N. She was devoted to him, God knows why, and he let her believe—he could be devilishly charming—that he felt the same way about her, when all he really cared about was her body. He used everyone he came in contact with, Dr. Haselmaus as much as anyone. He found that little screw the doctor had loose and exploited it. His own analyst! Disgusting."

He paused a moment, then added with a half-smile, "I suppose that disqualifies me in your eyes as an objective informant."

"Not entirely," I answered, "although that did cross my mind." I returned the half-smile, and squirmed. The phantom fingers were striking my belly now, and moving down towards my privates. "Even in his own narrative, Eichhorn doesn't come off as an especially sympathetic character. 'Grandiose' about sums it up. And your revelations about the, er, flaws in his version of the events are important for me to hear, even if I could wish the facts to be otherwise. But, you know [I shifted a little in my chair] I don't think one can accuse him of actually lying, not in the strict sense of the term. It's been established, surely, that he was delusional when he wrote those things. He really may have believed that his home life was idyllic. Such dissociations—as I'm sure you know—are far from uncommon, even among otherwise normal people who want to blot out some traumatic piece of their past." Her fingers slipped beneath the elastic band of my underpants. "And, as far as the authenticity of his homunculus goes, what Mrs. Eichhorn said about—"

"Gwynn," he snapped. "She got a divorce. I should have thought you'd know that, as a member of the family. But even without that information, you could hardly expect her to acquiesce meekly while—"

"Of course not. Please excuse me. A slip of the, er, tongue." Hers licked the inside of my naval. Her fingers ran through my pubic hair and curled around my testicles. I started to sweat. "I wonder," I asked him, "could I, er, have some more seltzer after all?"

"Certainly, sir. I will get it at once." He left the room. I used the time to whisper urgently to Anna—it had to be Anna—to please lay off, at least until we were decently out of the office. But Anna is *dead*, I told myself, you're the one who's losing your grip, not Dietz. You're turning into a Goddamn crazy man. "Ghosts can do anything, Johnny," came the answer from nowhere, and it was her voice saying it. "Whatever they like. *Graben, graben.*" But the fingers—if they were fingers, I was less and less sure of anything anymore—slowed down and stopped. By the time Dietz returned with my drink I was back to normal.

"Thank you." I took a sip and mopped my brow. "I don't know what came over me. But to pick up where I left off, if you don't mind, I was just going to say that Cousin Mary's—Ms. Gwynn's—statement, when you look at it squarely, doesn't rule out the possibility that Eichhorn really did make some sort of creature in the basement. No, Herr Dietz, please listen. She even supports him in one important detail—the broken jar. That doesn't prove there was no homunculus, far from it. It only suggests that she happened to come downstairs after the thing had escaped. Fritz's comment, 'not so good,' could just as easily have referred to the escape as to the whole experiment. And—even though you may discount them—I think you have to pay close attention to some remarkable facts about Schwank: his memory of his birth in a Mason jar, for instance—*in a Mason jar, Herr Dietz*—at the start of his most recent incarnation, as well as his extraordinary familiarity with the Caws story, which Eichhorn knew about but which was far from common knowledge. I don't know if you're aware of this, but homunculi traditionally have access to a vast amount of knowledge usually closed to the rest of us. Personally, I believe this information is transmitted along telluric pathways in the—"

"*Cease!*" He shouted. It was the first time I'd heard him raise his voice. "Cease, please, I beg you, sir. Save all that for your books. I'm sure your readers will adore it. They may even call it reasoning. Myself, I find it a bit much. Oh, I can readily understand your position; I can even sympathize with it. We all have our pet commitments, not lightly to be relinquished. You are committed to the paranormal for, let us say, professional reasons, and you wish to demonstrate the authenticity of this particular, uh, outstanding paranormality no matter what the cost. Or, failing that, you want to make it seem at least possible. You are very far from stupid, you speak well, you possess considerable ingenuity, and you mount a decent argument. But it still won't wash, Mr. Tiflis. You have to face one hard fact; homunculi have never existed in the real world of physical phenomena. And they never will—any more than Hyperborea."

He smiled his little half-smile, and went on. "Your reaction reminds me, I'm afraid, of Dr. Haselmaus and the resistance he put up when he heard Ms. Gwynn's story—although to be fair to you, sir, his response was far more hostile than yours and his arguments a good deal less than ingenious. On the other hand, in fairness to him, it must be said that his commitment had even deeper roots than yours. It came from a lifelong obsession which had finally, so he believed, been given positive, tangible confirmation. He would never have let that prize go without a fight. Still, his behavior with Ms. Gwynn was unconscionable. Let me tell you about it. It may even change your mind. Would you like some more seltzer?"

"No, thanks. I think I'm set."

"Very well. Our interview with her took place last year, as I think I've said, during the exhibition of her paintings here in Basel. It was a considerable display, well advertised in advance. She's become quite famous, your cousin. She sent Dr. Haselmaus an invitation to the opening reception. She had never met him—the doctor had been too distraught to attend Eichhorn's funeral—and I think she invited him simply as a matter of courtesy to the man who had been her son's psychiatrist and had cared for him.

"The doctor was eager to attend. He took me along as his 'interpreter,' as he called it, to explain the paintings to him. He has very little aesthetic sense, I'm afraid."

"When I saw the paintings, I was overwhelmed. I had almost forgotten that such freedom and expressiveness could exist in the world, much less be given such striking, visible form. The painting was so direct and open, the brush-work so alive, you could almost see her making the picture in front of you. It all brought back to me my years at art school, which were in many ways the happiest of my life. I needn't bore you with the details, Mr. Tiflis, but I have not had an easy time of it since then. It's possible that I've grown a little wiser as a result, and certainly a bit richer, but the élan I once felt eludes me.

"I bought three paintings in the first twenty minutes. Dr. Haselmaus, locked in his private fixation, assumed I did so because the artist was Eichhorn's mother. Nothing, of course, could have been further from the truth;

he had no inkling of the contempt I felt for that man. I tried to convince him that I was moved by the paintings themselves. I spent most of the reception explaining the pictures to him, not only the ones I had purchased but abstract art as a whole, the entire glorious procession—Kandinsky, Kupka, Klee, Matisse, on through Hofmann, Pollock and the rest—but I don't think any of it penetrated. I doubt he even listened.

"When the reception was over and the other guests had left, Ms. Gwynn graciously asked us to stay for a while. She was clearly impressed that I'd bought so much of her work, and wanted to find out something about me. She'd assumed I was a business man, which I'd actually been for a few years, pre-Stachelschwein, long enough to make quite a pile. But when I told her that before all that I'd been to art school, her face lit up. She wanted to know all about it. Were the schools over here different from those in America? How were the classes conducted? Were there group critiques, or was it just individual instruction? Did they put an emphasis on the history of art? She thought that was terribly important. And so on. But before I could say much, Dr. Haselmaus interrupted. He wanted to know all about the homunculus. I don't think she even realized at first what he was talking about—it can't have been uppermost in her mind at the moment—but at last she got it straight and told us the story, just as I have told you. The doctor was furious. He not only rejected her account out of hand, he practically accused her of lying and stormed out of the gallery. It was a most unpleasant and embarrassing scene. I confess I thought less of the doctor as a result. It was the beginning, perhaps, of the end."

"The end?"

"The end of my thralldom, Mr. Tiflis. I no longer thought of the doctor as a god. I began to see that he was not simply a human being, with roughly the same flaws all of us share to one degree or another, but a human being with enormous flaws, great gaping pits of malfeasance and misconception—not to put too fine a point on it—never before seen and unlikely, one hopes, ever to be seen again. There! I've said it, and it wasn't painful at all. It was a relief."

"So why do you stay with him?"

"Because it is my business to stay, sir. It is what I have done and do, and know how to do. I even, sometimes, cherish the illusion that I may be able to help the doctor, but that is not my real reason for putting up with him. I do it simply because I am able to, and therefore do not have to learn to do anything else. I am his dogsbody, I grant you, but I am not his dog anymore. I perform my duties, I carry out my instructions to the letter, but I keep the greater part of my mind, and my actions outside these walls, for myself alone. I am, I do believe, as free as it is possible to get in this world. To put it in psychological terms, Mr. Tiflis, the transference is broken."

He stood up.

"And now, sir, we come to another end, you and I. For you were the occasion of the doctor's final instruction, and I have completed it, completed it and then some, as you say in America, right down to the old Basie band and Desi Arnaz. I am, therefore—please forgive me for phrasing it this way—free of you, too. Or perhaps … perhaps that is putting it a bit strongly. Let us say simply that our sociality—and I do like you, Mr. Tiflis, please believe me when I say that—is now on a different footing. Perhaps we may soon be kinsmen. Who knows? I have an engagement this evening with your cousin."

✍

From *Die Schildwache*, Zürich, Switzerland, April 22, 2005:

The American writer John Khashurian collapsed here yesterday morning while walking on Minervastrasse, and died shortly thereafter, the victim of an apparent heart attack. Mr. Khashurian was the author of several highly successful works of non-fiction, including *Vampire Homunculi* and *The Invisible Homunculi of Gorakhpur*, written under the pseudonym of Llanvair K. Tiflis and dealing with unexplained phenomena and other aspects of the occult. A new volume is scheduled to appear this fall.

In a touch worthy of one of his books, witnesses reported a rain of white feathers on Minervastrasse at the time of his attack.

Mr. Khashurian had lived in Zürich for a number of years, with only occasional trips to the United States. He was born in Lichfield, New Jersey, in 1971, and attended the University of Zürich before embarking on his chosen career. He never married, and is survived by two cousins, the artist Mary Gwynn of Philadelphia and Jane Khashurian Robbins of Behemoth, Pennsylvania.

☙

I'd rather not tell this last part, frankly. I'm not sure yet what to make of it, and I damn well don't think it's anybody's business but mine, Johnny K_____'s. Still, it doesn't seem quite honest to leave it out. Writing this tale has changed me—or something else has, while I've been writing it—and in some pretty basic ways. I want you to know where I'm coming from now, and something about how I got here, if not why. The why I couldn't even begin to tell you. But as for the how, ladies and gentlemen, I give you, for whatever it's worth,

THE DAY IN QUESTION

After my interview with Dietz I had to go away for a little while. They found me later that day in the lobby of the Basilisk, crawling across the floor. I tried to convince them that I was only "looking for clues" in the patterns on the carpet. That's what they said I said, anyway, when I woke up in the hospital and demanded to know where I was. But even if I did say it, it wasn't true, not even a little bit. What really took place was this:

I was standing at the front desk, checking out of the hotel, feeling kind of jumpy from lack of sleep and not very satisfied with the way my mission had ended, when I felt a blast of cold air behind me. I turned and saw Anna coming through the front door. She was dressed to the nines, wearing the biggest, bulkiest, most expensive looking fur coat I'd ever seen, sable, I think, and about a pound and a half of jewelry—gold earrings, three or four necklaces and pendants, bracelets, rings on all her fingers. "Johnny!" She called. "I knew you'd be here, cha-cha-cha. At my very favorite hotel—where else would we meet. But what do I see here, Johnny, a suitcase? You're not leaving me already, are you? Oh, please don't go, *lieber* Johnny, please not yet." She started to whimper.

"Siskin!" I cried out. "Siskin, sweetheart, and after all this time! Pay no attention to the suitcase, dearest. You know I'd never leave *you*, never ever."

People were staring at me now, but I ignored them and rushed across the lobby to her. I must have fallen on the way, though, because the next thing I knew I was on the floor, looking up into the face of the manager.

Dietz came to visit me in the hospital. He was properly solicitous. Haselmaus had still not returned, he told me; he was beginning to doubt that he ever would. He gave me a cassette tape, "in lieu of flowers," he explained, *Count Basie's Greatest Hits*. I had nothing to play it on, but I appreciated the gesture.

I finally got out of the hospital, and caught a train back home to Zürich. By that time it was spring. Everything was coming alive again, even me. In the pile of unopened mail in my entry way I found an invitation to Dietz's and Cousin Mary's wedding, at the Leonhardskirche in Basel, no less, to take place on July 1. Leibniz's birthday, I reflected, pleased with myself that I still could recall such a thing. I decided to go, and RSVP'd my acceptance. The invitation was something in itself, worthy of framing, a print in three colors with an intricate design of knots and loops and the lettering running around the edges. I figured the church had been Dietz's idea and the print Mary's.

There was also something in that day's newspaper, delivered to my door, that must have interested Dietz if he saw it: a short piece, not quite buried back on page seven, informing the reader that Dr. P. C. Haselmaus, the prominent Basel psychiatrist who had disappeared several months previously, had been picked up in Oslo in a disoriented state, wandering through the back streets of the city. He claimed to be *en route* to a concert at the North Pole and finding his way there by the use of an object he called the Oracle, which he had in the suitcase he was carrying. He had been taken to the Oslo Psychomaladjustment Center for observation, before being returned to Basel. Wait until Anna Sprengel gets hold of *that* one, I thought.

I took *True Tales of the Paranormal* in hand and got it into shape in fairly short order, thanks to Eichhorn's narrative and the other material from Haselmaus. I sent the typescript (I will NOT use a computer) off to the publisher, making my deadline with half a week to spare, in spite of my little vacation. I had no other outstanding obligations. I was one hundred percent free. Art Baron and The Duke's Men were playing at the Adagio. I could go every night if I wanted. I should have been on velvet.

But there were complications. If the hospital had known about them, they'd have come right back and scooped me in again.

You see, I had started seeing things. In broad daylight, too:

a black Cavallini suit with nobody in it, dining with a man at the Brasserie Lipp;

a sign in front of an open-air vegetable stand announcing "PIZZLES AND SPOSH" for sale, along with the usual carrots, beets and turnips;

a long-haired yellow and white dog walking towards me on the Kreuzstrasse, who stopped, looked into my eyes and vanished when he was about ten feet away.

And hearing things as well. One night I was playing bass at the Fried Potato with the Day Jobs, a group I'd helped to start whose members all had their primary careers in other fields. We got the idea from that Herb Pomeroy record Haselmaus and I talked about, "life is a many splendored gig"—except that Herb's musicians were all terrific, whereas we, well, we were probably better at our day jobs. But at least nobody threw anything at us, and we did have a lot of fun. That night we were playing Monk's "Bright Mississippi" (as if we were really good enough—we had a lot of nerve, too!) and I was quoting from "Sweet Georgia Brown" during my solo. One of the things I always liked about that tune of Monk's was its kissing-cousin relationship to "Sweet Georgia Brown." But as I began my quotation, Anna's voice rang out from somewhere inside my head, singing along. Off-key, naturally—she never could carry a tune. Nobody else heard her, of course. But I stumbled over a passage, and Lowell, the advertising executive who was playing tenor, gave me a look.

Then came the visitations.

Every night, shortly after I'd gone to bed, just as I was dropping off, Anna would come into my room, put her glasses down on the bedside table, take off her clothes and get into bed with me. I don't think we spoke. We would make love all night, in every position imaginable. We were sixteen again, it seemed endless. But by the time I woke up the next day, she would be gone.

I call them visitations, not dreams, because they weren't anything like dreams. They were as concrete, as palpably immediate, as anything I'd ever experienced. And I remembered every second of them.

I remembered, too, the fate of Anna's other lovers: Hans the ethnobotanist, Wolfram the orthodontist and the rest. I remembered, and I did not care. I did not care a rap.

This was it. This was *IT*—everything I was born for.

On the day in question—it was to be the last, the last, that is, except this extremely long one, this never-stopping one, this whatever-it-is—I awoke to sunlight pouring in through the bedroom window. The shades were already drawn back. The clock on the wall said 9:20. Anna was still there. She'd gotten dressed—the Cavallini suit, no glasses. She looked absolutely gorgeous. But very, very serious.

"Johnny, sweet Johnny," she whispered. "Johnny, my loveliest Johnny K_____, the best K_____ I could ever imagine. I have to go somewhere. Empedocles just called. Did you not hear the telephone? Empedocles has found Prez, Johnny! 'Alive and cooking,' he says, just as he predicted. Is that not wonderful? 'Bells! Ding-dong!' He added. And 'simple panther.' He said that, too, over and over. 'Simple panther, simple panther.' What is 'simple panther,' Johnny?"

"Hmmm. I can't imagine. It wouldn't be '*sympnoia panta*,' would it?"

"Would it? Anyway, he kept saying it. He was so excited. I think I must go to him now. Do you want to come with me, cha-cha-cha?"

It didn't even occur to me to refuse. I got up and put on my clothes. We went out together into the street.

It was the street and it was not the street. The buildings were several shades lighter than I remembered them. The pavement felt squishy under my feet. She turned to the right, going towards Minervastrasse. I followed.

Music—jazz—was coming from somewhere. I thought of the old Basie band, with Prez and Billie and Helen and Jimmy—Mister Five By Five. I thought of Duke and Ivie. Of Eddie Barefield. Of Monk and Coleman

Hawkins. Of Ray Brown, Oscar Pettiford, Wilbur Ware. Of Mingus. Of Miles, Moten and Mulligan. Of Harold Ashby. Of Tommy Flanagan, Red Garland, Mary Lou Williams, Bud Powell, Bill Evans, Hampton Hawes, Elmo Hope, Jutta Hipp, Herbie Nichols, Jimmy Rowles, Lovie Austin, Julia Lee, Sir Roland Hanna, Jaki Byard, Willie the Lion, Art Tatum, Ralph Sutton, Dick Wellstood, Fats Waller, Teddy Wilson. I thought of New Orleans funerals, and Dr. Haselmaus' magenta pajamas.

Quite a few people were coming out of the houses ahead of us now, walking in the same direction we were. At the corner they all turned right, as we did again when we got there.

We were greeted by a burst of sunlight. "*Ach!*" Anna cried, and grabbed my arm. "Look, Johnny, look! *Ein Vogel!*" She pointed upward.

A shower of feathers fell from the sky. Everything went white in an instant. We

ACKNOWLEDGEMENTS

Begun more than twenty-five years ago as a four-page sketch written for the amusement of friends, this book, not yet a book, wouldn't let me alone. It stayed dissatisfied with itself, and with me, demanding more than I could at that time deliver. I added sentences, paragraphs, whole sections, rewriting and rearranging, without much success. At last, however, G. W. Leibniz—introduced at first merely as a name, dropped in as a little flourish to rescue an otherwise tedious passage—muscled his way into the text and refused to leave. He arrogated more and more space to himself, often taking over the narrative entirely. He seemed delighted by the chance to express himself anew—or rather a-old, since he mostly restated, verbatim, what he'd already said in previous writings. Perhaps he wanted people finally to get it.

Soon, though, not to be left out, Sir Isaac Newton blustered in, renewing his dispute with his old rival, bent on flattening him once and for all.

This, the dispute, is the Leibniz-Newton Effect of the title, not that term's usual meaning of contemporaneous invention by separate persons. Instead, it's a war to the death, and beyond death, too, as the old codger says in Chapter 8.

I hope it's obvious that I'm enormously indebted to both of them. Without Leibniz and Newton and their translators—Robert Merrihew Adams, Roger Ariew and Daniel Garber, Samuel Clarke, Daniel J. Cook and Henry Rosemont, Jr., G. M. Duncan, Richard Franks and R. S. Woolhouse, E. M. Huggard, Leroy E. Loemker, R. N. D. Martin and Stuart Brown, H. T. Mason, Benson Mates, George Montgomery and Albert R. Chandler, Andrew Motte and Florian Cajori, Mary Morris, David E. Mungello, G. H. R. Parkinson, Peter Remnant and Jonathan Bennett, Nicholas Rescher, Patrick Riley, G. MacDonald Ross, Donald Rutherford, Paul Schrecker and Anne Martin Schrecker, R. C. Sleigh, Jr., Teresa Tymieniecka, and Catherine Wilson—this book could not even have been thought of.

I'm especially grateful, in addition, to three friends, the poets Sascha Feinstein and Gerrit Lansing, and the artist and writer Kristine Roan, who have each brought their keen intelligence and sympathetic insight to bear on many,

many drafts of my text over a considerable number of years. In Sascha's case I benefited not only from his writing and editing skills but also from his experience as a jazz musician, who plays frequently in clubs and concerts. From Gerrit I've drawn eagerly on his amazing erudition throughout a great many areas, particularly his knowledge of metaphysical subjects. I thank him as well for the care and incisiveness of his writing critiques.

Kristine's work on the book has been nothing short of phenomenal, a product of sustained attention, meticulous care for detail, and bottom-line good will. She copied my manuscript onto a computer with an accuracy that astounded me when the two of us settled down to the arduous task of proof-reading. At my invitation, she sometimes suggested specific changes in the text, which I adopted in practically every instance. She also dealt quickly and capably with the numerous additions I wanted to make even at that late stage in the process. This book is greatly improved by her involvement with it.

Other friends have helped in a multitude of ways. I'm indebted to Frieda Arkin, Lisa Batchelder, Robin Blaser, Charles Boyer, Don Byrd, Lowell Cohn, Don Cooper, Linda Crane, Barbara Crawford, Constance Del Nero, Rosario Del Nero, George Dietz, Shana Dumont, Patricia Gray Feidt, Edward Foster, Michael Franco, Margaret Garrett, Mary Gotovich, Steve Hahn, Megan Hastie, Lucy Hull, Margaret Hull, Ken Irby, Jane Keller, John Kuhn, Sally Kuhn, Rebecca Laughlin, John McVey, George Quasha, Susan Quasha, Sabine Ralston, Charles Stein, Margery Theroux, Ashley Thompson, Joseph Torra, Elizabeth Warwick, Sylvia Welsh, Bruce Wolosoff, Elie Yarden and Nona Yarden.

I also wish to thank Keith Richmond and Marilyn L. Rinn of Weiser Antiquarian Books in York Beach, Maine, for years of support, encouragement and fellowship.

Portions of this book have appeared previously in *lift*, edited by Joseph Torra, and *Talisman*, edited by Edward Foster. Another portion, under the title "Miss Nightingale Meets the Big Dream," was published as a broadside by Imposition Press, directed by John McVey, at Montserrat College of Art.

ABOUT THE AUTHOR

THORPE FEIDT is a painter, writer and actor, who exhibits his work frequently throughout the Northeast. Since 1973, he has been on the faculty of Montserrat College of Art in Beverly, Massachusetts. He has often appeared on the stage in the New England area, especially the Player's Ring Theatre in Portsmouth, New Hampshire. *The Oracular Room* is his first novel.

CPSIA information can be obtained at www.ICGtesting.com
Printed in the USA
LVOW08s1115081115

461513LV00001B/1/P